Dear Reader,

Once again, I invite you to join me and the coal mining community in Hillsbridge. It's become a second home to me, which is hardly surprising, since it is a fictional recreation of my own hometown Radstock – once the centre of the Somerset coalfield.

Things have moved on since *All The Dark Secrets*, the first novel in my Families of Fairley Terrace series, though Sir Montague Fairley, the hated mine owner, is still alive and as much of a penny-pincher as ever, resentful of the fact that new legislation has meant he has to spend money to improve safety in his mines. But this novel centres around a roof fall in one of the mines, and the consequences for Lorna Harrison, wife of one of those seriously injured, and Bradley Robinson, the newly appointed Safety Officer.

I do hope you will enjoy reading about the way their lives are changed forever, their hopes and fears, and the mortal danger they face before the nightmare reaches its conclusion.

Please do visit my website www.jenniefelton.co.uk where I write blogposts on all kinds of events that have really happened in my life – and will continue to do so when I'm not sidetracked writing new books! And you can contact me on Facebook www.facebook.com/JennieFeltonAuthor or Twitter @Jennie_Felton – I do love to hear from you.

With love
Jennie xx

By Jennie Felton

The Coal Miner's Wife

JENNIE FELTON

HEADLINE

First published in 2023 by
HEADLINE PUBLISHING GROUP

First published in paperback in 2024 by
HEADLINE PUBLISHING GROUP

1

Cataloguing in Publication Data is available from the British Library

ISBN 978 1 4722 9676 4

Typeset in Calisto by Avon DataSet Ltd, Alcester, Warwickshire

Printed and bound in Great Britain by Clays Ltd, Elcograf S.p.A.

Headline's policy is to use papers that are natural, renewable and recyclable
products and made from wood grown in well-managed forests and other
controlled sources. The logging and manufacturing processes are expected
to conform to the environmental regulations of the country of origin.

HEADLINE PUBLISHING GROUP
An Hachette UK Company
Carmelite House
50 Victoria Embankment
London EC4Y 0DZ

www.headline.co.uk
www.hachette.co.uk

To all my lovely readers, for buying my books and letting me know how much you enjoy them.

Thank you all.

Acknowledgements

My thanks, as always, go to the amazing team at Headline, headed by Marion Donaldson, Executive Publisher, and including Rebecca Bader, Isobel Smith, Alara Delfosse, Rhys Callaghan, Sophie Ellis, Sophie Keefe and Zara Baig.

My usual editor, Kate Byrne, is spending a year in a different department, so this time around my thanks go to Flora Rees for the very helpful first edits, and to Jane Selley, copy editor extraordinaire.

My lovely agent, Rebecca Ritchie is on maternity leave – congratulations on the birth of your son, Kip, Becky, and thanks for all the work you did to ensure a smooth handover to Florence Rees and Harmony Leung at A. M. Heath. Great to get to know you both!

Thanks to my family and friends for their love and support – you know who you are!

And, last but not least, many thanks to all my readers. I've dedicated this book to you. I hope you enjoy it and continue to keep in touch with me. It's lovely to get messages from you, and hopefully I can answer any queries you may have too!

Chapter One

February 1911

The day that was to change Lorna Harrison's life began like any other. As always, she was up before dawn, cleaning the grate, laying and lighting the fire and setting the kettle on the hob so that she could make the strong sweet tea the way Harry, her husband, liked it. While she waited for it to boil, she unstoppered his stone bottle in readiness and fetched his snap from the cold slab in the larder. She wrapped it in a red and white striped neckerchief – two good thick slices of bread and a chunk of cheese, enough to sustain him through a long day underground hewing coal. At this time of year he never saw daylight during the working week. It was still dark when he left for the pit and dark by the time he emerged again.

As she worked, Nipper, their mongrel puppy, scampered around her heels and made vain attempts to reach the cheese snap.

'No! Bad dog!' Lorna reprimanded him. He wasn't big enough yet to steal food from the table, but it wouldn't be long before he was, and he might as well learn from the start that it wasn't acceptable. It was going to be an uphill battle, though, and training him would be all down to her. Harry hadn't wanted a dog – 'He'll just make extra work for you,' he'd said – but Lorna had fallen in love the moment she'd seen the little scrap, one of a litter of five, tucked under his mother's owner's coat with just his little face poking out. 'The children will love him, and it will be good for them too,' she'd pleaded, and eventually she had got her way.

Now, however, as she heard Harry's boots on the stairs, she caught Nipper by the collar and gave him a push in the direction of his basket behind the kitchen door. When he dug his heels in and tried to sit down, she reached for the bacon rind left from last night's tea and tossed it into the basket. Just in time. The door to the stairs opened and Harry appeared, clad in the heavy-duty shirt and rushyduck trousers that all the miners wore for work.

He wasn't a big man, but the muscles that came from almost twenty years of hard physical toil bulged beneath his shirt, and his veins stood out, ridges black with coal dust. Once Lorna had found it romantic, just as she had the weal around his waist caused by the guss and crook that he had worn in the days when he was a carting boy; now she worried about the unseen filth that was almost certainly clogging his lungs. Too many miners suffered from silicosis, which made them old before their time, and whenever she saw a man who had once been fit and strong sitting on a bench outside his cottage, coughing up thick black phlegm, barely able to breathe and unable to walk unassisted, she looked quickly away, trying to suppress the dread that one day in the not-too-distant future this could be Harry.

Nipper had made short work of the bacon rind, and almost as soon as Harry entered the kitchen he was out of his basket and rushing to greet his master, nearly tripping him up in his eager onslaught.

Harry swore. 'Bloody dog! He hasn't messed on the floor again, has he?'

'No, and I'll take him out to do his do's just as soon as I've got a minute. Sit down and have a cup of tea.'

'No time.' Harry was already shrugging into his coat. 'My snap ready, is it?'

'It's on the table, where it always is,' Lorna said, her tone a trifle tart. She was tired – for some reason Harry had been restless during the night, and his tossing and turning had kept waking her – and his attitude to the dog wasn't helping.

Harry wound a muffler round his neck, jammed on his cap and picked up the bag containing his snap and bottle of tea.

'I'm off then.' There was an edge to his voice, and for a moment Lorna wondered if he was worried about something. That might account for his edginess over the last few days and his restlessness during the night. Trouble at work, perhaps? She knew there was a lot of unrest brewing about pay and working conditions, and knowing Harry, he would be at the heart of it.

As he headed for the door, Nipper jumped up and Lorna grabbed his collar. She couldn't risk him following Harry down the lane and onto the main road. 'Not you, Nipper. I'll take you out when your boss has gone.'

Once the door had closed after Harry, she went to the foot of the stairs and called to the children. 'Are you awake, girls? It's time to get up.'

'Yes, I am. Daddy makes such a noise.' Seven-year-old Marjorie, the elder of Lorna's two daughters by just over a year, appeared at the head of the stairs, barefoot and holding her nightgown tightly around her against the morning chill. 'Vera's still asleep, though.'

'Wake her up then, and get dressed both of you. You can

wash your face and hands down here by the fire. I'm just going to take Nipper out, and then I'll get your breakfast.'

Lorna pulled on her coat and went to the front door, Nipper bouncing excitedly at her heels. The back door opened onto a track that provided vehicle access along the full length of the rank of ten miners' cottages – Northfield Terrace – with vegetable patches beyond the outhouses on the opposite side. But although the front garden extended to the lane that ran down to meet the main road, it was much better equipped to stop Nipper from straying, with flower borders and a small lawn surrounded by privet hedges. Lorna didn't want him running off until she was sure he was old enough to find his way home safely.

As the puppy circled the lawn, sniffing and cocking his leg frequently as if to mark out his territory, Lorna found herself wondering sadly what had happened to the Harry she had married. What had happened to *them*? Time was when she wouldn't have minded being disturbed by his tossing and turning, but enjoyed the warmth of his body next to hers. Time was when he'd have thanked her for getting his snap and bottle of tea ready for him and kissed her when he left for work. No more. True, even when they'd first met at a dance in the town hall, there had never been the breathless passion between them that she'd read about in the romantic novels she'd borrowed from the library in the days when she'd had time to read. But there had been familiarity, comfortable affection and trust. Now there was a distance, an all-too-ready tendency to become irritated with one another. She didn't like the company he kept either – George Golledge, who lived further up the rank, for one. They were nothing but trouble. Sometimes she wondered if she'd ever really known Harry at all.

Nipper had finished his business in his favourite corner under the privet hedge and was enthusiastically scraping his hind legs

f earth and wet grass flew out
oughts aside, called to the dog
ook him back into the house.
ow, washing at the sink, but
s click-clacking on the
ned her flannel into
hug him.
hool smock

on
beh
– wh

Bot
the mon Nipper's nail
linoleum t covered the floor, Vera dropp
the bowl, grabbed the towel and dashed over to

'Vera! His paws are muddy. He'll make your s
dirty.'

Sometimes, dearly as she loved her, Lorna despaired of her irrepressible younger daughter. The two girls could scarcely have been more different. While Marjorie was sensible and almost too serious, Vera was a bouncy chatterbox, always looking for mischief. She went through clean clothes twice as fast as her sister – only last week she'd come in with her knickers in a disgusting state after Arthur, the young son of Lorna's best friend and next-door neighbour, Flossie Price, had given her a ride up and down the rank in the trucks that he used for collecting horse manure. While Marjorie's hair, which was almost straight and the same nut brown as Lorna's, was tied into a thick plait so it was always tidy, Vera's was an irrepressible tangle of red curls, a colour she'd inherited from her father. And it was Vera who was constantly in some sort of trouble at school – chattering in class, spilling ink on her exercise book, breaking her chalks and pens. But for all that, she was popular with adults and other children alike. 'A little ray of sunshine,' someone had once said. And small and dainty though she was, she was far more robust than Marjorie, who seemed to catch every cold that was doing the rounds and get complications with every childhood illness while Vera sailed through with barely a cough or a sniffle.

When she had wiped Nipper's feet with an old towel, Lorna popped the pan of porridge she'd prepared last night onto the

trivet over the fire to ... making a fresh pot
of tea. It was a routine ... e followed in her sleep,
a never-ending round of t ... of a housewife and mother.
But she was determined to ... make the most of every precious
moment of her girls' chi ... dhood. All too soon they would grow
up, living lives in w ... ich she would have little part. She tried not
to think about ... that. Didn't want to dwell on a future when it
was just her ... and Harry. And mercifully, just now there was no
time ... for such things.

By the time the mantel clock in the living room was striking ten, Lorna had taken the girls to school, walked home again, washed the dishes, made the beds and lit a fire under the copper to heat the water for a load of washing. Time for a cuppa, she decided. She had just settled herself with a hot drink and a slice of the slab cake she'd baked yesterday when, as if on cue, there was a knock at the back door and a voice called, 'Coo-ee! It's only me!'

'Come in, Flossie,' Lorna called back. Her next-door neighbour – and close friend – Flossie Price often popped in for a cup of tea and a chat around this time of the morning.

Flossie was a big woman, as motherly in appearance as she was by nature. Her cheeks were round and rosy, her apron strained over an ample bosom, and her ankles, clad in grey woollen stockings, bulged over her black button shoes. From the moment Lorna and Harry had moved into the cottage, Flossie had taken her under her wing as if she was just another of her brood of chicks. There had been six of them, though only the two younger boys, Jack and Arthur, were still living at home. The oldest boy, Gerald, had moved to South Wales, where he'd heard conditions in the mines were better than here in Somerset, and the girls were away in service. With her wealth of experience,

Lorna knew she could rely on the older woman for a piece of sensible advice if she was worried about one of the girls, or a cup of sugar or flour if she ran out. Over the years, their friendship had blossomed, and Lorna had come to think of Flossie as a second mother. Her own had died of a brain haemorrhage when Lorna was just fifteen, and she really didn't get on well with Harry's mother, an unpleasant woman who never had a good word to say about anyone.

'Thought I smelled a brew,' Flossie said now by way of greeting.

'Don't you always?' Lorna smiled. 'Sit down then, and cut yourself a slice of cake if you fancy it.'

'I'm not goin' to say no. Your cakes are a real treat. I only 'ad a bit of toast fer me breakfast, an' I've bin on the go ever since. Not that it's bin any different fer you, I don't s'pose. It's high time you stopped runnin' up and down to the school, if you ask me. Those girls are big enough to see themselves home at least.'

It wasn't the first time she'd said as much, and perhaps she was right, Lorna thought. She wouldn't like them to go on their own in the morning – she'd only worry as to whether they'd arrived safely – but if they could see themselves home at lunchtime and at the end of the school day, it would be a great help. Perhaps after the summer holidays she'd try it. The trouble was, she couldn't be sure Vera wouldn't play Marjorie up.

'You'll never guess who's in the family way again,' Flossie said, taking a bite of slab cake. She didn't wait for Lorna to reply. 'Dolly Parsons. She came to see me last night, asking me to put the date in my almanac.'

Dolly Parsons lived at the far end of the rank, and since Flossie acted as local midwife, as well as being called on to lay out the dead, she was always one of the first to know of any expected new arrivals.

'Well.' Lorna didn't really know what else to say, but Flossie was far from finished.

'I've had my suspicions for a bit,' she went on. 'She's had that look about her. The end of the summer it's due, she reckons, but I wouldn't mind betting she's doin' a bit o' jiggling with the dates and it'll be a good while sooner.'

'Why would she do that?' Lorna asked.

Flossie nodded sagely. 'Her Wally had to go off up to Yorkshire back in the autumn when his father took bad and died, remember? Well, Desmond Hill's bike was propped up against her outhouse more than once while he was away. I saw it with me own eyes.'

'Oh Flossie, surely not?' Lorna didn't like gossiping, even with Flossie. 'I can't believe she'd do something like that. She goes to chapel regular as clockwork on Sundays – twice sometimes.'

'Well, folk like that can be the worst. Anyway, time will tell if I'm right or not. But don't you say anything, mind. This is between you, me and the gatepost.'

'Course it is.' But Lorna couldn't help smiling to herself. If there was anything in what Flossie said, it wouldn't be long before the jungle drums were beating up and down the rank.

They finished their tea and cake, Flossie regaling Lorna with an account of Arthur's latest mischief.

'Sorry, Flossie, but I'm going to have to get on,' Lorna said, stacking the used crockery and standing up. 'I've got a load of washing to do.'

Flossie sighed. 'Me too. Just wait till you've got six like I had – you'll wish 'twas just your two little girls then.' She hoisted herself to her feet and went to the back door. 'See you later, p'raps.'

Lorna followed her out, crossing the track to the outhouse to see if the water in the copper was hot enough for her to start on the washing. A horse and cart was just rounding the corner of the rank and heading their way, and she recognised Donald Davey the coalman perched in the driver's seat.

'You expecting coal today?' Flossie asked.

'No. Are you?'

Flossie shook her head.

They both stepped back into the doorway to let the cart pass, but as it drew closer it looked to Lorna as if it was empty, and her heart came into her mouth with a jolt. If a miner was involved in an accident and was hurt badly enough, a coal cart waiting for its load at the pithead was commandeered to serve as an ambulance. If that was what had happened today, then it must be a man from Northfield Terrace lying injured in the well of the cart. One of their neighbours? Or – please God no! – her Harry?

The cart was moving at such a slow pace it might almost be coming to a stop, and Flossie bustled towards it.

'Who you got there, Mr Davey?' she called, her hoarse voice betraying her anxiety.

''Tis all right, missus. Not your Albie.'

Flossie crossed herself. She was a lapsed Catholic, but in times of crisis, old habits died hard.

''Tis George Golledge. Could you go up and warn 'is missus we'm on the way?'

Now that she knew it was not her husband in the coal cart, Flossie quickly returned to her usual capable self. 'Course I will.' She hurried off along the rank.

As the cart jolted over a cobble, the injured man groaned in agony, and Lorna drew back into the doorway. She was shaking – her hands, her stomach, her legs – as much from relief as from the few moments of gut-wrenching fear. George Golledge. Not Harry. Oh, thank God! Not Harry! Not this time.

It was a fear she had learned to live with, but a constant worry nonetheless, that one day it would be him being brought home in who knew what state. And seeing the coal cart making its way along the rank had brought it home to her all too vividly.

The water heating for her washing forgotten, she went back into the kitchen, where she poured herself a fresh cup of tea from the pot that was keeping warm on the hob and sat down at the table to drink it.

What exactly had happened to Mr Golledge? she wondered. She hoped it wasn't too serious. She didn't much like the man: he was uncouth, couldn't complete a single sentence without swearing, and his wife, Lil, was a thoroughly unpleasant woman. But all the same, she wouldn't wish that on anyone. Harry always stood up for him, saying his bark was worse than his bite, but then they were pals. They both belonged to the Buffs – the poor man's equivalent of the Rotary Club – and they drank together with a few of their militant pals in the Miners' Arms.

By the time she'd finished her tea, her heartbeat had steadied and she told herself she really must get down to the washing. The water was surely hot by now. But as she opened the back door, she was surprised to find Flossie on the doorstep, her hand raised to knock. Her neighbour looked shaken – unusual for Flossie, who was used to dealing with crises as the one everybody turned to in medical emergencies.

'Is it bad?' Lorna asked, fearing the worst.

'Let's go inside.' There was something ominous in Flossie's tone, and a shiver that felt like drips from a fast-melting icicle coursed through Lorna's veins.

'Why? What is it?'

'Not out here,' Flossie said firmly, and a frightened and bewildered Lorna allowed herself to be ushered into the kitchen. 'Now, you'd better sit down,' her neighbour instructed.

Lorna spun round, trembling from head to foot. 'No! Tell me! It's Harry, isn't it? Is he . . .' She broke off, unable to bring herself to finish the sentence.

Flossie spoke gently. 'There's been a roof fall. That's how George Golledge got hurt. He was lucky, though. He escaped the worst of it. Just got hit by a gurt lump of stone. But Harry . . . well, they haven't been able to get to him yet.'

'You mean he's on the other side of it.' Lorna was desperately grasping at straws.

'No, my love. He's underneath it. Him, Ted Yarlett and a carting boy.'

'Oh dear God!' Lorna's knees went weak and she gripped the table for support.

A roof fall. It had always been one of her worst fears. Here in Somerset the seams were shallow and faulted. From time to time a section of the roof or the coal face would give way and come crashing down in a shower of rock and debris, sometimes without warning and in spite of the regular inspections that were carried out. The thought of Harry lying beneath it badly injured – or worse – was enough to spur her into action. She straightened, swallowing down the panic that had overcome her.

'I've got to get down to the pit.' She grabbed her coat from the hook on the back of the door, scrabbling her arms into the sleeves.

'I'll come with you.'

'There's no need. Mrs Golledge will want your help.'

'And she'll have to whistle,' Flossie said harshly. 'I'm coming with you whether you like it or not. An' somebody will have to

11

Jennie Felton

get the children from school if we'm still there waiting by dinner time. Just give me a minute to get me coat.'

She hurried out and Lorna followed, pulling the door closed behind her but not locking it. No one in the rank ever did.

Grateful as she was to her neighbour, Lorna had no intention of waiting for her. Flossie would know where to find her, and the only thing that mattered was getting to the pit as quickly as she could. Finding out for herself exactly what the situation was. Being there when they eventually got Harry to the surface . . .

Thoughts racing, emotions churning, Lorna started out along the track and down to the main road that led to Milverton Colliery.

Chapter Two

'Well, this is a tidy how-dee-do,' Shorty Dallimore said, with understatement that was typical of the miners, and Ticker Greedy and Moses Whittock grunted their agreement.

All three were pals and workmates of Harry Harrison and George Golledge, and they were among a small crowd that had gathered in the yard that fronted Milverton Colliery. Groups of other miners who had been brought to the surface squatted against the wall of the building that housed the manager's office and the Davy lamp store, smoking and discussing what had happened in low, shocked tones, while a few passers-by, attracted by the unusual activity, chatted amongst themselves, airing theories as to what was going on. A woman laden with shopping bags approached one of the miners, a man she knew, to ask why he and the others weren't at work underground at this time of the morning, and within minutes the awful news had spread like wildfire.

The loud honk of a motor horn interrupted the shocked discussions, and the little crowd parted like the waters of the Red Sea. A gleaming red Daimler chuntered into the yard and drew up in front of the manager's office. No one was in any doubt as to who it belonged to, and indeed, there was the man himself sitting in state behind his chauffeur.

13

Sir Montague Fairley. The owner of Milverton pit and half a dozen other collieries besides.

The reaction of the miners squatting outside the buildings was instantaneous and unanimous. To a man they despised Sir Montague, who was known as a tyrant who cared only for the profits that swelled his coffers and not for the men who spent their lives toiling in the dark tunnels that ran beneath his land. One spat contemptuously; others muttered darkly. If anyone was to blame for what had happened today it was Sir Montague. 'If this don't make 'im change 'is ways, I don't know what will,' one man opined, but others were more sceptical.

'Some hopes. After Shepton Fields 'twas better for a bit, but look where we'm at again now,' another pointed out, and the rest nodded sagely.

It was sixteen years now since the terrible tragedy at Shepton Fields Colliery when the winding rope had been severed and the hudge had gone crashing down, claiming the lives of all the men and boys who had been riding it. The tragedy was not something that could easily be forgotten. The hudge should have been replaced years before with a proper cage lowered on a steel rope rather than one made of hemp, but Sir Montague had delayed and delayed, not wanting to spend a penny before he was forced to. Even if he wasn't the one who had hacked through the rope, the tragedy would never have happened if it were not for his meanness, and the general feeling was that it would take something similarly disastrous to shock him into improving their working conditions.

'Bloody bastard.' Shorty turned to Saul Russell, who was standing nearby. Saul's uncle Archie had been one of the men to die in the Shepton Fields tragedy. Shorty didn't bother to lower his voice, and not one of the miners moved, though it was clear Sir Montague's chauffeur was doing his best to park the Daimler as close to the manager's office as possible. 'We bain't shiftin' to suit 'im,' their defiant refusal to vacate the spot seemed to say, and though the mine owner glared at them and gesticulated with his ivory-topped cane, they studiously ignored him.

Their scowls turned to smirks, though, as Sir Montague climbed out of the motor and headed for the manager's office.

''E bain't there, sir,' Moses called, then shrugged as the mine owner seemed not to have heard him.

A moment later Sir Montague emerged, an angry flush exacerbating his habitual whisky-fuelled high colour, and stood looking around him in obvious annoyance.

'Told 'ee so,' Moses said, under his breath this time. He didn't want to be the one to bear the brunt of his employer's fury.

A small, wizened man in miner's clothing emerged from one of the two cottages whose front doors opened almost directly onto the pit yard. On seeing the Daimler, he hesitated and seemed to be contemplating beating a hasty retreat, but too late. Sir Montague had seen him.

'Penny!' he bellowed. The man stood still, a rabbit caught in the headlights, and Sir Montague turned to his chauffeur. 'Fetch him, Waters.'

The interest of the squatting miners was captured now. Dick Penny had begun work in the coal mines as a carting boy and worked his way up until he was considered responsible enough to take charge of the shot-firing – the blasting that loosened the coal. The general consensus of opinion, however, was that he was getting too old for the job. If he had still been a collier he would have been forced into retirement long before now, but he loved his work, and since he had lost his wife, Flo, a few years back, the pit had become his whole life.

Now he approached Sir Montague warily, twisting his cap

between his hands, and his first words were evidence that he was afraid he was likely to be blamed for the explosion.

''Twasn't nothin' to do wi' me, sir.'

Sir Montague harrumphed. 'If you say so. Where is Mr Cameron? And Mr Robinson? Are they underground?'

Penny's worried expression lightened a little. 'Mr Robinson is, I think. But Mr Cameron's held up at Oldlands. Summat's gone wrong wi' the screens, I think.'

Sir Montague gave an impatient shake of his head. There was always some problem at Oldlands. Some three miles south-west of Milverton, it was one of the oldest of Sir Montague's collieries and he was in the process of winding it down in preparation for closure. And the sooner the better, in his opinion. The place was falling apart and it wouldn't have surprised him if the accident had occurred there rather than here at Milverton.

'Well, get Mr Robinson then,' he snapped.

'Like I said, sir, he's underground.'

'So? The cage here is still operational, I take it?'

'I believe so, sir.'

'Is it or isn't it?'

''Tis, sir.'

'Then have a message delivered to Mr Robinson to tell him that I am here and wish to see him. Come on, man – move! I haven't got all day.'

'Yessir.' Dick Penny moved away in the direction of the pithead with an alacrity that surprised even him, so relieved was he to escape the autocratic mine owner.

Bradley Robinson was less than pleased to be summoned to a meeting with the coal owner. As the newly appointed safety officer for all Fairley collieries, he believed his place was here, underground, lending some muscle when it was needed and overseeing the rescue operation. He'd been in the post only two short months, appointed reluctantly by the tight-fisted Sir Montague to fulfil the requirements of the new mines safety legislation that was passing through Parliament, and the team he'd recruited to deal with just such an emergency as this was as yet untried and tested. But he supposed it was not beyond reason that Sir Montague would want to be kept abreast of the serious situation. Duncan Cameron, the district manager, was still dealing with the problems at Oldlands and might not yet even be aware of the seriousness of the roof fall here at Milverton.

Bradley emerged into the cold grey morning, a tall, muscular figure in his early thirties, his hair matted with coal and stone dust and his face streaked black from wiping away beads of sweat with filthy hands. He wore overalls to cover his workaday clothes, but they had done nothing to protect the front of his collarless white shirt, and he doubted he would ever get it clean.

That was not his priority at the moment, though. First and foremost he was concerned with getting to the boy and two men who were still unaccounted for, and he would tell Sir Montague so in no uncertain terms if the man kept him too long with a barrage of as yet unanswerable questions.

Sir Montague was waiting for him outside the office, and as Bradley approached, he indicated that the safety officer should join him inside.

'Close the door,' he ordered by way of greeting, and pulled himself up to his full height, his cane planted firmly in front of him. Trying to emphasise his superiority, Bradley guessed, though he himself stood a full two inches taller.

'Sir Montague,' he said.

The coal owner huffed impatiently. 'What the devil is going on here, Robinson?'

Bradley held his gaze steadily. He was not intimidated by Sir Montague as so many of his employees were. His previous life as a cavalry officer had taught him to meet any challenge head-on.

'There's been a roof fall, sir, and at least one man has been badly injured. Others are trapped, but thanks to your authorising it, we have the very latest equipment and are working hard to free them.'

'I should darned well hope so!' Sir Montague snapped. 'It's cost me a pretty penny to get things ready to fall in line with the latest legislation.'

'But it is fortunate that a trained team were able to be on the scene so quickly, don't you agree? This is exactly the sort of incident the Act has been designed for.'

Sir Montague's bad temper was only worsened by what he regarded as a lack of respect from an employee at least thirty years his junior.

'What's caused this damned roof fall anyway?'

'I'm afraid it's too early to say, sir. Just now the most important thing is getting to the men who are trapped.'

Sir Montague huffed impatiently. 'That's as may be. But blame for what's happened must lie somewhere. Something must have been missed, and I want to know what. I can't afford for this sort of thing to become a regular occurrence.'

Bradley felt his own temper rising, and struggled to control it. The coal owner was more concerned about his profits than he was about his workers. He'd heard it said, but this was the first time he'd witnessed it for himself.

'As I'm sure you know, sir, the District Inspector of Mines will visit and report on his findings,' he said as levelly as he could manage. 'If he is unable to reach a conclusion, you have my assurance that I won't rest until I have some answers.'

'See that you do. And make no mistake, heads will roll if negligence is found to be the cause of this.' Sir Montague reached for his fob watch, stretched across his ample stomach. 'I have a meeting with my agent shortly, and it seems I am wasting my time here. In Cameron's absence, please ensure the men get back to work as soon as practicable, and don't make this an excuse for them to take the rest of the day off.'

'I'm not sending anyone back underground until I am satisfied it's safe to do so,' Bradley stated baldly.

Sir Montague shot him a thunderous look. But, presumably realising what the consequences for him would be should another roof fall occur, he did not argue.

'Keep me apprised of the outcome,' he said shortly, and stalked out of the office without so much as a backward glance.

A moment later, Bradley heard the engine of the Daimler crank into life. His breath came out on a sigh, and he sank into the manager's chair, resting his elbows on the desk and burying his face in his hands.

What a bastard Sir Montague was! But he was right about one thing. It wasn't usual for such a severe roof fall to occur with no warning. It was the deputy's job to check the safety of the roadways, and Ewart Moody, who had been in that role for years, seemed a conscientious sort. But Bradley had to bear some responsibility too. He'd made a cursory inspection himself only yesterday. Was it possible he had missed something? He hoped to God not. If what had happened was partly his fault, he didn't think he could live with himself.

For a moment he bent his head, massaging some of the tension out of his neck. What had happened had shaken him to the core. He'd come here with such enthusiasm; the prospect of being instrumental in minimising the chances of miners sustaining serious injury and perhaps even losing their lives had given him a new sense of purpose that had been lacking since his world had come crashing down around him.

In another life, Bradley had been a cavalry officer with the 14th King's Hussars. Just two years after he had completed his training, he had fought with them in the relief of Ladysmith. But bloody and gruelling as that had been, he'd never for one moment thought of a change of career. Until a disastrous accident had meant he was no longer fit to serve as a cavalry officer.

It was, he often thought, a cruel irony that after surviving the horrific bloodshed he'd seen in South Africa, this should have happened to him in peacetime, on what should have been a routine exercise. And all because of the pumped-up ego and incompetence of his commanding officer.

Bradley had been in the process of training a newly acquired horse, a fourteen-hand roan named – most aptly as it turned out – Fury. The horse had repeatedly refused at a jump that was often likened to Becher's Brook. Bradley had known he was becoming increasingly unsettled and it was unwise to push him further. But the CO thought otherwise and caught the reluctant animal a stinging blow to his rump. Fury's reaction was instantaneous. He bucked and reared, then took off at a gallop, completely out of control, and there was nothing Bradley could do to stop him. It was only when the horse came to a thick, high fence not unlike the one he had repeatedly refused that he came to a halt, so abruptly that he unseated his rider, then backed up, treading several times on Bradley's leg.

Even as he lay in agony on the sun-baked turf, Bradley knew that the career he loved was over, and so it had proved. His leg was so badly broken it was impossible for him to continue as a cavalry officer.

After a year in which he had descended into an abyss of pain and hopelessness, he had found employment as a pen pusher in the government-controlled Inspectorate of Mines. It was only when the inspectorate's districts were reorganised that things began to look up. An Act was passing through Parliament that required centres with proper equipment and teams of trained rescuers to be set up within a ten-mile radius of any colliery. Bradley had been trained in the new safety procedures that were to be introduced, and once he was qualified, he had applied for the post of safety officer for Sir Montague Fairley's group of collieries. To his delight he had been successful, and been informed that he would be based at Milverton Colliery where he would share an office with Duncan Cameron, the general manager.

He had also been allocated a house which had previously been occupied by the manager of Oldlands, the colliery where Cameron was this morning. The manager had recently retired, and since the pit was being run down for closure, Sir Montague had added it to Cameron's responsibilities rather than appointing a replacement. Bradley was more than satisfied; the house was surrounded by open countryside and wooded areas, and although as a single man he rattled around in it he counted himself very lucky.

The fly in the ointment was Sir Montague himself. There was something about the mine owner that reminded Bradley of his old commanding officer. Both came from aristocratic stock; both cared little for the men whose lives they ran. In Sir Montague's case it was money that mattered more; with 'Dimwit Dalton', as the regiment had called the CO behind his back, it was deference and control over those unfortunate enough to serve under him. There the resemblance ended, of course. Dalton was the younger son of a baronet whose father had bought a commission for him as compensation for missing out on inheriting the estate, while clearly Fairley had come into his title and all that went with it. But his attitude this morning had only confirmed Bradley's first impression. The man was a boor; ill-tempered and full of his own self-importance.

Bradley shifted his gammy leg, which was aching badly. He was lucky it had healed as well as it had, he told himself, and comparing his new employer to the man who had been responsible for the injury would help no one, least of all the poor souls still trapped deep underground. And neither would tormenting himself with the nagging worry that he should somehow have been able to prevent the roof fall.

He got up, leaning on the back of the chair while he swung his leg a few times to loosen the stiff joint. Time to go below again. There would be plenty of time in the days ahead to get to the bottom of what had happened. And just as he had promised Sir Montague, that was exactly what he intended to do.

Chapter Three

As she hurried down the incline that led to the main road, and even on the gentler slope when she reached it, Lorna's legs almost ran away from her. It wasn't far to the pit yard, and as she neared it, she was forced to slow down. Rails for trucks carrying waste, which were drawn in a long caravan by a team of ponies, crossed the road here on their way through the valley towards the batches, as spoil heaps were known locally, and she didn't want to catch her foot in them and fall.

She turned into the yard, where the small crowd of onlookers had been swelled by anxious womenfolk who had heard that something awful had occurred. A group of miners were squatting against the office wall smoking and speculating. The sight brought it home to her that this was really happening, and wasn't just some nightmare she had stumbled into.

She saw Dick Penny, the shot-firer, talking to Ewart Moody, the deputy; from their body language it looked as if they were arguing about something. It was common knowledge that the two men had little time for one another; Harry had told her Ewart made no bones about airing his opinion that it was high time Dick Penny retired. 'He's a fine one to talk,' he had said. 'They'm much of an age. They should both finish, the pair of 'em, and make way for younger blood.'

'Like you, you mean,' Lorna had teased him, but she knew it was close to the truth. Harry harboured ambitions. He wanted to move up the ladder to a more responsible job. But as long as the old brigade remained, there would be no vacancy. 'Waiting to fill dead men's shoes', he called it.

But whether Harry liked it or not, Dick and Ewart were the men most likely to know what was going on below ground. She'd ask them.

At that moment, however, a murmur ran like a stiff breeze in a field of corn through those gathered in the yard, and following their gaze, Lorna saw that the winding wheels had begun to turn, slowly, deliberately.

She stopped short, her heart racing once more, unable now to take her eyes off the wheels. Did it mean those trapped had been freed? Was the cage bringing one of them to the surface? Could it be Harry? And what sort of condition would he be in?

A tap on the shoulder made her jump as if she'd been shot, and she swung round violently to see Flossie right behind her.

'Steady up, my love.' Flossie was out of breath and red in the face. 'I'm here now.'

'Oh Flossie.' Lorna jerked her head in the direction of the pithead. 'Something's happening . . .'

Even as she spoke, the wheels stopped turning. The cage must have reached the surface. Flossie took her hand, and the two women stood silently, watching and waiting. Seemingly endless minutes passed before a group of four or five men emerged, clustered around what looked like a stretcher. But why weren't they hurrying to take whoever was on it to one of the coal carts that were waiting to act as makeshift ambulances? Dread rose, a barrier in Lorna's throat so that she struggled to swallow, speak or even breathe.

Flossie squeezed her hand. 'You stay here, my love. I'll find out what's what.' She hurried away in the direction of the pithead.

Lorna stood frozen with fear, unable to move a muscle. Without being told, without even having a clear view of whoever was on the stretcher, she knew he must be dead. There could be no other explanation for the delay. Or for one of the men taking off his coat and bending over the casualty. Covering him. He was covering him. Lorna's senses swam and it was all she could do to keep from collapsing. But a grim-faced Flossie was making her way back, and somehow Lorna steeled herself to take whatever was to come.

'Is it . . .' She grasped at the front of Flossie's coat.

'No, my love. 'Tis young Tommy Maggs. He's gone, though. Fifteen years old, an' he's gone.' She shook her head, the very picture of distress. 'Terrible thing. Terrible.'

It *was* terrible, of course. A tragedy – a young life snuffed out. But to her shame, in that moment Lorna could think only that Tommy was Harry's carting boy. He would have been with Harry, and perhaps not with the men who had been brought out, injured but alive. If Tommy had been killed, either outright, by the catastrophic fall of stone and coal that had come crashing down, or suffocated beneath it, what hope was there for her husband?

As if reading her thoughts, Flossie put her arm round Lorna's shoulders.

'They'm still working hard as they can to get him out, and Ted Yarlett too,' she said. 'Don't torment yourself with maybes, my love. There's hope for 'em yet.'

There was no room for Bradley in the narrow space where his team were working to free Harry Harrison and Ted Yarlett. He was only hampering their efforts. As he reluctantly shuffled backwards, his back brushed against the roof, and coal dust showered down, blinding him momentarily. His gut clenched. Was there going to be another roof fall? Were he and his team going to be the next casualties?

He coughed, trying to rid his throat of the dust he had breathed in, and as his vision cleared, he glanced up apprehensively. But the shower seemed to have stopped, thank God. Staying low, he inched back a little further and looked again, ready to yell to his men to get out if necessary. The beam of his Davy lamp caught what looked like a hairline crack in the roof. He leaned back on his elbows, studying it. But the surrounding rock looked stable enough. Gingerly he reached up, running his fingertips along the crack, but no more dust cascaded down. It seemed to run from the main roadway to the site of the roof fall. He frowned, puzzled. He certainly hadn't noticed it when he'd done his inspection earlier. But he was no geologist, no expert in rock formations. It would be up to the Chief Inspector of Mines to come up with an explanation – if there was one. At the moment, his main concern was getting the two men out – alive, he hoped. One fatality was bad enough, and in his opinion it could hardly have been worse. A boy. Just a boy, who should still be in the classroom, getting an education that would help him to better himself. The Act of Parliament that had raised the age at which lads could be sent to work underground had been an improvement, yes, but in Bradley's opinion it still didn't go nearly far enough. Children shouldn't be working in these conditions. And they certainly shouldn't be dying.

If he had been feeling bad about the accident before, the sight of the young lad lying dead in a grave of dust and rubble had hit him a hammer blow. He'd gritted his teeth and prayed to a God he no longer believed in as his team brushed away the last of the debris that covered the boy, and Petey Sawyer, the newly trained first-aider, felt for a pulse in his neck. But after a moment he had leaned back on his heels, shaking his head. Tommy was gone.

Bradley's first reaction had been a rising tide of anger, against the God who had ignored his prayers and the coal owner who cared so little for the safety of his men. Fairley should be here to witness the tragedy, but instead he was no doubt plotting with his sly agent, Fred Gardiner, how to evade responsibility for what had happened. And all the while savouring a tot of his finest single malt whisky, if his complexion and the purplish colour of his nose were anything to go by. What wouldn't Bradley give to land a hard punch on that nose!

But as the stretcher party moved slowly away with Tommy's body, he had thrust his anger aside. It would have to keep. There was still work to be done here, two more men to be pulled out of the rubble. He had little hope now of finding them alive, but they were owed the dignity of being laid out in daylight, rather than darkness punctuated only by the light of the men's Davy lamps, and their families needed to know their fate, whatever that might be.

He had set his team to work again, though they needed no telling, and now, as he squatted nearby, watching them work, a sense of having failed began to eat at him again, along with the nagging worry that he might have missed something, that somehow he should have been able to prevent what had occurred.

'I think we've got 'im,' one of his team called over his shoulder, and at once Bradley felt his throat tighten and his muscles tense as he prepared himself for whatever was to come.

The pit wheel was turning again, slow circles against the overcast grey sky. To Lorna the wait had been excruciating, and as the minutes crawled by her nerves stretched ever more tightly.

She was worried about Marjorie and Vera, too, anxious that they shouldn't come out of school and find no one waiting for them.

'Is it time for the children's dinner yet?' she'd asked Flossie.

'We'll hear the bell go,' Flossie had assured her. 'It won't take me five minutes to run under the subway and along to the school.' The subway was a passage that ran under one of the town's two railways. 'They'll have Harry out long before then if you ask me.'

Lorna hadn't answered. She couldn't trust herself to speak, and now, with the moving pit wheel signalling that someone was being brought to the surface, she was trembling from head to foot.

'Chin up,' Flossie said, squeezing her hand, but she was unable to conceal the anxiety that had crept into her voice. 'D'you want me to . . . ?'

'No. I have to. I'm his wife, Flossie.'

'Good lass. I'll come with you.'

The pit yard was less crowded now. The women who had satisfied themselves that their menfolk were safe had left – they had a full day's chores awaiting them at home – and most of the men had dispersed, heading for the Miners' Arms, where they would air their views on what had happened, and bemoan the loss of at least a half-day's pay over a much-needed pint of beer.

Lorna and Flossie made for the pithead. A burly miner Lorna didn't recognise had been stationed there to keep the curious from getting too close and hampering the evacuation of any remaining casualties.

'Step back now!' he said sternly, spreading his arms wide.

Flossie was undeterred. 'Harry Harrison's one of them wot's still trapped, Mr Milsom,' she said. 'And this be his wife.'

'Oh, right.' His expression softened to one of sympathy. 'You still need to keep the way clear, though. They'm bringing somebody up now.'

Flossie turned her head to one side so Lorna couldn't see what she was saying as she mouthed: 'Dead or alive?'

'Alive, I reckon. They took a long time getting 'im in the cage. Longer than they would if he were—'

'Is it Harry?' Lorna had heard what he'd said, and her words came tumbling out in an urgent rush.

'Sorry, missus. Couldn't say.' The cage had reached ground level and he turned towards it.

Lorna could hardly bear to look as the gate opened, but neither could she tear her eyes away. Her mouth was dry, the rapid beat of her heart echoed in her throat, and her fingernails bit deep crescents in the palms of her clenched hands.

The man lying on the stretcher was barely recognisable. Thick, muddy sludge matted his hair, and his face was black with coal dust. In several places the blanket that covered him was red with fresh blood, and one leg jutted out from under it at an unnatural angle. But his eyes were open, though he was blinking spasmodically to clear them of dust, startlingly blue eyes that Lorna would have known anywhere.

'Harry!' She pushed her way to the stretcher, shaking with relief. Tears starting in her own eyes, she reached for Harry's hand.

'Out o' the way, missus, the lead stretcher-bearer ordered brusquely. 'We gotta get 'im to hospital.'

Lorna barely heard him. For the moment, she was aware of nothing but her husband, his hand warm beneath hers. Dirty. Bloody. But warm. All the irritation with him she'd felt earlier this morning had been driven out by anxiety.

'Let them past,' Flossie urged.

It was a long moment before Lorna could bring herself to release Harry's hand. Then she touched his face gently, brushing away some of the dirt.

'You're safe now, Harry,' she whispered. 'It's going to be all right.'

As she straightened, he looked up at her directly, his eyes meeting hers.

'Sorry, m'dear,' he mumbled.

The threatening tears filled her eyes. 'Don't be so silly! It's not your fault!'

The stretcher-bearers moved off towards the waiting coal cart, and Lorna and Flossie followed.

'Be you comin', missus?' one of them asked as they heaved the stretcher onto the cart.

'You'll get yerself filthy, mind,' added another.

Getting covered in coal dust was the least of Lorna's worries at that moment, but Marjorie and Vera would be coming out of school soon. Uncertain as to what she should do, she glanced at Flossie pleadingly. Her neighbour didn't hesitate.

'Go on, my love. Go with 'im. I'll see to the children.'

'You'd best come up and sit wi' me,' the coalman called, and in a daze, Lorna let one of the stretcher-bearers help her up onto the driver's seat.

At that very moment, the bell signalling the school dinner break began to clang. Instantly Flossie sprang into action.

'Don't worry – they'll be fine,' she called to Lorna, and hurried off as fast as her legs would carry her.

By the time the coal cart reached the main road, to Lorna's relief, there was no sign of her.

Flossie heard the hubbub of children's voices as soon as she neared the school playground. After the discipline of the classroom, the excitement of the hour's freedom was too much for them to contain. Some of the older ones had already come running out, shrugging into their coats as they went, and the mothers of the little ones were fighting their way through the narrow doorway that led into the cloakroom.

A small boy almost crashed into Flossie as she hurried across the yard, and she tutted at him. 'Careful, me lad!' Of Marjorie and Vera there was no sign, but as she neared the door, Arthur came shooting out like a ball from a cannon, and stopped short in surprise to see his mother.

'What're you doin' here?'

'Collecting the Harrison girls,' she explained.

'They coulda come home wi' me!' he objected.

'You know their mother always fetches them,' Flossie said, a little impatiently. 'Where are they?'

'Still in there.' Arthur jerked his head in the direction of the cloakroom.

'Right. Just wait here for me. And no arguments,' she added firmly, putting a stop to what would have turned into a barrage of questions.

A handful of children were still in the cloakroom under the watchful eye of Miss Blanning, the infant teacher, who was standing at the top of the short flight of stone steps that led up into the classroom. Marjorie and Vera were at the far end of the long, narrow room; Marjorie, with her coat already on, was helping Vera into hers, at the same time keeping one eye on the doorway for her mother. When she saw Flossie approaching, her serious little face creased into a puzzled frown.

'Mrs Price! Where's Mammy?'

'Don't worry, my love. She's fine.' Flossie bent to button Vera's coat. 'I'm taking you home today, and you're going to have your dinner at mine. Now you two wait outside with our

31

Arthur. I'm just goin' to have a word with your teacher. I won't be a minute.'

'I don't understand . . .' Marjorie began, but Vera was tugging impatiently at her sleeve. Arthur Price was her hero. She'd told Marjorie that she was going to marry him one day.

'Go on now,' Flossie urged them. 'And no getting up to mischief.'

As they headed for the door, Flossie approached the teacher. She was a short, plump woman with a deceptively friendly face who could be something of a tyrant as far as the children were concerned, though she was unfailingly polite and even helpful towards the parents.

'Can I have a word, Miss Blanning?'

'About Arthur? He's not in my class any more. You need to see—'

'It's not about Arthur,' Flossie interrupted her. 'It's about the Harrison girls. They won't be in school this afternoon. There's bin an accident at the pit. Their father's bin seriously injured, so I'm taking 'em home with me.'

'Oh dear!' Miss Blanning looked flummoxed. 'I'm sorry to hear that. But wouldn't it be better for them to stay here? We can look after them in familiar surroundings until their mother is able to collect them.'

'Their mother will want them to be with me. They know me, and they'm used to bein' in my house,' Flossie said firmly. 'I live next door to them,' she added for good measure.

'Oh yes, of course. Well, if you're sure . . .'

'I'm sure all right. Now, I must get going if Arthur's to have his dinner and be back fer 'is afternoon lessons. I just thought I should let you know.' And without further ado, Flossie hurried off.

The children were waiting just outside, Marjorie looking

worried and holding tightly to Vera's hand, though her little sister was tugging at it impatiently, anxious to join Arthur, who was juggling a football that someone had left in the playground.

'Arthur! Come on! We're going now.' Flossie took hold of Vera's other hand. 'Let's step out, shall we? There's some nice new bread and tasty cheese for you when we get home. You like a bit of tasty cheese, don't you?'

'I don't,' Vera objected. 'It smells.'

'We'll find you summat else, then. I might have some ham if you behave yourself.'

'Ooh yes!'

If only everything could be solved so easily, Flossie thought. In spite of her reassurances, she was very concerned for Harry. She hadn't liked the look of him at all. And she was worrying too about how much she should tell the children, and when. Was it best to prepare them, or should she leave it for Lorna to tell them what had happened when she got home? And how was she going to get back anyway? The coal cart wouldn't wait for her.

What a day! Flossie thought. Just take things as they come – that was her motto. But she had to admit, this was testing it to its limits.

Chapter Four

This was not going to end well. Even before his team cleared the last of the rubble covering Ted Yarlett, Bradley knew it in his gut. It had taken too long to free him. Harry Harrison had been barely alive when he was pulled out, and that was almost an hour ago. As the painstaking work continued and hope faded, Bradley waited. His limbs were cramped and his leg ached badly, but he gritted his teeth and held on. He had to see this through.

Only when Ted Yarlett was freed and the first-aider had checked his pulse for signs of life and found none did he worm his way back to the roadway, take the cage to the surface and wait, sick at heart, for the man's body to be brought up. A man and a boy were dead. Two more had been badly injured, one of whom might not make it. Though Bradley had encountered death before, violent and bloody death, he hadn't felt responsible then as he did now. His guilt then had only been for surviving while others had died.

Had he made a bad mistake in taking the job of safety officer? he wondered. Accidents underground were almost inevitable, and not all were preventable. Whatever precautions he implemented, there would always be the man whose carelessness or lapse in concentration resulted in an injury of some kind. He'd known that, and thought he could accept it. But something of this magnitude occurring within months of his taking up the post had affected him badly, and at this moment he wasn't sure whether he wanted to carry on doing his best to save life and limb, or walk away.

But on one thing he was determined – he was going to get to the bottom of what had happened here today. And if the Inspector of Mines didn't come up with a cause, he'd investigate it thoroughly himself, just as he'd promised Sir Montague.

The sound of a motor interrupted his dark reverie. It wasn't the powerful roar of Sir Montague's Daimler, but the phut-phut of a much smaller engine, and he looked up to see a Ford motor entering the colliery yard.

Duncan Cameron, once manager of Milverton Colliery but now in charge of five of Sir Montague's pits. He must have sorted out the problem with the screen belt at Oldlands – or word had finally reached him of the disaster here at Milverton. Bradley crossed the yard to meet him, and guessed from his grim expression that it was the latter. Cameron already knew that something very serious had happened, and now it was up to Bradley to break the news that the death toll had risen to two.

'This is a bad business and no mistake,' Cameron greeted him.

He was a big man, not tall, but solidly built, and it matched his reputation of being hard but fair. Cameron kowtowed to no one, but was not too self-important to listen to opinions that differed from his own. It was he who had persuaded a reluctant Sir Montague to appoint a safety officer and invest in the equipment and facilities that would be needed in order to comply with the new laws. 'Better to get it done now than be forced into it later,' he had argued. 'Costs will rise, and it will be a bigger

Jennie Felton

expense in the long run.' He was also a good arbitrator in disputes between men and management, though even he had been unable to quell the unrest that had been stirring amongst the workforce for some months now.

'It's even worse than you may have heard,' Bradley said, and felt a sense of relief as he shared the details of the disaster with his superior.

'How badly are the two men injured?' Cameron asked as he finished.

'I think George Golledge will be all right, though how long it will be before he's fit to work again I couldn't say. But Harry Harrison . . .' Bradley spread his hands helplessly. 'It's in the lap of the gods whether or not he pulls through. He's been taken to the cottage hospital, but he's in a bad way. In fact, I'd like to go there myself and see how he's faring. My team have everything under control and I don't think there's anything more I can do here at the moment, apart from notifying the Inspector of Mines.'

He didn't need to explain to Cameron that the inspector would have to pay a visit and make a report. The manager was well aware of the protocol in case of an accident.

'I can do that,' Cameron said. 'Go and find out how Harrison is doing. Take my motor. I won't be going anywhere any time soon.'

'That's good of you, Mr Cameron.'

'Cam!' the manager exclaimed. 'I've told you before – I know that's what the men call me behind my back. You might as well call me it to my face.'

Bradley smiled briefly. 'I'll try to remember.'

'You'd better. Now off you go. I'll leave you to crank up the engine. You're younger than me by a good ten years.' He started towards his office, then turned, nodding at Bradley. 'Good work, Robinson. If it weren't for the team you've trained, we might have lost them all.'

Bradley nodded grimly. He didn't feel he was worthy of praise. Yes, his team had worked hard and well and put their training to good use when it was needed. But the feeling that he'd missed something still nagged at him.

Huffing breath over his top lip, he went to the Ford, gripped the starting handle and cranked the engine into life.

Lorna sat on a hard upright chair in the corridor outside the room where Harry was being assessed, a mug of tea clutched between hands that refused to stop shaking. At least it had warmed her, and she was grateful for that, but she only wished the kindly young nurse who had brought it to her had put in a tot of brandy instead of goodness only knew how many spoonfuls of sugar. She didn't often drink, but in times of stress she did pour herself a little measure from the half-bottle she kept in the dresser for medicinal purposes. Her mother had always had some on hand for when she suffered a bilious attack as a child, and for a long time afterwards the very smell of it had made her feel sick. Now, though, she'd grown to quite like the taste, and the warmth as it trickled down into her stomach, and there was no doubt it had a calming effect when her nerves were frayed. As they were now – only a hundred times worse than anything she had ever experienced before.

Harry hadn't spoken a single word on the journey to the hospital, hadn't even moaned. She'd cricked her neck turning to look at him countless times, just to make sure he was still breathing. 'Are you all right, Harry?' she'd asked, but he hadn't replied. It was a stupid question, of course. Perhaps he didn't think it warranted an answer. But she was very afraid that it was because he'd lapsed into unconsciousness.

It was the same when they'd stretchered him into the hospital. He'd just lain there, his leg jutting at that impossible angle beneath the blanket that covered it, and blood soaking the stretcher beneath it. He'd been whisked into an examination room and she'd followed, but a stern nursing sister in a starched white cap and apron had said she'd have to leave. She'd taken a seat in the corridor, trying unsuccessfully to hear what was going on behind the closed door. A doctor had arrived, coming in by the main entrance, wearing an overcoat and hat and carrying a medical bag. There were no resident doctors here; the cottage hospital relied on local general practitioners. He went straight into the examination room without so much as a glance at Lorna.

It was then that the young nurse had taken pity on her and asked if she'd like a cup of tea. Lorna had accepted gratefully, though in reality all she'd really wanted was to know exactly how bad Harry's injuries were, and what they were going to do to help him.

After what seemed an age, the doctor reappeared, shrugging into his overcoat while juggling his medical bag. This time he acknowledged Lorna's presence.

'You're the wife, I gather?'

Lorna placed her now empty cup on the vacant chair next to her and made to get up, but her leg was cramping and her feet felt like balls of cotton wool.

'How is he?' she asked.

The doctor put his medical bag down on the floor beside him and began buttoning his overcoat.

'Badly hurt, as I'm sure you know,' he said bluntly. 'It will be a few days before the extent of his injuries becomes clear. But one thing is indisputable. His leg is severely broken and will need an operation to give him any chance of saving it.'

Lorna swallowed hard. 'He's going to have to go to Bath?'

'Possibly. But we will attempt to do what's necessary here. We have a small operating theatre, and one of our local doctors – Mackay – is reasonably experienced in certain branches of surgery, such as the fitting of a restraint when there's an open wound. He'll assess him and decide on the best way forward.'

Lorna didn't understand what the doctor was talking about, and she didn't know what to think. On the one hand she was glad Harry was not going to be whisked off to the city, nine miles away; on the other, she didn't like the sound of 'reasonably experienced'. If Harry needed an operation, she wanted someone who knew what they were doing to carry it out.

'I'm sure Sister will explain things to you. But now I must leave you. I have calls to make on my own patients who are expecting me.' He picked up his medical bag. 'Goodbye, Mrs . . .'

He broke off. He'd already forgotten her name, Lorna thought. If that was the interest he had in Harry and his case, it didn't inspire confidence.

The door to the examination room opened again and the sister emerged, carrying a sheaf of notes attached to a clipboard.

'We're taking your husband to a ward now,' she said crisply. 'Perhaps you'd like to spend a few moments with him while we wait for the porter.'

'Can't I go with him?' Lorna asked.

'I'm afraid not. Visiting is between six and seven this evening if you'd care to come then. Unless of course he is being operated on. But I doubt that will be until tomorrow.'

'Oh.' Lorna was feeling completely overwhelmed.

'If you want to see your husband before you leave, I suggest you don't waste any more time,' the sister said, before bustling away along the corridor.

Lorna got up and approached the treatment room apprehensively. At first it appeared Harry was still in the same comatose state, but as she neared the bed, she saw that his eyes were open.

'Oh Harry!' She reached through the bars that had been raised on each side of the bed and took his hand. 'Are you awake now?'

For a moment he squinted at her with a puzzled expression creasing his face, which, now that it was cleaned of dirt and coal dust, she could see was covered with bruises that were beginning to change colour. He had a shiny lump the size of an egg on his temple.

'It's me, Lorna,' she said encouragingly.

'Oh . . . Lorna.' But he still looked uncertain. 'Where am I?'

She swallowed the knot that was tightening her throat. 'You're in hospital. They're going to take good care of you.'

'Why . . . ?' He broke off suddenly, his face contorting in agony. He must have tried to move his injured leg, Lorna realised.

'Just lie still, Harry. You've broken your leg, I think. It'll hurt worse if you move.'

He grunted, his features still twisted into a grimace of pain.

'Listen, Harry. They won't let me stay with you now, but I'll be in to visit you. Do you hear me?'

He nodded, an almost imperceptible jerk of his head.

'I won't be able to bring the children with me, but I know they'll send their love.' Tears were pricking behind her eyes and she blinked them away. She didn't want him to see her crying. She was taken aback when he spoke suddenly.

'Are George and the others all right?'

'Well, Mr Golledge is alive. They brought him home in a coal cart. But I don't know how badly he's hurt. I didn't wait to find out. I was too worried about you.'

She was saved from having to mention the fatalities as the door opened and the porter came in, followed by the kind nurse who had brought her a cup of tea.

'I'm sorry, but you'll have to go now,' the nurse said apologetically.

Lorna kissed her fingers and pressed them to Harry's cheek. 'I'll see you soon – promise,' she said, and hurried out, feeling the tears threatening again. Once outside she rounded the corner of the building, leaned back against the wall, and let them flow.

She was still sobbing, all the stress of this awful day pouring out, when a small motor came chugging up the path from the road. Horrified, she clapped her hand over her mouth. She didn't want anyone to see her like this, but there was nowhere she could hide. As the motor came to a halt, she hastily wiped her eyes with the back of her hand and tried to pretend she was waiting for someone, looking anywhere but at the motor. Perhaps it was the doctor who was going to operate on Harry's leg, she thought, and almost began crying again, thinking that he was in no fit state to be undergoing an operation.

But the man who climbed out of the motor didn't go into the hospital. Out of the corner of her eye she could see him coming towards her.

'Mrs Harrison?' he said. Lorna nodded, not trusting herself to speak. 'How is he?'

'I'm sorry?' Lorna had not the faintest idea who this man was.

'No – it's me who should apologise. You won't know me, of course. I'm Bradley Robinson, the mine safety officer. I'm very concerned about your husband. I've been told he has been brought here, and I've come to ask after him.'

Lorna swallowed hard. 'Well, he's in a bad way, Mr Robinson. He doesn't seem to know where he is or what's

happened, and they say he needs an operation. It's his leg . . .'
She broke off as the tears threatened again.

'I'm sorry to hear that.' He really did sound sorry, she
thought. 'Are you able to stay with him?'

She shook her head. 'They won't let me. They said I should
go home. And I suppose I should really. My children . . . my
neighbour's looking after them, but . . .'

'How are you going to get there?' he asked, concerned. 'You
live in Hillsbridge, I expect?'

'Walk, of course.' Her small scornful laugh turned into a sob.

'I can't let you do that.' He spoke decisively. 'I'm going back
to Hillsbridge. You can ride with me.'

Lorna gaped in astonishment. Ride? In a motor? With a pit
official? She'd never been in a motor, and never so much as
spoken to any of the bosses. 'Oh – I couldn't . . .'

'You can and you will. You're in no fit state to walk
anywhere, never mind all that way. Look – come and sit in
the car, and I'll be back just as soon as I've had a word with the
matron. And no arguments, d'you hear?'

In a daze, Lorna let him lead her to the motor and help her
into the passenger seat.

'I won't be long,' he promised.

She watched him disappear into the hospital. Whatever next!
When she'd got up this morning, everything had been as it
always was. Then out of the blue, her world had turned topsy-
turvy. The past few hours had been a living nightmare, and
now . . .

She breathed in the scent of soft leather, looked at the
gleaming dials in front of her. She wondered how long it would
be before she woke up and found that everything had returned
to normal. She clung desperately to the hope that it would be
soon.

* * *

'Drink up now, lads. 'Tis well past two, and we'm closin'.'
Walt Bray, landlord of the Miners' Arms, rang the bell that
hung above the bar as he called to the group of miners who
were seated in the inglenook. In view of what had happened
today, he'd already kept the pub open longer than the law
allowed, but he couldn't afford to get caught and lose his licence.

'Just finishing our drinks,' one of the men called back.

'Get on wi' it, then. You've got five minutes.'

'Keep your hair on, Walt. We'm goin'.'

But the men were in no hurry to leave. Walt knew they
wanted to be with their mates, wanted to talk about the disaster.
And air their grievances, as this particular little clique were all
too fond of doing.

He looked up at the clock above the bar. 'Right, that's it. Go
an' fetch their glasses, Mercy,' he instructed his barmaid, who
was wiping down the wooden counter.

Mercy Comer put down her cleaning cloth, picked up a tin
tray and slipped out from behind the bar.

She was a pretty girl, with a curvy figure and a mop of fair
curls caught up with a tortoiseshell comb, and her willingness to
flirt made her popular with the regulars. What they were
unaware of was that she knew a great deal more about each and
every one of them than perhaps they would have been comfortable with. Mercy would never have described herself as nosy;
she thought of her habit of listening in to customers' conversations
as taking an interest. And during her time working here she had
got to know them all pretty well. Who was happy-go-lucky and
who was a misery guts. Who spent too much of his wages
gambling on the horses or bought several copies of *The Umpire*
on a Sunday so as to cut out the coupons and try to win the
£300 cash prize on offer for predicting the results of football

matches. Who was having a tumble behind his missus's back. Who were the troublemakers, the most likely to call for a strike or some other action against the working conditions in Sir Montague's pits. And that would be the three men seated in the inglenook.

As she approached them, she gathered that that was what they were talking about now.

'It'll shake the bugger up. Bound to. Make him think again.' Moses Whittock, a strongly built man with close-cropped hair, spoke with grim certainty.

'Trouble is, he's not the only loser,' grumbled Shorty Dallimore, who, as his nickname suggested, was small and wiry. 'Our wages're gonna be down this week.'

'Oh ah.' A murmur of agreement. Then Ticker Greedy set down his pint with a hand on which, like all the other miners, the veins stood out black with inhaled coal dust.

'Don't forget there's two dead, poor sods. An' others hurt. I only hope 'twas worth it.'

'It 'ad better be . . .'

The conversation stopped abruptly as they realised Mercy was within earshot.

'Drink up now. You heard what Mr Bray said.'

'Gonna throw us out, is 'e?' Shorty challenged.

'I wouldn't tempt him if I was you,' Mercy said.

The mood around the table lightened.

'That's what *you* do all the time, ain't it, my girl?' Moses Whittock quipped, and pinched Mercy's bottom playfully.

'Right – that's it.' Walt had seen what was going on, and strode purposefully across the bar. 'Are you lot goin', or do I 'ave to call the law?' He picked up four of the glasses, two in each hand, holding them between finger and thumb. 'You take the rest, Mercy. And you lot . . .' he gesticulated with one hand,

and beer slopped out of one of the glasses, 'out. Now.'

'Who's pulled 'is chain?' Shorty grumbled.

'Not me,' Mercy quipped with a teasing look from behind her thick dark eyelashes. But as she carried the glasses through to the little kitchen and dumped them in the sink, she was wondering. What had Ticker Greedy meant when he'd said he hoped it was worth it? A very funny thing to say, in her opinion.

She tucked away the remark along with all the other snippets she'd overheard in the past weeks. She'd think about it when she had time. For now, she needed to get the glasses washed and go home.

As they drove, Lorna Harrison was silent, apparently lost in her thoughts, and Bradley's feeling of guilt and responsibility returned, stronger than ever.

It wasn't just the miners he had failed – if indeed he had missed something. It was their families too. Wives. Children. Mothers and fathers, brothers and sisters. He cast a sideways glance at the pretty young woman whose life might well be changed for ever by what had happened. A nerve ticked in his gut and he turned his attention back to the road.

As the Ford reached the point where the track that led to Northfield Terrace met the main road, Lorna came out of her reverie and spoke.

'You can drop me here.'

Bradley slowed. 'Are you sure?'

'Yes. That's my house just there.' She pointed towards the rank of cottages running away at right angles from the track. 'It's not a very good road, and it's quite steep. Sometimes people get punctures.'

'In that case, I'd better not try,' he said, though it was the suspension he was concerned about rather than the tyres. 'The car doesn't belong to me. It's Mr Cameron's, and he won't be best pleased if it gets damaged.' He leaned over and opened the door for her to get out. 'I hope all goes well with your husband.'

She nodded. 'Thank you. And thank you for bringing me home. It would have taken me ages to walk.'

'It's the least I could do.'

'Thank you,' Lorna said again, and climbed out, but Bradley didn't pull away immediately. He waited, watching her head along the track and thinking what a remarkable young woman she was.

Brave. Thinking nothing of walking four miles there and four back to visit her husband in hospital. Proud. He'd seen the way she'd been determined to hide her tears. And undeniably very attractive. Harry Harrison was a lucky man, he thought.

As she disappeared from sight, he released the brakes and moved away down the hill. But he was still thinking about Lorna Harrison.

Chapter Five

'I think we can safely say that this occurrence was an unfortunate accident, and I shall be reporting to the Chief Inspector of Mines accordingly.'

Horace Welby, the district inspector, settled himself comfortably in one of the brocaded chairs in Sir Montague Fairley's library. He was a short, stocky man with a face that appeared almost squashed – eyes that were too close together, a pug nose and a small mouth trapped between bulging cheeks.

It was just three months since he had been appointed to the position. Previously he had been a sub-inspector in South Wales, but when the districts had been reorganised he had been moved to Somerset and made an inspector. Just how he had managed to get the promotion was a mystery to his former colleagues, who considered him incompetent and lazy. The only explanation, they concluded, was that his superior had given him a glowing reference in order to get rid of him – vastly unfair, since there were others far more deserving.

Welby, however, was conceited enough to believe the opportunity was no more than his just deserts, and thick-skinned enough that he dismissed the criticism as nothing more than spite and jealousy. He basked in his new-found authority and the direct contact he was establishing with the gentry and self-made businessmen who had invested in the collieries. Those he had met so far in his short tenure had invariably treated him with the greatest respect and offered him their hospitality. After all, he reasoned, what was contained in his reports was important to them and the smooth running of their collieries.

Sir Montague Fairley was no different, he was pleased to discover. Anxious that something might come to light that would suggest bad management, dangerous practices, or failings in the infrastructure of his mines, the colliery owner had fallen over backwards to fete the inspector. He had welcomed him in person, and invited him for drinks at Fairley Hall when his inspection was completed a week after the accident.

'So there is no blame to be attributed?' Sir Montague said.

'I would question whether the safety checks were as thorough as they should have been, but at this point I see no point in attributing blame.' Welby was anxious not to report on anything that would result in more work for him. 'I would however recommend that you impress on your deputy and safety officer the need for regular and painstaking inspections, and that you take every precaution before continuing work in that particular seam. It may be that there are other areas that are unstable,' he added, in order to cover himself should his superiors in the inspectorate question his findings further.

'That goes without saying,' Sir Montague agreed. 'I wouldn't dream of putting my workers at risk.'

'I am sure you would not.' Practically every miner Welby had spoken to had said quite the opposite, but he wasn't going to jeopardise his relationship with Sir Montague by saying so.

'I think this calls for my finest single malt whisky.' Pleased with the inspector's findings, Sir Montague crossed to the pedestal table on which stood a decanter, two glasses and a small jug of water. 'Glenfiddich. Fifteen years old. Perfection, I think you will agree.'

'I look forward to sampling it.'

The mine owner poured two fingers of the golden liquid into each of the tumblers, then picked up the jug. 'Just a splash of water. Not so much as to drown it, but a drop or two brings out the flavour wonderfully.' He handed one of the tumblers to Welby, then lifted his own, swirled it and sniffed. 'The bouquet is a pleasure in itself, is it not? Tell me, Welby, what jumps out at you?'

Welby experienced a moment's panic. He didn't think he'd ever tasted single malt whisky before – his wife said that you could strip paint with the blend he drank – and to him this smelled remarkably similar. He sipped tentatively, surprised that it didn't burn his throat the way his usual tipple did, and a little disappointed at the lack of bite. But as he took another sip and rolled it around his tongue, he realised it had a distinctive flavour, and to his immense relief, he quickly identified it. His wife liked to serve toasted almond slivers on baked fish, and he was tasting them now.

'Almond,' he said triumphantly.

'Indeed. With just a modicum of smoke. And orange blossom. Can you not taste the orange blossom?'

'Oh yes, yes,' Welby agreed enthusiastically. 'A very fine whisky indeed, Sir Montague.'

'A toast.' Fairley lifted his glass. 'To what I am sure will be a good working relationship, a friendship even, and to Milverton Colliery being trouble-free from now on.'

To his shame, Welby realised he had drunk almost all his whisky. Attempting to hide the fact by clasping his glass tightly in his pudgy hand, he raised it and forced a smile.

'To all your collieries, sir.'

'Indeed. Would you care for another tot, Welby?'

Bradley Robinson was in his office at Milverton Colliery. He sat behind his desk, absently rubbing his leg, which was aching badly, and frowning. So the inspector hadn't been able to find a cause for the roof fall. He wasn't altogether surprised – the man hadn't exactly inspired him with confidence. Bradley had pointed out the crack in the roof that he'd spotted when he was waiting for his team to free Ted Yarlett, but Horace Welby had barely glanced at it. He'd wanted to make a cursory inspection and get out as quickly as he could, Bradley thought. He was clearly more interested in his own safety than he was in probing more deeply, and had seized on the crack as evidence of the roof being unstable. 'I'm only surprised it wasn't noticed before,' he'd said accusingly when they were safely above ground once more. 'Do you not ensure regular inspections are made as to the safety of the seams that are to be worked?'

'Of course,' Bradley assured him. 'I checked it myself to be sure that the deputy hadn't missed anything.'

'Then you clearly didn't look closely enough, and neither did the deputy.'

The barb struck home. Welby was going to lay the blame on him and Ewart Moody, which Bradley felt was deeply unfair and could well have disastrous consequences for both of them. He had spent sleepless nights going over and over it, wondering if he had missed the signs of a catastrophic roof fall, and coming to the conclusion that he had not. He'd shone his lamp over every inch of that seam and roadway and seen nothing untoward. And he'd pinned his hopes on the inspector coming up with some explanation that would set his mind at rest. But clearly that wasn't going to happen, and there was little point in saying that he believed the inspector was wrong. Sir Montague was unlikely to believe him, and speaking out would only make things worse for him.

He was far from satisfied, however. Milverton wasn't known for unexplained roof falls. He'd trawled through all the records of accidents there, and not one was as a result of a fault in the geological structure of the pit. Human carelessness was cited in most cases. A carting boy who had been dragged down a dipple and thrown over the top of the tub, scraping all the skin from his back but mercifully surviving. The lad had been suffering from a heavy cold and was unfit for work, and when he'd tried to jam his sprag into the wheel of the tub, he'd missed, allowing the tub to run away down the steep incline. In another case, someone had carelessly thrown away the smouldering butt of a lamp wick, which had ignited oil pooled on the ground beside the ventilation shaft where the lamp boys refilled their lamps. Fortunately the man employed to keep the area clean was nearby and spotted the fire before it gained hold. He'd managed to douse the flickering flames, but had burned his hands quite badly in doing so. And there were instances of men tripping over the rails, and even one when a miner waiting to go underground had actually fallen into the shaft. It was suspected he was drunk at the time, but incredibly he had come to little harm as he had landed on top of the cage. But there was not a single instance of a roof fall mentioned. And Bradley was reluctant to accept the blame for failing in his duty when his gut told him he had not.

In the days that had followed the catastrophe, he had been to see all of those affected by the disaster. He had visited Harry Harrison at the hospital and sympathised with the man, as he knew from experience just how painful a leg injury of this kind could be, as well as its potential long-term consequences. He had called on George Golledge, who was thankfully not as seriously hurt as Harry, but whose wife had taken it all very badly. And he'd been to the homes of the deceased and attended their funerals, where he'd witnessed first-hand the terrible distress of their loved ones. Both funerals had been harrowing, but it was the sight of the young carting boy's mother bent double with grief as she followed her son's coffin down the chapel aisle, sobbing uncontrollably and supported by a relative on either side, that still haunted him.

All this had only strengthened his resolve to find out exactly what had happened and whether there had been any warning. He'd talked to as many of the men who had been underground at the time of the roof fall as he could, but so far he'd learned nothing useful, and he doubted whether the ones he planned to catch when they finished their shift today would prove any more forthcoming. His hopes were mostly pinned on the members of his team, who he was meeting this evening in the Miners' Arms. He planned to treat them to a round of drinks to thank them for their tireless work on the day of the disaster. It hadn't seemed appropriate to do it too soon, but he'd known that today he would have the result of the inspector's report, and that provided a legitimate reason for a get-together that might otherwise have been tasteless. It would also give him the opportunity to pick their brains as to anything they might have noticed when they had been working to free the trapped men.

In the meantime, he would revisit all the information he had been able to find on the geology of the area and compare it with the map that Cameron had drawn up to comply with another new regulation, in the hope that he would discover something he had missed. Evidence of a fault, perhaps, that had opened up without warning and caused the roof to come crashing down. It was the only explanation he could think of. The only one that would exonerate him and Ewart from blame.

Fred Gardiner, Fairley's agent, had been waiting in the orangery while Sir Montague and the inspector talked. When Welby had left, driving away in a motor every bit as grand as the mine owner's, Sir Montague called Gardiner to the library.

He came straight to the point. 'So, Gardiner, have you been able to ascertain from Cameron how long it is likely to be before the men who were injured are fit to return to work?'

Gardiner was a man after Sir Montague's heart, intent only on ensuring that the estate as a whole was geared to bringing in a good profit, and to hell with working conditions and wages. He was universally disliked by both the men who worked the land and the miners, who saw him as a puppet who danced to his master's tune. Amongst themselves, they referred to him as Pinocchio for just that reason. He fitted the image well, with his long, thin nose, which they swore grew longer when he was reporting to Sir Montague. 'A lickspittle and a liar' he'd been called, though only once to his face, when he'd sacked a man he'd accused of stealing coal. ''Twas only a bit o' clinker! And you've twisted it to his lordship to curry favour,' the disgruntled man had claimed.

Now he perched in a brocaded chair, his long, thin legs stretched out in front of him so that his trouser legs rode up to display bony ankles.

'Golledge is making a good recovery by all accounts,' he said in his somewhat reedy voice. 'Harrison is another matter altogether. I've talked to his doctor, and he's doubtful the man will ever be fit for work again.'

Sir Montague huffed impatiently. 'You think we'll have to replace him?'

'Very likely, I'd say. I've already spoken to Cameron about it. He's anxious not to act too hastily, but if it's inevitable, he's keen to give the job to one of the carting boys. I pointed out that colliers are easier to come by than carting boys, and he should begin putting out some feelers. We may be able to attract an experienced man from South Wales if there are no local applicants.'

'Hmm.' Sir Montague considered the matter. 'We'll need Harrison to vacate his house, of course, if that's the case. But best give it a week or two. We don't want a strike on our hands, and that may well be the consequence if his workmates feel he is being treated unjustly.'

'That may be so.' Gardiner seldom argued with his employer. It was in his own best interests to toe Sir Montague's line. 'I'd advise that we shouldn't leave it too long, however. We don't want production to drop off.'

'What we lose in the short term will be nothing to the losses if the men take industrial action,' Sir Montague stated bluntly. 'Give it a couple of weeks and the position should be crystal clear. No one can reasonably expect me to keep on a man who is unable to return to work.'

Gardiner nodded. 'Very well, Sir Montague. I'm sure you're right.'

'Of course I am. Is there anything else you wished to bring to my attention? If not, you may go, Gardiner.'

'Thank you, sir.'

When the agent had left, Sir Montague crossed to the table and poured himself another large whisky. All the talking he'd been doing had made him even thirstier than usual. He sipped his drink. That was better! Now he intended to put to one side all the problems that attended owning a coalfield and relax with his favourite tipple.

Coal Miner

* * *

H
chan
upstairs and much to

Thank goodness for the sleeping
supplied, she thought as she made the be
clothes that needed washing. She'd asked the gi
but since they'd got home from school they'd been eng
a game of dominoes, Pippy Rabbit, Vera's favourite soft toy,
propped up on a chair between them as Vera had insisted she
would play too. But at least she'd have an hour or so now to see
to it herself. An hour or so when she wasn't constantly checking
on Harry and worrying about him. The trouble was that when
the medicine wore off, he was in dreadful pain, and he wasn't a
good patient. The metal contraption that had been fixed to his
leg was ugly and cumbersome and his moans and groans
whenever he tried to move tore at her heart, but sympathetic as
she was, the black cloud of depression that was making him
snappy and argumentative was beginning to get to her.

It was perfectly understandable, of course. It must be awful
for him, a fit and active man, to be reduced to this. But everything
she did or tried to do seemed to be wrong.

'Leave me alone, can't you?' he'd snapped this morning
when she'd taken up a bowl of water, soap and a flannel to wash
him down.

'You've been tossing and turning and you're all sweaty,' she
told him. 'I'll be as quick as I can.'

But as she went to turn back the covers, he lunged at her so
violently that she stepped back and kicked the bowl, and water
slopped onto the rag rug.

'I said leave me alone!' he snarled. 'Don't you ever listen to me?'

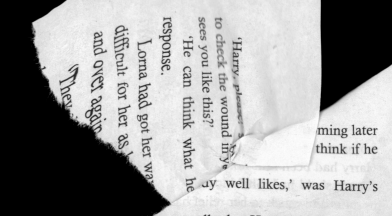

'Harry, please ...
to check the wound in y...
sees you like this?'
'He can think what he ...
response.
    Lorna had got her wa...
difficult for her as ...
and over again.
    'They ...

ming later
think if he

... uy well likes,' was Harry's

... y eventually, but Harry had made it as
... he could, muttering 'Bloody woman!' over
... until it was done.

... shouldn't 'ave sent him home,' Flossie had said when she'd popped in later to see how things were and Lorna had told her what had happened. 'He should be in hospital, anybody can see that.'

'They said they've done all they can for him and he'll be better off at home,' Lorna said.

'That's all very well, but nurses know how to take care of patients what kick up. 'Tis too much for you, my love, on top of everything else. An' I don't suppose you can expect any help from that mother of his.'

Lorna had pulled a wry face. Flossie was well aware of the situation with Harry's mother. 'I should be so lucky. I sent a note to let her know what had happened, but I've heard nothing back. No, it's my place to look after him, and I'll manage. I have to.'

But the truth was, she knew she could never have done it without Flossie's help. Her friend was taking the girls to school every morning because she knew Lorna would worry that they hadn't got there safely, though she had talked her into letting them walk home with Arthur. She'd made a big pot of mutton stew that would last them for two or three days since Harry was eating very little, and baked a batch of jam tarts. And it was her sound common sense that Lorna thought was keeping her sane. She really was the best neighbour anyone could wish for, and Lorna would be eternally grateful to her.

Now, as she gathered up the clothes and pillowcases that definitely needed to see the washtub, she heard footsteps on the stairs, then Marjorie's voice, loud and clear, coming from the bedroom next door.

'Would you like a cup of tea, Daddy?'

Lorna groaned inwardly, but before she could tell them not to disturb him, Vera chimed in: 'Here's Pippy Rabbit come to see you. I'll leave her with you if you like, so you won't be lonely.'

Lorna dropped the pile of washing and hurried to the other bedroom. Too late. They'd woken him.

'Can't you just leave me alone?' The same words, the same irritable tone he'd used with her this morning.

'But Daddy . . .' Marjorie sounded hurt.

Vera, flouncing out, almost collided with Lorna. 'Pippy Rabbit doesn't like you either,' she was muttering, loudly enough for Harry to hear.

Lorna caught her by the shoulders and turned her back into the room.

'Daddy is ill,' she said, addressing both her daughters. 'He just wants to rest quietly, like you do when you have a bilious attack. Tell him you're sorry you disturbed him, and then go downstairs and find a game to play.'

But Harry was already asleep again.

'We were just trying to make him feel better,' Marjorie said softly but earnestly as Lorna closed the door.

'I know you were. But really, you mustn't just go bursting in on him like that. Look – there are jam tarts in the tin on the shelf. Mrs Price baked them this morning. Help yourselves to one each, and then play nicely. I'll be down in a minute.'

'Sorry, Mammy,' Marjorie said penitently, but Vera was already racing down the stairs, eager now only to find the jam tarts, her special favourite.

'I know you meant well, Marjorie. Just think twice before you do it again.' Lorna gave her elder daughter a reassuring smile and went back to finish tidying the girls' bedroom.

In the public bar of the Miners' Arms, Bradley and his team of rescuers sat around two tables that they had pushed together to accommodate them all. He'd bought them pints, and dishes of cockles and pickled eggs, which they shared as they talked. They had accepted the inspector's report philosophically, and when Bradley steered the conversation to their opinions as to what had been the cause of the disaster, they had been unable to tell him anything beyond what he already knew. He was disappointed but not surprised – they had all been too focused on their Herculean task to notice anything beyond moving the mountain of fallen rock and coal.

He'd been hoping that the little clique of men who were pally with Harry Harrison and George Golledge would be here too so that he could have another word with them; he understood they were regulars in the Miners' Arms. Tonight, however, there was no sign of them – perhaps they'd got to hear that he would be there with his rescue team and had gone elsewhere in order to avoid him. But in any case, he doubted he'd have learned anything new. When he'd first talked to them, they'd stone-walled, and he was pretty sure that if any of them did know anything, they were unlikely to tell him.

He glanced at the clock above the bar. It was time he went home. He had an early meeting with Cameron in the morning, and then he was due to conduct an inspection at one of Sir Montague's other pits. He took a crown out of his pocket and put it down on the table.

'I'm going to leave you to it now. Have another drink on me. You certainly earned it.'

As he crossed the bar, he heard one of the men say: 'Decent sort, ain't 'e?' and smiled to himself.

He left by way of the snug. Amos Riddle was there, sitting on a stool beside the hatch into the bar. He was all alone, and it occurred to Bradley that it might be worth having a word with him. Amos was a general cleaner and handyman who did all the jobs nobody else wanted to do. He wasn't the sharpest knife in the box, but he had been underground at the time of the roof fall, sweeping up the used lamp wicks and covering any oil spills with sand.

'Evening, Amos,' he said.

Amos shuffled round on his stool, seemingly surprised that the safety officer was addressing him. He was a bulky figure, with a head that looked too big for his body and hands the size of hams. But he'd never been known to use them on anybody. Though he was the butt of many jokes and ribald remarks, he seemed to take it all in good part, and if he was wounded, which he surely must have been, he never showed it.

'Evenin', sir,' he mumbled.

Bradley tucked himself into the corner between the bar door and the serving hatch, and leaned back against the wall, hands tucked casually into his coat pockets. 'You were underground when the roof came down, weren't you, Amos?'

Amos nodded his big head. 'Aye, sir. I were, sir.'

'What did you make of it?'

He considered. 'Well, 'twere terrible, sir,' he said at last. 'Frightened I.'

'I'm sure it did,' Bradley sympathised. 'Was it sudden? Did anyone have time to shout a warning?'

Again Amos thought long and hard before replying. Bradley could almost see his brain ticking over. No wonder the other men made fun of him, he thought. He was so slow it was infuriating, but he waited anyway, and eventually Amos shook his head.

'I didn't hear nobody, sir.'

'So there was no warning at all?' Bradley was thinking that a rock fall was usually preceded by the sound of the earth shifting. It was a gradual process; the whole lot wouldn't suddenly come down without warning. It was what was still nagging at him, that he had seen no signs of impending disaster when he'd inspected the area the night before. No visible cracks, no sound of movement, no trickles of falling dust. What Amos had said seemed to confirm this. But if that was the case, what in heaven's name had triggered such a catastrophic roof fall?

'Well, sir . . .' Amos was speaking again, even more haltingly than before. 'There was summat.'

'What?' Bradley pressed him.

'Sounded like shot-firing. But it couldna bin that. Dick Penny weren't anywhere about. I don't know, sir, an' that's the truth. But 'twere very funny.'

'Thank you, Amos. You've been extremely helpful,' Bradley said, though he wasn't sure how much of what the man had said made sense. He had clearly been shaken by what had happened and it had made him even less coherent than usual. He glanced at Amos's beer mug; it was almost empty. 'Let me buy you another drink.'

'That be very kind of 'ee, sir . . .'

'Service!' Bradley called through the hatch, and almost immediately the blonde barmaid appeared. She must have been right there, and heard everything that had been said, he realised. 'Another pint for this gentleman, please.' He put a sixpenny bit down on the counter. 'You can keep the change.'

He said goodnight to Amos, then left the Miners' Arms deep in thought.

* * *

Mercy Comer set Amos Riddle's drink down on the counter with the provocative smile that she usually reserved for the men she enjoyed flirting with.

'Your lucky night!' she said. 'Mr Bray's closing up, but I managed to pull you this one when he wasn't looking.'

'Thank 'ee kindly.' Amos drained his glass and pushed it towards her, then reached for his fresh pint.

Time to get to the point, Mercy thought. 'Who was that buying you drinks?' she asked, pretending innocence.

'I can't mind his name.'

'You must know him, though. He wouldn't be buying you a drink otherwise.'

'Oh, I d'a know who 'e is all right.' Amos took a sip of his beer and smacked his lips.

'So who is he?' Mercy pressed him, frustration making her voice sharp. Getting sense out of Amos was like getting blood out of a stone. It would have been a lot easier to ask the miners in the public bar who it was who had been buying *them* drinks, but she couldn't do that right under Mr Bray's nose, and in any case, she didn't want them to know she was interested in the stranger. Didn't want them to think she fancied him – though she certainly did – or she'd never hear the last of it.

Amos took another pull of his beer, clearly anxious to finish it before the landlord realised he was still on the premises and kicked him out.

'Well,' he said at last, ''e's the new man in charge o' safety. An' I d'a mind his name an' all. Robinson. Mr Robinson.' He chortled. 'Not doin' a very good job, though, be he?'

'Are you still here, Amos?' Walt Bray appeared at Mercy's shoulder. 'Come on, time to go home.'

Jennie Felton

'You'm the boss.' Amos quickly downed the rest of his pint and shambled out of the door.

'I just couldn't get rid of him,' Mercy said, all innocence, as she followed Walt back into the bar and took Amos's mug to the sink. But as she was washing up, she was thinking. So, he was the new safety officer – and a bit of all right, too. He'd been talking to the men about the roof fall, she supposed. That was why he'd come in tonight, and why she'd never seen him before. He would drink in the George with the other bosses, and probably wouldn't set foot in the Miners' Arms again. More's the pity, she thought. He would certainly be quite a catch. Definitely a cut above the sort of man she usually came into contact with. And a lot better off as well!

But she was thinking too about what she'd heard Amos say – that he'd heard an explosion just before the roof came down. He must have imagined it, surely. He was as thick as two short planks. But if he was right, it might make sense of what she'd heard Ticker Greedy say when he and his pals had been drinking here on the day of the disaster: *I only hope 'twas worth it.* Was it possible that the roof fall had somehow been the result of a stunt they'd pulled to bring their working conditions to Sir Montague's attention?

Mercy's curiosity was piqued. When they next came in, she'd try to listen to what they were saying. Who knew, she might learn something, and that was all the excuse she'd need to make herself known to the new – and very fanciable – safety officer.

Chapter Six

There was nothing quite real about any of this, Lorna thought. It was as if she was fighting her way through a thick fog, and the passing days had all blurred into one. Cooking, washing, cleaning, just as she always did, except that now she had Harry to worry about too. He was improving slowly, though he still woke from nightmares screaming and sweating, and he became even more fractious and bad-tempered as he fought against his limitations. She was tired from lack of sleep, and worried. About Harry. About the children. She'd tried to keep things as normal as possible for them, and they were both being very good and doing what they could to help her. Even Vera – subdued, she guessed, by the state her father was in – was on her best behaviour most of the time. But most of all she was worried about money.

Mr Cameron had called, and after he'd spent a few minutes with Harry, he'd found her in the kitchen and told her Sir Montague had authorised him to give her five guineas in lieu of a week's wages by way of compensation – his way of trying to avert industrial action, she'd thought bitterly. At the time she'd been grateful for it – Harry had never given her more than fifteen shillings for housekeeping – but after Cameron had left, she'd got to thinking. Though five guineas looked and felt like riches it wouldn't last long if Harry was unable to work, and she couldn't see him being fit for that for some time yet. And knowing there would be doctor's bills to pay at the end of the quarter made it even worse.

She'd gone back upstairs to talk to Harry.

'I'm worried how we're going to manage,' she said, sitting down on her side of the bed. 'Mr Cameron's given me some money by way of compensation, but—'

'And so he bloody well should,' Harry grunted. 'Enough to keep us goin', I hope.'

'Not really.' Lorna twisted a corner of the bed sheet between her hands. 'But we'll have something from the Friendly Society when they get round to paying out, won't we?'

Harry turned his head on the pillow so she could no longer see his face and said nothing.

'Won't we?' she repeated, anxiety beginning to knot her stomach.

'Not a lot, no,' he mumbled into the pillow.

'But you pay into it so that we've got something to fall back on if we need to, don't you?' she pressed him.

Again it was a long moment before he replied, and her misgivings grew.

'I don't. I can't afford it,' he said at last, still talking to the wall and not to her.

Lorna was horrified. 'What do you mean, you can't afford it?'

'I just can't.' She could tell from his tone that he was beginning to lose his temper, as he did so often these days, but for once she didn't care.

'So where does it go then, your wages? Not on my housekeeping, that's for sure.'

'For God's sake, woman!' Harry exploded, turning back to

glare at her. 'It's not your place to question me about money. I give you enough to put food on the table, don't I? Enough for clothes and boots for the children? I don't have to answer to you for every bliddy penny piece.'

Lorna was stunned. Yes, Harry snapped at her sometimes, but that was only natural, wasn't it? She snapped too if she was annoyed – at him, at the children, at Nipper. And yes, he had been bad tempered and difficult to please since the accident, but never before had he ranted at her so viciously, as if a dam had burst and a resentment he'd been bottling up for a very long time had come flooding out.

Usually she did her best to keep the peace, but not this time. 'You're not the one who has to count the pennies to see if we can afford a pound of sausages or if it will have to be a half-pound – two for you, one each for the girls and none for myself. You're not the one who scrimps and saves to buy a Christmas present each for the children and a few little extras to make it special.' A sudden thought occurred to her – a problem she'd thought was behind them. 'Are you betting on the horses? Is that where the money goes?'

'Yes, that's it,' he snarled. 'Now for the love of God just leave me alone.'

'Well at least you won't be able to waste your money on that while you're laid up,' Lorna said with some satisfaction. 'If you think I'm going to place your bets for you, you've got another think coming.'

Harry grabbed the bed covers and heaved them over him, mumbling incoherently, and at the same moment Lorna heard a knock on the door.

'That might be the doctor now,' she said. 'Get yourself straight, Harry, for goodness' sake.'

* * *

As he stood on the doorstep waiting for an answer to his knock, Alistair Mackay shifted from one foot to the other trying to get some life back into them. He'd been called out to an accident on one of the outlying farms and had had to cross a ploughed field to reach it. By the time he'd delivered preliminary first aid and got the man back to the farmhouse, where he could assess and treat him properly, his boots were caked with near-freezing mud, his tweed suit trousers splattered with it, and he was chilled to the marrow. He'd gone home to change before calling on Harry Harrison. His wife, Jessica, had made him a cup of tea, which he'd drunk standing as close to the fire as he could, but still his feet and hands were numb and he felt as though he'd never get properly warm again. A suit, light overcoat and soft leather boots might be the right attire for taking a surgery or visiting the asylum at Catcombe, where he was a medical officer, but not for ploughing through acres of freezing wet mud.

He was about to knock again when he heard footsteps approaching and the door was opened.

'Ah, Mrs Harrison. I've come to see how your husband is doing,' he said in his warm Scottish brogue.

'Come in, Doctor.' Lorna Harrison stood aside.

She looked tired and harassed, he thought. This was taking its toll on her too. Hardly surprising, given the extent of her husband's injuries. Alistair had been the doctor who had set his leg and fitted it with a uniplanar, a fixation device to hold the bones together and allow them to heal. It had been a long and difficult operation and it would have been far better, in his opinion, if he had been attended to by a more experienced surgeon at the big hospital in Bath. But the trustees of the cottage hospital didn't like transferring patients there unless absolutely necessary, and he'd had no choice but to go along with their decision. He'd done his best under the circumstances – better

66

him than one of the elderly local doctors with whom he shared responsibility for the cottage hospital patients – but he was all too aware that his expertise was limited, and he was concerned that if he had made even a small error in the fixing of the screws, it could prove disastrous. At least Harrison was alive, but that wouldn't be much comfort if he was unable to work again.

'So how is he?' he asked as Lorna closed the door.

'Better than he was, but that's not saying much,' she said ruefully. 'I don't think he's in as much pain, but he's very low.'

Alistair nodded. 'That's to be expected, I'm afraid. Where will I find him?'

'Same as last time you called. In bed.'

'May I go up?'

'Course.' She lowered her voice. 'You mustn't mind if he's a bit rude to you. He doesn't mean to be.'

Alistair smiled. 'Don't worry, Mrs Harrison. I won't take it personally.'

Lorna followed him up the stairs, but not into the bedroom. She waited outside on the landing just as she had on his previous visits. 'He doesn't want you to think he needs his hand holding,' she'd explained. 'He's a proud man, is Harry.'

'Come to see how much longer I got then?' Harry said sarcastically as Alistair went into the bedroom.

'Oh, I think you've got a long while yet,' Alistair replied cheerily. Truth to tell, when he'd seen Harry immediately after the accident, he'd wondered whether he would make it – he'd been in a bad way. But the worst was over now. He wasn't going to die, just as long as gas gangrene didn't set in, and Alistair had stabilised the bone to prevent that.

'An' what about me leg?'

That was a much less certain prospect. 'Only time will tell us that, Harry,' Alistair said. 'It was a very serious break, as I'm sure you know. The hope, of course, is that it will heal well, but that is going to take time.'

'How long?'

'I'd say between six months and a year.'

Harry swore. 'I can't stay 'ere like this for all that time! I need to get back to work.'

'There's no question of that at the moment, I'm afraid. But the good news is you can get up and walk about now if you feel well enough. I've brought you some crutches – I left them in my car until I saw how you were. Didn't want to get your hopes up,' Alistair said with a smile.

'That's summat, I suppose,' Harry acknowledged. 'I can't stop here much longer, Doctor. 'Tis drivin' I crazy.'

'Well, just let me check the wound for any signs of infection, and then I'll fetch them. Your wife is managing to change the dressings, I see. And a very good job she's making of it too.'

A few minutes later, Alistair straightened and began repacking his medical bag. 'All good as far as I can see.'

Harry brightened. 'So I can get out'a bed then?'

'I think it would do you good. But use your common sense, and don't overdo it.'

By way of reply, Harry merely snorted.

As he'd expected, Alistair found Lorna lurking on the landing. She'd been listening outside the bedroom door and backed away when she'd heard he was about to leave, he guessed.

'So what's the verdict, Doctor?' she asked, all innocence.

He was unable to suppress a smile. 'Progress will be slow but steady, I hope,' he said. 'I've told him it would do him good to get out of bed, and I have some crutches in the motor. Would you like to come out and collect them?'

'Course I will, Doctor. But it won't be too much for him, will it?'

'Not as long as he takes things carefully. I'd expect him to be a little unsteady at first, but if you keep an eye on him and sit him down again if necessary, he should be fine.'

'I'm not sure he'd want me doing that,' she said ruefully. 'He wouldn't want to admit he needed any help.'

'Except that you and I both know that he does.'

'But at least he's alive, Doctor. Not like those other poor souls.'

Lorna followed Dr Mackay out onto the track, where he fetched the crutches from his motor and gave them to her. As she made her way back to the house, she saw Lil Golledge coming the other way, heading for the shops if the hessian bag she was carrying was anything to go by. Lorna hadn't seen her since the accident, and George hadn't been to visit Harry, though she'd heard from Flossie that he was up and about now, if not yet back at work.

'How's Mr Golledge?' she asked as they met.

Lil didn't so much as look at her. 'What would you care?' she muttered, walking straight past.

Lorna was taken aback. Though she knew Lil could be narky when the mood took her, this rudeness was quite uncalled for. But Lil might well be as stressed as she herself was, she supposed, and she had more to worry about than a snub.

Back inside the house, she went to the foot of the stairs. 'I've got your crutches, Harry,' she called.

'Bring 'em up then!' Harry called back.

'In a minute. I've got to get the potatoes on or they won't be ready for dinner.'

It was the truth, but not the whole truth. After their earlier exchange, she simply couldn't face him again just yet. It wouldn't hurt him to wait a bit, she thought. What with first Mr

Cameron and then the doctor calling, she was running late, and she must have the meal ready for when the girls got home. She propped the crutches in the corner of the living room and hurried into the scullery.

Bradley Robinson and Duncan Cameron sat in comfortable brocaded chairs across a table from one another in the lounge bar of the George Hotel. It was an impressive building, double-fronted, with a central balcony on the first floor overlooking the market square, and it was the favoured watering hole for those of standing in the community.

It was the first time the two men had met since the inspector had made his report – the spread of Sir Montague's coalfield meant that the odds of them being in the same place at the same time were low – and Cameron had suggested they adjourn to more convivial surroundings than the cold, cramped office at Milverton.

'I've a raging thirst besides,' he'd added with a wry smile.

Bradley had been more than happy to fall in with the suggestion. There was a lot to talk about. Better here than in the office, where they might be interrupted at any time. And at present they were the only two customers in the lounge bar – it was a little early for the solicitors and bankers who frequented the George.

'So, how are you finding Somerset?' Cameron asked once they had placed their orders with the barmaid.

'Challenging,' Bradley replied honestly.

Cameron straightened a beer mat. 'We'll get to that later,' he said with a nod towards the door by way of warning that the girl would be back with their drinks at any moment and what they would be talking about would be confidential. 'There are some lovely walks around Oldlands – across the fields, through the woods, along the river. I was amazed when I first came here. I'd thought nothing could match the bens and braes of my homeland. But I've come to love it here. And the winters are nae so harsh,' he added, raising his bushy eyebrows, his eyes twinkling wickedly.

'I've certainly enjoyed exploring,' Bradley said. He'd followed paths through the woods between the pit and his house, squelching across a carpet of rotted leaves, pushing his way between brambles, stepping over fallen branches, inhaling the scent of pine needles and wild garlic, listening to the birds calling and fluttering in the trees. He'd walked along the lane to the point where the fields fell into the valley below, and enjoyed the smell of the smoke billowing up from the trains on the line that bisected it. When the weather improved, he'd explore further afield; he was pretty sure that if he walked along the valley, he'd come to the village of Dunderwick, one bit of the locality that was not owned by Sir Montague.

'You've not seen it at its best yet. But the changing seasons, that's the thing. When the trees are in full leaf, you'll have to find your way about all over again . . .' Cameron broke off as the barmaid entered with their drinks on an enamelled tray, smiling at her to show his appreciation. 'Och, but you're a good wee lassie, Mary.'

The girl, immaculate in a black skirt, pristine white blouse and starched cap and apron, blushed. 'Just doing my job, sir.'

'We appreciate it, don't we, Robinson?' Cameron raised his glass in a silent toast and took a long pull of his beer.

When the door had closed after the barmaid, however, he became serious. It was time to get down to business.

'The district inspector has put the roof fall down to sheer bad luck,' he began. 'What's your opinion, Robinson?'

Bradley took a moment to sip his own drink before replying. What he was about to say was bound to be controversial.

'I'm not convinced,' he said. 'Ewart Moody swears there was no sign of movement when he made his inspection, and he's never given me cause to think that he's anything but reliable. But I do a check myself when I can, and it so happens I did one the previous evening. I didn't see anything to cause me concern either.'

Cameron frowned. 'So what are you suggesting?'

'I don't know,' Bradley admitted. 'But I'm not satisfied that Mr Welby was as thorough as he should have been.'

'In what respect?'

'He didn't visit the injured men, and spent hardly any time with those who were underground at the time of the accident. He barely questioned me, dammit. I tried to tell him that I spotted a crack in the roof when my team were digging out the buried men that I was sure wasn't there earlier. All he said was that the fall had most likely caused other fissures.'

Cameron wiped a smear of beer foam from his moustache. 'That's not an unreasonable assumption.'

Bradley bridled. 'There was nothing there to cause alarm before it happened,' he said emphatically. 'I'd stake my life on it.'

Cameron regarded him steadily. 'So what are you thinking, Robinson?'

'I don't know,' Bradley was forced to admit once more. 'I've questioned as many of the men as I could myself, but I've run up against a brick wall. Unsurprising really. They tend to stick together, and resent authority of any kind. But what I do know is that there is a lot of unrest over pay and working conditions.'

'You're not wrong there,' Cameron said. 'I've warned Sir Montague that there's trouble brewing if things aren't improved, but the man's as stubborn as a mule, and tight-fisted too. He's had to stump up a lot of money recently to pay your wages and all the equipment needed to set up your operation, and he doesn't want to spend any more. The men have a case, I agree. But surely you're not suggesting something was done to cause a roof fall in order to bring their grievance to Sir Montague's attention? A man and a boy died, Robinson.'

'I know that. I was there when they were brought out,' Bradley said bitterly. 'That wouldn't have been the intention, of course. If it was deliberate, they'd never have expected such serious consequences.'

Cameron thought for a moment and then sat back, shaking his head. 'I can't believe it. Have you seen any evidence of such a thing?'

'No,' Bradley admitted. 'But there's something else. Amos Riddle was underground at the time, cleaning up the wicks by the lamp oil station, and he says there was no warning at all. None of the men in that seam called out that the roof was crumbling – nothing. All he heard was what sounded like shot-firing, but he thought he must be mistaken as Dick Penny wasn't around.'

For a moment Cameron's eyes widened, then he shook his head again, clearly unwilling to consider what Bradley seemed to be suggesting.

'Amos Riddle is hardly a reliable witness,' he said. 'The man's half cuckoo. No, I think you will have to accept it was an unfortunate accident, Robinson. But rest assured, I shall do my utmost to see to it that the families who are suffering are provided with help and support.'

That was something, Bradley supposed. And it could be that both Cameron and the inspector were right. But he wasn't satisfied that was the whole story. If Amos was right – and it was a big if, he had to admit – and the roof had been brought down deliberately, whoever was responsible must have somehow got hold of explosives. The easiest access would be through Dick Penny. He'd speak to him again. He doubted the shot-firer would be any more help than the other men had been. But he needed to try and find out more.

Lorna was dishing up the meat and potato pie she'd made for dinner and putting the plates on the table in front of Marjorie and Vera.

'You'll have to make haste,' she said. 'I was late starting cooking today.'

'Why?' Vera asked.

'Never mind why. Just eat up and don't waste time talking or you'll be late, too, getting back to school. You don't want to get into trouble, do you?'

She broke off as a loud thumping sound startled her, and spun round just in time to see the door at the bottom of the stairs fly open and a bare foot come shooting through.

'Daddy!' Vera screamed.

'Oh my Lord! Go on with your dinner, girls.' Lorna hurried towards the stairs. 'Harry!'

He was spreadeagled over the bottom three steps, his head thrown back, his face contorted with pain. He had hit the door with his injured leg and the uniplanar had acted like a battering ram.

'What in the world do you think you're doing?' Lorna demanded shrilly.

'I wanted me crutches. You were supposed to bring 'em up.'

'So this is my fault?' Lorna snapped, at her wits' end.

He glowered at her. 'Help me up!'

'Oh Harry, I don't know if I can.'

'Shall I get Mrs Price?' She swung round to see the girls standing behind her, both looking shocked.

'Yes, would you, Marjorie? Vera, you stay here . . . and eat your dinner, for goodness' sake.'

'Can't you do *anything* without Flossie Price poking her nose in?' Harry grumbled.

Somehow Lorna held onto her temper. 'That was a silly thing to do, Harry. Who knows what damage you've caused?'

'Doctor said I could get up.'

'But not come down the stairs. All by yourself . . .'

Marjorie was quickly back with Flossie. Somehow, between them, they managed to hoist Harry to his feet and support him to the sofa in the living room, where Flossie questioned him as to any new injuries he might have sustained and instructed Lorna to fetch him a drop of brandy.

'That contraption'll 'ave protected his bad leg,' she said. 'At least I 'ope it will. But he'll be black and blue tomorrow, I shouldn't wonder. And . . .' she turned to Harry and spoke sternly, 'you're goin' to 'ave to stop down 'ere now. We can't get you up the stairs, and I wouldn't trust 'ee up there anyway.'

Lorna handed the glass of brandy to Harry and was relieved to see the colour returning to his face. She fetched the crutches and propped them up beside the sofa. 'Here they are. But don't you dare try them unless I'm here to help you,' she said.

And felt her heart sink at the thought of what the future held.

Chapter Seven

The next few days were every bit as bad as Lorna had anticipated. Flossie had offered Albie's help to get Harry back to his bed, but Lorna had refused it. She'd made him as comfortable as she could on the sofa, and at least with him in the living room she didn't have to run up and down stairs to attend to him, or worry about him attempting to come down again. Besides this, George Golledge had finally recovered sufficiently to walk down the rank to visit Harry. She didn't like the man, and wouldn't have cared for the idea of him being in her bedroom. She'd thought having the company of his pal for a bit might cheer Harry up, but it didn't seem to. Quite the opposite, in fact, as if seeing George up and about only highlighted his affliction, and from the tone of his voice it sounded as if he was getting ratty with his friend, though she couldn't hear what he was saying.

His constant ill temper had begun to fray her nerves, and anxiety for the future hung over her like a shroud. But there was no time to confront it. No time to make contingency plans if Harry was unable to return to work as a collier. Her days were so full with all the extra washing and nursing on top of her normal day-to-day duties that she didn't have a moment to herself. Even when she went to bed she couldn't relax, listening with one ear for anything untoward, with the result that she was permanently exhausted.

One night she'd heard noises in the kitchen, and when she'd gone down to investigate, she'd found Harry trying to heat a pan of milk over the fire, which she'd banked up for the night, with one crutch propped under his arm and the other lying on the floor, where he'd trip over it if he stepped backwards.

'What are you doing?' she asked in exasperation. 'If you wanted a drink, why didn't you call me?'

'I s'pose you think I'm bloody useless,' he snapped.

So it wasn't that he didn't want to disturb her. No, it was all about him. Yes, what had happened to him was dreadful, but why did he have to take it out on her and the girls? He snapped at them too whenever they went near him, and it just wasn't fair on them. But she couldn't see that she could do anything about it. He'd only shoot her down in flames if she mentioned it, and she just had to hope it wasn't upsetting them too much.

A couple of days later, however, she realised that that was a vain hope. She needed to go to town to buy groceries and other essentials, and decided to go early and walk the children to school as she used to do. As they approached the subway that ran under the railway, Vera tugged on her hand.

'Why is Daddy always so cross?' she asked plaintively.

'Vera! Don't say that! He's ill, and his leg is hurting him,' Marjorie piped up before Lorna could reply.

Vera pouted. 'I know. But he doesn't have to be so horrid.'

'Marjorie's right,' Lorna interceded. 'Daddy is in a lot of pain and he just wants to be quiet.'

'*He's* the pain!' Vera retorted. 'I hurt my knee when I fell over playing hopscotch, but I was very brave. You said so.'

At any other time Lorna would have been amused by the

childish comparison. But she was past finding humour in anything.

'Daddy's leg is a lot more painful than your scraped knee,' she said. 'You have to be patient with him. When he's better, he won't be so cross any more.'

'Good.' Vera let go of Lorna's hand and skipped ahead. 'Race you to school, Marjie!'

Lorna watched them run off up the slope that led to the school playground. When they were out of sight, she turned and walked back towards the town centre, still thinking of what Vera had said and hoping all this wasn't going to have a long-term effect on the girls' relationship with their father.

The shops were just opening, pulling up shutters, unlocking doors. She made first for the grocery store, which stood on the corner. As she went, she mentally counted how much money she had in her purse. It wouldn't go far; she'd have to be careful.

Inside, Mrs Hiscox, the shopkeeper's wife, was bent double as she opened a new hessian sack, and the aroma of fresh tea leaves filled the shop. As the bell above the door tinkled, she looked up.

'Oh, morning, Mrs Harrison. How's your husband doin'? We were only talking about him yesterday.'

Lorna was thoroughly tired of being asked that question. She didn't want to go into detail. 'Not good. I'm in a bit of a hurry, Mrs Hiscox. I have to get back to him.'

'Well, at least he's alive. Poor Mrs Maggs was in here yesterday and the dear soul's just a shadow of herself. 'Twouldn't surprise me if she didn't follow her lad to the grave.' The woman heaved herself up and waddled behind the counter. 'Now, what can I do for you?'

'Half a pound of bacon, please.' Lorna was glad of the change of subject. She didn't want to think about the dead carting boy and his grieving mother.

Mrs Hiscox lifted a side of bacon onto the slicing machine, cut off several rashers and weighed them. 'Anything else?' she asked as she wrapped them in greaseproof paper.

'Some tasty cheese.'

'A pound?'

'Say six ounces.'

As she positioned the cheese wire and sliced off a small chunk of Cheddar, Mrs Hiscox eyed Lorna with feigned sympathy. 'Money tight, is it?'

Something else Lorna didn't want to discuss. 'A bit.'

'No biscuits today, then?'

'Not today.'

Lorna could feel her cheeks burning. It was almost as if the woman was blaming her for not being able to afford treats for her family. And for all her supposed concern there was something almost hostile in her attitude that made Lorna uncomfortable. She paid hastily for her purchases and left.

Her reception in the greengrocer's, where she bought potatoes, onions, swede and a pound of sprouts, and the butcher's, where she spent most of her remaining cash on a pound of tripe and a half of pig's liver, was much the same. Was everybody in Hillsbridge talking about her and Harry? Blaming him, perhaps, for having survived when others, including a boy, had died? She still needed bread, and though she had just enough money left to buy a loaf, her heart sank at the thought of yet another interrogation and a dose of what felt like false sympathy. Besides, to get to the bakery she would have to cross the first set of railway lines, and the crossing gates were closed. A train must be coming. That decided it. She'd make a loaf of soda bread herself.

She cut back to the subway beneath the rail track and hurried through, then crossed the road and started back up the hill. She shivered as she passed the colliery; she didn't think she'd ever be able to forget that awful morning. Swallowing hard, she averted her gaze and headed for home.

'Can I have a word, Mr Penny?'

Bradley wasn't yet on first-name terms with the men he wasn't directly working with, and he saw the elderly man stiffen as he approached him.

'What be that about then?' Dick Penny's tone was defensive.

Bradley was uncomfortably aware that this conversation was not going to be easy, but there wasn't really any way to dress it up. He might as well be blunt.

'You haven't noticed any explosives missing recently, have you?'

The wrinkles that criss-crossed Penny's face deepened into a scowl.

'Wot be you sayin'?'

'It's a simple enough question, Mr Penny.' He met the man's gaze directly and saw the affront in his eyes.

'You'm not suggestin' I had anythin' to do with the bloody roof comin' down, I d'a hope.'

'No. I know you weren't underground at the time,' Bradley said evenly. 'But I have heard a suggestion that there was something that sounded like shot-firing just before it happened.' And so have you, he thought. Why otherwise would you jump to that conclusion? Perhaps Amos Riddle wasn't so stupid after all. He had just said straight out what others were saying in private.

'Well, I can assure you, mister, that if there were, 'tweren't any o' my explosives wot caused it,' Dick Penny said fiercely.

'I do keep all my stuff locked up, accordin' t' the rules. An' if anybody's said different, they'm a bloody liar.'

'Very well, Mr Penny. I'm sorry if I've offended you, but I had to ask.' Bradley could well have demanded to check the explosive charges himself, but he was inclined to believe the man, and he didn't want to upset him any further.

But he was more convinced than ever that there was more to the roof fall than a simple accident. Had one of the men, wanting to draw attention to conditions in the pit, got hold of some explosive and used it on the seam? Not being trained in stone blasting, he could well have used an excessive amount and caused a much worse roof fall than he'd intended. It would explain why ranks had closed to protect the perpetrator.

But if not Dick Penny, where could they have got the stuff from?

Lorna was just sifting flour and baking powder into a bowl to make soda bread when there was a knock at the front door. She dusted down her hands on her calico apron and went to answer it, wondering who it could be at this time of day.

To her dismay, it was Fred Gardiner, Sir Montague's agent, who stood on the doorstep. She'd never been face to face with him before, but she'd seen him strutting about town, looking down his aquiline nose at everything and everyone from beneath the brim of his black bowler hat. This didn't bode well. It wouldn't be out of concern for Harry's welfare that he was here. Quite the reverse.

'Mr Gardiner,' she said coolly.

The man nodded abruptly by way of acknowledgement but did not return the greeting.

'Is your husband home?' he enquired superciliously.

All the stress Lorna was feeling bubbled over at the

fatuousness of the question. 'And where else would he be?' she asked with heavy sarcasm. 'You do know he was dragged out from the roof fall at Milverton half dead?'

'That's the reason I'm here. I need to talk to him.' Fred Gardiner pulled himself up to his full height – all five feet two and a half inches – and puffed out his chest.

'Well, I'm not sure he's up to talking to you,' Lorna retorted.

The little man stood his ground. 'I'm afraid I must insist. I'm here on the instructions of Sir Montague.'

A voice from the living room. Harry. 'Who is it, Lorna?'

'No one,' she called back. A confrontation was the last thing Harry needed. But as she attempted to close the door, Fred Gardiner stopped it with the toe of his boot.

'I need to see you, Harrison!' he shouted.

Lorna was seething now. '*Mr* Harrison to you!' she flared. 'And I told you, he's not up to visitors. He's—'

She broke off at the sound of a crash, followed by a thud, from inside the house, her heart thumping in alarm. Had Harry attempted to come to the door and fallen? It certainly sounded like it. He still wasn't good on his crutches, and had had several narrow escapes since tumbling down the stairs.

Without another word, she turned and hurried back into the house, Fred Gardiner, who had seen his opportunity, following hot on her heels.

Sure enough, in the living room, Harry was struggling to get to his feet, supporting himself on the arm of the sofa. His crutches lay on the floor amidst the contents of the breakfast tray that he'd left on the occasional table beside the sofa and Lorna hadn't yet cleared away. Cold tea was pooling around an upturned cup, and a slice of bread and jam was face down beside the plate, which had broken in two. Harry himself was white as a freshly laundered sheet, his face contorted in pain.

'Oh Harry! Your leg's never going to heal if you keep trying to rush things!' she groaned.

He ignored her, glowering at Fred Gardiner. 'Satisfied?' he ground out between clenched teeth.

'I think I have the answer I was looking for, yes.' Gardiner spoke so smugly that Lorna wanted nothing more than to slap his gloating face. 'You'd better do as your wife says and stay where you are. But I'm afraid I still need to talk to you.'

Without being invited, he stepped over the mess on the floor and sat down in the easy chair that faced the sofa. 'Do you want to clear this up, Mrs Harrison?'

'It can wait.' Lorna had not the slightest intention of leaving this obnoxious man alone with Harry. She wanted to hear what he had to say, though already she had a pretty good idea of what it might be – the very thing she'd tried to put to the back of her mind. It was inevitable, she supposed, but she hadn't expected the crunch to come quite so soon.

Fred Gardiner fixed his supercilious gaze on Harry. 'From what I can see, it's clear there is no possibility of you returning to work in the foreseeable future.' He paused, letting his words sink in before continuing. 'Now, as you are aware, Sir Montague has most generously made a payment to those of you who suffered as a result of the roof fall . . .'

'He'd have had a strike on his hands if he didn't,' Harry interjected bitterly. ''Twas management's fault, what happened down there.'

'The inspector found no evidence of that. The roof fall was an accident that could not have been foreseen.' Fred paused to emphasise the point before going on. 'However, unfortunate as such an incident is, Sir Montague cannot support men who are unable to work. The coal mines are a business, and a business must make a profit. It will be up to the Friendly Society to provide help for you until you are fit for work again. You do pay into the Friendly Society, I assume?'

Harry said nothing. Lorna knew he'd be ashamed to admit he hadn't been keeping up with his payments, nor the membership fee for the Buffs either.

When he failed to reply, Fred shook his head disapprovingly. 'Prudence is a great virtue, Harry.'

So it was 'Harry' now, not 'Harrison', Lorna thought, but far from giving her any satisfaction, the familiarity jarred with her. What was this leading up to? It wasn't long before she was to find out.

'There's something else,' Gardiner went on. 'Should you be unable to return to work, this house will of course be required to accommodate the man who is employed to replace you. As I am sure you were made aware when you first took up occupancy, it is a tied cottage. Sir Montague is prepared to allow you a little longer to make a recovery, but if you are unfit to resume your normal employment within a reasonable period of time – and by that, I mean working as a hewer at the coal face – I'm afraid you will be required to vacate the premises.'

'What? You'd turn us out on the street?' Harry half rose, then fell back again.

'Let us hope it won't come to that.' Fred stood, smiling thinly. The bastard was enjoying this! Lorna thought bitterly. 'I'll bid you good day, Harrison.'

As he took a step towards the door, he inadvertently trod on the slice of bread that had fallen onto the floor, and jam oozed onto his highly polished leather boot. He glanced down and snorted in annoyance.

'This should have been cleared up,' he snapped at Lorna.

'And you should look where you're going.' She was in no mood to be spoken to as if she were a servant. Perhaps it was unwise to antagonise the horrible man, but even if she went down on bended knee and begged his forgiveness, it wouldn't change the situation. If Harry couldn't work, he'd not only be out of a job, but they would have to leave their home too.

Things could scarcely be bleaker.

When she returned from seeing Fred Gardiner out, Lorna found Harry struggling to balance on his crutches, his face contorted with pain.

'Harry, don't,' she begged him. 'You'll only fall again.'

He wobbled dangerously as he tried to face her. 'I got no bloody choice, have I? I got to get back to work.'

'Not while you're like this! Sit down, please!'

For a long moment he resisted, before collapsing back onto the sofa, breathless.

'Oh be buggered. I'm no use to man nor beast, an' 'tis all my own fault.'

'Don't talk so silly,' Lorna told him sharply. 'It should have been spotted if the roof was unsafe. It's management's fault, not yours.'

Harry snorted. 'They won't take the blame. They never do where there's money involved. Bloody money! It's all they care about. As for the likes of us, we're only any use as long as we'm making more of it for them. But how am I goin' to get back to work when I can't even drag myself across my own front room?'

'Not underground, perhaps, but they'll find you something,' Lorna said with more confidence than she was feeling. 'On the screens, perhaps.'

'Standin' all day? Pickin' bloody coal with the youngsters?' He snorted again. 'I don't think so. Even if I could manage it, the wage wouldn't be enough. We'm done for, Lorna.'

Lorna stifled a sigh. He was right. But she couldn't let him work himself into an even deeper depression than he was already in.

'Let me clear up this mess and we'll talk about it,' she said.

'What's there to talk about?'

Nothing, with him in this mood, she realised. Close to tears of despair, she went to fetch a dustpan and brush.

Lorna knocked on the door of the house next door, opened it a crack and called out, 'Are you there, Flossie?'

She shouldn't be bothering her friend. Flossie was sure to be busy. But if she didn't talk to someone, she thought she'd go crazy. Flossie would hear her out without either snapping at her or encouraging her to wallow in a morass of self-pity. It wasn't feasible to hope they might come up with a solution to her problems; there wasn't one that she could see. The best she could hope for was a cup of tea and a sympathetic ear, but that would be enough to give her the strength to carry on.

'Come on in!' Flossie called.

As Lorna went into the kitchen, a small bundle of wiry ginger hair scampered towards her, jumping up around her legs and barking excitedly.

'Nipper!' she exclaimed. 'What are you doing here?'

'I think you must've shut him out.' Flossie turned from the vegetables she was preparing, still holding the knife in one hand and a potato in the other. 'I heard him barking, and when I looked out I could see him scratching at your door. Thought I'd best bring him in here. You don't want him running out in the road and getting knocked over.'

'Oh my goodness.' Nipper must have escaped when she'd hurried into the living room after hearing Harry call. She hadn't even noticed he was gone. 'Thanks, Flossie. I don't know where my head is.'

'What you gotta put up with would drive anybody crackers,' Flossie said. 'I don't know how you'm doin' it, and that's the truth.'

'It's not just that.' Lorna felt a tide of hopelessness rising in her chest and tried to ignore it. 'We've had a visitor this morning. Not one I'd have chosen.' She laughed mirthlessly.

'Fred Gardiner,' Flossie said. 'I saw him, nasty little twerp. What did he want?'

'Oh Flossie . . .' Tears started to Lorna's eyes. She blinked them away angrily, but not before Flossie had seen them.

'Sit down, dearie. I'll make a cup of tea and you can tell me all about it.'

Lorna told her. When she had finished, Flossie tutted sympathetically.

'Only to be expected, I s'pose. What you gonna do?'

'I don't know.' Lorna cradled the teacup between hands that were trembling. 'I just can't seem to think straight.'

'Well then let's put our heads together. If the worst comes to the worst an' they do turn you out, you know I wouldn't see you on the streets. You'll have to come here for a bit. Till you can sort somethin' out.'

Tears pricked Lorna's eyes again at Flossie's generous offer. 'That is so kind of you. But we couldn't impose on you. You've got a houseful as it is.'

'We'll just 'ave to squash up a bit,' Flossie said, as if it was the most normal thing in the world.

'I can't let you do that,' Lorna said firmly. 'I suppose . . .' She broke off, thinking. 'I suppose Harry's parents might let us move back in with them. We lived with them when we were first married.'

'And you hated every minute of it. You've told me.'

She swallowed hard. The thought of going back to live with Harry's parents was a lead weight in her stomach. It had scarcely been the best start to their married life. She liked Harry's father – he was a good-natured, softly spoken man – but his mother was a nasty, overbearing woman. She was the one who wore the trousers in that house, not a doubt of it, and Harry's father would do anything for the sake of peace. He'd tried to speak up for Lorna when Rose Harrison was making her life a misery, but it never did any good. Always convinced that she was right and everyone else was wrong, she'd cut him down with scathing words and a display of her cold disapproval. Poor Joe would give up the argument and retire behind his paper or go out to potter in the garden. Lorna had felt like an intruder, which was precisely how Rose viewed her, she supposed, and the thought of being forced back into that claustrophobic atmosphere was a horrible one. Though it might be, of course, that they had no choice.

'Do you think we'd be allowed to stay here if we could pay the rent?' she asked, clutching at straws.

'Oh my dear, I couldn't say.' Flossie looked perplexed. 'But how would you manage to do that anyway, if Harry can't work?'

'I could get a job. More than one, perhaps. I'm not afraid of hard work, and Harry'd be at home for the children. There's always cards up in the paper shop window looking for women to do cleaning and such like. I could do that, no trouble.'

'True . . .' But before Flossie could continue, Lorna's hand flew to her mouth.

'Oh Flossie, I'm going to have to go. I was just making a loaf of soda bread when that man came and I forgot all about it. It won't be baked in time for the children's lunch if I don't get it in the oven.' She stood up. 'Thanks for the tea. And for being such a good friend.'

For a moment Flossie said nothing. Her eyes were narrowed, her brow furrowed in thought. Then: 'Now *there's* something you could do,' she said triumphantly.

'What?' She'd lost Lorna.

'Baking. Bread, biscuits, buns . . . Your specialities.'

'What are you talking about?'

'You could make things like that and sell 'em. There's not many that can bake as well as you can, an' I reckon they'd go like hot cakes.'

Lorna was still confused. 'Sell them? How?'

'We could spread the word. Our Arthur could put cards through folks' doors, for a start, and I 'spect the shops would take some if you asked them. But better still, there's a stall in the market goin' to be free sometime soon, from what I hear. Mr Johnson, the jeweller, 'as decided to retire, it seems. In luxury, I shouldn't wonder,' Flossie added with a knowing look. 'He's not short of a penny or two, an' that's the truth. You've seen his wife, strutting about in her fur coat like Lady Muck?'

Lorna smiled slightly. Mrs Johnson stood out like a sore thumb in the mining community, and there was always speculation about her morals and those of her so-called maid, Josie. Gossip had it that the two of them ran a sideline in entertaining men in exchange for money in the Johnsons' grand house. But this really wasn't the time for idle chatter.

'I can't stop to talk about it now,' Lorna said. 'But thanks again. For everything.' She glanced down at the little dog, who had curled up under the table. 'Nipper! Come on. We're going.'

Flossie's idea of using her baking skills to make some money was a good one, she thought as she made her way home holding tightly to Nipper's collar. But for the moment, she couldn't see for the life of her that it could ever be more than that.

Chapter Eight

'Excuse me, sir!'

Bradley had been to the bakery to buy a pasty for his dinner, and was just walking along the street on his way back when he heard the shout coming from behind him. He turned to see a young woman he didn't recognise hurrying after him.

'Are you looking for me?' he asked.

'Yes. You're the pit safety officer, aren't you?'

'I am,' he said, somewhat taken by surprise. 'How can I help you?'

'I wanted to talk to you about the roof fall.' She pushed a fair curl behind her ear. 'Look, I'm the barmaid at the Miners' Arms, and I've heard things I think you might be interested in. But I can't stop now. We're due to open at midday.'

'You want me to come to the Miners' Arms?' Bradley was intrigued now.

She shook her head. 'Not really. It's not very private, and I don't want to be seen talking to you.'

'So where do you suggest?'

She shrugged. 'Anywhere we won't be overheard.'

Bradley thought quickly. Duncan Cameron was at Milverton Colliery just now, but he intended to go to Oldlands when he'd finished there.

'I should be the only one in my office later on this afternoon. Shall we say about four?' he suggested.

The young woman frowned. 'Somebody might see me. What about down by the mill?'

The mill was just a few hundred yards from the pit, down a leafy lane. 'You do know that coal carts go that way to and from Lower Middlecote, don't you?' Bradley reminded her.

'We can keep out of the way,' she said confidently.

'Very well. I'll see you then.'

Mercy Comer smiled triumphantly as she headed for the Miners' Arms and her midday shift. This time her habitual snooping had given her a golden opportunity to make the acquaintance of the new safety officer. Ever since she'd overheard him talking to Amos Riddle, she'd listened even more intently to what the miners who were regular customers were saying, and she'd gathered enough to make her think that Amos might well be right when he said he'd heard an explosion before the roof fall. She would have liked something a bit more concrete in the way of evidence to present to the safety officer, but at least it had been enough to give her an opening, and she could offer to be his ears and eyes in the Miners' Arms from now on.

It would do the trick, she felt sure. Mercy was confident in her charms, and her ability to ensnare men. She'd never met one she couldn't wind round her little finger if she put her mind to it. Oh yes, she'd had plenty of practice while she was waiting for the right one to come along. And now he had! She could hardly wait to see him again. This was going to be the start of something special.

As she chopped vegetables for a stew for their evening meal, Flossie thought about her suggestion that Lorna should try to

Jennie Felton

make some money from her baking. If it meant they could manage to pay the rent, perhaps Sir Montague would let them stay in the house for the time being at least. The problem, of course, was that she couldn't see how Harry would ever be able to go back to his old job. She tried to suppress a wave of irritation with the man. He'd been badly hurt, yes, he was still in a lot of pain and that contraption on his leg wasn't helping, but he wasn't helping himself either in Flossie's opinion. On the one hand he was impatient, as witness when he had fallen down the stairs, intent on getting his crutches, and no doubt set back the healing process; on the other he was too depressed to do the gentle exercises the doctor had prescribed.

Flossie could see it was all getting on top of Lorna, but that was another good reason for her to take positive action. Baking, which she enjoyed, and was very good at, would give her something to focus on. Take her mind off her worries for a bit. She hadn't responded to the idea as enthusiastically as Flossie had hoped, but then she'd been upset, and in a rush too. If Flossie could come up with some concrete plans and offers of help, she felt sure she could talk her round. And talented baker as Lorna was, there'd be no shortage of customers once she'd put cards up in the shops in town and Arthur had dropped more through doors.

The biggest earner, though, would be the market stall, and it was the idea of that that excited her most. Flossie had always loved going to market on a Saturday, walking through the forecourt where the quack doctors Rainbow and Quilley peddled their pills and potions and a dentist pulled teeth in a wagon in full view of the shoppers. But best of all was wandering up and down the aisles inside the spacious market hall. She'd often thought she'd love to have a stall there herself. Well, this was her chance. The market ran from early morning until nine in the evening, and Lorna wouldn't be able to be there all that time.

The snag, of course, was that she couldn't see how Lorna could bake enough to stock the stall. Even with two bake ovens – her own and Lorna's – and enough coal to keep them going, it was a tall order. And not many things could be made in advance; the whole point was that the bread, scones and sponge cakes would be completely fresh. No, those would have to be just the main attraction. There would have to be other things to sell too.

As Flossie reached for another carrot to peel, it came to her in a flash. Albie, her husband, was a keen gardener. Besides their long vegetable garden, he rented an allotment, and the hours he spent tending the vegetables produced more than enough for their needs. They were fine specimens, too – he always walked away with more first prizes in the local shows than anyone else. The boom period wouldn't come until summer, but the rows of unpicked cabbages and the potatoes, carrots, parsnips and swedes they had stored in the garden shed would tide things over until the broad beans and other early vegetables were ready for harvesting.

There was a greengrocery stall in the market already, but Flossie always thought the produce looked a bit sad and she felt sure customers would prefer Albie's. But when Mr Johnson retired, there wouldn't be a jeweller's, and she was afraid that one from Bath or Frome might snap up the vacant stall in no time at all.

Flossie wasn't one to let the grass grow under her feet. She'd go and see Mr Baker the market manager this very afternoon, and stake her claim on the stall.

Lorna had always found baking relaxing, and by the time she took the loaf out of the oven, golden brown and nicely risen, her mood had lifted and a glow of satisfaction that owed nothing to the heat of the fire had brought a flush to her cheeks. She cut a hunk of it, still warm, spread it with butter and bit into it. It tasted so good! She put another slice on a plate with a bit of the precious cheese she'd bought earlier, and took it in to Harry together with a glass of brown ale. For once he didn't find anything to complain about, but ate every last crumb, increasing Lorna's feeling of satisfaction. Since the accident he'd had no appetite to speak of, and complained that the food was giving him indigestion, so this was a definite improvement.

Perhaps Flossie's suggestion wasn't such a bad one after all, she thought. She still couldn't see how she could make it pay well enough to solve their problems, but perhaps between them they could work something out.

Her good mood was short-lived, however. When the girls arrived home for their dinner, Vera was in tears.

'Whatever is the matter?' Lorna asked.

Vera was crying too hard to say a word, and it was left to Marjorie to explain.

'Reggie Bodman pushed her up against the wall and wouldn't let her go,' she said solemnly. 'He is such a bully.'

Lorna knew Reggie – a thickset boy who was tall for his age. It wasn't the first time he'd upset her girls. 'If I catch hold of him, I'll push *him* up against the wall. Don't worry, my love, I'll make sure he doesn't do it again.'

'Well . . .' Marjorie hesitated, reluctant to give her sister away. 'She did have his bag of marbles.'

'Didn't!' Vera spluttered between her tears.

'You did. You picked them up when he wasn't looking and hid them up your knicker leg,' Marjorie said, and Lorna sighed heavily.

'Oh Vera. Is this true?' Vera hung her head and said nothing.

'Yes,' Marjorie said. 'And she's still got them.'

Vera glared at her. 'Tell-tale-tit!'

'Let me have them,' Lorna said sternly and, reluctantly and a bit sheepishly, Vera hoisted up her petticoats, extracted a hessian bag from the leg of her bloomers and held it out to her mother.

'I'm surprised he didn't keep you there until you gave them back,' Lorna said, exasperated.

'He would have if it hadn't been for Arthur,' Marjorie said. 'He came to the rescue.'

'Well good for Arthur.' Lorna was cutting thick slices of her soda bread. 'But it wasn't a nice thing to do, Vera. Boys treasure their marbles, you know that. When you go back to school after dinner, you'll return them to him and say you're sorry.'

'I'm not going back to school!' Vera was crying again. 'I don't want to!'

'We'll see about that. Now sit down and eat your dinner, for goodness' sake.' Lorna loaded the bread onto a plate and put it on the table between them. She felt she was at the end of her tether again, and just to make things worse, Harry was calling out to know what the commotion was all about. 'You see? Now you've upset your father too,' she added crossly. 'I don't know what I'm going to do with you.'

She'd forgotten all about Flossie's suggestion, and once again felt as if she was drowning in a morass of never-ending problems.

Once their mother had left the room to collect Harry's dinner tray, Vera looked at Marjorie through tear-wet lashes.

'Why didn't you tell Mammy the nasty things Reggie Bodman said about Daddy?'

'Because it was rubbish,' Marjorie said quietly but firmly. 'And it would only have upset Mammy.'

'But she wouldn't have been so cross with me! And she wouldn't have said I had to say sorry to Reggie. I don't want to say sorry!' The tears spilled over again. 'He's horrible! I hate him!'

'Shh!' Marjorie whispered urgently. She hadn't understood what Reggie had meant as he pinned Vera against the wall and hissed: 'If you don't give 'em back, I'll tell. Your dad's a murderer! He'll go to prison.' Then Arthur had seen what was going on and come to their aid, and Reggie had shut up.

'This bread's lovely, Mammy,' she said as her mother came back into the room, and threw Vera a stern look that dared her to say another word about what Reggie Bodman had said.

The children had gone back to school and Lorna was elbow deep in soap suds washing the dishes when there was a knock at the door. Flossie popped her head in.

'Can you come round to mine for a minute?'

Lorna was surprised – it was unusual for Flossie to ask her to go next door at this time of day.

'What . . . ?'

Flossie nodded meaningfully in the direction of the sitting room, which puzzled Lorna more than ever. Whatever it was Flossie wanted to say, she didn't want Harry to hear it.

'Just let me finish up here,' she said.

Leaving the crockery and cutlery to drain on the oilcloth-covered cupboard beside the sink, she went into the front room.

'I'm going next door for a minute. I won't be long. And when I come back, we must get you trying to walk,' she said.

Harry muttered something unintelligible in reply, and Lorna took off her apron and left the house.

She found Flossie sitting at her kitchen table with a cup of tea in front of her.

'Pour yourself one,' she said by way of greeting. 'It's a fresh pot.'

Lorna found a cup in a cupboard – she knew Flossie's kitchen almost as well as she knew her own – filled it from the teapot that was warming on the hob and topped it up with milk from the jug on the table.

'What's this all about then, Flossie?' she asked, taking a chair opposite her friend.

'Well, I've most likely overstepped the mark,' Flossie grinned guiltily, 'but I thought you could do with a shove up the backside. I've been to see Mr Baker – 'im as runs the market – an' told 'im you're interested in taking over Mr Johnson's stall.'

'Oh Flossie!' Lorna spluttered over a mouthful of tea, which set her coughing.

'Well, he's 'ad a few enquiries already, it seems – word spreads awful fast. But 'e was very sympathetic, an' 'e says 'e'll let you 'ave it fer a trial period if you think you can make a go of it.'

Lorna put down her cup and covered her mouth with her hands.

'I know, I know,' Flossie went on. 'Like I say, p'raps I shouldn't'a done it. But I want the old Lorna back, an' doin' summat positive will be a proper tonic, not to mention putting some readies in yer pocket. I reckoned the stall would be gone if you took too long shilly-shallying, an' I wasn't far out.'

'Oh Flossie, I don't think I can. I wouldn't know where to start! And how would I pay the rent?' Lorna protested weakly.

'You just do what you do best – baking,' Flossie said firmly. 'I'll take care o' the rest. I'll write out some cards for our Arthur to drop through people's doors, an' if you haven't got enough wares to sell, I'll bring a nice lot of Albie's vegetables to fill the gaps. As for the rent, I'll see to that until you get goin'.'

'Oh Flossie, I couldn't let you do that!' Lorna protested.

'I'll be doin' it as much for meself as for you. I've always fancied a stall in the market. So let's have no more excuses. Fresh bread, buns and scones – that's what I'll be tellin' folk you'll be sellin'. An' as for what you'll need . . . well, I'll let you have some eggs from my hens, and if there's anything else you can't afford right now, I'll help you out with that too.'

Lorna was dumbstruck at Flossie's generosity. 'You can't do that,' was all she could manage.

'Stuff and nonsense!' Flossie said. 'I don't wanna lose you as a neighbour. Goodness only knows who they'd put in next door if they turned you out. We'm the best o' friends, bain't we?'

'Well, yes, but . . .'

'It's up to you, o' course.' She shrugged, as if to say she'd done all she could. The rest was up to Lorna.

'I'll have to talk to Harry,' Lorna said.

'I wouldn't if I was you. Not yet anyway. From what I can see, he'd only put the kibosh on it, the mood he's in. Get it all sorted out first, and then tell him. An' be firm about it.' Flossie fixed her with a straight look. ''Tis high time you started standing up to 'im, my girl. The more you kowtow to him, the worse it'll be.'

Lorna nodded. 'I expect you're right. And I've got time to think about it, haven't I? But it's a big step, Flossie. I don't want to get in over my head. Besides, I don't know how I'd find the time to do all that baking and spend most of Saturday in the market on top of everything else.'

'I've said I'll help you, haven't I? And it wouldn't hurt the girls to do a bit more,' Flossie said decisively. 'They'm big enough now to do some dusting and cleaning up. An' they'd love goin' to the market with you.'

Lorna smiled faintly. 'They would. I always have to drag

them away when I've finished my shopping.'

'Well there you are. But just don't take too long makin' up yer mind. Mr Baker won't keep the offer open for ever.'

'I won't,' Lorna promised. 'And thanks again, Flossie.'

'You goin' to stop fer another cup o' tea?'

'I'd better not. Harry will be wondering where I am.'

'Let 'im wonder,' Flossie said scathingly. 'I don't know 'ow you put up with 'im, an' that's the truth.'

'He's my husband,' Lorna said simply. Head spinning, she left Flossie and walked back along the track to her own door.

Mercy Comer was trembling with anticipation as she crossed the river and walked up the lane towards the mill. She'd allowed herself plenty of time in case there was a train due on the track that ran between her home and the bridge. As the main line to and from Bath, it was often busy, and she didn't want to be late for her meeting with the safety officer.

But today there had been no delay, and she had time to spare.

As the mill came into sight, she could see a wagon drawn up beneath the pulley system and a sack of grain suspended above it, moving jerkily downwards. She cursed inwardly. She didn't want the wagon driver or the mill hand to see her here. As a barmaid, she was well known in the locality, and the men were bound to wonder why she was hanging about near the mill. She'd walk a little way in the opposite direction, she decided.

To her dismay, however, she hadn't gone far before she heard the clip-clop of a horse's hooves coming from behind her and the creak of a wagon as it bumped over the uneven track. As the safety officer had said, the lane led to Lower Middlecote pit, a mile or so away, and she guessed it would be a cart on its way to collect a load of coal. As she stepped onto the grass verge so that it could pass safely, a cheery voice called her name. It was Fred Thomas, the haulier.

'Hoi, Mercy! What be you doin' down 'ere?'

'Can't a girl go for a walk in the fresh air? It's a free country as far as I know.' She tossed her head, giving him a withering glance, and the coal cart rumbled on in the direction of Lower Middlecote.

She delayed for a few minutes, then walked back towards the mill. The wagon had gone, so she headed for the small patch of woodland that bordered the river where it flowed into the mill pond. At the same time, a man turned into the lane from the main road. The safety officer. Her heart skipped a beat.

'You came then?' she said, pretending indifference, as he reached her.

'So it seems,' he replied drily. 'I'm curious to know what it is you want to say to me.'

Mercy glanced around warily. She wasn't convinced that one of the mill hands wasn't still close enough to overhear.

'Let's go over the bridge,' she suggested.

He raised a quizzical eyebrow, but followed her without a word.

'This should do,' she said when they were midway across. It wasn't how she'd planned it, but they were far enough away from both the mill and the railway sidings now, and that was the most important thing for the moment. 'I'm Mercy, by the way. And you're Mr Robinson, I'm told.'

'Bradley Robinson. Yes. So what is this all about?' he asked.

'The roof fall – I told you that.' Mercy rested a hand on the wooden railing. She was feeling uncharacteristically nervous. 'And like I said, in my job I hear a lot of things.'

'Such as?'

She took a deep breath. 'I don't think it was an accident.

I think it was planned. The men are all fed up with the conditions in Sir Montague's pits, and I think they wanted to highlight just how dangerous working there is. There was an explosion, wasn't there, just before the roof came down?'

'I have been told that,' Bradley agreed. 'But why would anyone risk their life, and those of their colleagues, just to make a point?'

'Well, they wouldn't have meant for anybody to be killed. Something must have gone wrong,' Mercy said.

'That's possible, I suppose.' He paused. 'What proof do you have? And who do you think was involved?'

'I don't have any proof yet,' Mercy admitted. 'And I don't know for sure who actually did it, so I'm naming no names. What I do know is that there's talk about it. And I ought to be able to find out more if I use my ears and eyes and ask the right questions. It's risky, though, meeting you in broad daylight. If the men realise I've been talking to you, they'll make sure I don't know anything I shouldn't. Look,' she went on, emboldened by his silence, 'Mondays and Tuesdays are my nights off, an' it's dark by six or so. I could come to your office when all the men have gone home.'

Bradley gave her a straight look that she didn't much care for.

'I wouldn't bother you unless I had something definite to tell you,' she said, realising her charms were not working as they usually did with men, and trying a different tack.

'And how will you let me know, if you're so anxious not to be seen talking to me?' he asked reasonably. 'Look, let's put an end to all this cloak-and-dagger stuff. I'll call in to the Miners' Arms from time to time. Just come to the hatch in the snug and you can tell me if you've discovered anything new. That way no one in the bar will see me. How does that sound to you?'

Mercy nodded. What a let-down! She must be losing her touch. But really she had no option but to agree. 'All right,' she said, hiding her disappointment.

She might have to play her cards a little differently, she thought as she watched him walk away, heading back to Milverton. He wasn't an uncouth miner but an intelligent and educated man. And Mercy was determined he wasn't going to be the one that got away!

Chapter Nine

Since Flossie had suggested baking as a way of making some much-needed money, Lorna had thought of little else. She'd weighed up all the pros and cons, and in the end come to the conclusion that she had nothing to lose. But if the plan had any chance of working, it was imperative they were allowed to stay in their house. She could hardly bake bread, buns and cake to sell in the market or anywhere else if they were out on the streets, or forced to move back in with Harry's mother and father. Before confirming arrangements with Mr Baker, she needed to settle the matter of their tenancy, for the time being at least.

But how? She'd never be able to approach Sir Montague himself. Mr Gardiner, his horrible agent, was his gatekeeper, and she'd get nowhere with him. She had to find another way.

She thought of the general manager. Mr Cameron was noted for being fair-minded if tough, and he might well be sympathetic to their plight and put it to Sir Montague that they should be given more time. The problem was that now he was responsible for four pits besides Milverton, he might be at any one of them at any given time.

Then there was the safety officer. Mr Robinson. He'd been very kind to her on the day of the roof fall, giving her a lift home from the hospital, and she felt he was more approachable than any of them. Employees' accommodation wasn't in his remit, of course, but perhaps he would plead their case with Mr Cameron if she couldn't speak to him herself. But as he too was responsible for all the Fairley pits, he might be as difficult to locate as Mr Cameron.

She'd go to Milverton and hope to find Mr Cameron there, she decided. But she wouldn't tell Harry. He'd only say it was useless, and if he was proved right, it would send him even further into the depths of depression.

'I'm just popping out,' she told him. 'I need a few things from town. I won't be long. You'll be all right, won't you?'

'For crying out loud!' he grumbled. 'I'm not a babby. I don't need a nursemaid.'

'Well, just be careful you don't fall again,' Lorna cautioned.

'I thought you wanted me to do a bit of exercise.'

'Yes, I do. But wait till I'm here to steady you if you get dizzy.'

She buttoned her coat, picked up her shopping bag, and left before he could ask her any awkward questions.

A chill whispered over her skin as she walked into the pit yard. The ponies that pulled the spoil trucks across the road at the start of their journey to the batches were harnessed up and ready to go, but not even this evidence of life here having returned to normal could dispel the sinking feeling in her stomach or the echo of the dread she'd felt the last time she'd been here.

She was heartened, though, to see Cameron's motor drawn up outside the office block. It looked as if she had struck lucky. A knot of nervousness constricted her throat. This was it then. For one horrible moment, everything she had planned to say deserted her, but, grimly determined, she forced herself to keep going. She'd come this far; she wasn't going to turn back now.

Clenching her fist to keep it from shaking, she knocked on the office door.

'Come in!' It was Cameron's distinctive Scottish burr.

Lorna opened the door. But he wasn't alone. Seated in the visitor's chair opposite him was the safety officer. For some unaccountable reason she felt hot colour rising in her cheeks. She'd thought of him as a potential ally; now, coming face to face with him so unexpectedly, she was embarrassed and shy.

'Mrs Harrison, isn't it?' He sounded surprised – and pleased – to see her.

'I was hoping to speak to Mr Cameron,' she blurted, then addressed the general manager directly. 'If you're not too busy, that is, sir.'

Cameron's mouth twisted upwards in a wry smile. 'I'm always busy. But since you're here . . . What was it you wanted me for, Mrs . . . Harrison, isn't it?'

'That's right. Her husband was one of those badly injured in the roof fall,' Bradley said. 'I expect it has something to do with that. Am I right, Mrs Harrison?'

There was unspoken encouragement in his dark hazel eyes, and Lorna nodded, wishing the heat in her cheeks would subside and her heart would stop pounding in her chest.

'It's had terrible consequences for us, Mr Cameron,' she began, and then the words came tumbling out. 'I'm really sorry to bother you, but I'm going out of my mind with worry. As you know, my husband can't work at the moment – he's still on crutches – and Sir Montague's agent is threatening us with eviction. We've got two small children, and I don't know what we'd do if he put us out on the streets. Please . . .' Her voice faded as sudden tears thickened her throat. 'Please! Can you do anything to help us?'

Before the general manager could answer, Bradley rose from

his chair and gesticulated towards it. 'Sit down, Mrs Harrison. You're upset. Understandably. I'll leave you to talk to Mr Cameron and I'm sure he'll be sympathetic to your plight.'

He turned for the door, but Cameron stopped him. 'Don't go, Robinson. Since this is as a result of a safety issue, it concerns you too. And Mrs Harrison, please do as Mr Robinson suggests, and take a seat before you fall down.'

The colour that heightened in Lorna's cheeks was now shame. But it was true: her legs were shaking uncontrollably, and the last thing she wanted was for them to give way beneath her in front of the two men. 'Thank you,' she managed, and sat in the chair Bradley had vacated.

'So.' Cameron leaned back in his own chair. 'Let's have the details. What notice have you been given? Was it in writing?'

She shook her head. 'Mr Gardiner came to see us. He said if Harry can't get back to work at the coal face within a reasonable time, then they'll need our house for whoever gets his job.'

'No actual time frame was mentioned?'

'No, but to be truthful, sir, it's going to be a very long time before he's fit for anything, let alone going underground. The doctor said six months at least. And from what Mr Gardiner said, they won't be prepared to wait that long.'

'I see.' Cameron picked up a pencil, twisting it between his thick fingers. 'Then I'm sorry, Mrs Harrison, but I don't see what I can do. A new collier will have to be taken on, and he'll need a place to live. Besides that, I presume Sir Montague has concerns with regard to the rent you'd be obliged to pay him. With no wage coming in, ye'd have difficulty with that, I'd imagine.'

Lorna sat forward in her chair. 'I've thought of that, sir. It's what I wanted to tell you. I have a plan for earning some money.

se...

makin... ...support yoursel...
itself, never mind paying rent on your h...
bake a great many cakes to do that, and fin...
customers.'

'I hope I can do just that, sir.' Lorna lifted her chin, me...
his gaze squarely. 'My neighbour is willing to let me use her
bake oven as well as my own, and help me out financially until
I'm up and running. I've got the offer of a stall in the market of
a Saturday, and that should turn a good profit – you know how
busy the market gets. I've done some sums, and I believe I can
make this work.'

'You seem to have the makings of a successful business-
woman,' Cameron said, not troubling to disguise his admiration.
'What's your opinion, Robinson?'

'I agree.' The safety officer, too, seemed impressed.

Cameron tapped his pencil on the desk for a few moments,
looking thoughtful. 'You must realise I play no part in the
allocation of tied accommodation?' he said at last. 'It's Sir
Montague's agent who is responsible for that, and he's a stickler
for running things in the way they've always been done.'

'Oh.' Lorna's heart sank.

'However,' he went on, 'if ye leave it with me for the time
being, I'll see what I can do.'

Lorna's breath came out on a little gasp. 'Oh thank you, sir!'

'Don't thank me yet,' Cameron cautioned. 'I'll raise the
matter with Sir Montague when I've given it some thought. But
there is no guarantee he'll be amenable to anything I may
suggest, and in the meantime, it would be wise for ye to consider
other options.'

'Yes, of course. I understand.
this time from embarrassment.
otherwise, even for a moment. 'A
for saying you'll try.'
'I think we owe yo...
the pencil and
interview...

...er cheeks burned,
...he should have thought
...nd I'm really grateful to you

...u that much, lassie.' Cameron put down
...rose from his chair, and Lorna realised the
...was over.

...ne slipped the handles of her bag over her arm and stood up. 'Thank you, sir.'

As she left the office, she was uncomfortably aware of two pairs of eyes following her, and even when the door had closed behind her, she could still feel them.

What were they saying about her? she wondered. That she was a pathetic, deluded woman who was chasing rainbows? Well, perhaps she was. But better that than giving up without a fight.

She steadied her breathing and walked across the pit yard with her head held high.

'That is quite a woman,' Cameron said as he sat down again.

'Indeed,' Bradley agreed. 'With her spirit and determination it wouldn't surprise me if she was able to make a go of this idea of hers. But if she's forced to leave her home, it will be dead in the water. There's no way she could produce bread and cakes without access to a bake oven.'

'Quite.' Cameron picked up the pencil and tapped it on the desk again, a habit of his when he was deep in thought, Bradley had learned. Just now he was clearly trying to come up with a way to get around the problem.

Not wanting to interrupt the general manager's deliberations but anxious to know what conclusion he reached, Bradley looked at the district inspector's report again.

replaces … d altogether, and the … aying where they
make an exception to what … un … return to his old … ve to go to whoever … ade Sir Montague to … an unwritten rule.
But . . .' He paused.

'Yes?' Bradley said expectantly.

'Oldlands is being run down for closure, as you know,'
Cameron continued. 'There are three cottages providing
accommodation for some of the men who work there. You must
know them. You pass them on the way to your house.'

Bradley nodded. Yes, he knew them. They sat in a dip in the
lane not far from a little crossroads, one arm of which led to the
colliery. If they weren't such a long walk from the town, it would
be an idyllic place to live, surrounded by fields and a copse, and
the houses themselves appeared to be more spacious than the
long ranks that straddled the slopes around Hillsbridge. He had
noticed, though, that they were beginning to fall into disrepair,
which was unsurprising given that Oldlands wouldn't be a
working pit for much longer.

'Harrison's mother and father live in one – Harrison senior
drives the winding engine at Oldlands,' Cameron went on.
'Another is occupied by Widow Parfitt and her son, a strange
fellow who works on the screens when he manages to turn up;
and the third is vacant. If the Harrisons could afford to pay a
peppercorn rent, I see no reason why Sir Montague wouldn't
agree to them moving there.'

'That certainly makes sense,' Bradley said. 'If the house is
unoccupied, a small rental income would be better than none.'

'It may be, of course, that Sir Montague decides to sell off all

three cottages wh...
a solution to the Ha...
Hopefully to g...
sufficiently to...
Cameron slapped...
Montague about st...
'When will tha...
'I've an appo...
let's...

provide

ing at least.

e recovered

apacity or other.'

ood up. 'I have to see Sir

er matters. I'll raise the subject then.'

Bradley asked.

intment with him tomorrow morning. Now, let's go and see what the man you're hoping to recruit to your team has to say for himself.'

Bradley watched with interest as Cameron cranked the Ford into life.

'You really must look at getting a motor. It's not fitting for a man in your position to have to rely on a bicycle to get about,' the manager said as they drove out of the pit yard and headed for Lower Middlecote.

'It's not ideal,' Bradley agreed. 'I've been making some enquiries, and I think I may well be the proud possessor of a little Ford myself before long.'

Cameron changed gear noisily. 'And not before time,' he said with feeling.

The interview with the man Bradley had selected as a possible rescue team leader was over. It had gone well, and soon Lower Middlecote would have a trained squad of its own. Now Bradley was back in his office, sitting at the desk deep in thought. But it wasn't the new team he was thinking of. It was Cameron's suggestion of alternative accommodation for the Harrison family. Would he be able to persuade Sir Montague to go along with it? Bradley was very much hoping he would. For two reasons.

The first was that he felt genuine sympathy as well as

admiration for pretty little Mrs Harrison. Unsurprisingly, she was dreadfully worried at the prospect of losing her home, especially as there were apparently two young children to think of, but rather than accepting the hopelessness of the situation and weeping and wailing, she was fighting every step of the way, and her resourcefulness deserved to be rewarded.

The second reason, he acknowledged, was less altruistic, and not something he was proud of.

He was still determined to get to the bottom of the cause of the roof fall if at all possible. The rumours he'd heard, and his gut instinct, told him that it had been no accident, but caused deliberately to highlight the dangerous conditions in Sir Montague's collieries. What Amos Riddle had said – that there had been an explosion immediately before the fall – had deepened that suspicion, but Amos was a lone voice in a wilderness of silence, and not a very reliable one at that. The miners who had been underground at the time of the disaster had been evasive, shifty almost, when he'd questioned them. He'd formed the distinct impression that there was something they were not telling him, and what the barmaid, Mercy, had said seemed to confirm that. He could well picture them clustered around the tables in the Miners' Arms discussing what had happened – a plan that had gone horribly wrong – not realising that the girl was listening to every word they said.

But it was all still speculation. The Inspector of Mines had deemed the roof fall an unavoidable accident, and without concrete proof, Bradley couldn't ask for the case to be reopened. Now, though, he thought, he might have found a chink in the wall of silence.

Harry Harrison had been right there when the roof had come down. He, George Golledge and Ted Yarlett had taken the brunt of it, along with the unfortunate carting boy. Bradley was aware that all three men were known troublemakers. If someone had set off an explosion, they must have been aware of it. In on the plan, even. Now, given the serious injuries Harrison had sustained and the threat of losing his home, he might well be feeling resentful towards whoever it was who had made the disastrous mistake that had caused the roof fall and be ready to talk. If Cameron was able to persuade Sir Montague to allow the family to move into the Oldlands house, it would provide Bradley with an excuse for contact with Harry. Perhaps even a bargaining chip. And if he was reluctant to dob in his mates – there was a code of brotherhood amongst the miners – Mrs Harrison was a very different proposition. She certainly wouldn't want to risk losing the chance of a roof over their heads. Through her, Bradley might well be able to get the evidence he needed to have the investigation reopened and set his mind at rest that the disaster hadn't come about because of his carelessness.

His mind was made up. He would do whatever it took to achieve that end.

Chapter Ten

'Well, well! So you've taken my advice. And very impressive, I must say.' Cameron nodded in the direction of the black Ford parked outside the office.

'Not as smart as yours, but I must say I'm pleased with it.'

He walked around the motor that Bradley had purchased in Bath only the day before, inspecting a scratch here and there, and a dented fender.

Bradley smiled ruefully. 'That's the reason I could afford it on my salary. Don't worry, I plan to get it fixed when I've put a bit more aside.'

'Well, now that you have transport, perhaps you'd like to make use of it.' Cameron looked at him, a wry smile crinkling the deep furrows in his face. 'I've good news for Mrs Harrison, and it's my opinion you should be the one to break it to her. And her husband, of course,' he added.

'Sir Montague has agreed to your proposal, then?' Bradley said, pleased.

'Aye, he has. It took some arm-twisting, mind you. I told him the men would all be up in arms if the Harrisons lost their home through no fault of their own, and a strike was more than likely if he didn't do something to make amends. As I'd hoped, the old miser decided it would be for the best.'

'That's good news,' Bradley said. 'But don't you want to tell them yourself?'

'I've a busy day ahead of me, laddie. And if I'm not much mistaken, you'd be glad of the chance to talk to them. From what you said before, you're not convinced the roof fall was an accident. Harrison might well be the one to tell you the truth of what happened down there that day. Do you still think it was caused deliberately?'

'Yes, I do. As I mentioned before, Amos Riddle told me he'd heard an explosion, and while I agree he is not the most reliable of witnesses, I tend to believe him. He wouldn't have imagined something like that.' Bradley deliberately didn't mention Mercy, since as yet she hadn't supplied him with proof of what she had said.

Cameron got out his pipe and twisted the stem between his finger and thumb. 'It's a serious allegation, Robinson. A matter for the police.'

'Since the inspector has recorded what happened as an accident, I doubt the police would take any action on the basis of what I have at the moment,' Bradley said.

Cameron's brow was furrowed. He put his pipe in his mouth and lit it, clearly deep in thought. At last he spoke.

'You're most likely right about that. But if there's any substance to what ye're suggesting, we need to get to the bottom of it. We can't risk something like that happening again.'

'Exactly,' Bradley agreed. 'But what we need is hard evidence.'

'And Harrison may well be ready and able to provide that. I'd speak to him myself, but I think you'll get further with him than I could.'

'I'll certainly do my best,' Bradley promised.

'I'm sure you will. And Mrs Harrison might be willing to talk to you too,' Cameron added with a wicked twinkle.

Bradley ignored the implication that he had a soft spot for Mrs Harrison, though it was not far from the truth.

'I'll go and see them right away,' he said.

'And I expect you to report back to me if you find out anything of interest.' Cameron was serious again.

'That goes without saying.'

Bradley didn't use his new motor to visit the Harrisons. It wasn't far to the rank of cottages where they lived – for now, at least. He put on his coat, walked up the hill and turned along the track to the back doors. He could smell baking – a delicious smell wafting out from one of the bake ovens on the opposite side to the houses – and it tickled his taste buds. If this was evidence of Mrs Harrison's skills, he thought her enterprise stood a good chance of success.

He knocked on the door of number 3. Pans clattered, and a moment later the door opened. Lorna's apron was dusted with flour, and as she wiped her hands on it, a little cloud flew off and settled on the doorstep. Her face was rosy, from the heat of the oven, Bradley guessed, and he was struck again by what a pretty woman she was.

'Mrs Harrison.' He smiled. 'I've news for you and your husband. Might I come in?'

To his surprise, instead of the relief he'd expected, her expression was one of apprehension bordering on panic, and she stepped outside, pulling the door closed behind her.

'I'd rather not talk in front of my husband, if you don't mind. He doesn't know I came to see you, or anything about my plans. I didn't want to get his hopes up.'

'I see.' Bradley thought quickly. 'I do need to speak to you both, but I don't have to say anything about your visit to Milverton if that would make things difficult for you.'

Lorna relaxed visibly. 'Oh, I'd be so grateful if you didn't mention it. I don't want him to know I've been going behind his back. It's silly, I know, but things aren't easy at the moment.'

'I can imagine,' Bradley said sympathetically. He nodded towards the door. 'So?'

'Oh yes, come in. But you mustn't look at the mess. I've been baking sausage rolls – I thought I could give them out as samples.'

Bradley wondered how she was managing to do all this without Harry realising something was going on, but he didn't ask, simply followed her into the kitchen. It was small but cosy, and much tidier than he'd expected, given her apology. Just a pastry board and rolling pin on the table, with an earthenware jar of flour, pats of butter and lard, and a slab of what looked like sausage meat on a piece of greaseproof paper beside it. Two rag dolls sat side by side in a rocking chair by the fireplace, and a small dog was asleep on a folded blanket, beside which was a tin dish of water and another containing what looked like biscuit.

The dog raised its head questioningly, then, seeing a stranger, was up in an instant, barking.

'Quiet, Nipper! Lie down!' Lorna gave the animal a little push, and it sat, still eyeing Bradley warily.

'He won't hurt you,' she assured him. 'He's just a puppy. But he doesn't always behave very well.' She raised a finger, pointing directly at the dog. 'Stay!'

'Who's there?' Harry's voice came from what Bradley guessed was the sitting room, and he didn't sound best pleased.

'You've got a visitor,' Lorna called back, nodding to Bradley to go through.

'Not that bliddy Fred Gardiner again, I 'ope . . .' Harry broke off as Bradley entered the room. 'Oh! What are you doing here?' His tone was less than welcoming.

'I'm sorry,' Lorna said softly to Bradley, then addressed her husband. 'Don't be like that, Harry.'

Bradley took charge of the situation. 'How are you, Mr Harrison?'

Harry huffed impatiently. 'Not at me best, as you can see. Not that you'd care. What d'ya want, anyway?'

'I've come with what I hope will be welcome news,' Bradley said evenly. 'Though I can well imagine that's not quite what you were expecting.'

'I don't expect nothing from the likes of you and the rest of the *management*.' Harry imbued the word with unmistakable scorn.

'Then I think you'll be pleasantly surprised. May I sit down?' Bradley was refusing to rise to the bait.

'You'll do as you damned well like if I know anything about it.'

'Harry!' Lorna exploded. 'For goodness' sake stop being so rude. I'm ashamed of you!'

Harry shrugged, unwilling to back down. 'Go on then, say what you gotta say and then you can get out.'

Bradley took a seat in one of the easy chairs and gave the Harrisons the news.

'Well, that's better than nothing, I s'pose,' Harry said grudgingly when Mr Robinson had finished. Though he'd had the wind taken out of his sails, he still couldn't bring himself to show due gratitude.

'It's a huge relief to know we won't be homeless.' Unlike Harry, Lorna was doing her best to hide her dismay at what had been proposed, but secretly she couldn't help but agree with him.

The location of the house they were being offered was far

from ideal. It was a good two miles out of Hillsbridge, a long way for the children to walk to school, and she wouldn't be happy for them to do it alone. The lane was narrow, bordered on both sides by thick hedges with only farmland beyond, and when they reached the main road they would have to cross it, as there was no pavement on their side on the first stretch, and then cross back again to reach the subway. She could make them sandwiches so they didn't need to come home for their dinner, but she'd still have to make two trips into town each day if she was to be sure they were safe. And how on earth would she be able to get her wares all the way to the market on a Saturday?

Worst of all was the prospect of living so close to Harry's mother. At least they wouldn't be in the same house, but they would be near enough for her to interfere, which she undoubtedly would. And Lorna wasn't very happy that they would be living next door to the Parfitts either. Old Mrs Parfitt had always reminded her of a witch – thin and bent, with a hooked nose and chin and long, straggly grey hair – and Gilroy, her hulking son, was none too bright and had the look of generations of inbreeding. When they'd been living there, Lorna had also suspected him of being something of a peeping Tom.

Besides all this, she would miss Flossie dreadfully. But she knew she must put all her reservations to one side. She couldn't say or do anything that might jeopardise the offer of a roof over their heads. And hopefully when Harry was fit to return to work they'd be able to find somewhere more suitable.

'Thank you so much,' she said. 'I don't know how we can ever repay you.'

'It's Mr Cameron you should thank. He's the one who came up with a solution and put it to Sir Montague. I'm just the messenger. But if you really want to show me some gratitude, I wouldn't say no to a cup of tea.'

'Oh, of course! I'm sorry – I should have offered you one. I don't know where my head is today.'

She went into the kitchen and set the kettle to boil on the hob. Nipper was restless, running between the sitting room door, which she had closed after her, and the door to the garden, whining and pawing at both.

'You want to go out, Nipper?' she asked, though she wasn't sure that was his priority. He wanted to check out the stranger, if she wasn't much mistaken. But just in case he did need to relieve himself, she took him outside. She didn't want a puddle on the kitchen floor, especially not where Mr Robinson might inadvertently step in it.

He really was a very nice man, she thought. More than nice, actually. She liked that he hadn't tried to take the credit for the offer of the house, as many would have done, though she thought it was more than likely his doing that Mr Cameron had put the suggestion to Sir Montague in the first place. He hadn't taken offence at Harry's rudeness either, for which she was grateful.

When Nipper had lifted his leg against several shrubs, he ran back to the door. Lorna opened it and followed him in. The kettle was singing but wasn't yet on the boil, so she set her best bone-china cups and saucers, a jug of milk and the sugar bowl on a tray, and poured some of the hot water into the pot to warm it. Then she went to the living room door and tried to hear what Harry and Mr Robinson were saying.

It wasn't easy – she could only catch snatches through the closed door – but it sounded as if they were going over the conditions of the lease and how what Mr Robinson described as 'a peppercorn rent' would be paid.

The kettle was boiling now; she heard it bubbling and spitting on the hot coals. She spooned tea into the pot and poured the boiling water onto it, protecting her hand from the handle with a patchwork pot holder. Then, shooing Nipper away, she took the tray into the sitting room.

'Ah, tea!' the safety officer said with an appreciative smile.

'I hope it's to your liking.' She cast a rueful glance at Harry. 'My husband says I don't make it like his mother does.'

'You don't let it brew long enough,' Harry said. 'You're always in too much of a hurry.'

Lorna ignored the criticism. She took the lid off the teapot and gave the contents a stir. 'Nearly ready.'

She moved the occasional table so it was within Mr Robinson's reach as well as Harry's, arranged the cups and saucers on it and poured the tea.

'I'll leave you to add what sugar you want.' She pushed the bowl in Mr Robinson's direction.

'Thanks, but I don't take sugar,' he said.

'Really?' Lorna was surprised. 'Harry likes his really sweet, don't you, Harry?'

'I used to,' Mr Robinson admitted. 'But when I was with my regiment in South Africa, we often couldn't get hold of it, and I got used to going without. I'm afraid I lost the taste for it entirely.'

So he'd been in the army! Lorna thought. Yes, she could just imagine him in uniform.

She smiled, nodding at her husband, who was stirring a third spoonful into his own cup. 'Do you hear that, Harry? If you had a bit less, you'd soon get used to it too.'

'For crying out loud! Give it a rest, can't you, woman?'

'Perhaps I would if I didn't have to keep letting your trousers out,' Lorna replied. She didn't often say anything that might upset Harry, but for some reason just now she felt emboldened, and she saw the corners of Mr Robinson's mouth quirk in amusement. But he must have been aware that Harry was on the point of retaliating, and intervened quickly to prevent the row that was brewing.

'I was just saying to your husband, I expect you'd like to have a look around the house before you actually move in, Mrs Harrison.'

Lorna was already familiar with the general layout, since she guessed the house would be identical to the one Harry's parents occupied, but that wasn't the same as standing in a room, imagining where their things would go. Then a thought suddenly occurred to her.

'The last people did take their belongings with them, didn't they? They haven't left a lot of old furniture and things?'

Mr Robinson looked nonplussed. 'I don't know,' he admitted. 'I'll have to find out. But if they did leave furniture you don't want, I'll see that it's taken away. And if the house has been left in a dirty state, we'll get someone in to clean it up.'

'Oh, there's no need for that,' Lorna said. 'I can do any cleaning that needs to be done. But we would appreciate it if you could get rid of furniture – we'll want to take our own with us. And if there's any old rubbish that won't go on a bonfire, you could have that taken away too.'

Harry snorted. 'I'd bet me last farthing there'll be plenty of that. The Higginses never threw anything away.'

'Of course, I was forgetting – you must have known them well.' Once again Mr Robinson was attempting to keep things on an even keel, without any great success.

'I wouldn't say well, but I knew 'em, course I did,' Harry said scathingly. 'Funny lot. The place is goin' to be a proper mess if you ask me.'

The Higgins family hadn't seemed that bad, Lorna thought. When they'd been living with Harry's parents, she'd often seen

Mr Higgins working in the long strip of garden, planting runner beans and potatoes and cabbages, and Mrs Higgins hanging out the washing once a week, regular as clockwork. But of course Harry had grown up next-door-but-one to the family, while she had only been there for a short time. Perhaps he knew things about them she didn't. But that he should malign them was inevitable in his present mood.

Mr Robinson took a sip of his tea. 'I've got myself a motor, so when it's convenient for you to take a look at the place, I can take you there myself.'

'Oh, we couldn't put you to that trouble,' Lorna said quickly.

'It's no trouble. It's a fair way from here, and in any case, I'll need to open up and let you in.'

'Well, if you're sure . . . Certainly Harry wouldn't be able to walk it,' Lorna said.

'I don't need to look at the place anyway,' Harry grumbled.

Ever more annoyed with his truculence, Lorna spoke up. 'It's very kind of you, Mr Robinson. Thank you.'

He put down his cup. 'I have a busy day tomorrow, but shall we say the day after? And what time would suit you best?'

'In the morning, perhaps about half past nine or ten o'clock? The children come home for their dinner and I need to be back by then,' Lorna said.

'Ten, then? That should give you plenty of time to have a good look round and measure up for curtains and so on.'

'Yes. That sounds perfect.' Lorna didn't mention that there would be no money for new curtains if their own didn't fit the windows.

Mr Robinson got up. 'Good. I'll see you then. And you too, I hope, Mr Harrison. But I must get going now.'

'Of course. You're busy I expect. But thank you again for everything. We really are very grateful, aren't we, Harry?'

Harry only grunted. Lorna showed their visitor out, restraining Nipper as they went through the kitchen and holding onto his collar when she opened the door. Then, still burning with embarrassment at the way her husband had behaved, she went back inside.

What a boor Harrison was, Bradley thought as he walked back to Milverton. He understood and sympathised with the man, knowing from personal experience what he was going through, but it was really no excuse for the despicable way he treated his wife. She must have the patience of a saint to put up with it, and she certainly deserved far better. But he supposed she had no choice. It was the lot of working-class women to work their fingers to the bone day after day for little reward. They bore and raised large broods of children, and all too often saw one or more of them go to an early grave. Sometimes, of course, there was love to lighten the load, but he'd seen little evidence of that in the Harrison home, and his heart went out to the brave, resourceful, loyal and undeniably pretty Mrs Harrison.

He was more convinced than ever that Harry Harrison was exactly the sort of man to have been mixed up in some act of rebellion against his employer, and possibly stupid enough not to appreciate what the consequences might be. And he was determined to do whatever it took to get to the bottom of the matter. He didn't like to think of the hurt and hardship his investigations might cause to an innocent woman and her children, but if Harrison was involved, he had to be brought to justice.

'Oh Flossie, you'll never guess what's happened. We've got to move to Littleton Lane!'

As soon as she could, Lorna had gone to tell her neighbour the news, and Flossie's face had fallen.

'They're really turning you out then. Oh Lorna, what can I say? I can't imagine you not being next door. An' Littleton Lane! That's right out in the wilds!'

'I know. I can't see there's any way I can take the market stall now. I couldn't carry bread and cakes all that way. So don't go paying Mr Baker the rent he asked for in advance, whatever you do. And I don't know how I'd be able to deliver orders either.'

Flossie chewed her lip. 'Oh, that is a shame. I can see the market might be out of the question, but our Arthur could collect the orders from you and deliver them. The exercise'd do 'im good.'

'Let's talk about it another time. I can't think straight right now. My head feels fit to burst.'

Flossie reached out and took her hand. 'Oh my dearie, I don't want you to go.'

Tears filled Lorna's eyes. 'I don't know what I'll do without you, Flossie.' She wiped her cheeks with the back of her hand. 'I'd better go now. Me and Harry have got a lot to talk about.'

Trying to find a positive in all this, Lorna left her friend and returned to what was, for now, still her home.

Chapter Eleven

The man who stormed up the three shallow steps and into the public bar of the Miners' Arms was short and thickset, with a low, jutting forehead and beetling eyebrows that were all but obscured by the peak of his cloth cap.

As the door banged shut behind him, the group of miners clustered around their usual table looked up from their pints through a fug of cigarette smoke. Tonight was something of a celebration – the first time George Golledge had joined them since he'd been hurt in the accident. His arm was still in a sling and his ribs were bandaged beneath his shirt, and although the bruise beneath his eye where a lump of rock had caught him had faded to a dirty yellow, that side of his face was still swollen, as if a toffee apple had been jammed into his cheek. But at least he was here, back with his pals. He'd bought the first round of drinks, and had been regaling them with tales of the horrors of being taken home in the back of a coal cart and the indignity of being at the mercy of his nagging wife while he recovered, which was causing some merriment.

'Doctor said I weren't to 'ave any hard liquor, and she made bliddy sure I didn't,' he'd grumbled. 'Put a stop to me nip o' whisky at bedtime, miserable cow. I'd 'ave walloped her one if I could, I can tell 'ee.'

'Bested by a woman! Dearie me, that don't sound like you, George,' Shorty Dallimore had said solemnly, and Moses Whittock guffawed.

'Reckon she 'ad you just where she wanted you, me son.'

A barrage of ribald comments had followed.

'It bain't funny! 'Tweren't for me, anyways,' George had growled, but his mates had continued their joshing and were still chuckling when the thickset man made his entrance.

'Who be that?' Ticker Greedy asked in a low voice, and the others shook their heads, equally mystified. It was highly unusual for a lone stranger to walk into their local.

'Well, he bain't a barrel of laughs by the look of 'un,' Shorty said, and that set them chuckling again.

The stranger stood for a moment glancing around. His gaze flicked over Mercy, who was behind the bar, and Amos Riddle, who sat alone in the inglenook, before settling on the group of miners and striding purposefully towards them.

'Which one of you be George Golledge?' His tone was aggressive, his expression dark and surly.

The men exchanged puzzled glances, and George's eyes narrowed.

'Who wants to know?'

'You, is it?' The stranger focused his gaze. 'I want a word wi' you.'

'Better look out, George. He's bigger than your missus,' Ticker quipped, but nobody was laughing now. Trouble was brewing, and they knew it.

'I don't talk to folk I don't know,' George said shortly and dismissively, and picked up his pint. But before it was even halfway to his mouth, the stranger was behind his chair, grabbing him by the collar as if to hoist him to his feet. Beer slopped from the mug down George's shirt front and into his lap, and a strangled gasp escaped him as pain shot through his injured shoulder.

For a long moment his pals were too taken by surprise to react.

'What the . . . ?' Shorty's muttered words seemed to act like a wake-up call.

The stranger had pulled George's collar so tight around his neck that his face was turning red and his eyes were bulging. Ticker and Moses leapt to their feet, each grasping one of the man's arms in an attempt to force him to let their friend go, while Shorty balled his fists, ready to intervene if necessary. But the man was strong, and fuelled by determination and anger. His hands were like hams, his thick fingers might have been glued to George's collar, and as Ticker and Moses tugged him backwards, the chair rocked and toppled over with a crash. George was pitched onto the floor, and all three men were momentarily thrown off balance. Moses, a useful amateur middleweight who was a stalwart of the local boxing club, was the first to recover. His fist shot out and he caught the stranger with an uppercut that in his younger days would have knocked a lesser opponent off his feet. The man staggered but recovered himself, and was about to throw a punch of his own when Shorty grabbed him from behind and he whirled round, tripping over the legs of the upturned chair and landing half on top of George, who lay moaning on the floor.

'Oi! Leave it out, the lot o' you!' The authoritative roar came from Walt Bray, who had been fetched from the back room by an alarmed Mercy. He strode across the bar threateningly and the three friends backed off like schoolboys caught brawling by the headmaster.

''E started it!' Shorty said indignantly, jerking his thumb in the direction of the stranger, who was picking himself up.

'He did!' Mercy, watching from a safe distance, confirmed it.

Walt turned on the man furiously. 'I don't know who the hell you are, but get out of my pub before I set the law on you. Go on!'

'All right, all right, I'm goin'. Fer now. But you . . .' he pointed a stubby finger at George, still sprawled on the floor, 'you ain't heard the last of this. An' the rest of you'm just as bad. My sister's boy is dead because o' you. An' you needn't think you'm gettin' away with it.'

'Out! Now! This is yer last warning!'

The stranger held up his hands in surrender, but his face was still distorted with rage.

'Bloody murderers, the lot o' them,' he called over his shoulder as he headed for the door.

'Well bugger me!' Moses muttered.

'Fer pity's sake give me a hand, Moses!' Shorty was struggling to help a white-faced George to his feet. He was groaning loudly and clutching his ribs with his free hand. Ticker righted the chair and they lowered George onto it.

'Did 'ee hurt th'self, George?'

'Course he did! Couldn't save 'imself, could 'e? Do you want a brandy, my son? Walt, get the man a brandy!'

'We could all do wi' one, I reckon.'

The three friends now looked, and sounded, chastened, sheepish almost.

'A brandy for George,' Walt called to Mercy, who was still watching proceedings round-eyed. 'Just make sure 'e pays for it.'

'Aw, come on, Walt. The man's hurt. An' we'm all in shock.' That was Shorty.

'I'll not reward goings-on like that in my pub,' Walt said

sternly and decisively. 'This is a respectable house. Just think yerselves lucky I'm not throwing you out as well.'

''Tweren't our fault! Like I said, he started it,' Shorty protested.

But Walt was unrepentant. 'P'raps wi' good reason.' He shook his head, tight-lipped. 'I hope ye're pleased with yerselves, the lot o' you. And make sure George gets home safe. There's no coal carts to call on at this time o' night.' With that, he turned and walked away.

'He'll come round,' Moses said. 'Course he will. We'm his regulars, after all.'

Ticker looked at Mercy. 'Make that a brandy all round, love. Put it on the slate and I'll pay when I get me wages on Saturday.'

Now that things had calmed down, Mercy Comer could scarcely contain her jubilation. The fracas had scared her – though she'd seen scraps in the bar before, this one had been particularly nasty – but she'd learned more in those few minutes than she could have hoped for. She had tried to listen to what the miners were saying so as to get confirmation of what she'd gathered from the stranger, but they were in a tight huddle and she was only able to catch a word here and there. She could tell from their demeanour, though, that they were worried, and not just about George, who did look as if the fall had exacerbated his injuries. They weren't joking and laughing now, and they hadn't even tried to flirt with her when she'd served them their brandies.

As she collected empties and wiped down the bar, Mercy's brain was working overtime.

My sister's boy is dead, the stranger had said. Presumably he'd been referring to the carting boy who had been killed in the disaster, which must mean he was Mrs Maggs's brother, and he'd come here looking for someone to blame for the tragedy.

Mercy was already sure that the little clique of regulars knew something about what had happened that day. To a man they were troublemakers. But she was puzzled as to why the stranger had singled out George Golledge. And how had he known where to find him? Tonight was the first time he'd been in since the accident.

From what Walt had said, she rather thought he wasn't completely in the dark over all this either, and she'd tried asking him what the trouble had been about but had got nowhere. 'Don't go poking your nose into things that don't concern you. It's over and done with,' he'd said, his tone indicating that the conversation was closed, and though Mercy was itching to learn more, she'd known better than to press him.

What she had was enough of an excuse to ask the safety officer to meet her again. But that in itself posed a problem. If anyone suspected she was running to him with tittle-tattle and Walt got to hear of it, she could lose her job as well as her chance to get close to him. But she couldn't let this chance slip away. Somehow she had to keep their meetings secret, for the time being anyway.

Throughout her shift, Mercy worried away at the dilemma, and by the time the pub closed at eleven, she had the germ of an idea as to how she could get him to meet her – and this time, hopefully, she could work her charm on him.

She was still mulling it over as she walked home along the road beside the railway track. The row of cottages where she lived with her parents and brothers was the lowest of three that straddled the hillside and from here could be reached by way of a cinder path that ran between the long gardens on one side and a copse on the other. Mercy had used this path countless times and never been nervous, even as late as this. Tonight, however, she felt a niggle of unease. She looked round but could see nothing in the fitful moonlight except the gently swaying shadows of the trees. Yet the feeling persisted. Was there someone there? Don't be so stupid! she scolded herself. It's just the excitement getting to you. But she quickened her pace anyway. The houses up ahead to her right were all in darkness, and she found herself wishing she'd taken the longer route home by way of the main road.

She was about halfway up, her breath coming fast now, partly from hurrying up the steep incline and partly from nervousness, when a shout from behind her made her heart leap into her mouth. A man's voice, harsh and loud in the quiet of the night. 'Hey, you! Wait!'

Mercy wheeled round, and by the light of the moon, which had emerged from behind a cloud, she saw him. Short, thickset. The man who had attacked George Golledge in the pub. Somehow she found her voice. 'Go away! Leave me alone!'

He ignored her, coming closer. Mercy took a step backwards, staring at the man like a rabbit caught in the beam of a poacher's torch.

'It's all right. I'm not goin' to hurt you.' His voice was gruff. 'I just want to know where that bugger Golledge lives.'

'I don't know,' she said desperately.

'Don't give me that.'

'I don't!' It was the truth. There were ranks of miners' cottages all around town; it could be any one of them.

'Course you do.' His voice had the same undertone of threat she'd heard earlier, and one of his big hands shot out and caught her by the arm.

Suddenly, despite the fear that was making her tremble, Mercy was furiously angry. 'Get off me!' she yelled, and startled, the man released her. 'I've told you, I don't know! They come to the pub for a drink and they go again. I can't know all of them.

And even if I did, I wouldn't tell you,' she added defiantly.

'He needs to be taught a lesson,' the man growled.

'Maybe so, but I can't help you. An' now I'm going home, and if you're still following me when I get there, my brothers'll give you a good hiding, an' they're a lot bigger and younger than you.'

She turned her back on the man and started off up the path, and to her relief he didn't follow. At the top, she turned and looked back. There was no sign of him. Her breath came out on a sob. She was shaking from head to foot now, but feeling oddly triumphant. She'd sent him packing. And now she really did have something to tell the safety officer, and she knew exactly how she was going to get hold of him.

Noel Comer, Mercy's younger brother, had been working on the screens at Milverton since leaving school the previous summer. When he arrived to begin his shift the next morning, he was brimming with self-importance. A note addressed to the safety officer was burning a hole in his pocket alongside a bright new sixpenny piece Mercy had given him.

'See that he gets this,' she'd instructed him. 'Don't give it to anyone else, and if you're asked, don't mention my name. If he gives you a note to bring home to me, you keep quiet about that too. Do you understand?'

'Yes, but . . .' Noel was puzzled.

'Do as I say, and if you bring me back a reply, there'll be another silver sixpence for you. But if you tell anybody, there won't be. An' I shall tell Ma you stole this one out o' my purse.'

Mystified, but proud that he'd been entrusted with Mercy's secret and gleeful at the prospect of more riches coming his way, Noel made a detour to the office on his way to the screens. He knocked on the door, fishing the note out of his pocket but keeping it half hidden under his coat as he waited for a reply. None came.

He chewed his lip, uncertain as to what to do. He could push the note under the door, he supposed, but Mercy had explicitly said he should give it to the safety officer in person. A motor drew up in front of the office, and he felt the beginnings of panic. He knew that car. It belonged to Mr Cameron, the general manager, no less. He tried to push the envelope containing the note back into his pocket, but it stuck half in and half out, and Mr Cameron was climbing out of his motor and had seen him.

'Can I help you, laddie?' he called.

Noel flushed scarlet. 'I was looking for the safety man,' he blurted.

'You mean Mr Robinson? He won't be here today. Can I help ye?'

Another dilemma! This was proving more difficult than Noel had expected. He was supposed to give the note to the safety officer and no one else, but he certainly wouldn't earn another silver sixpence if he took it home again. And he could trust the general manager, surely?

The matter was taken out of his hands when Cameron caught sight of the envelope sticking out of his pocket.

'Is that for Mr Robinson?' He held out his hand. 'Let me have it, and I'll put it on the desk where he'll see it when he comes back.'

Still Noel hesitated, unsure. 'He will get it, won't he?' he asked anxiously.

'I said so, aye.' Cameron twitched his fingers. 'Come on, laddie. I won't bite. An' shouldn't you be at your work?'

Reluctantly Noel handed over the envelope and sloped off to the screens.

* * *

133

The children had only just left for school with Arthur, and Lorna was clearing away the breakfast things, when there was a knock at the back door. Nipper ran to it, barking, and Harry, who was still sitting at the table over yet another cup of tea snapped: 'Can't you keep that bliddy dog quiet?'

Lorna ignored him and went to open the door, grabbing Nipper's collar. To her surprise, it was Lil Golledge on the doorstep. In all the years they had lived here, Lorna didn't think Lil had ever called at their house, and she was at a loss for words. Her first thought was that George had been taken worse – died suddenly, even – although he'd seemed much better when he'd called to see Harry.

Lil, who was wearing her coat loose over her apron and house dress, pulled it closed around her thin chest. Although the weather was slowly improving, it was still cold first thing in the morning, and a nasty wind was blowing along the rank.

'George wants to see Harry,' she said without preamble.

'Oh!' Lorna said. 'He's just finishing his breakfast.'

'What's up?' Harry must have heard; he appeared in the scullery at Lorna's shoulder.

'George wants to talk to you.'

'He d'a usually come down here.' It was clear that Harry didn't like being virtually ordered to go and see his friend.

'Well not today. He's not fit.' Lil stood her ground.

'Oh? What's wrong wi' 'un?'

'He went out for a drink last night and got into a fight. That's what 'e wants to talk to you about.'

'I'd better come up to you then,' Harry agreed reluctantly. 'In about half an hour, say?'

'Mind you do.' Lil Golledge, as satisfied as such a miserable woman could ever be, departed.

Harry finished his tea and tied a muffler round his neck.

'You're only going up the rank, not to the North Pole,' Lorna said.

He didn't reply, and when he'd left, limping off on his crutches, she heaved a sigh of relief. It had come to something, she thought, that she was actually glad to see the back of him. She hoped he and George would take their time over whatever it was they were going to talk about. And that when he came home, by some miracle he would be in a better mood.

It was a vain hope. If anything, when he returned Harry seemed to be in a worse temper than ever. His expression was thunderous, and when she asked him what George had wanted, he told her sharply to mind her own business. Really, Lorna didn't know how much more she could take. And the prospect of moving to Littleton Lane just made things worse. The nightmare was continuing, seemingly never-ending, and she felt as if she was caught in a trap from which there was no escape.

Cameron was still in the office at Milverton when Bradley returned late that afternoon.

'I saw the Harrisons yesterday about the house in Littleton Lane,' Bradley said when the two men had exchanged greetings. 'I'm going to take them there tomorrow morning to have a look at it.'

'Good. Sir Montague is anxious for them to vacate Northfield Terrace as soon as possible. They were pleased, were they?' Cameron asked.

'I think so. But Harrison is a miserable sod. It's hard to tell what he's thinking.'

'Could be he's worried about how they're going to find the rent,' Cameron suggested. 'It'll be some time before his wife's baking business makes any real money – if it ever does.'

'I must say I'm concerned about that too,' Bradley admitted, but Cameron was no longer listening. His eye had fallen on an envelope propped up against the filing tray on the desk.

'Och – there's a note there waiting for you.'

Bradley picked up the envelope. It was indeed addressed to *The Safety Officer*, but he didn't recognise the writing, and couldn't think who it could be from.

'Did someone deliver it?' he asked, curious.

'That laddie Comer who works on the screens.'

The name meant nothing to Bradley. He reached for the bone-handled paper knife and slit the envelope open. Cameron didn't so much as glance up from the paperwork he was sifting through, and when he saw the signature at the bottom of the page, Bradley was glad of that.

Mercy. The barmaid at the Miners' Arms. Her surname was Comer, he seemed to recall.

It wasn't a long note; it simply said that she had something new to tell him that she thought would interest him. Could he meet her in the same place as last time after her lunchtime shift tomorrow? He could send her a reply by way of her brother, Noel, who worked on the screens, and she would be there by about a quarter past two.

Bradley thought quickly. He was taking the Harrisons to view the cottage in the morning, but after that he was free. For some reason he was slightly wary of meeting Mercy; he had an uncomfortable feeling that she had some kind of agenda she was keeping to herself – why else would she be so anxious to essentially spy on her regular customers? But if she really had found out something of interest to him in his investigation, he couldn't afford to miss the chance of discovering what it was.

He checked the clock on the office wall. With any luck he could just about catch the brother before he left work. He found a sheet of paper, wrote a short reply saying he would be there, and used the same envelope that Mercy's note had arrived in, scribbling out his own name and replacing it with hers.

'I have to pop out for a minute,' he said to Cameron, who was so engrossed in his paperwork he merely nodded. Then he set out in search of Mercy Comer's brother.

Chapter Twelve

Bradley knocked on the door of Number 3, Northfield Terrace just as the town clock was chiming the hour. Punctuality was one of his watchwords. After a few moments it was opened by Lorna. She was wearing an outfit that was much smarter than her usual workaday attire: a pink blouse that seemed to mirror the rosy glow in her cheeks, a bright sash cinching the waistband of her skirt and a cute little boater hat of the sort that had been fashionable some years ago, but which suited her perfectly.

'All ready then?' he greeted her.

'Yes. But Harry isn't coming. He's not feeling too well this morning.'

That's his excuse, Bradley thought, but he couldn't say he was sorry. This trip would be a good deal more pleasant without him and his ill temper.

'That's a shame,' he said nevertheless.

'I'll just get my coat.' Lorna popped back into the house and he could hear her telling the dog, Nipper, to lie down, and instructing Harry not to let him out.

'I've left the motor down on the road,' he said when she re-emerged. 'I've only had it a few days, and as you pointed out before, the rough track wouldn't do it much good.'

'Your own motor!' she said. 'I'm impressed.'

'Don't expect luxury,' he warned her. 'It's not as good a specimen as Mr Cameron's.'

'I'm impressed anyway,' she said, smiling. And it seemed to Bradley that her smile lit up the dull grey morning.

At the bottom of the track, they crossed the road and Bradley handed her up into the passenger seat of the motor. As he cranked the starting handle and the vehicle began to shake and rattle, Lorna felt a stab of nervousness, but as he pulled away, she realised it wasn't just riding in this strange contraption that was making her stomach churn. It was the thought of going to Littleton Lane, where she had been so unhappy when they'd lived with Harry's parents.

When Bradley turned off the main road and started up the winding lane that led to Littleton Cottages, the feeling of being trapped closed in around her like a shroud, and only intensified as the Ford chugged along between hedges and open farmland for a mile or so. She really didn't want to be doing this. Didn't want to live in the little terrace of three houses. Didn't want to see her mother-in-law. She'd rarely visited since they'd moved out; Harry almost always went alone, or took the children with him. But she had no more choice now than she'd had back then. Less, since she had Marjorie and Vera to think of too. Somehow she had to put the past behind her and be grateful that they were not going to be homeless.

'Here we are then,' Bradley said, slowing and turning into the track that ran along between the fronts of the houses and a row of outhouses. 'This is the one – at this end – but I expect you know that.'

At first glance, Lorna could tell that the cottage had been empty for some time. The net curtains at the windows were a dirty grey and the paintwork on the little lean-to that provided shelter for the front door was peeling. But what had she been expecting? Sir Montague would never have agreed to them moving in if he'd had any use for it. Perhaps he intended to sell it when Oldlands Colliery closed and was hoping she and Harry would smarten it up a bit so it would be more appealing to prospective buyers.

Bradley turned off the engine, told her to wait for him to help her down, and clambered out himself. As she rose from her seat, she realised her legs were trembling and was glad of his hand holding hers firmly. The ground was rutted and uneven, and he helped her over it before releasing her hand to find the key to the front door on the twist of wire that was a makeshift key ring. Lorna cast an anxious glance along the front of the other two houses; nobody had emerged to see what a motor was doing parked there, but she did see the curtains of the next-door house twitch, and caught a brief glimpse of someone there looking out. Mrs Parfitt – the old witch – no doubt.

It took Bradley some minutes to get the key to turn in the lock – it seemed to be rusted with disuse. But at last he managed it, and the door creaked halfway open, scraping over the stone floor before jamming.

'It'll need sanding off, but Harry will be able to do that, won't he?' he said. 'Can you squeeze through?'

'I expect so,' Lorna said. But she was less sure that Harry would bother to take the door off its hinges to work on it before hanging it again. She had visions of having to squeeze through the restricted space many times before that happened – if it ever did.

A cobweb brushed her face as she stepped inside. She flicked it away with a shudder. The lean-to was festooned with them, hanging from the ceiling, clumped in the corners, draped down the walls and the windows. The door that led into the little living room was equally stiff, and the stench that wafted out when it eventually opened was so overpowering that Lorna took a step backwards, colliding with Bradley.

'What is that?' she gasped, covering her nose and mouth with her hand.

Bradley had caught her arm to steady her; still holding it, he reached past her to pull the door closed.

'Dead birds, I imagine,' he said grimly. 'They come down the chimney and are trapped.'

'Ugh! I can't go in. It's disgusting!' She wasn't usually squeamish, but this was just a step too far.

'I'm sorry. I should have checked the place before bringing you,' Bradley apologised. 'Let's get some fresh air.'

When they were outside again, he brushed a cobweb off the sleeve of his coat and added ruefully: 'I don't suppose you're quite as anxious to do the cleaning-up yourself now?'

'Not really, no,' Lorna admitted, searching in her bag for the little bottle of eau de cologne she kept there. 'I didn't realise it was going to be this bad.'

'Nor did I. Don't worry, I'll arrange something. I'm sure Amos Riddle would like the chance to earn a bit of a bonus.'

Lorna didn't know who Amos Riddle was, but she sent up a silent prayer of thanks anyway. She tipped some eau de cologne onto her handkerchief and sniffed deeply. Better, but not much. She thought she would still be smelling the odour of decay at bedtime.

'Would you like some?' she asked Bradley.

Bradley tried to smile at her. 'Thanks, but no.' He didn't want to admit that the stench had made him feel nauseous too; nor, as very much a man's man, did he like the idea of smelling of cologne himself. 'You stay here. I'll check if there's anything that needs getting rid of. Furniture or rubbish, I mean, not poor dead birds.'

'How can you go back in there?' Lorna asked, looking awestruck.

'I won't be staying long, you can depend on that. I just want to get an idea of how big a cart we'll need to clear the place.'

'It's an awful lot of trouble for you.' Lorna took another sniff of her handkerchief.

'Least I can do. You and your husband have been treated very badly.' He remembered suddenly that he had intended to use this opportunity to learn anything he could about the roof fall. 'None of what happened was your fault after all, was it?' he said, trying to steer the conversation in that direction.

'No.' If she did know anything, there was nothing in her demeanour to give it away, he thought. 'Are you really going to get whatever's been left there taken away?'

'Of course. And I'll arrange for the transportation of your furniture and belongings when you move in.'

'That is so kind!' Lorna said gratefully, and he felt a twinge of guilt at his duplicity. He had turned to go back to the house when she spoke again, a little diffidently. 'Could I have a look at the bake oven while you're gone?'

'Oh – yes.' It hadn't occurred to him that she'd want to see the outhouses, but if she was to set up in business, the bake oven would be a necessity. She'd never be able to batch-bake in the tiny oven beside the living room fire.

He searched the bunch of keys for one that looked as if it might fit the array of doors on the far side of the track, not even sure which one would house the bake oven, though that scarcely mattered. He really should check the other amenities while he was here.

The first one he opened was a cramped privy, which in its

own way smelled almost as bad as the house. It was served by way of a septic tank, he guessed, and made a mental note to make sure that it was emptied regularly. The second was a coal house cum tool shed, with a corner blocked off by planks of wood built high enough to contain the coal – there was still some there; enough, he thought, to last a few weeks at least. A saw, a lump hammer and various gardening implements hung from hooks on the wall. And there was the bake oven. It hadn't been cleaned – the fire tray was still full of cinders and ash – but at least it looked reasonably serviceable. A few stray leaves had been blown in under the door in the winter gales, but that was no problem. It was the size of the oven that took him somewhat aback.

'Is this going to be big enough for all your baking?' he asked dubiously.

Lorna shrugged. 'It'll have to be, won't it? In any case, I'm only going to be filling orders. The market stall will be out of the question if I'm going to be so far away. And if necessary, once I've got the fire going I can do several batches one after the other.'

Her answer reminded him of his misgivings – and Cameron's – regarding her ability to make enough money to pay the rent while Harry was unable to work, but for the moment he didn't mention it.

'I'll leave you to look around then.' He pulled his handkerchief from his pocket and added with a mischievous grin: 'I don't suppose you could spare me some of that scent after all?'

She rummaged in her bag again.

'Don't worry, I was only joking,' he added hastily, and headed back to the cottage.

Left alone, Lorna inspected the bake oven more closely. The interior and the cast-iron racks were going to need a good scrubbing before they were fit for use, and she didn't suppose the man Bradley brought in to clean the house would do that. It would be just another job that she would have to do when they moved in.

Her heart sank again at the thought of it, a heavy lump in her chest like undigested dumpling and the lingering stench of the decaying birds making her feel sick. Stop it! she scolded herself. Just think yourself lucky you'll have a roof over your heads.

She was staring unseeingly at the bake oven, desperately trying to dispel the negative thoughts, when a voice from behind her made her almost jump out of her skin.

'Wot d'you think you'm doin'?'

She wheeled round.

It was the witch woman, Mrs Parfitt, and to make matters worse, crossing the track towards her, glowering fiercely, was Harry's mother. Lorna realised she'd been right in thinking Mrs Parfitt had been peeking out of the window when they'd arrived, and she must have hurried next door and told Rose what she'd seen. She hadn't realised they were that friendly, but there was no other explanation.

What had she ever done to either of the women to warrant such antagonism? she wondered wretchedly. But she mustn't rise to the bait. She was going to have to live alongside them soon.

'Mrs Parfitt,' she said evenly, and nodded in Rose Harrison's direction. 'Mother.' It stuck in her craw to call the nasty woman that, but it was what was expected of her.

'I asked you a question,' the witch woman snapped. 'Wot d'you think you'm doin'?'

Lorna swallowed her pride. They'd find out sooner or later, and it was best they heard it from her. 'We're moving into this house. Harry's still not fit to work, and we have to leave Northfield Terrace.'

'What?' Rose Harrison was bristling with indignation. 'What be you on about? Our Harry's so bad he can't work, an' you couldn't be bothered to let us know?'

'You knew he was hurt in the accident underground,' Lorna said, trying to remain calm. 'I sent you a message. My neighbour's little boy delivered it.'

Rose huffed. 'Oh, him. 'E should'a washed 'is hands. That note was covered in dirty finger marks.'

Was she trying to pretend she hadn't been able to read it? 'You could see what it said, though?' Lorna asked. 'Surely Arthur didn't make it that dirty?'

'Oh, I read it all right,' Rose conceded. 'Not that it told me much.'

'I had too much on my plate to write a long letter,' Lorna said, still trying to be conciliatory, but Rose had the bit between her teeth.

'You should'a made it clear he was hurt bad. We don't get to 'ear much of wot's goin' on in town all the way out 'ere. I've bin wondering why he hasn't bin to see us, an' worrying meself sick. I'm his mother when all's said an' done. But I don't suppose that matters to you.'

Finally Lorna had had enough. 'If you were so worried, you could have come to see him,' she said flatly.

'Don't you speak to your mother like that, Miss Toffee-Nose!' Mrs Parfitt's bony chin was thrust forward, her beady eyes glittering with indignation. 'If you'm comin' to live 'ere, you'd do well to learn a bit of respect!'

It was the last straw. Setting her jaw, Lorna shook her head and made to walk away from the horrible pair, but they stood their ground, blocking her path.

'Excuse me!' she said with all the hauteur she could muster.

For what seemed like an eternity, neither woman moved,

145

then reluctantly Mrs Parfitt stepped to one side, muttering 'Stuck-up cow,' and at the same moment, to Lorna's immense relief, she saw Mr Robinson emerging from the house.

She hurried across the track and touched his arm with a trembling hand. 'Can we go, please?'

'You've seen enough?'

She gave a short, humourless laugh. 'More than enough.'

'I'll lock up then. Do you want to wait in the motor?'

Grateful though she was, Lorna was horribly embarrassed that he might have witnessed at least part of the altercation. Perhaps he thought she'd started it, but she wasn't going to explain. She was inexplicably ashamed that she should be the object of such hatred, and she didn't want to admit to him that the very thought of living here filled her with dread. Most of all, she didn't want him to see that she was on the verge of tears of despair and anger that they should treat her this way.

She kept her face turned away as he handed her into the motor, and fought hard to compose herself while he locked the outhouses. Harry's mother and Mrs Parfitt stood watching as he did so, silent now, arms folded across their chests like two gargoyles. Mr Robinson nodded at them, but they barely responded, and their malevolent stares followed him back to the motor.

'I take it one of those women was your mother-in-law,' he said once he had manoeuvred back onto the lane.

'Yes,' she managed, not trusting herself to say more.

'What's wrong?' His tone was kind, concerned.

'Nothing.'

Even as she said it, the irony of it struck her. Everything was wrong. Everything. At that moment she couldn't see any way out of the nightmare her life had become. The threatening tears gathered in her throat and pricked her eyes.

There was a gateway up ahead, the grass verge flattened and a gap in the hedge to allow access for farm vehicles. Bradley slowed the motor, drew into the opening and pulled on the brake, then turned to her.

'I'm not surprised you're upset. The state of the place is a disgrace. But I'm going to have it all fixed before you move in. You won't recognise it as the same house by the time I've finished with it.'

'Thank you,' she managed. But she couldn't look at him.

'There something else, isn't there?' he asked.

The tears she was trying so hard not to shed were a hard knot in her throat, and before she could stop herself, she was saying aloud in a choked whisper the mantra that was repeating itself inside her head. 'I can't live there.'

'Oh Lorna. I don't know what else I can do,' he said wretchedly.

She barely noticed that he had used her Christian name for the first time, couldn't know how her distress was affecting him. But as his arm went around her shoulders, the last of her defences crumbled and the tears that had threatened for so long coursed down her cheeks. Her shoulders were shaking as the horrors of the last hour, coming on top of the stresses of the past weeks, overcame her, and she buried her face in his shirt front, sobbing uncontrollably.

'Lorna . . . Lorna . . . don't . . .' His voice seemed to come from a long way off, but his kindness only made her cry harder, long streams of sobs punctuated by agonised inhalations of breath. It was several minutes before they began to quieten to hiccups and sniffs with just the occasional gasp.

'Better?' he asked gently, and Lorna was suddenly, painfully aware of what had just happened. She pulled away abruptly, hot now with shame.

'I'm sorry.'

'Don't be,' he said. 'You've had a terrible time of it lately. A lot of people would have fallen apart long ago.'

'But . . . your shirt! It's all wet.'

He laughed shortly. 'Don't worry about my shirt. It's you I'm concerned about. I realise that house is far from ideal, and I'm guessing those women upset you too.'

'They did.' Her hat had gone askew. She pulled it off, setting it on her knee, found her handkerchief, wiped her eyes and blew her nose. 'Harry's mother has never liked me, and Mrs Parfitt . . . she reminds me of an old witch. I shouldn't take any notice of them, but I'm just so worried about everything. About Harry. It's a nightmare really.'

'I'm sure it is,' Bradley said. 'Look, I need to be getting back now, but let's talk again. I can't promise I can find you another house – that's up to Mr Cameron, and in the last resort Sir Montague himself. But if there's anything I can do to help, I will.'

Lorna swallowed hard. 'You're so kind. I don't know how to thank you. And I really am very sorry, disgracing myself like that.'

'You didn't disgrace yourself. Forget it. I have.'

As they drove, Lorna watched the fields and hedges give way to houses, nice houses with tiled arches over the doors and windows that sparkled as they caught the sun, which had just come out from behind the bank of cloud. She thought how lucky the people who lived in them were. But who knew? They might feel just as trapped as she did and not have a shoulder to cry on as she just had.

She glanced at the safety officer. In profile, his features above the upturned collar of his coat were rugged and strong, and something sharp and sweet twisted deep inside her. A sensation she had not felt in so long that she had quite forgotten how emotive it could be. How sensuous. Yet at the same time something about him made her feel safe. As if he could save her from the storms that were tearing her world apart.

She found herself wishing that she could remain here in this safe harbour with Bradley Robinson for ever.

Bradley was working his way through a pile of paperwork with one eye on the office clock. He didn't want to be late for his meeting with Mercy Comer, though he wasn't hopeful that what she had to tell him would offer concrete proof that the roof fall had been no accident, or take him any closer to identifying the perpetrators. In fact, he was no longer sure he wanted that.

And all because of Lorna.

Bradley still believed that if there had been a plot, Harry had been one of the conspirators. They hadn't reckoned on such disastrous consequences, of course. Something had gone badly wrong. But a man and a boy had died, and along with his desire to be sure he was not in any way to blame for what had happened, Bradley had felt very strongly that whoever was responsible should face the full force of the law. Now, however, his resolve was beginning to waver. If Harry was at least partly responsible, he had already paid a terrible price. But worse, so had his wife.

He pushed the pile of paperwork to the back of the desk; concentration was impossible. He could think of nothing but Lorna. Her courage in the face of overwhelming odds. Her loyalty to her boor of a husband, who treated her abominably and certainly didn't deserve her. Her determination to keep the family together and salvage something, anything, from the wreckage of their lives. But today had pushed her to the limits of her endurance.

He rested his elbows on the desk, massaging his temples and seeing again her tear-wet face, feeling her whole body shaking with sobs as he tried to comfort her, smelling the sweet fragrance of her eau de cologne and the scent of her freshly washed hair. And experiencing again his own feeling of helplessness. She didn't deserve any of this, and he couldn't see that it was going to end well. He could have the cottage put to rights as he'd promised her, but he couldn't do anything about the unpleasant neighbours or her despicable husband. And he was still concerned, too, that her proposed business venture would never provide sufficient income to meet their needs.

A thought occurred to him suddenly. A way he could perhaps make things easier for her. It was far too early to suggest it to her, but it was something he would bear in mind.

The wooden case clock began to chime the hour, snapping him out of his reverie. He should be making his way down to the mill. But whatever Mercy Comer had to report, he would tell her he was dropping the investigation and she was not to summon him to any more secret meetings. If he didn't put a stop to it, he had a horrible feeling that he was going to find himself entangled in a web from which he couldn't escape. And right now, the only thing on his mind was how he could help Lorna out of the hell she had found herself in.

Chapter Thirteen

There was no sign of Mercy when Bradley reached the mill. Perhaps she'd been late leaving work. There were two routes she could take to get here from the Miners' Arms – the main road or by following the railway line – so he stood beside the entrance to the copse to wait.

It wasn't long before she appeared, coming from the direction of the bridge where they had talked the last time, and he began walking to meet her. She looked nervous, he thought, and wondered if she would want to go back to the bridge again. But today there was no wagon outside the mill, and none of the mill hands anywhere to be seen, and when they met, she hustled him towards the copse, pulling him between the trees. Dead twigs cracking underfoot, the occasional flutter of wings above them and the rush of water into the mill pond were the only sounds.

'Is all this secrecy really necessary?' he asked.

She wheeled round. 'Don't you realise the risk I'm taking to help you?'

He was bemused. He'd thought the only risk involved was that if it was known amongst the militant miners that she was his eyes and ears, they'd make very sure they didn't say anything that might incriminate them in front of her.

'What are you talking about?'

'I was followed home the other night. I thought he was goin' to attack me.'

Bradley was even more confused. 'One of the miners?'

'No. The man who beat up Mr Golledge.'

'Someone beat up George Golledge?' Bradley knew nothing of this.

'Yes. A real nasty piece o' work. Not local. He said the carting boy who got killed was 'is sister's son.'

This was getting more complicated by the minute.

'I think you'd better start at the beginning. You're not making any sense,' Bradley said. Despite having more or less decided to put a stop to his investigation into the cause of the roof fall, his curiosity was aroused.

'Well, it started in the pub,' Mercy said, and went on to relate the events of the evening.

The altercation in the bar was startling enough, and seemed to confirm Bradley's suspicions of foul play, but that the strange man should have threatened Mercy too took things to a whole new level.

'Are you saying this man actually accused George Golledge of being responsible for causing his nephew's death?' he asked when she had finished.

'Yes. He'd 'ave given 'im a real goin' over if the others hadn't stopped him. 'Twas bad enough as it was. And when Mr Bray threw 'im out, he waited for me to try an' get some idea where he could find Mr Golledge so he could 'ave another go.'

'But you didn't tell him?'

'I don't rightly know where Mr Golledge do live,' Mercy said. 'He didn't believe me, though, an' he turned proper nasty. Frightened me half to death, an' that's the truth.'

'I'm sure he did,' Bradley said.

Mercy laid a hand on his arm, looking up at him, her blue eyes wide. 'You won't let him hurt me, will you?'

Realisation that she was making a pass at him jolted Bradley away from trying to make sense of her revelations. He'd thought she might have an ulterior motive for offering to spy on the miners, but if this was it, it was far from subtly done.

'I'm sorry you had such a horrible experience, and I'll certainly try to find out who this man is and warn him of the consequences if he tries something like that again,' he said. 'Beyond that, I don't know what I can do.'

'Couldn't you at least see me home safely when I finish in the evenings?' Her eyes were still fixed pleadingly on his, and the warning signals were clear.

'I don't think that's a good idea,' he said firmly.

'But . . . you have a motor, don't you? No one need see us together.'

His motor. Word must have spread around Milverton and her brother had got to hear of it. What had seemed a blessing now appeared to be more of a curse.

'I'm sorry. I can't possibly commit to that. Couldn't one of your brothers meet you when you finish your evening shift, at least until I've found the man who threatened you and warned him off?'

'My little brother wouldn't be much good. He's only thirteen. And the older ones play skittles for the Railway Inn. They've got an away match tonight. They won't be home in time.'

Bradley hardened his heart. Though he wouldn't have hesitated if it had been Lorna who had called on him for help, all his instincts were warning him not to risk any more involvement with Mercy. This had already gone further than he'd ever intended it should. It was time to put an end to it once and for all.

'I'm sorry,' he said. 'If you're really worried, perhaps the landlord would walk you home. Or if one of your regulars goes your way, maybe he'd wait while you clear up?'

Mercy knew when she was beaten. It didn't happen often, but it was happening now. Reluctantly she removed her hand from Bradley's arm.

'Just as long as you do catch up with that horrible man and make sure he leaves me alone in future,' she said.

'I've already said I'll do that. But now I must get back to work.'

He turned away and set off in the direction of the road. He sincerely hoped that was the last he'd hear of Mercy Comer. But she'd certainly given him something to think about.

'That house is in such a state, you'd never believe it,' Lorna said.

It was mid afternoon, and she had gone next door to fill Flossie in on the latest developments. Harry had been no help at all. When she'd told him about the visit to Littleton Lane, he'd only snorted in typical Harry fashion.

'What did I tell you? They'm tryin' to fob us off with a place that bain't fit to live in. A waste o' time you goin' out there.'

'I suppose you knew what it was like. You'll have seen it going downhill when you've been out to see your mother,' Lorna said. 'And speaking of her, she had a real go at me. Made it quite clear I'm not welcome there.'

Harry had merely shrugged. 'She'll have to put up wi' it, same as us.'

Now, once again, Lorna found herself turning to Flossie. When she no longer had her friend to talk things over with, she didn't know what she would do.

'Mr Robinson has promised to get it all cleared up, but it's going to take an awful lot of doing,' she said forlornly.

'Well, that's good, isn't it?' Flossie said encouragingly. 'He seems a nice sort of chap. It'll work out, you'll see.'

Lorna's cheeks burned at the reminder of how she had broken down and cried into his shirt front.

'He is. But I let myself down in front of him good and proper. I was that upset with it all I just couldn't help myself. I don't know what he must think of me.'

'He understood, I'm sure. 'Tis hardly surprising it's all got on top of you,' Flossie said. 'But things'll work out, just you wait. I've finished writing out the cards to let folk know you'll bake whatever they'd like to order, and I'm goin' to get Arthur to push them through the neighbours' doors when he gets 'ome from school.'

'That is so kind!' Lorna was overwhelmed.

'Fiddlesticks,' Flossie said. 'What are friends for? But to change the subject, I ran into Lil Golledge this morning. It seems George is in a bad way again. Albie did say he'd heard at work there'd been a bit of a scrap in the Miners' Arms and George was involved, but from what Lil said, it was worse than that.'

'I knew he'd been in a fight. Lil came down this morning to ask Harry to go up and see him. I don't know any details, though, Harry wouldn't tell me.'

'Well, it seems George has done his shoulder in again an' he's in awful pain with 'is ribs. Lil's worried they'm goin' to find themselves in the same pickle as you if he can't get back to work soon.'

'He's a nasty piece of work, and so is she, but I wouldn't wish that on anybody,' Lorna said.

Flossie gave her a straight look. 'Could be he's asked for it. I haven't said anything before, but p'raps I should. My Albie said—'

She broke off abruptly as the back door flew open and Arthur came bursting in with all the energy of a nine-year-old, making straight for the biscuit barrel on the kitchen shelf.

'Oh, is it that time already?' Lorna exclaimed. 'I'd better go. If Arthur's home, the girls will be too.' She managed a smile at the lad. 'Thanks for seeing them home safe.'

Arthur was too busy helping himself to a garibaldi to reply, but Flossie said: 'It's no trouble. He enjoys it. Makes 'im feel important.' She lowered her voice. 'Look, you know where I am, any time . . .'

'Thanks, Flossie.' Lorna was heading for the door, wondering what her friend had been about to say, then forgetting all about it as she summoned her reserves to return to her duties as a wife and mother.

Bradley was mulling over what Mercy Comer had told him, and wondering what exactly he should do about it. Though he'd more or less decided to abandon his investigation, this new information put a different slant on things, and he would be failing in his duty if he didn't pursue it.

The first thing he needed to do was ascertain what evidence, or lack of it, the man who had attacked George Golledge had for believing he was involved. But since no one appeared to know him, Bradley's first problem was finding him. The obvious person to speak to was his sister, the mother of the dead carting boy, but Bradley was reluctant to approach her unless there was no other option. She was grieving, probably still in shock, and he didn't want to cause her unnecessary distress. Nor did he want to publicise what he was doing by asking the miners who had worked with the boy. In any case, they might well remain as tight-lipped on the subject as they had been when he had questioned them about the roof fall.

But for this unknown man to have laid into Golledge in the way Mercy Comer had described, he must have been pretty sure he shared at least some of the responsibility for what had happened. Bradley hadn't questioned Golledge in any depth at the time of the accident – interrogating the men who had been badly injured had seemed insensitive, to say the least – but if he was sufficiently recovered to go to his local for a drink with his pals, a visit from the safety officer seemed perfectly reasonable. Even if he had suffered a setback as a result of being assaulted in the pub.

He'd go and see Golledge again, he decided. But first he'd make arrangements for the house in Littleton Lane to be cleared and cleaned. He was as sure as he could be that Cameron would agree to Amos spending a day or two getting the house in a fit state for occupation, and there was no need to seek his authorisation first. And while he was speaking to Amos about that, he would also ask him some more questions about the explosion he claimed to have heard just before the roof came down.

He found the man lurking just around the corner of the winding shed, smoking a cigarette that looked as if he had rolled it himself – it was so loosely packed it hung limp between his thick fingers.

'Amos,' he said.

Amos nearly jumped out of his skin, taking one last quick drag on his cigarette before hastily dropping it, and stubbing it out with the toe of his boot.

'I ain't bin 'ere long!' he stuttered, his tone rising in a combination of guilt and indignation as he scuffed a bit of coal dust over the remains of the wilted cigarette.

'You're entitled to a few minutes' break, and I'm glad I've caught you,' Bradley said. 'I've a special job for you tomorrow, but I'm afraid it's going to be hard work.'

As he outlined what he expected Amos to do, the man gawped open-mouthed.

'But 'ow be I goin' ta git there?' he asked when Bradley had finished.

'I'm sure you're quite capable of walking, but you'll need a broom and cleaning materials, so on this occasion I'll take you.'

'In your motor?' Amos asked, as if he couldn't quite believe it.

'Yes. So make sure you're not wearing those filthy trousers. I don't want my seats covered in coal dust. And you'd better take a spare pair with you so that you can change before I collect you. It's going to be dirty work.'

'I only got these an' just the one other pair,' Amos objected.

'Then I'll find a pair of overalls for you,' Bradley said.

'Oh, awright.' Amos nodded, satisfied. 'They be good. I'd get meself a pair if I could afford it.'

'Now, there's something else I want to talk to you about,' Bradley said. 'The explosion you said you heard on the day the roof came down.'

Amos was shaking his head. 'I might'a bin wrong about that, sir.'

Bradley's eyes narrowed. 'What do you mean?'

'Well, don't seem like nobody else heard it.'

'What makes you say that?'

'They do all reckon I must'a imagined it.'

'Who?'

'The men.'

The dental surgeon who pulled teeth in the market square in full view of the shoppers must have an easier time of it than this, Bradley thought. He tried a different tack.

'Who was in the vicinity that day?'

'The wot?'

'Close to where you thought you heard the explosion.'

'Well, I don't exactly know, sir. I wasn't where it 'appened.'

'Think, man,' Bradley said, exasperated. 'George Golledge, Harry Harrison, Tommy Maggs, the carting boy, and Ted Yarlett. We know those four were there. Who else?'

'There weren't nobody that I remember.' Amos was beginning to become agitated, and Bradley realised he was going to get nothing more out of him.

'All right, Amos. Never mind,' he said. 'I'll leave you in peace. But just remember – don't be late tomorrow. You've got a long day's work ahead of you.'

Frustrated, he set out for Northfield Terrace.

A broad lane ran from the main road to the rank of houses that straddled the hillside, and long front gardens ran down to meet it. The Golledges' home was closer to the road than the Harrisons', which was towards the far end. Bradley pushed open the little wooden gate and stepped inside. The lawn was not well tended – it was mostly covered with moss – and the flower beds that edged it were overgrown with weeds. George Golledge clearly wasn't much of a gardener.

The front door looked as if it had been painted fairly recently, but the lattice porch around it was falling to pieces and the honeysuckle that clung to it couldn't have been cut back in years. Bradley pushed aside a long brown stem festooned with dead leaves and raised his hand to knock, then hesitated.

The angry raised voices of two men were coming from within. George Golledge – and Harry Harrison. Clearly the two of them were having a right old ding-dong.

Harry said something Bradley couldn't quite catch, but he heard George's response clearly enough. ''Tis all your bloody fault! I got done over because of you. Look at the state o' me! I can't hardly bloody move!'

'Don't you go blamin' me! 'Twas your idea in the first place!' Harry had raised his voice sufficiently so that Bradley could hear what he said now. 'I only did what I was told.'

'An' see where that's landed us! We're all fer the high jump if it gets out. An' it will, you can bet on that. Somebody's bin talkin', or that lad's uncle wouldn'a come after me, would he? I thought I could trust you, y'bugger. Could I? Like hell.'

'Stop it, you two! D'you want the whole rank to hear you?' A woman's voice now. Mrs Golledge must be intervening.

'Shut up, woman. You'll be doin' yer own fair share o' blamin' 'Arry here if we lose our 'ouse like he's losing 'is.' George again. 'Brought that on 'isself awright. An' 'e's gonna drag us down as well.'

'Bugger you, ya bliddy turncoat! I'm not stoppin' t' listen to this. You an' all the lads know damn well you're every bit as much to blame as me – more so.'

Bradley took a backwards step, not wanting Harry to come bursting out of the door and find him there on the step, but things went quiet and the door didn't open. He must have gone out the back way.

He walked quickly back across the lawn to the track. He didn't think this was the best moment to call on George Golledge, and he'd heard enough to know he'd been right all along. He still wasn't sure exactly what they'd done, or who the main culprit was – most likely they were as much to blame as one another. But he was no longer in any doubt that Harry Harrison and George Golledge were in this up to their necks.

He now felt sure Amos was right when he'd said there was an explosion before the roof came down. But if explosives had been used, how had they got hold of them? He was inclined to believe Dick Penny when he'd said it couldn't have been any of his shots that had been used. The man might be past his prime, but keeping dangerous charges safely locked away would be second nature to him, and he wouldn't have been open to persuasion from known troublemakers. He was too close to retirement, and had too much to lose. So how in the world had Harry and George Golledge managed it?

By the time he was out of sight of the houses, Bradley had begun to wish he'd intervened while the two men were at one another's throats. It had sounded as if George Golledge was blaming Harry; if he was angry enough, he might have been tempted to tell Bradley just what it was Harry had done, in order to save his own skin.

Was it too late to go back now and confront him? he wondered. Tell him what he'd overheard and hope he would be sufficiently shocked to give something away? But if he denied everything, claimed the row had nothing to do with the roof fall, Bradley would be no further on than he was now. And the two men, and whoever else had been involved in the plot that had gone so horribly wrong, would be warned of the danger of being found out.

No, best to wait rather than go in all guns blazing. He rather thought he was going to have to talk to Tommy Maggs's mother, little as he wanted to. She must know something.

He sighed deeply. He was now certain there had been foul play. And however sympathetic he felt towards Lorna, it was his duty to get to the bottom of it.

Lil Golledge threw more coal on the living room fire and turned angrily to face her husband, brandishing the shovel as if to strike him.

'You're a damn fool, George. I could happily murder you for

landing us in this pickle. You should'a known Harry Harrison couldn't be trusted. He couldn't run a piss-up in a brewery.'

'Think I don't know that now?' George was supporting his injured shoulder and gritting his teeth against the pain.

'Bit too late to be wise to that, when we'm in danger of losing our home.'

'It'll turn out awright, s'long as we keep our 'eads down,' George argued.

'Oh yes, an' 'ow's that? Look at you! 'Ow d'you think you can work when you can't move that arm? It's gonna be weeks afore you'm fit, an' I can't see 'is lordship keepin' yer job open fer you that long.'

'That's not my fault!' George objected. 'I were doin' well till that bugger picked on I!'

'An' that's another thing.' Lil was far from finished. 'How did 'e know you 'ad anything to do with it? Somebody's bin talking, and if management gets to 'ear of it, you won't just be out of a home and a job, you'll be up before the magistrates. In prison, I shouldn't wonder.'

'Aw, stop mithering, woman!' George exploded. But he looked worried as well as angry. 'Haven't I got enough on my plate without you goin' on about it? You'll drive me to drink.'

But Lil was no longer listening. She'd heard the sound of the letter box snap open and shut.

'Wot's that? It's a bit late for the second post.' She went to the front door, picked up the card that was lying on the mat and looked at it. 'Well!' Her tone was one of outrage. 'You'll never guess wot! Lorna Harrison's goin' to start bakin' bread and cakes to sell! She's got somebody dropping cards through folks' doors askin' if we want to order any! Wot a cheek!'

George shrugged. 'Good luck to 'er with that.'

'Knowin' her, she'll make a go of it,' Lil said, and sniffed to show her disgust. 'She'll come up smellin' o' roses, while God alone knows what's gonna become o' you an' me. It's just not fair! Jumped-up little madam. If you ask me, it's about time she got cut down to size!'

Furiously she tore the card in half and in half again, crumpled it into her clenched fist and threw it on the living room fire.

Chapter Fourteen

'Mammy! Mammy! Wake up!'

Lorna fought her way through the mists of deep sleep. A small hand was tugging on her arm, and by the fitful light of the moon slanting in through a gap in the bedroom curtains, she saw Marjorie leaning over her.

'What is it?' she mumbled.

'Fire! Come quick!'

Instantly Lorna was wide awake. 'What? Where?'

'Outside! Come on, Mammy!'

Though her first thought was that Marjorie had been frightened by a bad dream, there was no mistaking the panic in her voice. And it was very unusual – Vera was the one who sometimes had nightmares.

Lorna threw back the blanket, pushed herself upright and swung her feet to the floor in one fluid movement. For a moment her head swam, but Marjorie was still tugging urgently on her arm, and she recovered herself and followed her daughter out onto the landing.

The girls' bedroom was at the back of the house, directly opposite her own, and even from here she could see the flicker of flames illuminating it. She could smell smoke too; it must be filtering in through the gaps in the draughty sash window. She thrust Marjorie to one side and ran into the room, where Vera stood on tiptoe leaning against the sill, mesmerised by the drama unfolding outside.

Lorna leaned forward herself so as to be able to see out, and gasped in disbelief. The seat of the fire appeared to be in the cubbyhole that housed the bake oven, but surely that couldn't be? The oven was perfectly safe when the fire was lit beneath it, and in any case she hadn't used it today. But now flames were leaping high and bright, like nothing she had ever seen before. A thin line of flickering flame had already reached the coal house and was licking at the piece of wood behind which the coal lay – a fresh load, half a dozen sackfuls, had been delivered only last week.

Momentarily Lorna froze in shock, then, yelling to the children to stay where they were, she rushed downstairs, almost tripping over in her haste. She was aware of a faint oily smell coming from the kitchen, but for the moment it barely registered. She threw open the front room door, shouting at Harry to wake up.

'Wha . . .' he mumbled sleepily, but before she could explain, she was interrupted by someone thumping loudly on the front door. She flew to open it, scrabbling with the heavy old iron key that was only ever turned at night.

It was Flossie, a coat pulled on over her nightdress.

'There's a fire round the back!'

Lorna had never been more glad to see her friend. 'I know!' Her voice was sharp with panic.

'What's goin' on?' Harry, struggling along on his crutches, was behind her, wearing nothing but his round-necked woollen vest and long johns, and Nipper, woken by all the commotion, leapt out of his basket and ran round the kitchen barking.

'A fire!' Flossie repeated. 'Don't open your back door,

Jennie Felton

whatever you do. Fetch a bucket an' come round to ours through the front. Albie an' our Jack are doin' their best to put it out, but they need help. Quick sharp now, if you don't want the whole place goin' up.'

At last Harry seemed to realise that action was needed, even if he still didn't fully appreciate the urgency of the situation.

'Just let me put some clothes on . . . An' I need a dose of Newton's. Me indigestion's terrible,' he said.

Flossie threw up her hands in exasperation and turned to Lorna. 'You'd best get the girls and bring them round to mine too. Just in case. Our Arthur's gone on his bike to raise the alarm, but the Lord alone knows 'ow long it'll take for the fire brigade to get here.'

Lorna nodded and hurried up the stairs.

The children's bedroom was still aglow with a strange orange haze, and shadows flickered like branches in a gale.

'Put on your dressing gowns, girls,' she said, trying, and failing, to sound calm.

'Why?' Vera asked, frightened now, and on the verge of tears.

'You're going next door to Auntie Flossie's. Just for a bit, until the fire's out.' Lorna took Vera's dressing gown from its peg and held it out. 'Come on now, there's a good girl.'

'Is our house going to burn down?' Marjorie asked. She sounded frightened too.

'Of course not. And you'll be safe with Auntie Flossie.'

Lorna eased Vera's arms into the sleeves of her dressing gown, but struggled to tie the sash around her waist as Vera had begun to squirm.

'I have to get Pippy!'

'Here she is.' Lorna reached for the soft toy, which lay on Vera's pillow, and the little girl grabbed it, hugging it to her chest.

166

'What about Nipper?' Marjorie asked anxiously.

'We'll take him with us too.'

By the time the three of them were downstairs, however, there was no sign of the puppy, nor of Harry and Flossie. Lorna hoped that Nipper had followed them. If he'd escaped when the door was open, heaven only knew where he'd run off to. But for the moment that was the least of her worries.

She looked under the sink for her bucket before remembering she'd left it in the washhouse, then ushered the children out of the door and along the path. Flossie's door was ajar and they went straight in. Their neighbour was at the big stone kitchen sink filling a bucket with water.

'We'm dowsing down the coal in the coal house,' she said over her shoulder. 'If that catches, it'll be the devil's own job to put it out. Oh, an' don't worry about the dog. I've shut 'im in the front room.'

As if to confirm this, Nipper began barking shrilly and scratching at the door.

'I just can't believe this,' Lorna said. 'How in the world did it start?'

'Never mind about that fer now.' Flossie turned off the tap and hefted her bucket. 'Put the children in the front room with the dog and give me a hand here. There's another bucket under the sink.' She hurried out.

'Go on, children. Do as Auntie Flossie says. But don't let Nipper out, whatever you do.'

Lorna found the spare bucket and began filling it with water. When it was full, she took it to the back door, which Flossie had pulled to after her to keep out the stench.

Outside, the smell was almost overpowering. The seat of the fire had now died down. It was still glowing, and it flickered intermittently as it discovered new pathways, but mostly it resembled nothing more than a spent bonfire. Fragments of ash swirled in the air like dead leaves before crumbling and disappearing. Alongside the smoke, Lorna caught a whiff of the same oily smell she'd half noticed in her kitchen, but most disturbing of all, a thin line of flame that resembled the touchpaper on a firework was inching its way across the track towards her back door, flaring up every so often with a strange bluish tinge.

Horrified at the thought of what might happen if it reached the door, she hoisted her pail of water and was about to throw it over the snaking line of fire when an urgent shout stopped her.

'No! Don't do that!' Albie, who had been working to damp down the coal in the coal house, rushed towards her, his hand raised in warning. 'Don't!' he said again. 'Not there! You'll only spread it!'

'But our house . . .' Lorna was still holding the bucket at an angle.

'There's paraffin or some'ut. You'll make it ten times worse.'

Paraffin! By the light of the moon she could see it now, floating on the puddles of water that had collected outside the coal house as Albie and Jack soaked the wooden partition that kept the coal from tumbling out onto the track. That was what she had smelled in the house! But why? Her blood ran cold as it dawned on her. Someone must have poured paraffin under the door.

'It's inside!' she gasped. 'It goes right inside!'

Albie didn't hesitate. Without another word, he took off his heavy overcoat and threw it over the snaking trail of flame.

'Your coat . . .' Lorna said stupidly, but Albie wasn't listening. He was too busy stamping on it. Jack came running over to help him, taking off his own coat and stuffing it along the bottom of the door, then taking Lorna's bucket and pouring water directly onto it until it was thoroughly soaked.

'That should do it,' he said.

'Oh thank you, thank you . . .' Lorna was shaking from head to foot, tears of sheer relief gathering in her eyes.

'Well,' Flossie said, regarding the two ruined coats. 'Let's just 'ope the worst of the cold weather is over.'

Some of the other neighbours were out now, a couple of the menfolk doing what they could to help, the women peering out of bedroom windows. In all the mayhem, it hadn't occurred to Lorna to wonder where Harry was. Now she looked round and saw him sitting on the bench outside Flossie's kitchen door, rubbing his chest and saying something to Arthur, who had just arrived back and was balancing his bicycle against his hip.

'Not much more we can do now,' Albie said, philosophical as always. 'Fire brigade'll be 'ere soon, I should think.'

He'd barely spoken when, through the blood roaring in her ears, Lorna heard it. The faint jangle of a bell coming up the hill. And the clip-clop of horses' hooves, loud in the quiet of the night.

'Sounds like they'm on their way,' Flossie said. 'Thank the Lord fer that!'

'A quick turn-out,' Albie said approvingly.

Lorna's knees felt weak, as if they would no longer support her.

'D'you mind if I . . .'

'Go an' sit down, girl,' Flossie ordered her.

She made it to the bench where Harry was resting and sank down onto it before her legs could collapse beneath her.

There would be no more sleep that night for any of them. The sky was lightening for the dawn of a new day before the weary firemen finished damping down and rolled up their hoses.

Flossie made them cups of tea, for which they were truly grateful, while their chief, Bert Francis, escorted Harry and Lorna into their house by way of the front door now that it had been deemed safe to enter. When she saw the state of the kitchen, Lorna was horrified. The floor was awash with water and the stench of smoke and paraffin was sickening. Bert, who by day was a supervisor at a local joinery, was more interested in telling them of his suspicions than he was discussing the mess, which he said was unavoidable.

'This was arson, not a doubt of it.'

'You mean somebody did it on purpose? Surely that can't be right,' Harry protested, but Lorna agreed with the assessment. It was only what she had suspected after all. But thinking about the implications was beyond her just now.

'I'm afraid so,' the fire chief said. 'Setting a fire so close to the buildings is proof enough, and the trail of paraffin leading to your back door and more inside confirms it.'

'Wot be you suggestin'?' Harry demanded aggressively. 'If you be accusin' me of some'ut, spit it out.'

'I'm not accusing you of anything, Mr Harrison,' Bert said equably. 'Just that it's my opinion the fire was started deliberately, and with intent not just to cause damage but to endanger life.'

'Poppycock!'

Bert ignored the remark. 'I'm going to have to report this to the police as a criminal offence. You were clearly targeted, and whoever is responsible must have had some reason for doing what they did. Can you think of anyone who might bear you a grudge?'

'No, I bloody well can't,' Harry snapped. 'I'm the injured party here. Look at me! Not fit even to 'elp me neighbours tryin' to save me 'ouse from burning down.'

Though he'd kept his temper admirably, Bert had had enough.

'If I were in your shoes, I'd give it some thought before Sergeant Love comes to see you, as he undoubtedly will. He'll be asking you the same question, I feel sure.'

'An' I shall tell 'im the same as I've told you.'

'You must do as you think fit, Mr Harrison.' The fire chief turned to Lorna. 'I'm sorry about the mess, Mrs Harrison, but as I said before, it couldn't be helped. And better than having your house burn down.'

'We're really grateful to you, Mr Francis,' Lorna replied. 'And all your men too. It can't be much fun being called out in the middle of the night when you've got work next morning. Will you thank them for us?'

'It's what we do, Mrs Harrison, and we're only too glad to be of assistance, but I will pass on your thanks.' He smiled slightly. 'Though I suspect the tea your neighbour made for them will be thanks enough.'

Lorna managed a smile in return. 'That's Flossie all over.'

'Now, I'd better stand the men down,' Bert said. 'As you so rightly say, they all have jobs to go to, and though on the whole their employers are very understanding, I don't want them to be any later arriving for their day's work than is necessary. I'll bid you good day.'

'Good day,' Lorna echoed, but Harry only grunted dismissively.

When the fire chief had left, she turned furiously to her husband.

'Did you have to be so rude? That man and his crew just saved us from losing everything.'

Harry snorted. 'We 'aven't got anything to lose.'

'Don't talk such rubbish. What about our furniture? Our

171

clothes? The children's toys?' Lorna retorted, and Harry snorted again, even more derisively.

'There's stuff in the junk shop better'n ourn.'

'But at least it's bought and paid for. And there are some things you could never replace. Letters. Cards. The drawings the girls did when they were little. That lovely poem Marjorie wrote about snow—'

'Just more junk.'

Finally Lorna snapped.

'What is the matter with you, Harry? I'm fed up with the way you've been acting lately. I know you've been through a lot, but so have I. I've tried my very best to look after you on top of everything else, and all I get in return is your filthy temper. It's high time you took a good look at yourself. Saw yourself as others see you. I warn you, there's a limit to my patience. And if things don't change . . .'

'Oh yeah? Wot?'

Lorna didn't trust herself to answer. She left the room, slamming the door behind her.

But tired as she was, sleep eluded her, and as her anger cooled, she sank ever deeper into the depths of despair.

News of the fire at Northfield Terrace was the talk of Milverton Colliery. Lionel Percy, one of the volunteer firemen, was an overman there as well as being a member of Bradley's rescue team, and he'd been full of it when he'd arrived bleary-eyed for work.

When Bradley pulled into the yard, he was surprised to see Cameron's motor parked outside the office block. He'd thought the general manager was visiting one of the outlying collieries today. He turned off his engine and breezed into the office, unbuttoning his coat as he went.

Cameron was sitting behind the desk, drumming his fingers on the ink-stained surface. His pipe, which seemed to have gone out, was still jammed between his teeth.

'Good morning,' Bradley greeted him.

Cameron grunted. 'Not so good, all things considered. The Harrisons will have to move to Littleton Lane without delay.' The words were muffled by his pipe, but Bradley caught the gist of them and frowned.

'It's not fit for habitation yet. I'm taking Amos Riddle out there today to get it cleaned up. But it's going to be a good couple of days' work, I should think. It's in a hell of a state. And I need to arrange transport too, to get the rubbish that was left taken away and the Harrisons' stuff in. I'd say it will be at least a week before we can move them.'

Cameron shook his head, grim-faced, and Bradley frowned.

'What's the hurry? Is Sir Montague getting impatient?'

'Ah. You won't have heard.' Cameron removed the pipe from his mouth and twiddled the stem between his fingers. 'There was a fire last night, a serious one, at the Harrisons' place.'

Bradley's gut clenched and he stopped short, one arm in and one arm out of his coat.

'Are they all right?'

'Aye, from what I hear of it. But they can't stay there, Robinson.'

'The house is badly damaged then?'

'Not as bad as it could've been. According to Lionel Percy, it's a wonder the whole place didn't go up. It's not that that's concerning me.'

'What then?' Bradley was confused.

Cameron found a box of matches, struck one, and stared for a moment at the flame before answering.

Jennie Felton

'By all accounts it was arson,' he said at last. 'The fire was set deliberately. And with the intent of doing the Harrisons serious harm.'

Before he could stop himself, Bradley uttered a profanity.

'Aye. Quite,' Cameron said grimly. 'Now I've been sitting here and asking myself why anyone would do such a terrible thing, and I can come up with only one answer. You'll doubtless come to the same conclusion.' He applied the lit match to the bowl of his pipe, looking at Bradley meaningfully through the haze of fragrant smoke.

'The roof fall,' Bradley said.

Cameron nodded. 'You told me you were of the opinion that that was no accident either. And if you were right, and Harrison was involved in some way, this could be an act of retribution.'

Bradley was silent. He could only agree with Cameron's conclusion. If he himself had suspected that Harry had been involved in what had happened, then others would have done so too. Especially those who knew a great deal more than he did about the plotting that had gone on, or been underground at the time and seen something suspicious. They'd closed ranks when he'd questioned them, but they wouldn't be so reticent amongst their own. Lives had been lost. Relatives were grieving for their loved ones. It was all too plausible that they would want revenge on the author of the tragedy. An eye for an eye. A life for a life.

'It's not safe for them to be in Hillsbridge just now,' Cameron went on. 'If the house in Littleton Lane isn't ready for them, maybe they've relatives they could stay with until it is. Go and talk to them, Robinson. Tell them they've got to get themselves out of harm's way.'

Bradley nodded. 'I'll go and see them just as soon as I've taken Amos out to the cottage. I presume under the circumstances

174

I can offer him overtime so as to make the place habitable as soon as possible?'

He didn't mention that he had already promised Amos this, and Cameron agreed readily, just as Bradley had known he would.

'Aye, do whatever you think is necessary. In the meantime, I'll have a word with Sergeant Love. See if he can offer protection of some kind. Though I wouldn't hold my breath on that score.'

'There'll be an investigation, though, surely, if the fire chief has reported it as arson?' Bradley said.

'I suppose so. Of sorts. Though it wouldn't surprise me if the powers-that-be in Bath don't leave that to Love too. They've no appetite for wasting their time out here in the sticks if they can avoid it. Whoever did this was canny starting the fire in the bakehouse. They'll write it off as nothing more than carelessness if I know anything about it. A fire left unattended before it was properly out. Nippers playing with paraffin. It'll be recorded as an accident, mark my words.'

'An accident. Exactly what the roof fall was passed off as.' Bradley shook his head in disgust. 'You can be sure of one thing – I shall be redoubling my efforts to get to the bottom of that. And maybe that will lead us to the guilty party in this case too. But my first priority is getting that cottage cleaned up and ready for the family in case they don't have any alternative accommodation. They should be safe there so long as we keep their whereabouts quiet. I'll tell Amos he won't get a penny piece for his day's work, never mind overtime, if he blabs about what he's been doing, and why.'

'You can leave the arrangements for the transport wagon to me,' Cameron said. 'We don't want to use one that has any connection with the colliery. I'll look into hiring a haulier from

Bristol way. One who won't have any interest in goings-on in Hillsbridge.'

'That sounds like a plan,' Bradley agreed. 'I'll be on my way then. The sooner I get Amos out to Littleton Lane, the sooner the place will be cleaned up and ready for them to move in.'

Leaving Cameron puffing thoughtfully on his pipe, he rebuttoned his coat and went in search of Amos.

Chapter Fifteen

When Bradley drew up outside the cottage in Littleton Lane, he saw the curtains twitch at the window of the house next door and smiled to himself. The woman who had been so unpleasant to Lorna was undoubtedly a nosy parker who wanted to know what was going on. He hoped that she and Harry's mother were the only ones who knew that the family were going to be moving into number 1. It was vital their whereabouts were kept secret. He was fairly sure the occupants of the cottages in Littleton Lane were too far out of Hillsbridge for them to gossip about it to the townsfolk. They would buy their provisions in the small general store in Littleton, he guessed. As for the men, both Harry's father and Mrs Nosy Parker's son would be working at Oldlands for the foreseeable future, and the skeleton workforce there drank and socialised in the village and formed a completely different clique from the Milverton miners.

As far as Amos was concerned, Bradley had warned him not to say anything to anyone, but he had no worries on that score. Getting anything out of Amos was like getting blood out of a stone.

He unloaded the cleaning equipment he'd brought with him, and Amos carried it across the track while Bradley found the door key amongst all the others on the unwieldly bunch.

'Knock down those cobwebs so we don't get covered in them,' he instructed as the door grated open, and Amos obediently lifted the long-handled broom and attacked the offending webs.

'That'll take some gettin' off,' he observed sagely, trying to extricate the sticky mess from the bristles and dusting his hands off on his borrowed overalls.

'There are plenty of rags in that box.' Bradley was anxious to make light of the daunting task that lay ahead of the man.

He need not have worried, he realised, as Amos merely nodded. 'Oh ah.'

He looked similarly unperturbed by the filthy state of the cottage, taking it in his stride just as he did any unsavoury jobs that came his way during the course of his day's work.

Bradley, however, was disgusted all over again. It would certainly take at least a couple of days to clean the place from top to bottom, and longer still to rid it of the foul stench. He went around opening windows to let in some fresh air, and warned Amos that he'd better keep his coat on if he didn't want to catch his death of cold.

'Oh, don't 'ee worry about I,' was the stoic reply. 'I s'pect I shall get 'ot workin'. An' I got me bottle o' tea.'

'Did you bring something to eat too?' Bradley asked.

'Oh ah.' Amos's stock response. 'Me bread an' drippin'.'

'Where is it then?'

'Well, 'tis in yer motor. Under the seat.'

Bradley sighed. Would the man have let him drive away with his day's sustenance if Bradley hadn't mentioned it?

'I have to go now, so you'd better come out and fetch it,' he said, grateful that he had a good reason to leave both the filthy house and the irritating man.

As he left, he saw the curtains of the house next door twitch again, and wondered how long it would be before Mrs Nosy Parker ventured out to satisfy her curiosity. But he wouldn't mind betting she wouldn't want to stay long once she'd sampled the awful stink at number 1. No one in their right mind would.

Very quickly, though, his mind returned to the problem of the Harrisons' safety. After what had happened last night, he wasn't happy for them to remain in Hillsbridge, and neither was Cameron. The danger of another attack was too great. Was there any possibility that they could move in with Harry's parents for the time being? It wouldn't be for long; once the cottage had been cleaned up, they'd be able to lend a hand getting it shipshape, and the job would be completed all the sooner.

Lorna wouldn't be best pleased about it, of course. She'd made it clear that she dreaded the idea of living in close proximity to her in-laws, and certainly the confrontation he'd witnessed between her and Harry's mother was proof of bad blood between them and didn't bode well for the future. But surely that was preferable to living in fear of her family's lives? And surely Mrs Harrison senior wouldn't want them to be put at any further risk?

He made up his mind. He'd go and speak to the woman now. Spell out the seriousness of the situation and ask if she couldn't take the family in temporarily. He walked to the house at the other end of the little terrace and knocked on the door.

While waiting for an answer, he looked around. Unlike number 1, it was well kept, exceptionally so. The paintwork was fresh, the flagstones around the door looked as if they were swept and scrubbed regularly, and the brass knocker – in the shape of a fox's head – gleamed. In spite of the recent bad weather, the windows were sparkling. Mrs Harrison senior was clearly a house-proud woman. When he turned to look at the long garden that ran away from the houses up a gentle slope, he could see that in contrast to its neighbours it was well tended, and most likely provided all the vegetables the family needed and more. Proof, if any were needed, that this could be a pleasant spot to live, even if it was somewhat isolated.

The flip-flop of carpet slippers on tiles within the house drew his attention, and he turned back to face the door as it opened smoothly.

Bradley had seen Mrs Harrison only briefly on his previous visit, and had been more concerned with what was going on between her and her daughter-in-law than with her appearance. Now, coming face to face with her, he was struck by the similarities with her son. Though now shot through with grey and somewhat faded, her hair had obviously once been the same fiery red, and she had the same strong features. Perhaps they were more suited to a man, but Bradley had no doubt that she had once been a handsome woman, before discontent and a bad temper had etched frown lines into her forehead and between her nose and mouth. Just as they would with her son if he continued to think, act and speak as he did at present.

'Yes?' Her tone was surly, her voice gravelly. It could almost have been a man speaking.

Bradley introduced himself, and explained that as Harry's injuries made it extremely unlikely that he would ever be able to return to his former job, he and his family were being moved into number 1.

'Tell me some'ut I don't know,' she said off-handedly, not displaying so much as a hint of concern or compassion for the situation her son found himself in.

'There is a problem, though,' Bradley went on. 'The house is in a bad state.'

'I could 'ave told 'ee that.'

'And it doesn't end there, unfortunately,' he continued

smoothly. 'There was a fire last night at your son's home. He and his family need rehousing urgently, and as number 1 is nowhere ready for them to move into, I was wondering if—'

'Caught the kitchen afire, did she?' Once again Mrs Harrison interrupted him. 'Well, that don't surprise me.'

'Nothing like that,' Bradley said. 'It's not because of fire damage that they need to move out urgently. The fire officer believes the blaze was started deliberately. That someone with a grudge against Harry intended them harm.'

'Huh!' Mrs Harrison snorted. 'Trouble follows my son around like a dog after a bitch on heat. What's 'e done this time?'

'I really couldn't say.' Bradley had no intention of telling this unpleasant woman of his suspicions. 'All I know is it's not considered safe for him to remain in the town just now. But we have no other accommodation we can offer the family, and I wondered if you might be able to find room for them until number 1 is made habitable.'

'*What?*' Mrs Harrison practically spat the word at him. 'If that's why you're knocking on my door, you might as well know you're on a fool's errand. The answer's no.'

Bradley wasn't going to give up so easily.

'Even if his life and the lives of his family are in danger?'

Mrs Harrison's mouth was set in a tight line. Her eyes blazed. 'Our 'Arry's made 'is bed an' 'e'll 'ave to lie in it. I 'ad 'im and that stuck-up wife of 'is livin' 'ere once before and it didn't work out. And I certainly can't be doin' with kiddies about the place, with their noise and their bliddy muddles, thank you very much. Not at my age. So there you are, Mr Whatever-yer-name-is. You might as well save yer breath.' Without more ado, she shut the door in his face.

Bradley shook his head in disgust. Clearly moving in with Harry's parents was not an option. But he couldn't help wondering what had happened between them to cause such deep-rooted antagonism. That a mother could refuse to help her own son even if his life was in danger was beyond him. It went against all the laws of nature. An unpleasant person she might be, but even so, there must surely be a reason for such callousness.

And why had she called Lorna stuck-up? She certainly wasn't that. Because she was better-spoken than the Harrisons, with their rough Somerset accents, perhaps? Or was there another reason? Something of which he knew nothing? Whatever the case, it rankled with him, and he felt angry on Lorna's behalf.

What he needed to concentrate on, however, was finding a solution to the problem of moving the family out of Hillsbridge before whoever had set last night's fire made another attempt on their lives. He couldn't take the risk of letting them stay where they were.

He cranked the engine of his motor to life, climbed into the driving seat and reversed out onto the lane, turning over the few options he could think of, and by the time he parked on the road beneath the track that led to Northfield Terrace, he had come to a decision.

Lorna was on her hands and knees scrubbing the kitchen floor. When she'd collected the children, who had spent the night next door, Flossie had already lit a fire under her boiler to heat water for Lorna to clean up, since she wouldn't be able to use her own, and offered to come round and lend a hand as soon as she'd cleared away the breakfast things and made the beds.

Good as her word, she had appeared an hour later armed with a mop and a handful of cleaning rags, and was now washing cooking pots, crockery and cutlery, all covered in smuts and splashes of dirty water, and setting them to drain on the oilcloth-covered cupboard beside the big stone sink.

'What a to-do,' she said, wiping a soap bubble off her chin.

If Lorna hadn't been so tired and worried, she might almost have smiled at the understatement. As it was, she could barely summon the energy to speak. Grateful as she was for Flossie's help, there was a part of her that wished she hadn't come round. All she wanted was to get on with what had to be done, so that she could begin to come to terms with what had happened.

'You could say that,' she managed. 'Is there any more hot water in your copper? I could do with some fresh.'

That too was an understatement. The water she was using was filthy.

'There's plenty,' Flossie said. 'I topped it up half an hour ago, so it should be hot by now.'

Armed with a fresh bucketful, Lorna tossed a rug onto the kitchen floor before kneeling down and immersing a cloth in the soapy water.

'Wot's Harry up to?' Flossie asked. 'Couldn't he lend a hand?'

'He's asleep in the front room. He's tired out,' Lorna said.

Flossie snorted. 'Aren't we all? He could have washed these things up. That shouldn't be beyond him.'

'But he can't stand for long,' Lorna said, ready as always to jump to his defence, though she sometimes wondered why she did it. Out of loyalty, she supposed. A loyalty she was beginning to wonder if he deserved. 'Anyway, he'd most likely break half the crockery and glasses,' she added. 'And we've no money to buy new.'

They worked in silence for some minutes, then Flossie said: 'D'you think it was deliberate?'

'Harry breaking things? No, he's just clumsy.'

'Not Harry. The bugger wot started the fire.' She plonked a

saucepan upside down on the cupboard to drain.

'That's what Mr Francis said. I can't believe it, though.' Lorna sat back on her heels and stretched her aching neck. 'Who would do such a thing?'

'One o' the folk 'Arry's made an enemy of,' Flossie said flatly. 'Did you know there's talk goin' round that 'e 'ad summat to do with the accident at the pit?'

Given the unpleasant way folk were treating her, Lorna had wondered if that might be the case. But it wasn't something she wanted to think about. 'Oh, please don't say that, Flossie,' she said.

'Just tellin' it like it is. Let's hope there's nothin' in it. But they'll want to get to the bottom of it, you can bet your last farthin' on that.'

Lorna sighed. 'Mr Francis said he'd have to report it,' she said miserably. 'I'm expecting a visit from Sergeant Love . . .' She broke off as there was a knock on the door. 'P'raps that's him now.'

'Well, if it is, I'll make meself scarce.' Flossie began to dry her hands on her wraparound apron, and Lorna got to her feet, doing the same.

When she opened the door, however, it wasn't the police sergeant on the doorstep, but Mr Robinson.

Her hands immediately flew to her hair, which had come loose from its pins and straggled limply over her face.

'Mr Robinson . . .' She knew she sounded flustered.

He cocked his head to one side with a wry smile. 'I really wish you'd call me Bradley.'

'Bradley.' It was an automatic response. 'We're in an awful mess here, I'm afraid.'

'So I see.' He looked round at the evidence of last night's conflagration. The burned-out remains of the fire, the pools of water with telltale streaks of blue oil suspended in them, the charred strips of rag that the firemen had swept against the walls of the outhouses.

'You've heard, then?' Lorna said.

'It's all over Milverton.'

'I suppose it would be,' she said resignedly.

'Look, I expect you're up to your eyes in clearing up, but I really do need to talk to you and Harry.'

Lorna tucked a stray end of hair behind her ear. 'You'd better come in then. Only, would you mind . . .' She indicated the boot scraper beside the door. 'I don't want all that black mud tracking in again.'

'I'll do better than that.' Bradley bent and removed his boots, stepping over the puddles of water and into the kitchen one stockinged foot at a time.

'This is Mr Robinson,' Lorna said to Flossie, aware of a flush creeping into her cheeks and hoping Bradley wouldn't notice as she turned to him. 'My neighbour, Mrs Price. She's helping me clean up.'

'Pleased to meet you, Mrs Price.'

'I'll leave you to it, Lorna.'

Both of them had spoken at once.

'There's no need, Flossie. We'll be in the front room,' Lorna said, but her friend was clearly uncomfortable.

'It's awright, Lorna. You don't want me hearing talk wot's private. I'll be back in a bit.'

Flossie bustled out, and Lorna showed Bradley into the front room, where Harry was asleep on the sofa.

'Wake up, Harry. Mr Robinson's here.'

He rolled over, almost toppling off the sofa, and swore.

'Wot do 'e want?'

'Don't be so rude, Harry,' Lorna said, speaking her mind in

front of company for once. 'Would you like a cup of tea, Mr Robinson?'

'I wouldn't dream of putting you to the trouble when you have so much to do,' Bradley said smoothly. 'I won't keep you for long, but in view of what's happened, I do need to speak to you both.'

'I could do wi' a cup,' Harry said. 'My mouth's like the bottom of a parrot's cage.'

Lorna ignored him. 'Sit down, Mr Robinson.'

'Bradley. Remember?' He sat in one of the easy chairs, and Lorna perched on the edge of the other.

'Oh, *Bradley*, is it?' Harry muttered, and Lorna flashed him a warning look.

'I'll get straight to the point,' Bradley said. 'If the fire was started deliberately—'

'Who said it were?' Harry interrupted.

'The chief fire officer.' Bradley tossed it at him, almost a throwaway line, before continuing. 'If he's right – and I have no reason to doubt him – it's really not safe for you to remain here. Do you have any friends or relatives away from the district you could stay with until the house in Littleton Lane is ready for you? And before you suggest your parents, Harry, I must tell you I was out there this morning and floated the idea to your mother. I'm afraid she was adamant that staying with them isn't an option.'

'You've spoke to my mother? What business did you 'ave doin' that?' Harry demanded indignantly.

'No, she wouldn't want us there,' Lorna said. 'And to be honest, I wouldn't want to be there either. But to answer your question, Mr Robinson – Bradley – there isn't anyone. My mother and father are no longer with us, and their families are all up in Yorkshire. I haven't seen them for years.'

'Harry?' Bradley looked at him quizzically, and for a brief moment an almost sheepish look replaced his usual scowl, before it was gone again. 'Wot's this?' he grumbled. 'Why're you trying to palm us off on whoever will 'ave us? Bloody Fairley wants us out so 'e can move some other bugger in, I s'pose.'

'Not at all,' Bradley said equably. 'We are concerned for your safety, that's all. If someone means you harm, they may well try again, with more success.'

'An' why would anybody do that?'

He met the other man's eyes squarely. 'You tell me, Harry.'

Harry muttered something unintelligible, and Bradley turned back to Lorna.

'We're not willing to risk leaving you and your children here,' he said. 'Nothing else may happen, of course, but we can't take the chance. This was a pretty determined effort to start a serious fire, as I understand it. And I for one won't stand by and allow your lives to be endangered. Which is why I have a proposal to put to you. The house that came with my job was built as a family home, and being single, I rattle around in it. There's no reason why you shouldn't all move in with me until the cottage in Littleton Lane is ready.'

'Oh, that is so kind, but we couldn't impose on you.' Colour was flooding Lorna's cheeks again.

Harry spoke scathingly. 'Not bloody likely!'

Once again Bradley ignored him and spoke directly to Lorna. 'It wouldn't be an imposition. In fact you'd be doing me a favour. I haven't yet had time to advertise for a housekeeper, or even someone to come in a couple of days a week to keep the place clean and tidy. It would be marvellous to have meals prepared for me rather than having to cobble something together myself. The prospect of freshly baked bread alone is enough to make this an offer I hope you'll feel able to accept. And I shall sleep a good deal more easily in my bed if I know you are safe.'

'You know what you can do with your "offer",' Harry growled, but Lorna was close to tears of gratitude.

'That is so kind!' she said again.

'No it bain't,' Harry snarled. 'Wot 'e wants is an unpaid skivvy. Well, it won't work, mister. We'm stoppin' 'ere, an' that's me last word.'

Lorna had had enough. She rounded on her husband furiously.

'You can stay here if you like, Harry, but I'm not, and neither are the children. Thank you, Mr Robinson. You're not the only one who will sleep more soundly if we're somewhere safe. It was terrible last night.' She bit her lip, remembering the shock of being woken by Marjorie and seeing the dancing flames outside the window. 'I don't think I could get a good night's sleep here ever again,' she finished.

'Good.' Bradley rose from the chair. 'I'm glad that's settled. I have to collect Amos Riddle, who's working on the cottage as we speak, and bring him back to town. I'll come and collect you after that. It'll be somewhere between six and seven, I imagine.'

'We'll be ready.' A sudden thought struck Lorna. 'What about Nipper?'

Bradley glanced at the puppy, who was happily chewing a sock Harry must have discarded.

'Oh, bring him too. There's a good-sized garden, and plenty of nice walks round about. He'll enjoy it, and so will I. We always had dogs at home when I was a boy.'

'I don't know how to thank you,' Lorna said.

Harry said nothing.

When Bradley had left, Lorna turned on her husband.

'I mean it, Harry. You must do as you like, but I'm taking

the children and moving out. I'm not willing to put their safety at risk, even if you are.'

'Over my dead body. I won't be driven out of me own house,' Harry said stubbornly.

She groaned in exasperation. 'Face facts, Harry! Someone's got it in for you. I don't know who or why, but they meant business last night, and there's every chance they'll try again.'

'Codswallop! 'Twas just some drunken layabout.'

But there was something in his expression that told Lorna this attitude was nothing but bravado. Could it be there was something in what Flossie had said, and people thought Harry had had something to do with the roof fall?

'Tell me the truth, Harry,' she said quietly. 'I think you know very well what's behind all this.'

'Just leave it, woman,' he growled. His eyes were avoiding hers, and Lorna's conviction deepened. But she could see she was getting nowhere. He wasn't going to admit to anything, and she was too tired to pursue it.

'Please yourself,' she said wearily. 'But I'm telling you, I'm leaving with the children and you can't stop me.'

'I can have a damn good try!'

Already in the doorway, Lorna turned and faced him again.

'I'll have a word with Sergeant Love when he comes to see us and ask him what right you have to stop me taking the children to a place of safety. I'm expecting him any time. And you can be sure he'll be asking you the same questions I just did. But he won't give up so easily. Now I've got work to do.'

With that, she returned to the kitchen and resumed the gargantuan task of clearing up.

Sergeant Love was just about to leave for Northfield Terrace when a woman came hurrying up the path to the police house that doubled as a station. His heart sank as he recognised Agnes Tiley, the local busybody who lived in one of the houses at the bottom of the hill on the road that led to Bath.

'Sergeant, there's cows all over the main road just up from my house. They must have got out of the field. You'd better come quick before there's an accident.'

'Does the farmer know?' Sergeant Love asked.

'He's nowhere to be seen, and if you think I'm going all the way to his farm, you've got another think coming.'

'All right. Leave it to me.'

Under normal circumstances, Sergeant Love would have been furious with the woman, but now he was quite glad of the excuse to delay investigating last night's fire. Even more annoying than Mrs Tiley was the way the detectives in Bath pushed jobs they didn't want his way, the jumped-up lazy sods. Well, they'd just have to wait. And when he'd taken care of the escaped cows, he'd find a few more things to keep him busy, he decided. It was high time he showed that self-important detective inspector that he was nobody's lackey.

Chapter Sixteen

Just what changed Harry's mind was something of a mystery to Lorna. He was usually stubborn as a mule. Perhaps when he'd calmed down, he'd realised that if someone did launch another attack on him, he was in no fit state to defend himself, but was too proud to admit it.

'I'm not 'avin' you stoppin' with that man on yer own,' had been his excuse. 'I reckon 'e's got designs on you.'

'Of course he hasn't,' Lorna had scoffed, but she had been annoyed to feel herself blushing, and had turned away quickly so he wouldn't see it.

'His sort're always ready to try it on if they get half a chance,' Harry had continued. But Lorna felt sure he knew more than he was letting on about why the fire had been started, and she found herself remembering once again Lil Golledge's hostile attitude towards her in the aftermath of the roof fall. Then there was George's reluctance to visit Harry, although she'd always thought they were bosom pals.

She couldn't shake the bad feeling that folk were blaming Harry for what had happened in the pit. But there was no point in asking him again. Sergeant Love hadn't turned up with questions of his own either, and she was glad of that. She really didn't want to have to revisit the events of the previous night. It had been too horrendous to think about.

She went upstairs to look out clean clothes, bedding, and anything else they would need. She had to head off Harry, who was attempting to come up to do his own packing – she didn't want him falling again! As she busied herself in the bedrooms, she tried to put her growing suspicion out of her mind.

They were ready and waiting when Bradley arrived soon after dark, a suitcase, a rucksack and a large carpet bag stacked beside the door.

Vera, excited by what she thought of as an adventure, was unable to stay still.

'We're going to ride in a real live motor!' she'd cried, clapping her hands and dancing round the kitchen. She'd gone outside now to watch for the amazing contraption. Marjorie, predictably, was solemn and wary, while Harry was sullen and silent. Lorna wondered if he'd change his mind yet again and refuse to leave when the time came, but she remained determined not to spend another night in this house whatever he did.

'Mammy! Daddy! The motor's here!' Vera came rushing in, Nipper yapping at her heels.

'Are we all ready then?' Lorna said. 'We don't want to keep Mr Robinson waiting.'

'I'm ready!' Vera piped, and Marjorie, still looking worried, fetched her coat.

'What about Pippy?' Lorna reminded her younger daughter.

'Oh!' Vera rushed upstairs.

Lorna glanced at Harry, who had made no move. 'Are you coming with us or not?'

'I told you. I'm not havin' you go off with that bugger on yer own.'

'Well, I just hope you'll be polite to him,' she said.

'Don't you want to say goodbye to Flossie bloody Price?' Harry asked sarcastically.

'I already have.' Lorna was determined not to let him see how much she hated leaving her friend. They might not be actually moving out yet, but this still felt horribly final.

She went to the door and opened it. Bradley was on the doorstep, about to knock.

'Ready?'

'I think so. We're all coming. Harry too.'

'Fine.' Bradley's tone gave nothing away. 'I've risked bringing the car up to the end of the track. I didn't know how much luggage you'd have.'

'Not too much, I hope. I've tried to keep it to the bare essentials. But with the children . . .'

'Of course. Let me help.'

For some reason there was an awkwardness about him that Lorna hadn't felt before, even when she'd broken down and cried on the visit to Littleton Lane. He had always seemed supremely self-confident. A man who was comfortable in his own skin, who took everything in his stride. It was oddly disconcerting.

Marjorie was behind her now, clutching a bag containing books, pencils and a jigsaw puzzle, and Vera appeared with Pippy in her arms.

'You haven't met my daughters, have you?' Lorna said, glad of the distraction. 'This is Marjorie, and this little terror is Vera.'

'Pleased to meet you,' Bradley said solemnly, but he was smiling.

'Are we really going to ride in your motor?' Vera asked.

'Do you want to?'

'Yes!'

'Then so you shall. But you'll have to sit on your mother's lap. I'm afraid it's going to be a bit of a squash.'

'I don't mind! Can it be in the front?'

'Vera, stop!' Lorna warned. 'Daddy is going to sit in the front.'

'Where is Daddy?' Marjorie asked, noticing that he hadn't joined them.

Lorna felt a stab of unease. Harry had still been muttering about wanting something from upstairs when she'd been doing the packing. But at that moment he emerged from the living room, leaning heavily on his crutch. He nodded brusquely to Bradley, but to Lorna's relief made no rude remark.

'I s'pose we'd better lock up,' he said. 'Not that we've got anythin' worth stealing.'

Lorna clipped on Nipper's lead and the little procession moved off along the path, Bradley carrying the case and Nipper's basket and with the rucksack slung over his shoulder, Lorna with the carpet bag, and Marjorie in charge of Nipper.

The motor was loaded and the seating arrangements decided upon. Harry would sit in the front passenger seat, and Lorna, Marjorie, Vera and Nipper in the rear. It was a tight squeeze, Vera on Lorna's knee, Marjorie nursing Nipper, but at least it wouldn't be for long.

'Amos made good progress with the house today,' Bradley said as they drove. 'He might be a bit on the slow side in some departments, but he's a hard worker. And Mr Cameron has arranged for a wagon to take away any rubbish that's left, so hopefully you'll be able to move in sooner than I first thought.'

'Wanting to get rid of us already, are you?' Harry said, and Lorna cringed. But Bradley seemed unfazed.

'Not at all. But I'm sure you'll be much happier when you have a place of your own.'

'It won't be ourn, though, will it? Fairley can turn us out whenever he likes.'

'I'm sure he'll be in no hurry to do that,' Bradley said smoothly.

They rode up the hill and along Littleton Lane in silence, and Lorna's stomach clenched as they passed the cottages. She'd never feel at home there, she knew. But beggars couldn't be choosers.

The motor chugged up a little rise, then turned into the lane that led to Oldlands Colliery, bumping along for a quarter of a mile or so before coming to a halt outside a house that was barely visible in the pitch darkness.

'This is it.' Bradley turned off the engine. 'Let's go in, and please do make yourselves at home. It's not ideal, I know, but at least you'll be safe in your beds.'

'You don't know what a relief that will be,' Lorna said.

Bradley showed them around the house: two reception rooms, one leading off a big farmhouse-style kitchen, plus – wonder of wonders! – an indoor privy. The three bedrooms were up a steep flight of stairs, which Harry baulked at. There was no way he could manage them; he'd have to sleep downstairs on the sofa as he did at home, he said. Bradley's room was off to the right of a small square landing, and the two spares were to the left, one leading directly into the other. He suggested the girls should have the farthest room.

'That way they won't be able to get out and go wandering about in the middle of the night without you knowing about it,' he said, and Lorna was quick to agree. Vera sometimes walked in her sleep, and in a strange house she might very well tumble down the stairs.

Bradley suggested that a cup of tea was called for – he'd set

195

the kettle to boil before showing them around – but Lorna was anxious to get the children settled; it was already well past their usual bedtime.

'D'you mind if I make up the beds first?' she asked.

'Whatever suits you best,' he said.

'And I'm sorry to have to bother you, but could I have some warm milk for the girls?'

'Lorna, you don't need to ask.'

When she'd made up the three-quarter-size bed that Marjorie and Vera were to share and got them into their nightdresses and dressing gowns, she took them downstairs to fetch their milk. Bradley was in the big kitchen, stoking up the fire, and Nipper had made himself comfortable on the rag rug in front of it, but of Harry there was no sign.

'He's lying down,' Bradley said in answer to her unspoken question. 'After a broken night and with the burden of that heavy contraption on his leg, he's done in, I expect.'

Lorna didn't mention that Harry had been either asleep or resting most of the day. It was good not to have to worry about his ill-tempered behaviour towards Bradley for a little while at least.

Bradley poured warm milk into two mugs and offered the children the biscuit barrel. 'Only Osborne, I'm afraid,' he apologised, but they took one each anyway before leaving for bed.

'They've had an evening meal, I presume?' he said.

'We all have. Harry and I ate with them.' Lorna was still conscious of the aura of awkwardness, and thought it must be because, like her, he was feeling his way in this unfamiliar situation.

'Well, I haven't. I'm going to have some bread and cheese, and you're welcome to join me if you're still hungry.'

'No, really, thank you. But I would like a cup of tea if I'm not too late.'

'It's keeping warm for you.' Bradley indicated an earthenware pot that stood on a trivet over the range, and a cup and saucer, milk and sugar set out ready on the table. 'And you can pour me another cup while you're about it.'

As Lorna attended to the tea, he fetched bread, cheese and butter and laid a place for himself.

'I'm afraid I don't have much food in the house. I should have gone to the shops today, but time ran away with me. There's more bread, and blackcurrant jam, which should suffice for breakfast, and tomorrow is Saturday, so I'll drive you into town and we can get whatever you think you'll need.'

'Saturday – of course it is! Market day.' Lorna couldn't help thinking of the stall she'd planned to take there herself. So much had happened in the last weeks, it seemed a very long time ago. In another life almost. 'Can the children come too? They love the market.'

'By all means.' Bradley sawed off a chunk of bread and spread it thickly with butter.

The tea was calming Lorna's nerves, making her feel more relaxed.

'I'll get something nice for dinner. What do you like?' she asked, setting her cup down.

Bradley grinned. 'Anything I don't have to make for myself. I take it you're offering?'

'Of course I am! So what's it to be? A shepherd's pie? Liver and onions? Beef stew? No, it'll be too late for that by the time we get back. I can do that another day. What about mackerel? The fish from the market is always lovely and fresh. And I'll bake bread, too, and make a lardy cake ... .'

'It sounds as if I am going to be thoroughly spoiled.'

'Oh, I promise, you are!'

Things were easier now. Far more comfortable.

Nipper stretched, yawned, got up from his place in front of the fire and went to the door. Suddenly Lorna was anxious again.

'I ought to take Nipper out to do his business,' she said.

'I'll take him,' Bradley offered. 'It's very dark out there. I don't want you tripping over. Can he wait a few minutes, do you think?'

'I expect so. He's very good for a puppy.'

Bradley smiled. 'Well trained.'

'I hope so.'

Perhaps, Lorna thought, this was going to work after all.

'That were a tidy how-de-doo last night, weren't it?' Moses Whittock wiped beer foam from his stubbled chin and looked at his pals, who sat around the table in the public bar of the Miners' Arms. 'You must've 'ad a grandstand view, George. Accordin' to Lionel Percy, they damn near burned in their beds.'

'No more'n he deserves.'

It was the first time George Golledge had ventured out for a pint since he'd been attacked, and he'd been given a hero's welcome by his friends. Now, however, they glanced at one another uncomfortably, and for a long moment no one spoke.

It was Shorty Dallimore who broke the loaded silence.

'That's a bit much, George. I d'a know you and he 'ave fallen out, but nobody ought to meet an end like that. An' wot about 'is wife, an' the little 'uns?'

'I s'pose,' George said reluctantly.

'Well, I heard 'twere done deliberately,' Ticker Greedy ventured.

There was a general murmur of agreement. What Lionel Percy had said had been thoroughly aired during the long day's shift.

'Who the devil would do a thing like that, though?' Shorty asked the question that had been on everybody's lips.

'Well, it's pretty bliddy obvious to me,' George said bitterly. 'The same bugger that tried t' beat me up. You seen wot 'e was like. A mad bull. He'd'a put I in the 'ospital if it hadn't been fer you lot.'

'So why didn't 'e set fire to your place then, George?' Moses asked.

'Got the wrong house, I reckon. He'd made up 'is mind somebody were goin' t' pay for wot were done. His sister's boy dead an' all that.'

'Ah, you might be right,' Shorty agreed.

'An' then again, maybe 'e didn't,' Ticker said enigmatically. 'Maybe 'e's going after Harry as well. He were right there, weren't 'e? He—' He broke off as Moses, who had noticed Mercy Comer taking rather a long time wiping down one of the nearby tables, interrupted abruptly.

'I 'ear Stanley Bristow's puttin' on a concert to raise money for the families of them wot lost their lives or was hurt.'

'Gettin' a bit past it, in't he?' Ticker suggested.

Stanley was quite a celebrity in Hillsbridge, well-known and well-loved for the concert parties he had been putting on at the Town Hall for almost as long as anyone could remember. Besides the variety of acts he assembled from local talent he himself was one of the main attractions for his polished monologues and comic songs.

'He were as good as ever last time I saw 'un,' Shorty insisted. 'Had my wife in stitches, 'e did. An' 'e gets some good turns too.'

'Yeah, yer right. His voice might be going, but 'e can still tell a joke better'n most,' Ticker agreed reluctantly.

The friends had all cottoned on to the danger Moses had warned them of with a nod and a wink. Discussing the roof fall amongst themselves was one thing. Being overheard was quite another. Especially by Mercy. They all liked the barmaid – she was a pretty little thing, and flirty with it – but none of them would trust her with information that was best kept amongst themselves.

As they discussed the shows Stanley Bristow had put on over the years, Moses's suspicions were confirmed: in no time at all, Mercy had stopped cleaning the table next to theirs and gone back behind the bar, disappointed, no doubt, that she would hear no more tonight.

They were wrong in that regard. Before they'd changed the subject, Mercy had heard enough to lift her spirits. As she polished glasses, her mind was working overtime, mulling over what the miners had been saying. It didn't entirely make sense to her, but it might to the safety officer. Most importantly, it gave her the perfect excuse to see him again. And that was exactly what she had been hoping for.

Bradley was finding sleep elusive. As a general rule, he slept easily. But tonight his thoughts were running in never-ending circles, and each time he began to drift off, they jolted him awake again, relentless as an incoming tide.

First and foremost, he was more certain than ever that Harry was one of those responsible for the disaster that he was convinced had been no accident. Everything seemed to point to his involvement. The fact that he had been right there on the very spot where the roof had come down. The argument he'd heard between Harry and George Golledge, who had himself been set upon by the dead carting boy's uncle. Bradley couldn't help thinking that a guilty conscience might account for Harry's surly attitude, along with the knowledge that he'd brought all his troubles on himself. He couldn't believe the man had always been so objectionable. Surely Lorna would never have married him in the first place, nor be so loyal to him now if she wasn't hoping and praying he'd get back to his normal self as his body slowly healed. He must have been a good husband and father once. Either that or she was a saint to put up with the appalling way he treated her.

Lorna. Something sweet yet painful twisted in his gut. How could she have taken hold of his every thought, every emotion so fast? But she had. From the first time he'd met her at the hospital, little by little she'd worked her way into his heart, and he was stunned and bewildered at the feelings that consumed him. He'd never expected to experience them again, and nor had he wanted to.

He'd been a young officer when he'd met Ella, and the brief affair they'd shared had been intense, all-consuming passion. Two hearts that had seemed to beat as one. Shared secrets. Laughter. Love. Tenderness. Quite simply, he'd worshipped her. When he had been posted to South Africa, she'd wept and promised to wait for him, and fool that he was, he'd believed her. Her father was an officer in his regiment, after all, and however hard it was to be parted, he'd thought she would understand. Throughout the bloody conflict, his memories of the time they'd spent together and his hopes for the future had sustained him.

But when he returned to England, wounded and battle-scarred, there was no joyous reunion. In his absence, Ella had married a handsome and well-to-do solicitor she had met at a charity ball. Bradley had been devastated. More hurt than he would ever have believed possible. And he had vowed never again to trust a woman. There had been flings, and he was not proud of the fact that he might have broken other hearts as his had been broken. But no one had touched his soul as Ella had, and he'd set up his defences so as to be sure no one ever would.

Yet now, just when he had least expected it, those defences had been breached. By a woman he scarcely knew. A woman he had no business feeling this way about, who was another man's wife. And whose world would fall apart if he found proof that Harry Harrison's actions had caused the deaths of a man and a boy.

Angry with himself for his weakness, Bradley thrust aside the blankets, pulled on his woollen dressing gown and went downstairs. He could hear Harry's snores coming from the parlour, and he thanked God the man's injuries prevented him from climbing the stairs. If he had been in bed with Lorna, Bradley didn't think he could have borne it.

He poured himself a generous whisky, added a splash of water and took the drink upstairs. On the landing, he paused for a moment outside the room where Lorna was sleeping and imagined her lying there, her hair fanned out across the pillow. Fancied he could smell the sweet scent of her as he had when she'd cried into his shoulder. Imagined how soft her skin would feel beneath his touch. Felt his body responding to the very thought of her . . .

He shook his head, even more angry with himself for such foolishness, and returned to his own room and his empty bed.

Lorna was dreaming. Unlike Bradley, she had fallen asleep the moment her head touched the pillow. Though she was in a strange bed, the little sleep she'd had the night before and the busy and stressful day that had followed had exhausted her, and at first a deep and dreamless slumber had enveloped her. It was only much later that a vivid scenario began playing, a little like a moving picture, but one of which she was a part.

She was in the field above Northfield Terrace that ran down to the railway line, and Marjorie, Vera and Nipper were there too. Marjorie was plodding along behind her on a well-worn path on one of the long ridges that might almost have been giant steps into the valley below; Vera had run ahead with Nipper, throwing a stick for him to fetch.

Lorna was feeling tired, as tired as she had been when she'd fallen gratefully into bed, and the grass – as long and lush as it would be in high summer – looked inviting. She sat, then lay down, looking up at the sky, clear blue with fluffy white clouds like lace, and feeling the grass tickle her cheek and bare arms. It was sheer bliss. Until a sudden wave of anxiety prickled over her skin, sharper and more insistent than the teasing grass. She sat up, looking around, and was somehow not surprised to find she was no longer in the field, but in the pit yard, with the headgear towering over the office block and the rail lines along which the team of ponies dragged cartloads of waste headed for the batches.

She saw the pit every day as she passed it on her way into town and never gave it a second glance, so familiar was it. But not now. The sun was shining, but the whole place appeared to be in deep shadow, the air heavy with claustrophobic fear, a fear that seemed to emanate from the crowds of people who were milling about. The dream was slipping into nightmare, and Lorna looked around, frantically searching for her daughters. She couldn't see them anywhere.

She called their names, but her voice was lost in the cries and murmuring of the gathered throng, and when she tried to push her way through it, it closed in around her. Her anxiety was becoming panic. Where were the children? Where *were* they? Something terrible had happened. She knew it with every fibre of her being, and her panic grew. Oh dear God, where were they?

And then she caught sight of Bradley. She wondered briefly why he was wearing his overcoat on a warm summer's day, but it was a fleeting thought only. She had to get to him. He would know what to do. Miraculously a path opened up in the mass of bodies that had hemmed her in, and she began to run towards him, but her feet seemed to be sinking into quagmire. He'd be gone before she reached him.

'Bradley!' she called. And he looked up and saw her. Came towards her, moving swiftly across the ground that had bogged her down.

'The children!' she gasped. 'I can't find the children!'

'It's all right,' he said. 'They're safe. It wasn't them.'

She didn't stop to wonder what he meant by that. If Bradley said they were safe, they were. She sobbed with relief. And then his arms were around her, her face pressed into his shirt front. The moaning crowds had vanished, and the two of them were alone. His hands were in her hair, undoing the pins so that it fell loose to her shoulders. She lifted her face. His was close, so close. Happiness surged through her. Everything truly was all right. He'd made it so, just as he always did. Oh Bradley . . . Bradley . . .

His mouth was on hers, gentle at first, then harder, more urgent, and she felt herself responding. Wanting him. Suffused with joy that he wanted her . . .

The dream was fading. She was rushing up towards wakefulness as a diver might rise from the seabed, and however hard she tried to cling to the dream world, it was receding.

Yet the aura of wonder and happiness remained, warming her through. She lay for a long moment not daring to move. Savouring it. Not wanting it to end. Ever . . .

'Mammy.' Reluctantly she opened her eyes. Vera was beside her bed, one hand rucking up her nightgown between her legs. 'I need the potty, Mammy.'

'It's under your bed, Vera.'

'I can't find it. Oh hurry, Mammy. Please!'

'All right. I'll come and help you look.'

Lorna hauled herself out of bed and back to reality.

A dream, that was all it had been. A dream. One she had no business having. But what a dream! Awful. Horrifying. And then . . .

She followed Vera into the children's room. And the blissful aura went with her.

Chapter Seventeen

It was the chatter of the girls in the next-door bedroom that finally woke Lorna. She opened her eyes to full daylight, something that usually only happened during the summer months. For a moment she was puzzled by the unfamiliar surroundings and wondered too why she felt so happy – happier than she'd felt in a long time. Then it all came flooding back. The upheaval of the day before. And the dream that could be the only reason for the way she was feeling, its aura still warming her through and lifting her heart.

She couldn't stay here thinking about that now, though. If it was daylight, it must be late. Nipper would need to be let out, the girls would be wanting their breakfast, and most importantly, she didn't want Bradley to think she was taking advantage. She got out of bed, went to the window and opened the chintzy curtains to bright, cold spring sunshine.

Her room at the rear of the house looked out over a long garden. Immediately below the window was a flagstone yard, and beyond that a patch of lawn, a garden shed, some fruit trees and a stretch of bare earth that must be the vegetable plot. As she watched, a pair of magpies landed on the grass, then took off again, flapping away towards the woodland that bordered the garden on either side. One for sorrow, two for joy, Lorna thought, and smiled.

'Mammy! You're awake!' Marjorie was in the doorway that connected the two bedrooms, Vera beside her.

'Why aren't you dressed, Mammy?' Vera demanded accusingly.

'Because I've only just woken up,' Lorna said. 'I don't know what the matter with me is, sleeping so late.'

'You were tired, I expect,' Marjorie said, sensible – and kind – as ever.

'Yes, I was. Very tired. But I must get on now. Mr Robinson will think we're lazy lie-a-beds.'

'*We're* dressed,' Vera offered.

And so they were. They'd put on the same pinafores they'd worn the day before. Marjorie's hair was plaited and tied with ribbons, and for once it looked as if Vera had brushed hers.

'Can we go downstairs?' Marjorie asked.

'And explore!' Vera was now at the window looking out in wonder at the expanse of garden.

'You'd better wait for me. I won't be long.' Lorna crossed to the chair where she had left her clothes in a neat pile the night before.

There was a jug and basin on a marble-topped washstand in one corner of the room, but the jug was empty. She had been too tired last night to even think of filling it.

She dressed quickly, and as she brushed her hair and twisted it up into a pleat, she found herself thinking again of the dream. Bradley taking out the pins, running his fingers through her nut-brown curls as they cascaded to her shoulders . . . A little thrill ran through her, tweaking a nerve deep inside her, and she felt the all-too-familiar flush rising in her cheeks. She had to stop thinking about that dream, she warned herself. Just now she was alone except for the children, who probably wouldn't notice. But it would be a different story if it happened when she was with Bradley – or Harry. But she didn't want to stop thinking about it. Oh, she really didn't want to!

She licked her fingers and wiped the last of the sleep out of her eyes.

'All right. You can go down now. But please, do remember you are guests in someone else's home, and try to behave yourselves.'

An oak-cased grandmother clock stood at the foot of the stairs in the narrow hallway, and when she glanced at it, Lorna was shocked to see the hands pointing to almost eight. She could scarcely believe she'd slept so long, and her sense of guilt only increased when she heard voices coming from the kitchen and realised that both Bradley and Harry were already up and about. The children, who had run down the stairs ahead of her, stopped in the hallway, shy suddenly, and it was left to Lorna to lead the way.

With some trepidation, she pushed open the door. The table was set with crockery, bread, butter and jam, and the two men were sitting at it nursing mugs of tea.

'I'm so sorry. I overslept,' Lorna said.

'Lazy mare,' Harry grunted, and Lorna saw Bradley shoot him a look of disgust.

'Don't apologise. You must have needed it,' he said pointedly. 'I'll make some fresh tea.'

'Oh, I can do that,' Lorna began, but he was having none of it.

'Sit down. That's an order. And what would the children like?' he added as Marjorie and Vera crept in behind her.

Marjorie looked to her mother uncertainly, but Vera piped up: 'Milk, please.'

'Vera!' Lorna warned, embarrassed, but Bradley only smiled.

'Lucky I've already been to the farm then, isn't it?'

'Oh! Does the milk come straight from the cows?' Vera said in wonderment. 'The milkman brings ours. In bottles.'

'I'm afraid he doesn't deliver this far out,' Bradley said, amused. 'I have to go every morning and collect mine. In a jug.' He indicated an enamel pitcher that stood on a Welsh dresser. 'You can come with me tomorrow if you like.'

'Oh yes please! Will we see the cows?'

'I shouldn't think so. They'll be either in the milking shed or out in the fields.' Bradley was busying himself spooning tea into the pot and reaching for the kettle, which was singing on the big old range.

'I'd better take Nipper out. He'll be crossing his legs,' Lorna said, and the dog, hearing his name, emerged from under the table and circled her feet expectantly.

'There's no need,' Bradley said, depositing the pot of tea on a trivet in the centre of the big table. 'He's already been out. I took him up to the farm with me. Just sit down and relax. He can wait until you've had your breakfast, I'm sure.'

'Have you had yours?' Lorna asked.

'No, we were waiting for you. Weren't we, Harry?'

Harry scoffed, but said nothing. The implication was clear. He didn't see why he should have had to wait if Lorna couldn't be bothered getting up at a reasonable time.

'Shall I cut some bread?' Lorna asked, anxious to cover the awkward moment. 'Sit up, girls. You need to make a good breakfast. We're going to the market today, remember.'

'Yes!' cheered the irrepressible Vera.

By the time they reached it, the market was already busy. Smasher the Chinaware Man was advertising his crockery in the

big yard that fronted both the main entrance and the neighbouring
George Hotel, throwing plates into the air so that they shattered
as they fell to the ground, and the children were eager to stop
and watch for a bit. They never tired of the noisy promotion,
although they were anxious to move on when a young miner,
cheered on by his mates, climbed into the dentist's wagon, where
the dentist was waving aloft a large pair of metal pincers, to the
delight of the crowd that was gathering.

'That is so horrible!' Marjorie said, and Vera wondered
aloud if the young man would get a threepenny bit if he left his
extracted tooth under his pillow, as she did when she lost a milk
tooth.

Lorna shuddered. 'He deserves more than a threepenny bit
for what he's putting himself through!'

'Better than days and nights of raging toothache,' Bradley
pointed out.

Passing the fruiterer's stall, and the quack doctors Rainbow
and Quilley, they went into the main market hall. The children
made a beeline for the sweet stall, and Bradley bought them
each a paper twist of jelly babies, then left them at the stall that
sold small toys and novelties, where they could browse to their
hearts' content while he and Lorna shopped. As they made their
way to the far end of the market, where a plump farmer's wife
sold butter, cheese and bacon from a marble slab, they passed
the stall that would have been Lorna's if she had gone ahead
with her plan. She felt a twist of regret, but at the same time she
knew that it had been a pipe dream that would probably never
have worked, and would have caused her a great deal of worry
and hard work into the bargain. She could still do orders from
home, though, if Arthur was willing to make the deliveries.

Along the way they bought mackerel as she had planned,
fruit and vegetables from the greengrocer, and chuck steak,

pig's liver, and a leg of pork from the butcher. Bradley insisted on paying for it all.

'You must let me get the cheese and bacon,' Lorna said, feeling guilty. 'We're the ones eating the lion's share, after all.'

'We'll see,' was all he said.

There was a long queue at the farm stall. Lorna was enjoying watching the farmer's wife cutting slabs from a big round cheese with a wire, and slicing ham from the bone with a terrifying long and sharp knife, when she saw the two children weaving their way through the shoppers. She'd expected them to be happy enough looking at the toys and novelties for a while yet, and was surprised to see that they were both looking anxious.

'What's wrong, girls?' she asked.

'It's Mrs Golledge,' Vera said. 'She was asking us lots of questions, and Marjorie didn't like it, did you, Marjie?'

Instantly Lorna was on high alert. 'What sort of questions?'

'Where we'd gone to.'

'You didn't tell her, I hope.' Lorna spoke sharply.

'We said we didn't know,' Marjorie said, but Lorna could tell it wasn't the whole truth. Marjorie was as transparent as the day was long.

'Are you sure?'

'That's what *I* said.' Marjorie was looking both anxious and guilty. 'And Vera only . . .'

'I said I didn't know too! And I don't. Not really.'

'But you did say it was up a long lane where Daddy used to take us when we went to see Granny and Grampy,' Marjorie reminded her.

Vera pouted. 'I don't understand anyway. Why shouldn't I tell Mrs Golledge? Or anybody?'

The queue had shortened without Lorna noticing, and Bradley touched her elbow.

'You're next.' He lowered his voice. 'Leave them to me.'

'Yes?' The farmer's wife was a woman of few words and sounded impatient. Somehow Lorna managed to ask for the things she wanted, still worrying about what the girls had said, and what might happen if their whereabouts got out. She paid for the butter, cheese and bacon as she'd promised, then hurried across to Bradley and the girls, who had retreated to the market's rear entrance. Marjorie still looked anxious, but Vera had seemingly forgotten all about the breach of confidence. She was hopping up and down with impatience, and grabbed Lorna's arm.

'Mr Robinson says we can buy a windmill each!'

Lorna shook her head in exasperation, and Bradley caught her eye.

'Stop worrying!' he mouthed.

If only it was that easy! Her life these days seemed to be a rocky road riddled with potholes, and she was at a loss as to how to negotiate them. She followed Bradley and the children back to the toy stall, keeping a wary eye out for Lil Golledge. There was no sign of her now, but Lorna couldn't wait to get back into Bradley's motor and leave the bustling market – and the risk of meeting someone else she knew.

Lil Golledge wasn't the only one who'd seen Lorna and Bradley together in the market.

Mercy Comer had gone there to buy chrysanthemums. Her mother liked to put fresh flowers every week on the grave of a child she'd lost as a toddler so that it looked cared for when folk went to church on Sunday. Today, however, her rheumatism was playing her up and she had asked Mercy to do it for her.

The flower stall was quite close to the main entrance, and while she waited to be served, Mercy glanced around idly. When

212

she spotted Bradley, her initial reaction was delight – she'd already decided she would send him another message by way of her brother on Monday, telling him she had more information, but a chance to speak to him without having to wangle a meeting was even better.

Her pleasure was short-lived, however, because he wasn't alone, but with a woman and two children!

As she gawped, shocked, they disappeared from her sight down the aisle that ran parallel to the one where the florist sold his wares. But she'd seen enough to realise that the man she'd set her sights on was involved with someone else, seriously involved by the look of it, and she felt sick with dismay.

By the time she'd purchased the chrysanths and walked through town to the churchyard, however, she'd begun to gather herself together. She wouldn't give up so easily. By fair means or foul she was going to fight for this man. It wasn't just that she found him compellingly attractive; until he'd rebuffed her, she'd even dared to dream he might marry her and give her the sort of life people of his standing enjoyed. As for this woman, well, Mercy knew she was younger and prettier than her, and her way with men had never before failed her. Oh, it might take her a little longer than her conquests usually did, but he was a prize worth fighting for. She just had to persevere. And perseverance, Mercy thought, was her greatest strength.

Bradley parked the motor in the drive, and he and Lorna carried their purchases into the kitchen while the two children stayed outside playing with their paper windmills, which were spinning merrily in the brisk breeze. Harry was nowhere to be seen. Lorna wouldn't have been surprised if he'd gone back to bed. But Nipper hadn't come out to greet them either, which was unusual. When she'd stowed the perishable food away in the pantry – a walk-in pantry, no less, with high wooden shelves and a marble cold slab – she went into the parlour to see if the dog was there, He wasn't, but Harry was reclining in a comfortable chair, his bad leg propped up on a leather pouffe.

'Where's Nipper?' she asked.

Harry shrugged. 'He's around somewhere, I 'spect.'

'He's not in the kitchen or the dining room.'

'Upstairs, then.'

'He shouldn't be. He knows he's not allowed.'

But she went to check anyway, hoping the puppy wasn't up to mischief. He had a penchant for socks, and she hoped he hadn't found some of Bradley's and started chewing holes in them. But he wasn't upstairs either.

Beginning to feel concerned, she went back downstairs. Bradley was fiddling with the knobs of a wireless set, from which a tinny voice was emanating. Under normal circumstances, Lorna would have been fascinated. They didn't have a wireless set at home, and how a simple square box could transport what someone was saying miles away in London was a mystery to her. But just now she was too worried about the puppy to take the slightest interest.

'I can't find Nipper,' she said.

'Perhaps he's in the garden,' Bradley said, still twiddling the knobs.

'I don't think so. If he was, he'd have come running when he heard the motor.' Not waiting for Bradley's reply, she went back to the parlour. 'Did you let Nipper out, Harry?'

'Yeah. He was bothering, like 'e does.'

'And you didn't watch him? Oh, you are hopeless!' She dashed out through the kitchen and into the garden, frantically calling the dog's name. There was no response.

Bradley had followed her out, and by the time she had

reached the end of the vegetable patch, he was coming down the path towards her.

'He's not here!' Her voice was rising to near hysteria. 'Harry let him out and he's gone!'

'He could be in one of the fields.' By contrast, Bradley was the calm voice of reason. 'The wall's not very high. He could have got over it. Look, I'll try one, you try the other. I'll give you a hand getting over.'

He was right. It wasn't a high wall, just three layers of rough stone piled one on top of the other, but there were no footholds that Lorna could see, and she knew she'd have difficulty climbing over it without help. Bradley made a stirrup of his hands and hoisted her up so she was able to scramble onto the top and drop down on the other side.

From here she could see that the field was dotted with clumps of bramble bushes that were beginning to sprout new life. But of Nipper there was no sign. There was always the chance that he was ferreting behind one of the hedges or in the bushes, though, and she started across the field, soggy from the recent rain, calling his name. There was no response.

Eaten up by anxiety and a sick feeling of dread, she walked back the way she had come, hoping against hope that Bradley had had more luck. If Nipper had gone out onto the road, heaven only knew where he'd ended up, and if he was in the woods . . . There were old mine shafts that weren't properly covered in there, Harry's father had once warned.

One of the stones on this side of the wall had come loose, and taking enormous care, she managed to get a toehold on it and haul herself up and over, landing with a thud on the path beneath.

As she regained her balance, she saw Bradley scrambling over the wall on the other side of the vegetable patch. She looked at him hopefully, but he shook his head. Her heart sank again and tears of despair pricked her eyes.

'We're never going to find him, are we?' she said.

'We will,' he assured her. 'He might be trying to make his way back to Northfield Terrace. Dogs have an amazing instinct about these things. I'll go back to town and look for him.'

'I'll come with you.'

The two girls had run to greet them, anxious for news. When they'd realised Nipper was missing, their windmills had been forgotten, though both still clutched them in the folds of their pinafores.

'Can we come too?' Vera piped up.

'No. I want you to stay here in case Nipper comes back,' Lorna said.

'But Daddy's here,' Vera pointed out.

'I don't trust Daddy not to let him run off again.'

The children looked startled. Lorna never criticised Harry openly in front of them, but this time she didn't care.

As Bradley cranked the engine to life, Lorna climbed up into the passenger seat, then they set off along the track, both scouring the hedgerows that bordered it on either side as they drove. Down the dip to Littleton Lane and up the other side. Around the bends and down to the main road. But no sign of Nipper. At the foot of the poorly made-up track that led to Northfield Terrace, Bradley brought the motor to a halt, and Lorna clambered down.

Together they walked up the track, looking into the gardens of the other houses in the rank as they passed. They didn't see anyone they could ask, but then it was approaching dinner time and no doubt everyone was inside. In any case it was too cold to be sitting out, and too early in the year to be tending rose bushes or planting bedding.

The gate to number 3 was open. 'It'll be that blooming postman again!' Lorna said. 'He never closes it after him.' Since they'd had Nipper, she'd cursed him silently almost every day when she'd had to go out in all winds and weathers to shut it. But though it was one of his favourite spots, Nipper wasn't in the garden. They trudged the rest of the way up the track, and when they reached the corner of the rank, Lorna reached for Bradley's hand, anticipating the horrible moment when they would discover that the dog wasn't here either. His fingers squeezed hers and she clung to them, panic and despair a tight knot in her throat.

But . . .

'Oh my God!' Her breath came out on a gasp of disbelief.

Lying outside the back door, head between his paws, was Nipper.

Lorna dropped Bradley's hand and began to run along the trackway between the houses and the outbuildings, but before she had gone more than a few steps, the puppy was bounding towards her, frondy tail wagging furiously, leaping up at her with such enthusiasm that he almost bowled her over.

'Oh Nipper! Nipper!' Tears of joy and relief were streaming down her cheeks as she lifted him into her arms and buried her face in his fur. 'You bad dog! You gave me such a fright!'

'Well, you've got him back. That's the main thing,' Bradley said, and she raised her head, her wet eyes full of gratitude.

'Oh thank you so much! You were right! But how did you know?'

'Just a hunch.'

'I'd never have thought of it. He could have been waiting here for someone to let him in for goodness knows how long. Though I suppose Flossie would have found him eventually. I'm only surprised she hasn't already.'

217

'Perhaps no one's been out the back door.'

'I suppose . . .' Lorna stiffened suddenly. Someone had emerged from one of the houses towards the far end of the rank. Someone she most definitely didn't want to see.

'Lil Golledge!' she hissed, thrusting Nipper into Bradley's arms, finding the key in her pocket and unlocking the door. 'Come on! Quick! Let's get in.'

She rushed into the house, Bradley following, still carrying Nipper.

Quite suddenly Lorna saw the funny side of it and collapsed in a fit of giggles.

'What?' Bradley asked.

'Us! Two grown people running away from a miserable old woman!' she managed between chuckles.

Bradley set Nipper down. 'I wasn't running away from anybody,' he protested. But he was grinning broadly. 'I don't suppose there's any hope of a cup of tea,' he added.

'I think I could do with something stronger! A glass of brandy is what I need,'Lorna said with feeling.

'You little toper!'

She giggled again, then regained control of herself. 'It's for medical emergencies,' she said primly.

She went into the front room and retrieved the brandy – a quarter bottle – and two glasses from the chiffonier. 'Here we are. You'd like some too, I expect.'

'If you insist.'

Nipper, who had been running around sniffing as if to make sure everything was still in its proper place, lay down on the hearthrug with a deep sigh and curled himself into a ball, head tucked between his rear legs.

'He's tired himself out,' Bradley said with a smile.

'I should think he has, the little monster.' Lorna poured

brandy into the glasses, then handed one to Bradley and raised the other in a toast.

'To finding Nipper!'

He clinked his glass with hers. 'Amen to that,' he said ruefully.

Lil Golledge stood, hands on hips, thin lips curled in a sneer, watching the back door of number 3. Something was going on there and no mistake. She hadn't been close enough to identify the man, but sure as eggs were eggs, it wasn't Harry.

Lil waited, hoping to see them come out again, her arms wrapped around herself for warmth, but eventually the cold wind got the better of her and she was forced to go back inside. But her numb fingers and toes couldn't detract from the glow of satisfaction that came from her belief that Harry Harrison was being cuckolded, and anticipation of the shame he'd feel if – when – it got out. She sniffed and wiped away a dewdrop that had run down her nose. Shame and disgrace were no more than that man deserved.

Chapter Eighteen

Bradley and Lorna sat side by side on the sofa Harry had used as a bed since the accident, sipping their brandy.

'Where did you get this?' Bradley asked, teasing. 'It could strip wallpaper.'

'We can't all afford the best stuff.' Lorna, who couldn't stop smiling, took another mouthful and tried not to cough.

'I suppose it would be fine for setting the Christmas pudding alight,' he suggested.

'Or making the children sick when they feel bilious.'

'That too. Definitely,' he agreed.

'It's just what I needed, though, after the fright I had. The thought of losing Nipper . . .'

'I know.' He was silent for a moment, clearly thinking something over. 'While we're alone, there's something I wanted to talk to you about.'

'Oh yes, and what's that?' she asked playfully. She thought she'd forgotten how to flirt, but she was flirting now, and she didn't care. This was something else the cheap brandy was good for – making her forget her inhibitions.

But Bradley was being serious. 'I know you're worried about being able to pay the rent on the cottage when you move into it,' he said. 'And I could really do with some help around the house

– tidying up, preparing a meal, washing my socks, that kind of thing. As I told you before, I haven't yet got around to finding someone. If you were prepared to fill the vacancy, it could solve both our problems.'

'Oh!' Lorna was taken by surprise and it sobered her up momentarily. She had thought of looking for some kind of cleaning job, before the idea of a baking business and the events that had followed had put it out of her mind, and she couldn't think of anyone she'd rather work for than Bradley. But was it wise, given her newly discovered feelings for him?

Then there was the question of how she would fit everything in. She was going to have to walk all the way into town and back again twice to take the children to school and collect them, even if she made them sandwiches so they didn't have to come home for dinner. And besides all that . . .

'I'm not sure Harry would be agreeable,' she said reluctantly.

'Surely he wouldn't object given that he's unable to provide for you and the children,' Bradley reasoned. 'You need to make some money, Lorna, and you'll be living a fair way out of town. Getting to my house would be much easier for you. It's no more than a ten-minute walk, and if the weather happened to be really bad, I could always fetch you or drop you off.'

Lorna was silent, biting her lip. She was tempted, oh so sorely tempted, but anxious too about the probable consequences. Harry's unpredictable temper and constant ill humour had been unbearable since the accident, and she had a nasty feeling that if she accepted this job, things would become impossible. She thought of what he'd said when he'd changed his mind about moving in with Bradley: *I'm not 'avin' you stoppin' with that man on yer own*. No, she couldn't see there was any way he'd agree to her working for him, and if she defied him, goodness only knew what his reaction would be.

'It's really kind of you,' she said, 'but Harry—'

Bradley frowned. 'It's time you stood up to him, Lorna. He rides roughshod over you from what I can see of it. You can't be happy living that way.'

His tone had become hard, and Lorna bent her head, unable to meet his gaze. No, she wasn't happy; if she was honest, she hadn't been happy for a very long time. She'd been merely existing. Too busy to even stop to think about it really. The love she'd once felt for Harry – *thought* she felt – had long since faded. There was nothing left but a sense of duty and, yes, resentment.

And what were his feelings for her? Something else she hadn't had time to think about, and now it struck her that he regarded her as little more than a convenience. A drudge. Someone to cook his meals and wash his clothes and do her wifely duty in bed when he felt like it. He wasn't violent towards her, unlike some, and though he'd raised his hand in anger on occasion, he'd never actually struck her. She wasn't even sure he meant to be unkind, but he certainly had no regard for her feelings. Never seemed to notice if she was feeling tired or down. Was impatient with her on the rare occasions she was ill, as if she was being intentionally awkward. Never offered to take the children off her hands to give her a break, had never so much as changed a nappy when they were babies, though she wouldn't really have expected him to. That was a mother's job. But he'd never got up to them if they cried in the night either. His excuse was that he had to work the next day. As if she didn't. And he never took her out. Seemed never to want her company. Always preferred to drink with his mates in the pub or the club. Goodness, he'd spent more time with George Golledge than with her – until they'd fallen out.

But there was one thing she had to be truly grateful to him

for – her children. They were her pride and joy. Her whole life, really. She had to humour Harry to ensure their home was a place where they felt safe, comfortable and loved. The inevitable rows they would witness if she crossed him would be upsetting for them, and she didn't want that. He might even take out his bad temper on them. In order to give them the stability they needed, it was vital they felt part of a happy family. For that she was more than willing to sacrifice her own happiness.

She raised her head, looked at Bradley. 'I'm sorry, but I have to think of the children,' she said. 'If I went against Harry's wishes there would be ructions, and I don't want them to be caught in the middle of something like that.'

There was a bleakness in his eyes. 'Oh Lorna,' was all he said. But the wealth of meaning in those two words spoke so very much more.

There was nothing for it; he'd have to take the bull by the horns and speak to the dead carting boy's mother, Bradley decided reluctantly. She must know who was responsible for the roof fall that had taken her son's life, otherwise she wouldn't have talked to her brother about it and he wouldn't have set out to attack George Golledge. Surely, he thought, she would want the perpetrators brought to justice and would be prepared to tell him what she knew? He wasn't sure where she lived, but he could find out the lad's address from the records kept in the colliery office, and this was as good a time as any to go there and check.

Lorna was in the kitchen peeling potatoes to go with the mackerel for their evening meal. It wasn't what she was used to – she'd told him that normally she ate at midday with the girls and warmed Harry's on a plate over a saucepan of simmering water when he got home from work. But by the time they'd found Nipper, it had been too late to cook a midday meal. In

Jennie Felton

any case, Bradley guessed she knew he was accustomed to eating in the evening and was anxious to disrupt his routine as little as possible.

'I just need to pop out for a bit. I won't be long,' he said, shrugging into his coat. He kept it deliberately vague. He wasn't yet ready to tell her that he believed Harry was one of those who had caused the roof fall. That would be hard enough when he had the evidence. Hard, but unavoidable.

When he reached Milverton, he was surprised and none too pleased to see Cameron's Ford parked outside the office block. He'd have to explain his reasons for being here, and though he thought the general manager was coming around to his way of thinking, he was afraid he would say that visiting a grieving mother and asking probing questions that might well upset her was inappropriate.

Cam was behind his desk, pipe in mouth as usual, studying the records of the week's coal yield at the various collieries under his control. He looked up as Bradley came in.

'Bradley! What brings you here on a Saturday?'

Bradley decided he might as well answer honestly. 'I want to look up the home address of the carting boy who died in the roof fall,' he said. 'I'm still trying to get to the bottom of what happened, and I think his mother has a pretty good idea who was behind it.'

Just as he'd expected, Cam frowned. 'I'm not sure it's a good idea to bother her at a time like this.'

It was warm, even stuffy, in the office, and the strong smell of paraffin suggested that Cam had been here some time with the little Aladdin stove going full blast.

'It's the only way I can think of to be sure I'm on the right track,' Bradley said, unbuttoning his coat.

'Sit down then, laddie, and let's talk about it.' Cam produced

224

a stone tea bottle from beneath the desk and a hip flask from his pocket. 'Get yourself a mug and we'll have a wee drink. The tea's a bit stewed, but it's still warm, and the brandy will make it taste better.'

Bradley fetched a mug from the cupboard on the wall and Cam poured milky tea into it and added a generous measure of cognac. The smell of it, tickling his nostrils, reminded Bradley of the cheap brandy he'd shared with Lorna. This was very different, no doubt about it. But even if it was the finest on the market, that experience had been far more enjoyable than he expected this one to be.

Cam relit his pipe and nodded at him. 'So, let's see if we can come up with a plan of action,' he said.

By the time they were done, they had consumed another tot of brandy and the bottle was empty.

'I can't say I like the idea of calling on the mother,' Cam said, 'but if it's necessary, so be it. We can't have hotheads working in our pits, and the sooner we get to the bottom of it all, the better.'

'My sentiments exactly,' Bradley said. 'I can't help feeling sorry for Lorna – Mrs Harrison – though. This is going to turn her world upside down, as if she hasn't suffered enough already.'

'Lorna, is it?' Cam sucked on the stem of his pipe. 'Watch your step there if you know what's good for you.'

'There's nothing . . .' Bradley began defensively, then bit off the words. If she accepted his offer of work, Cam would get to hear of it, and he was shrewd enough to know that it hadn't been made solely out of sympathy. 'She's a fine woman,' he said. 'She deserves better than the scumbag she married and the trouble he's caused her. And if I can help her when all this comes out, then I intend to do so.'

'It's your business, laddie.' Cam knocked his pipe out into the ashtray on his desk and nodded towards one of the shelves laden with files and ledgers. 'You'll find what you're looking for on the far left. Go and see the carting boy's mother with my blessing. And it's my opinion you should do it without delay.'

'Thank you, sir.'

In truth, they were long past such formality, but somehow at that moment it felt right to Bradley.

He fetched the ledger and found the address he needed. He'd go there now and hope to catch her in, he decided.

The house was one of a rank of six, which looked to Bradley to be privately owned. They were larger than the long row of miners' cottages opposite, from which they were separated by a narrow track leading to open fields that dropped down to the Hillsbridge valley.

He stopped his motor at the kerb outside, opened the gate and walked down the path between two strips of lawn. The grass was beginning to grow for spring, but clumps of last year's leaves still lay under the laurel hedge, depressingly brown and soggy.

He knocked at the front door, and after a few minutes it was opened by the small, wiry woman he'd last seen at her son's funeral. On that occasion she had been dressed all in black; now she was enveloped in a floral wraparound apron, but the pinched cheeks and the haunted look in her eyes was just the same.

'Mrs Maggs, I don't know if you remember me from when I called on you before, but I'm Bradley Robinson, the colliery safety officer.'

She sniffed, almost contemptuously, and it wasn't hard to guess what she was thinking.

'I'm sorry to disturb you,' he went on, but she cut him off.

'I don't want any more o' your lot 'ere. I've already 'ad Fairley's agent askin' wot 'e could do fer me, an' I told 'im nothing, thank you very much. If you can't bring my boy back, just leave us alone.'

As she went to close the door, Bradley's heart sank, but he wasn't about to give up so easily.

'Please hear me out, Mrs Maggs. My reason for wanting to speak to you is quite different. I don't believe, as Sir Montague seems to, that the roof fall was an accident. I think it was caused deliberately, and I'm working to get justice for Tommy. I want those responsible to face the full force of the law.'

For a long moment she looked him up and down silently, tiny muscles working in that ravaged face, as if trying to decide if she was being told the truth. Then she sniffed again, somehow injecting all the bitterness that accompanied her grief into that one little sound.

'If that's right, you won't get very far. They won't tell you nothin'.'

'Which is why I've come to you, Mrs Maggs. I'm as angry as you are about the way the truth of the matter hasn't been properly investigated, and I think you may be able to point me in the right direction to get the inquiry reopened.'

After another pause, she seemed to make up her mind. She opened the door fully and stood aside.

'You'd better come in.' Relieved, Bradley did as she said, finding himself in a long, narrow hall. She closed the door and indicated that he should follow it towards the rear of the house. 'Down there. Second on yer right.'

It was, he realised, the living room. A polished gateleg table with a crocheted runner on which stood a yellow glass jug and bowl was surrounded by four high-backed chairs; a sofa was backed up to the longest wall, and there were easy chairs each side of the fireplace. A small, wizened man sat in one of the fireside chairs, hawking into a khaki-coloured handkerchief. From the look of him, Bradley surmised this must be the boy's grandfather.

'This is the colliery safety man, Jim,' Mrs Maggs said. And to Bradley: 'My husband. Tommy's father.'

The man hawked again, struggling for breath, and Bradley recognised the symptoms of pneumoconiosis, the miners' lung disease. Clearly it had aged him far beyond his years.

'Mr Maggs,' he said, then, as the man attempted to rise from his chair, he added: 'Don't get up, please.'

Jim Maggs sank back gratefully, but regarded Bradley suspiciously, his rheumy eyes narrowed.

'Wot do 'e want?'

'Says 'e's tryin' to make sure somebody answers for wot 'appened to our Tommy.'

'Huh! Fat chance o' that. You ain't told 'im anythin', I 'ope, Edie.'

'I 'aven't said anythin' yet.'

'An' you bain't goin' to neither. 'Tis none o' 'is business.' The man spoke forcefully, and the effort set off a bout of coughing.

Bradley waited until it subsided.

'It's my intention to see the men who did this punished,' he said. 'To do that, I need your help.'

Mr Maggs spat phlegm into his handkerchief and rallied. 'You'll get nothin' out'a me.'

Despite his loss, despite what his years underground had done to his health, it was clear that the spirit of comradeship and solidarity that existed amongst the miners was still the most important consideration to him.

His wife, though, had other ideas. 'How can you say that, Jim? They didn't care who got hurt, an' now our son's dead.'

'I d'a know that. But you don't grass up your mates.'

Another man spoke from the doorway. 'Don't be a bloody fool, Jim. Tell 'im wot you told me.' He was thickset, swarthy, a day's growth of stubble shadowing his face. Bradley realised straight away that in all likelihood this was the man who had attacked George Golledge in the Miners' Arms. The one who had followed Mercy Comer home and demanded to know where Golledge lived. Mrs Maggs's brother, though he looked nothing like her.

'You keep out'a this, Mark Wheeler. 'Tis none o' yer business,' Jim Maggs snarled.

'Yer wrong there, my son.' Wheeler strode into the room. 'Tommy's my flesh and blood too, an' so's his mother. If you won't speak out, I will.' He swung round to face Bradley. 'I went after one o' them. Golledge. I'd've beaten the livin' daylights out'a 'im if it hadn't been four against one. O' course, they was all in on it. But Golledge was one o' the ringleaders, him an' another chap . . . wot did you say 'is name were, Edie?'

Mrs Maggs cast a nervous glance at her husband, then muttered, 'Harrison.'

So he'd been right, Bradley thought grimly.

'And they were the ones who brought the roof down?' he asked.

'No doubt about it. They'd been planning it fer a while t' show his lordship 'ow dangerous 'tis underground, an' 'ow they deserve t' be a lot better paid. 'Twas Ted Yarlett's widow told Edie wot 'appened.' He turned to his sister. 'You reckon she felt bad about Tommy getting killed 'cos Ted knew about the plan an' kept quiet about it, isn't that right, Edie? Tell 'em wot she said.'

Edie plucked at a fold in her apron. 'She said Ted 'ad 'eard some'ut was afoot, but 'e couldn't believe they'd go through with it so 'e never said nothin',' she said tremulously. 'But she reckoned that when he saw what they were up to, 'e tried to stop them an' Tommy must've followed. That's why they were right there when it 'appened.'

Bradley wasn't sure that was the whole truth, but since Ted Yarlett was dead too, it scarcely mattered. He couldn't be held accountable now.

'Stop them doing what exactly?' he asked.

'Well, set off the explosives, o' course,' Wheeler said derisively.

'So there was explosive involved?'

'Course there were. An' a lot stronger than what they expected, I reckon.'

'And how did they come to get hold of it?' Bradley asked.

Wheeler shook his head. 'That I couldn't tell 'ee. You don't know, do you, Edie?'

'Mrs Yarlett didn't say.'

Bradley frowned. 'Nor who set it off?'

'No. But it would'a bin one o' them two – 'Arrison or Golledge, that's fer sure. They were the agitators.'

Bradley nodded, satisfied. 'Well, thank you very much. You've been a great help,' he said. 'I won't disturb you any longer.'

'Just make sure you get 'em,' Mark Wheeler grated. 'Or so help me, I'll do fer both the buggers.'

'No!' Edie said sharply. 'We don't want any more trouble brought to our door. An' it won't bring our Tommy back.'

'She's right,' Bradley cautioned. But it crossed his mind to wonder if it could have been this man who had started the fire in Northfield Terrace. He was certainly angry enough, and from what Mercy had said, he had been prepared to stop at nothing to avenge the death of his nephew. Yet another reason to ensure that those who had been responsible for the roof fall were brought to justice without delay.

'Thank you, Mrs Maggs,' he said as she showed him out. 'You've been a great help. And you have my word I'll do everything in my power to get justice for your boy.'

At least his own suspicions as to who the perpetrators were had been confirmed, Bradley thought as he drove away. But he still didn't know where the explosives had come from, and that would be vital evidence. He knew that once again he would be faced with a wall of silence from the miners, and the only way he could think of overcoming the problem was to go back on his vow to cut contact with Mercy Comer and ask her if she could try to gain the confidence of the clique of men who frequented the Miners' Arms. He was in no doubt now that they had all been in on what was planned, even if they had taken no active part. Could she be persuaded to do more than simply eavesdrop on their conversation? Ask the questions he so badly wanted the answers to? He rather thought she could. And she was resource-ful enough – and popular enough with the men – to pull it off, if he wasn't much mistaken.

He dared not risk going to the Miners' Arms over the weekend, though. The men were likely as not to be there. There was nothing for it but to wait until Monday, when they'd be underground during the day. He itched with frustration and impatience. He really wanted to make some progress with his investigation sooner rather than later.

As he approached the centre of town, he was not best pleased to see that the level crossing gates for the line to Frome were closed and the signals down – a train must be expected, and if the engine needed to take on water, he could be there for some time. He pulled up, looking for the first sign of it; as yet there was none, and he couldn't see anyone waiting on the platform. But he did see a woman standing on the pavement on his side of the road, waiting to cross, and he could scarcely believe his eyes. From behind, it looked for all the world like Mercy, almost as if she'd materialised simply because he'd been thinking of her.

He tooted, and when she turned round, he could see that it was indeed her, with a laden shopping basket over her arm. He waved and gesticulated, indicating that she should climb into the front passenger seat of the motor, and she did so rather too eagerly.

'Mr Robinson! What a surprise!'

'A stroke of luck,' he said. 'I wanted to speak to you.'

'Really?' She gave him a coy look.

At that moment, a goods train appeared, smoke billowing – an engine pulling three trucks. The driver blew his whistle, and the train ran through the station without stopping. A moment later, the gates were opened by a man in the uniform of a railway employee.

Bradley realised he couldn't say all he wanted to say sitting here in the middle of the road; the only course of action open to him now was to drive her home. Since he'd seen her cross the second set of railway lines when they'd met at the mill he guessed she lived in one of the plethora of miners' cottages on the far side of the valley,

'I expect you'd be glad of a lift. Your basket looks heavy,' he said, pulling away and bumping over the rails. 'Where exactly do you live?'

'The top rank of The Batch,' she said. 'I can easily walk down if you drop me by the Rose and Crown. But you shouldn't go out of your way for me.'

'No trouble.' He drove across the second set of railway lines and turned right past the corner of the market square and into the road that rose steeply. 'As I said, I've been hoping to see you, but I wasn't sure of the best time to catch you.'

'And I've been hoping to see you.' She managed to make the words into a double entendre, pausing slightly before going on. 'I've been eavesdropping on the clique of troublemakers, and I've got a lot to tell you.'

'That sounds interesting,' Bradley said non-committally.

'Oh, it is.' Mercy paused again, waiting for his reaction. When none came, she said, 'There was a fire, wasn't there? At Harry Wot's-is-name's house?'?'

'Harry Harrison. Yes. Luckily the family escaped unharmed, but it could have been a very different story,' Bradley said grimly. 'What about it?'

'Well, George Golledge thinks it was deliberate. He reckons it was the same man as attacked 'im – the carting boy's uncle – wot started it, to get 'is own back for wot 'appened at the pit. T'would make sense, after all. If you ask me, George an' Harry were in it together. They're both as bad as one another.'

She drew a quick breath, her eyes going wide with horror as a thought struck her.

'Oh my Lord! If 'e's out for revenge he might try again! Do some'ut even worse!'

There were no flies on Mercy, Brad thought.

'Don't worry,' he said. 'I've moved them to a place of safety.'

'That's all right then,' Mercy said, relieved.

They had reached the track leading down to the Batch houses where she lived. Brad stopped the motor but left the engine running.

'You've done well, Mercy, and I'm grateful,' he said. 'But I still need more detail. Where they got the explosives that brought the roof down. Which of them actually set it off. And why what was intended as a protest turned into a disaster. Do you think you could take things a step further? Gain their confidence and fill in the blanks for me?'

Mercy frowned. 'I can try.'

'Good girl.' He climbed out of the motor, took her heavy basket from her and helped her down. 'Can you manage from here?'

She nodded, clearly reluctant to leave him. 'How do I keep in touch with you?'

'Give your brother a note for me.'

'And will you take me for another ride in your motor so that I can tell you what I've found out?'

Bradley smiled. He didn't want to lead her on, but this was too important to risk losing her help.

'We'll see,' he said enigmatically.

There was a spring in Mercy's step as she walked down the track, her basket hefted onto her hip. If she could find out what he wanted to know she'd be able to see him again. Just as long as he wasn't seriously involved with the woman she'd seen him with in the market, perhaps there was hope for her . . .

She stopped short as a sudden thought struck her. Was it possible that the woman was Harry's wife? The two little girls his children? Was the place of safety he'd taken them to his own home? Suddenly it all came together, making perfect sense. Where better to have them where he could ensure no harm came to them? That was who they were, she was sure of it now.

But why would he have Harry under his roof if he believed

he had been involved in whatever it was that had caused the roof to come down?

Mercy shook her head, utterly confused. But hers not to reason why. She'd just try to do as he'd asked and hope for the best.

Chapter Nineteen

Flossie was in the garden cutting a cabbage to go with the leg of mutton she was roasting for their Sunday dinner. She straightened up, lifting her apron to make a cradle for it, and surveyed the row that still remained – far more than they'd need before the spring greens were ready to eat. They'd finish up on the compost heap, she supposed. What a waste! If Lorna had been able to go ahead with the plan for the market stall, she'd have been able to sell them to folk who could do with them. As it was . . .

A sudden thought struck her. What was stopping her from taking the stall herself? It was something she'd always fancied doing. She ran a thoughtful eye over the rest of the garden. There were still plenty of parsnips and carrots waiting to be harvested, and trays of potatoes, apples and pears stored in the shed. There were even some sprouts still coming on – Albie always planted in stages, and not many were keen enough on gardening to make time to do that.

A big smile lit up Flossie's face. She'd seen yesterday that nearly everything had been sold from the jewellery stall, and those items that remained had been reduced in price. It wouldn't be long before it was vacant; as long as it hadn't already been let, she was going to stake her claim to it.

This was just what she needed to fill the hole left in her life since Lorna had moved out of the house next door. Oh, she still had Albie and Jack and Arthur of course, but she couldn't talk to them the way she could to another woman, and she'd missed her girls terribly since they had left home and gone into service.

She slipped her old knife into her pocket and hurried indoors to tell Albie what she planned to do.

Thinking things over, Bradley came to the conclusion that he should talk to Lorna about Harry's involvement in the roof fall sooner rather than later. If Mercy Comer was able to gain the confidence of the other conspirators and come up with evidence that he could take to the authorities – and the police – the whole sorry tale would be out in the open. Harry would almost certainly be charged with a serious offence, and the consequences for Lorna would be devastating. If he could prepare her for what was to come, at least it wouldn't be quite such a terrible shock. Give her the chance to come to terms with the inevitable before the heavy arm of the law fell on Harry's shoulders.

But how to break it to her? Where to begin? He honestly didn't know. And how would she react? Would she tell Harry what was going on? Fly at him angrily for being fool enough to do something so dreadful? Or try to make excuses for him? If Harry got to know about it before Mercy had managed to infiltrate the circle of men who knew exactly what had happened that fateful day, would the ranks close even more tightly?

It wasn't likely that Harry would be able to warn his mates, though, Bradley thought. He was in no fit state to walk all the way into town; he'd scarcely been able to walk along Northfield Terrace to Bradley's motor, or up the path from the road to his

Jennie Felton

house. But he was improving much faster than Bradley had expected. He was getting used to managing the contraption on his leg, he supposed, and it certainly seemed to be doing what it was meant to.

Bradley sighed. He felt as if he was chasing his tail in ever decreasing circles, and that wasn't something he was used to. As a cavalry officer he'd been nothing if not decisive. Even when it was a matter of life or death he'd kept a clear head, swiftly weighed the options and acted. But then, of course, there had been no Lorna in the picture. It was because of her, and his feelings for her, that he was torn now, and he cursed silently. After losing Ella, his first love, he'd vowed never to allow himself to be at the mercy of a woman again. But he had ignored the warning signs when he'd first met Lorna, and by the time he'd recognised the way she was affecting him, it was too late. Now a battle was raging between his heart and his head, and somehow he had to find middle ground.

But in the last resort, he knew it was Lorna that mattered most.

He still hadn't reached a decision as to how to broach the subject with Lorna when an opportunity that was too good to miss presented itself. It was early on Sunday afternoon. Lorna had cooked a midday meal – the leg of pork they'd bought at the butcher's yesterday, potatoes and greens – but Harry had done nothing but criticise and complain. The crackling on the pork wasn't crisp enough for his liking. The cabbage was overcooked, the gravy too thick.

'I'm still getting used to Mr Robinson's range. I'm used to a hob and an oven beside the fire,' Lorna had explained, but Harry had only scoffed.

'Can't be that different. Call yourself a good cook? Our

238

Marjie could'a done better.' To emphasise his point, he had pushed the offending crackling to the side of his plate.

'Well, I'm enjoying it,' Bradley said. 'You've done a great job, Lorna.' The children had agreed, tucking into what was one of their favourite dinners.

When they'd finished, and Nipper had made short work of the rejected crackling, Harry went off for a 'snooge', as he called it. The girls took Nipper into the garden, where they found a stick under one of the trees to throw for him to retrieve, while Lorna set to work clearing up the used crockery and pans. To her surprise, Bradley fetched a tea towel and offered to dry as she washed up. In all their married life, Harry had never done such a thing.

'I'm sorry about Harry,' Lorna said apologetically as she immersed the glasses they'd used in soapy water. 'I don't know why he's behaving like this. He's always had a short fuse, it's true, but since the accident he's become impossible. I can only think it's because he's ashamed that he's unable to support us as he thinks he should. Feels he's less of a man.'

'That might be part of it,' Bradley said carefully.

'Or perhaps a big stone fell on his head. I've heard something like that can change someone's personality.'

It was something Bradley had wondered about. There was something almost insane about Harry's behaviour, and he seemed to be getting steadily worse. He'd seen it happen with a man in his regiment, and it hadn't ended well. But now was not the time to warn Lorna. What he was going to tell her would be shock enough for the moment.

'You've never wondered if it's because he feels guilty?' he said carefully.

'For not being able to provide for us? That's what I said.'

'No. Not just that. Because he knows he was at least partly to blame for what happened and his injuries are his own fault. Worse still, a man and a boy are dead.'

He saw Lorna's whole body stiffen, then she swung round, soap suds flying from her hands. 'What are you saying? That Harry was responsible for the roof fall?'

Bradley had no way of knowing if she had suspected this much herself. 'I don't think it was an accident.' His tone was gentle but firm. 'There was a lot of unrest among the miners. I think they believed some kind of accident would draw attention to their working conditions. I don't suppose for one moment they intended it to be as catastrophic as it turned out. But something went horribly amiss. Perhaps I'm wrong – I sincerely hope I am – and Harry had nothing to do with it. But I have to get to the bottom of it. Ensure nothing similar can ever happen again. I'm sorry, Lorna, but there it is. I'm the safety officer. It's my job to make working underground as safe as it can possibly be. And if I do find out that Harry was involved, I shall have to report him, just as I will any other guilty parties.'

For a long moment Lorna was silent, and he saw a succession of emotions that he couldn't interpret chase one another across her face. Finally she spoke, and what she said cut him to the quick.

'Is that the reason you've offered me a job? Been kind to us? Or pretended to be? To worm your way into my confidence? Did you think I knew something that would help you build a case against Harry? Well, I don't know anything. And if I did, do you really think I'd betray my husband? My children's father?'

'Lorna . . .'

'Don't "Lorna" me! I trusted you, Bradley. I really trusted you. And all the time . . .' There was no mistaking the hurt in her voice.

Her soapy hands were balled into fists half hidden in the folds of her apron, and he reached for them, but she batted him away.

'Don't touch me!'

Shocked as he was at the violence of her reaction, he recognised it for what it was. The primitive instinct of survival. Not for herself, nor for Harry. She was a lioness fighting for her cubs. And he knew too that there was some truth in what she was accusing him of. But even now, painful as it was that she should think so badly of him, he couldn't turn his back on what he knew was right.

'A boy died, Lorna,' he said. 'A boy whose mother loved him just as you love your girls. And a man, too, who's left a grieving widow and children. They deserve answers. To see justice done. I'm truly sorry, but I do believe Harry was one of those responsible for the roof fall, and I'd be failing in my duty if I didn't pursue the matter.'

'Even if it destroys us?' Her tone was bitter.

'Believe me, I don't want that. It's the reason I'm being straight with you now. So that it won't come as a complete shock to you, and you'll be able to begin to come to terms with it. Make plans . . .'

'How noble of you.' Her voice wavered a little, but the bitterness was still there, more pronounced than ever. 'Is the cottage ready yet? Even if it's not, we'll move into it. Or we'll go back to Northfield Terrace. I don't want to spend another night under your roof. Not now that I know why you've brought us here.'

Bradley shook his head despairingly. 'You're not thinking straight, Lorna. You'll be putting the children's lives in danger if you go back there. We'll talk again when you've calmed down. Then, if you still feel the same way, I'll make every effort to see that the cottage is made fit for you to move into as soon as humanly possible.'

'And what are you going to do about Harry? Are you still going to pursue him?'

'I'm sorry. You must see I have to.'

She turned back to the sink, plunging her hands into the soapy water that was now cold and scummy.

'Then just leave me alone.'

Defeated, Bradley tossed the tea towel down onto the draining board and walked away.

Left alone, Lorna emptied the greasy water into the big stone sink, then covered her face with her wet hands, frightened, but desperately hurt too. How could she have been such a fool? How could she have believed for a moment that Bradley Robinson cared one jot about them? Worse, how could she have secretly wished he could be more than a friend in need, her knight in shining armour? Fool, fool, fool! He was just like the rest of the upper classes. Hard. Uncaring. Working only in his own interests. And duplicitous.

And now, just when she'd thought things couldn't get any worse, the darkest cloud yet was looming on the horizon. Enormous. Ominous. Moving ever closer. Yes, she'd had her own suspicions that Harry might have been involved in the plot that had brought about the tragedy, but she'd tried to dismiss them, or at least play down his part in it and the consequences. From the way Bradley had spoken, however, it seemed he believed Harry was one of the prime movers rather than simply a stupid man who'd gone along with it. And little as she wanted to believe it, her gut instincts were telling her he was right.

She thought again of the animosity she'd encountered from

Lil Golledge, and the uncomfortable way others in the town had made her feel. Though they were keeping quiet about it, amongst themselves they blamed Harry. Then there were his dark moods. She'd tried to put them down to the pain and disability he was struggling with. But it could well be that they stemmed from guilt, as Bradley had suggested. Guilt . . . and regret, though that was probably most likely for the injuries he'd brought on himself.

What would happen to him if Bradley found the evidence he was looking for? She hardly dared think about it, but she couldn't escape the dread of what would follow. Not so much for Harry; if he'd done this dreadful thing, he deserved whatever punishment was meted out to him. But the children shouldn't have to bear the burden of the condemnation of a community. The shame. They'd done nothing wrong, but they'd be tarred with the same brush. Stigmatised. Bullied, no doubt, by their classmates who would have heard their parents calling Harry a murderer. How could Bradley do this to them?

In a way, she could see he had no choice. But that didn't make it any easier. And it didn't stop the sick ache in her heart. Though that hardly mattered now. She had more important things to worry about. Never mind the stupid dreams she hadn't even really dared to dream. Survival for her and her children had to be her first and only consideration.

Bradley was cursing himself. Hating that he'd hurt Lorna and that he had nothing to offer her but the stresses and strains of what lay ahead. Wondering what the hell had happened to him that he could think of nothing but her. And why it hadn't occurred to him that she might react as she had to what he'd had to say. He knew it would have been even worse if she'd only learned his part in Harry's downfall when the truth finally came out, but that was small consolation.

Why hadn't he realised that she might think she had been used and be angry and bitter about it? As an army officer, he'd prided himself on thinking through every eventuality and weighing the consequences of every decision. He was slipping. Going soft. Well, the damage was done now. She despised him – not without reason – and knowing it hurt more than he'd have believed possible.

Through the window he could see that the girls were still in the garden, playing with the puppy. He put on his coat, found the dog's lead and went outside.

'I'm going to take Nipper for a walk,' he said.

'Can we come?' Vera asked excitedly.

It was the last thing Bradley wanted. He would have liked some time alone, out in the open air, attempting to clear his head. But neither did he want them going into the house and finding their mother upset, or perhaps even discussing with Harry the impending disaster that would tear their lives apart.

'If you'd like to,' he said, and both girls nodded eagerly. 'I just need to tell your father that you and Nipper are with me, or he and your mother will wonder where you've got to.'

'I'll tell them!' Vera volunteered, but Bradley refused the offer firmly.

'You can put Nipper's lead on and wait by the gate. I'll only be a minute.'

Harry was lying on the sofa, his eyes closed. But Bradley didn't think he was asleep, and didn't much care if he was.

'I'm taking the girls and the dog for a walk,' he said, and sure enough Harry's eyes opened immediately.

'Just as long as they don't expect me t' do the same when we'm out'a here,' he said ill-temperedly, reminding Bradley once again – if a reminder was needed – just what a boor he was. The thought of Lorna with him turned Bradley's stomach.

'Not much chance of that, I imagine,' he said shortly, and went back into the garden, where Marjorie, Vera and Nipper were waiting.

The atmosphere around the tea table was strained. Even the children sensed it, though Lorna was obviously making an effort to hide her feelings from them and keep things as normal as possible. She'd made sandwiches with the ham they'd bought yesterday, and stewed some bottled plums she'd found in the larder, evidently left behind by the former manager of Oldlands when he had moved out. But she studiously avoided Bradley's eyes, and spoke only to the girls, in a tone of forced cheerfulness. Harry, of course, was being Harry, complaining that there was too little mustard on the ham and the plums were too sweet. 'Makin' my teeth ache,' he'd commented sourly. But he exhibited no sign of being aware of what had passed between Bradley and Lorna, and for that Bradley was grateful. The longer he remained in the dark, the better.

Towards the end of the meal, to his surprise, Lorna spoke directly to him for the first time since the altercation. But although her tone was even, giving nothing away, the hurt and hostility in her eyes was unmistakable.

'Could you give me a lift into town when you take the girls to school tomorrow? There are some things I'd like to collect from our old home.'

'Of course. Get whatever you need, and I'll drive you back again before I go into work.' He matched his tone to hers.

'Thank you.' Cold. Formal.

'I could do with comin' too,' Harry said.

'If you tell me what you want, I'll fetch it for you.' Lorna

245

spoke as coldly to her husband as she had to Bradley. 'You know it's a squeeze fitting us all into the motor.'

'We managed before,' Harry retorted. 'Want to be on your own with your man friend, do you?'

A wash of colour flooded Lorna's cheeks. She glared at Harry, locking her eyes with his and nodding surreptitiously in the direction of the children. 'Don't talk such nonsense, Harry.'

He smirked. 'Hit a nerve, have I?'

Bradley intervened quickly. 'We'll make room for you if you want to come along.'

'As it 'appens, I do, yes.'

'That's settled then.'

'Would you like some more plums, girls?' Lorna asked in an attempt to divert this uncomfortable conversation. Vera responded with her usual enthusiasm, but Marjorie shook her head, looking anxious.

She didn't miss much, Bradley thought. He wondered how they were all going to get through the next few days, when this tension and awkwardness could only get worse.

'Well, you fellas, aren't you the clever ones!' Mercy Comer said flirtatiously as she delivered a fresh round of drinks to George Golledge and his pals.

'Wot you on about?' Shorty Dallimore asked.

'Ah!' Mercy tapped her pert turned-up nose. 'I think you know very well, Mr Dallimore. You were lucky to get away with it, though. An' none of you hurt too bad.'

The men exchanged glances, all concern suddenly, and Mercy pressed home her advantage.

'Have things improved for you since the roof fall? Better pay – that's what it was all about, wasn't it?'

'Now look 'ere . . .' George Golledge began, but Ticker Greedy silenced him with a look. If George lost his rag, as he so often did, it would only make things ten times worse.

'I don't know what you d'a think you know, Mercy, but wotever it be, there's no truth in it.'

'Really? Mercy fluttered her eyelashes at him, pleased that for once she had the upper hand. 'You'd be surprised what I do know, I reckon. Where the Harrisons are, for instance.'

The men's surprised expressions would have been almost laughable if this wasn't so important to Mercy – and to George Golledge, who could no longer contain himself. He was desperate to know where Harry was. If things turned nasty, he didn't want to be the one left carrying the can.

'Where's that then?' he asked sharply.

Mercy tossed her head. 'Wouldn't you like to know!'

'You're just sayin' it,' Moses Whittock scoffed. 'You don't know any more'n we do.'

'You're wrong there. But I'm sayin' nothin' unless we do a trade,' Mercy said archly. 'I'll tell you where the Harrisons are if you'll answer a question I've got fer you.' She waited a beat to let her words sink in, then leaned low over the table, and momentarily the men were distracted by the ample cleavage on view. She looked at each of them in turn, a little smile playing about her mouth, her eyes teasing, yet full of promise.

'Wot I'd like to know is . . . where did you get the explosives? And who actually set them off?'

Instantly the appreciative leers were replaced with expressions of shock and consternation. They hadn't for one moment thought the pretty barmaid was acquainted with any of the details of what had happened. They'd assumed she was only repeating the gossip and supposition that was rife amongst those who hadn't been in on the plan. But if she was asking questions

---

about explosives, she must know more than they'd credited her with. And it followed that others might be putting two and two together and coming up with the right answers.

George Golledge looked from one to the other of his mates, a question in his eyes, and each of them nodded. It was almost as if they were able to communicate by telepathy, and perhaps they could. The very nature of the hard and dangerous job they did forged bonds that were in many ways inexplicable. Having obtained their agreement, he pushed away his glass and leaned his elbows on the table.

'Tell us where Harrison is, an' mebbe we'll tell you what you want'a know.'

Mercy hesitated, wondering just why these men – and Golledge in particular – were so keen to know where they could find Harry Harrison. It wasn't to ask him to join them for a glass of beer, that much she was sure of. More likely they wanted to even a score. Mercy didn't much care if they gave him a beating – it was beginning to look as if he deserved it. But the children were a different kettle of fish entirely. And she couldn't forget about the fire that could easily have claimed their lives. Supposing it was these men who had started it, blaming Harry for a plan that had gone disastrously wrong? Much as she wanted some information to take back to Bradley, she couldn't risk something like that happening again. And in any case, there was no guarantee that they had any intention of telling her where the explosive had come from.

'You first,' she said.

The men looked at one another again. Perhaps Mercy didn't know anything that would incriminate them after all. She'd just heard idle gossip and was angling to see what more she could find out.

Moses spoke for all of them. 'All we'm sayin' is, if you d'a know where Harry is, you'd do best to ask 'im.' He winked at her, and sat back in his chair with a satisfied grin.

Mercy straightened, and tossed her head. 'I might just do that.'

She collected the empties, loaded her tray and flounced back to the bar, frustrated. She'd done her best. For the moment, there was nothing more she could do.

Chapter Twenty

Next morning, as she prepared breakfast and made packed lunches for the children, Lorna was feeling every bit as hurt as she had done the previous day. She couldn't blame Bradley for thinking Harry might have played some part in the roof fall at the pit when she'd suspected the same thing herself. But that he had been using her, as she saw it, to try to get evidence against him was something else entirely.

The atmosphere around the table as they ate was strained, and even the girls were subdued. They only brightened when they trooped out to Bradley's motor. Nothing could quite quench the excitement of another ride in this amazing contraption, though Vera was not best pleased that she had to ride in the rear seat again with her mother and Marjorie rather than in the front. 'I'll be sittin' there. I need the room fer me leg,' Harry had told her.

'There's plenty of room in the back today since we've left Nipper at home,' Lorna pointed out.

Bradley stopped at the junction with the track leading up to Northfield Terrace. 'I'll be back for you in about half an hour,' he said.

As Lorna and Harry were climbing out of the motor, they saw Arthur running down the incline on his way to school, and the irrepressible Vera did not hesitate.

'Oh – can we take Arthur too?' she piped up. 'He's our friend!'

'Vera!' Lorna reprimanded her sharply, but Bradley merely smiled.

'I don't see why not.'

'And can I sit in the front with him?'

'You'd better stay where you are unless you want to be late for school,' Bradley told her. 'You can ride in the front on the way home.'

A surprised Arthur, goggle-eyed with excitement, clambered nimbly up into the motor and Bradley drove away.

As Harry and Lorna walked up the sloping track, Harry said bad-temperedly: 'I s'pose you want'a go and see your pal Flossie Price. You might as well get it over with first as last.'

Lorna would have liked nothing better. Homesickness for this place and her friend was a dull ache in her chest. But she knew this would have to be a flying visit.

'I don't know if I should. We don't want to keep Mr Robinson waiting.'

Harry huffed scornfully. 'You don't want'a worry about he.'

It was on the tip of Lorna's tongue to tell him he should be very worried indeed about Bradley, though for a different reason, but she didn't. Harry had brought it all on himself, she thought bitterly.

As they turned the corner of the rank, there was Flossie, going across the track to the coal house carrying an empty scuttle. Her face lit up when she saw them.

'Lorna! You're back!'

'Only to collect some more of our things,' Lorna said ruefully.

'Well come in an' 'ave a cup o' tea, do! Lord, it in't the same wi'out you. Just let me get a bit o' coal.'

'I don't think I ought to stop, Flossie. We've only got half an hour.'

'Oh go an' 'ave a gas wi' yer mate. You know you want to.' Harry slotted the key into the door and turned it. 'I'll go on an' get wot I came for.' He went into the house, closing the door behind him.

'Well knock me down wi' a feather!' Flossie said. 'Wot's up wi' 'im all of a sudden?'

'Goodness knows. I don't.' Lorna was as puzzled as her friend. It was unheard of for Harry to take her wishes into consideration. 'I really don't think I should stop for tea, but I'll come in for five minutes.'

'Come on then. The coal can wait.' Flossie opened her door and Lorna followed her into the kitchen. 'So how're you gettin' on?'

'To tell the truth, I'm worried to death,' Lorna said. Though they were alone, she lowered her voice conspiratorially. 'Bradley – Mr Robinson – thinks Harry had something to do with the accident.'

She had expected her friend to be shocked, but Flossie merely sighed and shook her head. 'Didn't I say Albie'd heard all sorts of talk? 'Twas all done on purpose to make management sit up an' take notice. Harry an' George Golledge were thick as thieves before it 'appened, and now . . . well, they've fallen out, 'aven't they? There's something fishy there, don't you think?'

'I don't know what to think, Flossie. But what's going to happen to Harry if Bradley can prove it? What's going to happen to us?'

'It'll work itself out, you'll see,' Flossie said, reverting to her usual motherliness. 'An' truth to tell, if 'Arry gets sent to jail, you'll be well rid of 'im. You bain't happy wi' 'im, that

I do know. An' I'll tell you straight, I'd like t' see you with a man who treats you right. There, now I've said it.'

A wave of emotion rose in Lorna, threatening to overwhelm her. Wasn't that exactly what she'd been dreaming of? A man who treated her well. A man who loved her. A man like Bradley . . .

'I'd better go, Flossie,' she said. 'I'll come back and see you when I get the chance and we can have a proper talk. But not now.'

'I certainly 'ope so, 'cos I got some'ut to tell you.'

Flossie moved as if to envelop her in a hug, but Lorna headed quickly for the door. Just now, any display of kindness and affection would be her undoing.

'I'll see you then,' she said brightly, for all the world as if nothing was wrong, and hurried out. Back to Harry. Back to the nightmare her life had become. Back to insoluble problems, and disappointment and heartache.

Flossie wasn't for a moment fooled by Lorna's attempt at chirpiness. But she knew when to butt out. Lorna wouldn't thank her for saying any more now. Her pride would be badly hurt if she let anyone, even Flossie, see her cry. But if everything went pear-shaped, as Flossie feared it was going to, she'd be here, ready to do whatever she could to pick up the pieces. And in the last resort, Lorna would come to her, she felt sure. For the moment there was nothing she could do. Except say a prayer for her, perhaps. Flossie wasn't a religious woman. She hadn't been to church for years. But she thought that tonight, when she went to bed, she'd take her rosary with her, say as many Hail Marys as she could before she fell asleep. And hope that someone would hear her, and answer her prayers.

* * *

'I'm going to get Mr Robinson to drop me off at Littleton Lane,' Lorna said as she and Harry waited for Bradley on the main road. 'I want to see how it's coming along and do what I can to speed things up.' She indicated the cloth bag she was carrying. 'I've brought soap and wax polish and some rags for cleaning. Do you want to come and give me a hand?'

'I just want to get back and sit down,' Harry said. 'Me leg's paining me.'

This came as no surprise to Lorna He was carrying his old attaché case so he must have managed to get upstairs to fetch it, and that would have done him no good at all, she thought.

'You might as well take the things I've brought for the girls with you, then,' she said. 'It'll be less for me to carry when I'm done and ready to walk back to Mr Robinson's. They'll go in your case, won't they?'

'No, they won't,' Harry snapped, cradling the battered case to his chest as if he expected her to try to take it off him. Lorna was puzzled as to why he should want it, but she wasn't going to ask. Harry was old enough and ugly enough to decide for himself what he needed, and he'd probably have told her so if she'd questioned him.

At that moment, Bradley's Ford appeared round the corner at the bottom of the hill. 'Here he is now,' she said.

The motor chuntered up the slope and stopped for Harry and Lorna to get in. 'Did the girls get to school all right?' she asked unnecessarily as she settled into her seat.

'I watched them in.'

'And thanks for giving Arthur a ride too. He's a good boy.'

'One extra was no trouble.'

The conversation was civil enough, but the distance between them was as marked as before. As they turned off the main road, Lorna asked Bradley if he would drop her at Littleton

Lane. He didn't ask her why; that was taken as read – that she wanted to get things ready so as to move in as soon as possible, Lorna guessed.

'You'll need the keys,' he said, fumbling in his coat pocket and passing them back to her. 'I'm bringing Amos out later, but he has work to do at the pit first. I think you'll find he's done a good job so far, though.'

'It's really kind of you to spare him,' Lorna offered.

'It's the least we could do under the circumstances.' Bradley pulled over to pass a woman and a boy who were trudging up the steepest part of the hill. 'Now there's a lad who should be in school,' he added, hastily changing the subject as if he found her gratitude embarrassing.

'Old enough t' be at work if you d'a ask I,' Harry snorted.

'The leaving age has been raised since your day, if you remember,' Bradley said. 'And not before time.'

'Didn't hurt I, leavin' at twelve,' Harry retorted.

Neither Bradley nor Lorna bothered to answer him, and they rode the rest of the way to Littleton Lane in silence.

'Will you be home for your dinner?' Lorna asked him as she climbed down.

'I'm not sure. It all depends.'

'It will only be cold cuts anyway,' she said. 'I won't be finished here in time to cook.'

'Don't worry about it. I had a good breakfast and I can always get a sausage roll or a pasty from the bakery.'

Lorna nodded. The familiar sick feeling was turning her stomach over and over as it always did the minute she was in the vicinity of Littleton Lane. She watched Bradley's motor disappear round a bend, then swallowed hard at the knot in her throat and walked towards number 1, every step an effort of will. The curtains of the next-door cottage twitched as she was nearing the door: Mrs Parfitt, the witch woman, on the lookout again. Did she spend all her time at the window? Lorna wondered. Or did she simply keep a sharp ear out for a motor or the clip-clop of a horse's hooves and then rush to find out who was there?

She found the right key on the bunch Bradley had given her and fitted it into the lock, which was still stiff with disuse. When it finally turned, she gave the door a determined push, and it scraped over the stone flags as it would continue to do until Harry got around to planing it down. But at least this time there were no cobwebs to negotiate, and she could see that the floor and walls had been washed. The smell of putrefying birds still lingered, but now it was just a faint whiff that she might not even have noticed if she hadn't been expecting it.

She went from room to room throwing the windows open in the hope of dispelling the last of the stench, and was pleasantly surprised to see that they too had been thoroughly cleaned, as had the steep, narrow staircase and one of the two bedrooms. The other, though, had not yet had the benefit of Amos's attention. There was a thick layer of dust on a mahogany tallboy that must have been left by the previous occupant, a couple of manky rag rugs that felt damp to the touch, and black mould growing around the window casing. She cleared it as best she could, got the window open and tossed the rugs down onto the path below. Then she dusted the tallboy, which she'd decided to keep, and cleared the drawers of the yellowing newspaper that lined them, swept the floor and scuffed a bundle of her cleaning rags over it with the toe of her shoe.

What she really needed was a bucket of water, but no pipes had been laid to deliver it so far out of town. She knew where the well was, however – she'd drawn water from it often enough when they had been living with Harry's parents. There wouldn't be time for it to heat up in the copper before she had to get back to Bradley's to make Harry his dinner, but cold water would be better than nothing.

She went downstairs again. She remembered seeing a heavy bucket in the outhouse last time she'd been here, so she let herself out and went to fetch it, resisting the urge to look around to see if Mrs Parfitt was watching. Ignoring her was the best policy, she had decided. She found the bucket and started up the gravel path that ran the length of the garden alongside the neglected vegetable patch until it reached an earthen walkway that served all three cottages. The well was positioned more or less centrally along this. She attached her bucket to the cast-iron crook on the end of the waxed rope, then dangled it over the mouth of the well and began turning the handle to lower it until she heard the satisfying splash as it hit the water below. It didn't take long to fill. The springs that fed the well had been swollen nicely by the heavy rains they'd had recently. She turned the handle more slowly now, jiggling the rope, the knack coming back to her as she did so, although it was a good many years since collecting water for the Harrison household had been one of her chores.

She was less used to carrying a whole bucketful of water, though. When she'd cranked it up and attempted to lift it onto the low stone wall that surrounded the well, she was quite shocked by its weight. She had to use both hands, and even then some splashed out and onto her shoes. I suppose I was ten years younger then! she thought ruefully.

She'd managed to get the bucket inside the house and was contemplating how best to carry it upstairs when there was an imperious knock at the door. She cursed silently. There was only one person likely to be calling on her here. Presumably the Littleton Lane grapevine had been active again, and Mrs Parfitt had told Harry's mother that she was here. Reluctantly she went to answer it, and there sure enough was Rose Harrison, her face set in the miserable lines that were an unpleasant harbinger of the way Harry would look very soon if his bad mood persisted.

'Mother.' Lorna used the term that was expected of her, though as always it stuck in her throat.

'Is Harry there?' Rose demanded without preamble.

'No,' Lorna said shortly. 'He's not.'

'Then you'd better come.'

'Where? Why?'

The thin lips tightened. 'There's somebody wants to speak to 'im. Since he's not 'ere, you'll 'ave t' do.'

'Who wants to speak to him?'

Mrs Harrison jerked her head back and sideways. It was the woman and boy Bradley had overtaken on the rise away from the main road. The woman's maroon coat and black hat, and the boy, tall and skinny, in clothes that looked too small for him, were unmistakable. But before today, Lorna had never seen them in her life, and she couldn't imagine why they would be looking for Harry.

'Who are they?' she asked her mother-in-law, who snorted.

'You'll find out soon enough. She'll tell you. 'Tis nothin' t' do wi' me.'

She marched back to the pair and Lorna heard her say: 'That's 'er. His wife. An' much good will it do you.' Then she stalked off up the track.

The woman was hesitating, as if unsure what she should do. Curious and a little perturbed, Lorna stepped outside, pulling the door partially closed behind her. As she approached, she could see that the woman was a good ten years older than her, though hard work and deprivation could age a person, and if the lad was her son, he'd likely be the youngest of a large family.

He looked to be about eleven or twelve, but his head was bent, chin almost resting on his chest, and really all she could see of him was a shock of ginger hair that had been cut with a pudding basin. He appeared to have outgrown his clothes by at least a couple of inches.

'I'm sorry – I don't think I know you,' she said. 'But if you wanted to see my husband, I'm afraid he's not here. We haven't moved in yet. Can I give him a message?'

The woman eyed her with suspicion. 'Are you sure he's not 'ere?'

'That's what I said.'

She sighed as if Lorna was being deliberately obstructive, and when she spoke again, her tone was bitter. 'Tell 'im I want to know why 'e's stopped sendin' Frank's money. An' when I can expect wot I'm due.'

Lorna couldn't make head nor tail of any of this. 'I think you've mistaken me for someone else. Who is it you're looking for?'

'No mistake,' the woman said firmly. 'It's Harry Harrison I'm after. Last I knew, 'e was livin' 'ere with his mother.' She nodded in the direction of Rose Harrison, who was standing outside her own house, watching the encounter from a distance.

'I really don't know what you're talking about. Who are you? And who's . . . Frank, did you say?' Lorna was utterly confused now, but also disconcerted.

The lad had been hanging back, head still bent, eyes fixed on the ground in front of him, hands thrust defensively into the pockets of his too-small trousers. Now the woman pushed him forward.

'This is Frank. Harry Harrison's son, that's who. An' I'm Mrs Presley. His auntie, wot looks after 'im.'

Lorna's world seemed to tilt on its axis. Her head spun, her vision blurred.

'Harry doesn't have a son,' she protested dazedly. 'He's got two little girls. Our children.'

'He most certainly does,' the woman scoffed. 'This is 'im right 'ere. 'Is son by 'is first wife, wot took bad and died. An' I've bin lookin' after 'im ever since.'

'This is nonsense!' Lorna barely knew what she was saying, and the woman – Mrs Presley – threw her a pitying glance.

'Didn't you know he'd bin married before? Hasn't 'e told you?' She shook her head. 'That's 'im all over. Oh, 'e were married all right – to my little sister, Greta. An' when she died, 'e couldn't get away quick enough. Left the boy with me and came back 'ome. Course, 'e'd 'ad the sack from the quarries by then.'

'The quarries?' Lorna repeated stupidly.

'Yeah. Out at Charter'ouse. That's where 'e was workin' when 'e first took up wi' our Greta. I warned 'er 'e was a bad lot, but would she listen? No, she married 'im anyway. Anythin' to save 'er good name. I've always said 'twas the shame and worry of it that killed her, though doctor reckoned it were a growth, an' they missed it because they thought 'twere milk fever. Terrible, t'were.'

She broke off, her eyes misting, then pulled herself together. 'Anyway, 'Arry promised me he'd pay fer Frank's keep if I'd look after 'un, and give 'im 'is due, 'e did, though not hardly enough to keep body an' soul together. But now I haven't 'ad so much as a brass farthin' fer weeks. That's why I'm 'ere.' She looked at Lorna. 'I don't s'pose any o' this is your fault. 'E's took you in just like 'e took in our Greta. But you can tell 'im from me, if 'e don't pay up sharpish, I'll be back, an' next time I'll be leavin' Frank with 'im. He's a good lad, no trouble really, but I've got nine o' me own, an' much as I'd like to keep 'im wi' me, I can't afford to feed ten.'

She touched the boy on his shoulder. 'Come on, Frank, we'd best be gettin' back. We got a long walk ahead of us. A good eight mile.' She nodded to Lorna. 'I'll bid you good day. But mind what I say – I'll be back, an' you and he can shoulder a burden wot's rightly 'is.'

'Wait!' Lorna was suddenly overwhelmed by a rush of guilt. This poor woman had been left not knowing why the money for the boy's keep had suddenly stopped, and she had come all this way because she was desperate. She couldn't let her leave empty-handed. 'Harry was hurt in an accident underground and hasn't been able to leave the house since. Without his wages we're hard pressed ourselves, but I'll give you what I can. Just let me get my purse.'

She hurried back inside, grabbed her purse from her bag and emptied it onto the kitchen worktop. She took the silver coins – five florins – went back to where the woman and boy were waiting and thrust them into her hand.

'That's all I've got. It's not much, but at least it will tide you over.'

Mrs Presley examined the coins and nodded. 'I s'pose it's better than nothin'. But I mean what I say. If I don't start gettin' some money regularly, Frank will 'ave to come back and live with you.'

With that, she turned and walked away down the track, the boy following her.

Chapter Twenty-One

When the pair had disappeared from view, Lorna went back into the cottage. She was in shock, dazed and trembling, her legs carrying her forward as if she was an automaton; they didn't even seem to belong to her. She felt sick, and her breath came in shallow gasps, but she couldn't stop moving about from one side of the room to the other, as if standing still would allow all this to become real. Her mouth was bone dry, even her lips felt parched and swollen, and she went into the kitchen, found a cup, dipped it into the pail of water she'd drawn from the well what seemed a lifetime ago, and drank. Then she leaned against the wall and slid down it to sit on the bare flagstones, knees drawn up to her chest, arms wrapped around them, head resting on top.

And still her thoughts churned, so that one minute she was thinking this couldn't be true, and the next she was overwhelmed by the enormity of it.

Harry had a son. A boy of about eleven or twelve from the look of him. He'd been married before. And she hadn't known. He'd never told her. Never even tried. Everything they'd been to each other had been built on a lie. The love she'd once thought they shared. The plans they'd made together. The children. Their life as a family. How could he do that? How could he keep something so important from her?

She straightened up, resting her head back against the wall, feeling the damp chill of it through the fabric of her blouse. Shocking as the revelation was, it explained a lot of things that had worried and puzzled her. His moods. The silences when he was lost in thought. But most of all the fact that they were always short of money. She'd thought that he was gambling on either the football results or the horses and losing his hard-earned wages to a bookie. But she'd been wrong. He'd been sending money to that woman towards his son's upkeep.

And now that he was no longer able to do that, she was threatening to bring the boy back and leave him with his father. She'd do it, Lorna had no doubt. She might even have left him today if Harry had been here. And what would they have done then?

A sudden flash of anger consumed her. How dare Harry place her in such a position? Presumably he'd thought he could get away with it and she'd never be any the wiser. Well, she knew the truth now. The time for reckoning had arrived.

Full of purpose now, she pushed herself up from the wall. Her mouth was dry again, so dry that it was an effort to swallow. She dipped the cup back into the pail of water and drank every drop. Then she put on her coat, picked up her bag and went out, locking the door behind her. She didn't want to talk to Harry, didn't want to ever see him again – the very thought of it made her stomach churn with revulsion. But she had no choice. This had to be done, and done now.

Anger and hatred driving every step, she set out along the lane.

As she let herself into Bradley's house Nipper came bounding out to greet her, but for once she ignored the little dog.

'Harry? Where are you?' she called.

When there was no reply, she went through to the parlour. Sure enough, there he was, sprawling on the sofa with a cup of tea at his elbow. He looked up bad-temperedly, as if annoyed at the interruption, though as usual he was doing absolutely nothing.

'Wot's up wi' you? Didn't expect you 'ome yet.'

'We need to talk, Harry,' she said shortly. 'I think you owe me an explanation.'

'Wot you on about? Explain wot?'

Lorna sat in one of the easy chairs so that she was at eye level with her husband.

'Why you never told me you were married before, and have a son.'

Momentarily Harry's face was blank with shock. Then he recovered himself.

'Wot bloody stupid gossip 'ave you bin listenin' to?' he blustered.

'No gossip. I have it from the horse's mouth.'

'My mother? She's goin' funny in the head. I've thought so fer a long time.'

'Not your mother – although there's no doubt she knew all about it. She liked knowing something about you that I didn't, I expect. And when they turned up looking for you, she was quick enough to bring them down to our cottage and leave them with me.'

'Who?'

'Your son, Frank. And a woman who said she was his aunt and has been looking after him ever since his mother died.'

All the colour drained from Harry's face. His mouth worked, but not a single word came out.

'She wanted to know why you've stopped sending money for his keep,' Lorna went on. 'And she said that if you don't pay up, she'll bring the boy back and leave him with you.'

'That bitch . . .' Harry mumbled.

'She didn't seem like a bitch to me,' Lorna said. 'Just a woman at the end of her tether. She's done right by him, looked after him because you wouldn't.'

'Couldn't,' Harry corrected her.

'Why not? You're his father. You could have brought him home with you when you came back to Hillsbridge. You were living with your mother, the woman said. She could have taken care of him while you were at work.'

'She wouldn't,' Harry said. 'She reckoned I'd got meself into the mess and I'd 'ave to get meself out of it.'

Lorna had no answer for that. She could well believe her mother-in-law would have taken that attitude. But it didn't excuse what Harry had done.

'Then you should have found somebody else to mind him. Not just walked away and abandoned him.'

'I paid 'er sister.'

'And now you can't,' Lorna said flatly. 'The poor woman was desperate. I gave her as much as I could—'

'You did *wot*?'

Lorna ignored him. 'How could you do it, Harry? Just leave your son like that? How often have you seen him since? When you took his aunt the money for his keep? Is that where you've been going when you told me you were at the pub?'

'I posted it. Regular as clockwork.'

'So you haven't even seen him. Why not? Did you just want to forget about him? Pretend he'd never existed?'

Harry was beginning to regain his usual belligerence. 'You've got it. I didn't want a millstone round my neck. I wanted to forget the whole bloody thing ever 'appened.'

'And that's why you never told me, I suppose.'

'Would you 'ave married me if I 'ad? I don't think so. You

wouldn't 'ave wanted to be saddled with a babby that weren't yours.'

'If you'd been honest, I might well have. I'm not completely heartless. I might have been a bit shocked at first, but I'd have understood. We'd have worked something out.'

'I wasn't goin' to risk it,' Harry argued. 'I just wanted a normal life, like everybody else.'

'How could it be normal when you were deceiving me like that?'

He changed tack. 'I never meant fer any of it to 'appen. I never intended to marry Greta. 'Twas only ever a fling. When a man's offered it on a plate, who's goin' t' say no?'

'A man with some principles. Who's prepared to take responsibility if there are consequences. I suppose the poor girl's father forced you into it.'

'Said he'd make sure I lost me job if I didn't make an honest woman of 'er. But the mud stuck anyway. Soon as she was in 'er grave they gave me me marching orders.'

'So you took the easy way out. Came back here to the mines. Met me, let me think you were a bachelor, and married me without telling me the truth. And you've kept it up all this bloody time.'

'Swearin' now?' Harry taunted her. 'That's not like you, Lorna.'

'I feel like swearing! I feel like . . . Oh, I just don't know who you are any more. And Bradley says you were behind the roof fall at the pit. Were you?'

Harry's face changed again. Grim. Feral, almost.

'Wot's 'e bin sayin' t' you?'

'Just that he doesn't think it was an accident. He thinks you and George Golledge and some of your cronies planned it so as to push Fairley into paying you more.'

'An' you believe 'im?'

'I don't know what to believe any more, Harry.'

'You think I wanted to end up crippled?'

'Of course not. Something went wrong. But—'

"Twas a fault. The inspector said so.'

'Bradley says the inspector took the easy way out.'

'Bradley, Bradley, bloody Bradley! Who does 'e think 'e is?'

The grandmother clock in the hall whirred and began to chime. Lorna listened with growing dismay.

'Oh my Lord! Is that the time? If he does come home at dinner time, he'll be here soon and nothing's ready.'

"E'll 'ave to wait then, won't 'e?'

She ignored the ill-tempered remark. 'We'll talk later.' She hurried into the kitchen, put some potatoes on to boil, and began setting the table.

Bradley didn't come home at dinner time, and Lorna was relieved. It would have been almost impossible to hide the raw antagonism between her and Harry, or the fact that she was so upset by this morning's shocking events. Her hands were still shaking, and she knew it would show in her face too. She just wasn't ready yet to share any of this. It would come out eventually, but for the moment at least it was between her and her husband.

They ate their meal of cold cuts and mashed potato in silence, and she was glad of that too. It was hard enough as it was to swallow a single mouthful. Harry, however, managed to wolf his down as if nothing had happened.

When he'd finished, she decided it was time to tackle him again.

'So what are you going to do?' she asked, fixing him with a steely stare.

'Wot about?'

'Your son. I don't know how much you've been paying for his aunt to keep him, but whatever it is, we can't afford it now, can we?'

He shrugged as if he didn't care one way or the other. 'Not unless there's anything left out'a wot Fairley paid us in compensation.'

'Not much,' Lorna admitted. 'Especially since I felt obliged to give that poor woman something. I've made it go as far as I can, and for now we're living on Bradley's generosity. But we shall have to pay our own way when we move into the cottage, and I don't know how we're going to manage, with you still unable to work.'

'Wot d'you expect me to do with this contraption on me leg? 'Ow long will it be on, anyway?'

'I'm not sure. We'll ask Dr Mackay when he next calls. Or perhaps Mr Robinson would take you into town to his surgery, though I hardly like to ask.' This time, Lorna deliberately avoided using Bradley's Christian name, as it would only set Harry off on another rant. 'He's done more than enough for us already.'

Harry snorted in disgust. 'Huh! Like accusin' me of bringing the pit roof down! As fer lookin' for work, town's the only place I'd get any, an' I can't walk there and back every bloody day. 'Twould kill me. Can't you find some charring work or summat?'

'Well . . .' Lorna waited a beat, knowing that what she was going to say would be fuel to the flames. But the time had come for straight talking, and she really didn't care any more what Harry thought. As for the secret feelings she had for Bradley, she wasn't going to think about those. 'As it happens, I've already been offered a job,' she said. 'Here, working for Mr Robinson.'

Harry's face was a picture. 'Doin' wot?' he demanded.

'Cooking, cleaning, washing . . . What do you think?'

'And a few perks thrown in, I dare say.'

'You're a fine one to talk, Harry Harrison,' Lorna flared, furious again. 'Mr Robinson doesn't have a son by some poor girl he only married because he had to – not as far as I know, anyway. And if you think I'm going to spend my hard-earned wages sending money to that woman, you've got another think coming. My first priority is our girls. Your son's keep is up to you. As for getting into Hillsbridge, when you're fit enough you'll just have to get yourself a bike. If you have to push it up the hills, at least you'll have something to lean on.' She paused to take a breath, and then went on. 'I'll give you what's left of the compensation to satisfy Mrs What's-her-name so that she doesn't come straight back here with Frank, but after that it's up to you. Do I make myself clear?'

'As day,' Harry said bitterly. 'I don't know what's got into you, Lorna.'

'I don't think you need me to tell you that,' Lorna said shortly, though she barely knew herself. But it felt good standing up to Harry at last. And like most bullies, he'd backed off in the face of it.

Why, she wondered, hadn't she done it sooner?

Bradley drove the girls home from school, but didn't stop to come in.

'Have you had a good day?' Lorna asked them, trying to inject some normality into the toxic atmosphere.

'Yes, really good,' Marjorie said. 'I got nine out of ten in the spelling test. And three big red ticks and a "well done" for the story I wrote about Nipper.'

'And I didn't get told off once!' Vera announced triumphantly.

'Well done. Now sit up and eat your tea. I've made an egg and bacon pie.'

'Aren't you going to have any?' Marjorie asked, seeing that only two places had been laid.

'We'll have ours later, when Mr Robinson gets home,' Lorna said. She didn't feel in the least like eating yet, and she suspected Harry didn't either.

When Bradley came home at about half past six, Lorna was still feeling nauseous, but she supposed she really should eat something – she'd had nothing but a few mouthfuls of ham since breakfast. But the pastry was like cardboard in her mouth and she could only manage the egg and bacon filling.

They'd almost finished eating when Marjorie and Vera came in from the parlour, where they'd been playing snap with a pack of cards Bradley had got out for them.

'Mammy, can we have tuppence each to take to school tomorrow?' Marjorie asked. 'We're collecting money to send to poor dogs and cats whose families can't look after them.'

Harry snorted contemptuously, but without hesitation Bradley put his hand in his pocket and came out with two silver sixpences. 'Will this do?'

Marjorie's eyes lit up at the sight of the coins. 'Oh thank you, Mr Robinson!'

But Vera looked dubious. 'Will they be heavy enough?' she asked her sister.

'Vera!' Lorna scolded.

'I think pennies would be better,' Vera said, unabashed. 'The collecting box has a little wooden dog, and you have to put the money on a tray in his mouth and then he drops it in the box.'

'Well, take the sixpences anyway, and I'll see if I've got some pennies,' Bradley said, amused.

'I've got some,' Lorna said quickly. There had certainly been coppers amongst the small change left in her purse when she'd given the florins to Frank's aunt. 'I'll get them.'

She got up and fetched her bag, but to her dismay her purse didn't seem to be in it, and suddenly it dawned on her. She'd emptied it onto the kitchen worktop at the cottage and been in such a state she'd forgotten to put it back.

'I'm going to have to go back to Littleton Lane,' she said. 'I've left my purse there.'

'Typical!' Harry grumbled.

'Hardly surprising, given what I needed it for,' Lorna shot back, no longer caring that Bradley and the children were listening. Harry would know what she meant, and he could put that in his pipe and smoke it.

She went into the hall to fetch her coat, and Bradley followed her.

'I'll come with you.'

'There's no need.'

'I don't want you going along the lanes in the dark on your own.'

'I'll be fine.'

'Just the same . . .' He reached for his own coat.

Realising there was nothing she could say to dissuade him, Lorna shrugged and made for the door. He caught up and fell into step beside her.

'I wanted the chance to speak to you in any case,' he said. 'I've upset you, I know, and for that I'm sorry.'

'It's all right,' she said tonelessly.

'No, it's not. But as I tried to explain before, I thought it was only right to be straight with you.'

'In the hope that I'd be shocked into telling you something incriminating.' Lorna's tone was bitter.

Bradley looked away. 'It wasn't that at all,' he said quietly. 'I care a great deal about you, Lorna, and the children too. I worry about you and what all this is doing to you. But you must understand I have a duty to the families of those who died too. I very much hope I'm wrong about Harry being involved in some way, but . . .'

Lorna stopped walking, and when he did too, she turned to face him.

'As a matter of fact, I think you may well be right,' she said bluntly. 'I've thought it myself for a while now. I didn't want to believe it, but I've learned things today . . . Well, to be honest, I've seen a whole new side of him that I never knew existed.'

'Are you talking about the roof fall?'

'No,' she said. 'Nothing to do with that. And I really don't want to talk about it. Let's just say it opened my eyes to what he's really like. And I can see why you have to find out the truth.'

'I didn't mean to hurt you, Lorna. That's the last thing I want. Can you forgive me?'

A tiny sad laugh escaped her. 'I expect so.'

'Oh Lorna . . .'

Rain had started to fall, gentle at first, then with such force that they could hear the relentless patter on the leaves of the trees and hedges that lined the lane. Water began to trickle down inside the collars of their coats.

'Come on – we're getting soaked.' Bradley grabbed her hand and they began to run, down the slope that led to the cottages.

The rain was still coming down in stair rods when they reached number 1. Reluctantly Bradley let go of Lorna's hand – it had felt so good in his – and fished in his coat pocket for the bunch of keys that she'd given back to him earlier. He found the right one, unlocked the door and pushed it open with some difficulty. The wet weather had evidently swollen the wood even more. He let Lorna go in first, then followed, striking a match and lighting a taper he had brought, knowing the cottage would be in pitch darkness. As it flared, he noted with some satisfaction that at least the floor was clean now, and there were no cobwebs festooning the corners. Amos had done a good job.

'Oh my goodness! What a storm!'

Lorna was brushing the worst of the rain from her face, and with it long strands of hair that had come loose from its pins. She looked small and vulnerable, and a sudden rush of tenderness made Bradley's heart turn over.

More than anything he wanted to take her in his arms. Protect her. Show her all the love that seemed to be missing from her life. But it wasn't his place. He had no business feeling this way about another man's wife.

'Have you seen a lamp anywhere?' he asked in an attempt to cover the moment.

'There's one in the living room window.' She flipped more rain from her coat. By the light of the taper it glistened on the flagged floor, along with the puddles thar surrounded their soaking boots.

'We'll get that lit then so we can see what we're doing. We might be here a while if that rain doesn't ease.'

He found the lamp, checked that there was oil in it, and lit it from the taper. Then he held it aloft, surrounding them in an aura of soft golden light. 'Let's find your purse then,' he said.

'I think I left it in the kitchen,' Lorna said. She headed that way and he followed. Sure enough, there was the missing purse, surrounded by coins. She began to scoop them up: a sixpence, a couple of threepenny bits, but mostly pennies, halfpennies and farthings. He was shocked to see how little there was.

'Is that all the money you've got?' he asked before he could stop himself.

'Oh, I've got some more put away for safety,' she said, but he wasn't convinced.

'There's no shame in being short of money, Lorna,' he said gently. 'Harry's not been earning and isn't likely to any time soon. Have you thought any more about the job offer I made you? You've done yourself proud these last few days.'

'I've done my best. And actually I've enjoyed it.' Lorna slid the last few coppers into her purse and fastened it. 'Apart from when I thought you'd been using me,' she added with a mischievous smile.

'I thought we'd settled that,' he said, matching her tone. 'But to go back to the housekeeping job. You said before that Harry wouldn't want you working for me. Is that still the case?'

Lorna looked up, her eyes meeting his directly. 'To tell you the truth, I don't much care any more what Harry wants.'

'Because you think now that he had something to do with the roof fall at the pit?'

She looked away, turning her purse over and over between her hands.

'Not just that.' She paused, and the silence seemed to pulse with what was unsaid. 'If I took the job, could it be live-in for me and the girls?'

Her words came as a total surprise to Bradley, and he was at a loss to know how to interpret them. But whatever she was thinking, moving in without her husband would certainly result in raised eyebrows and a great deal of gossip.

'I can't be with him any more,' she went on tonelessly. 'Not here in this cottage or anywhere else.'

Dear Lord, she really was suggesting she wanted to leave Harry. Did she realise the seriousness of what she was contemplating? Did she think she could somehow obtain a divorce? If so, she was whistling in the wind. Bradley knew that the Victorian laws had been under review for the last year or so, with a Royal Commission examining ways in which they could be reformed, but no agreement seemed to have been reached, and as things stood it was not only difficult but extortionately expensive to end a marriage. Even then the stigma remained. Divorce was almost as scandalous as 'living in sin', which was very likely what folk would assume they were doing if she moved in with him.

She must be desperate to consider such a move, he thought, and he could see from the look in her eyes, begging, pleading, that she was counting on him to offer her a way out of her miserable existence.

For a long moment he was silent, torn between his head and his heart, but if he was successful in bringing Harry to the justice he so richly deserved, public sympathy would almost certainly be with Lorna, he reasoned. He made up his mind.

'Perhaps we could work something out,' he said. 'But what about Harry?'

'He could still move into the cottage – as long as he can find the rent.'

Or he might be in jail, Bradley thought but didn't say.

'It might not be just him anyway,' Lorna went on.

'You mean . . .' Bradley frowned. Surely she could mean only one thing. But he could scarcely bring himself to put that into words either. 'There's someone else?' he asked tentatively.

Lorna laughed, a short, mirthless sound that might almost have been a sob.

'No, not now. It's not what you think.' She raised her hand and held her purse out as if it were an exhibit in a court case. 'I expect you're wondering why we're so hard up. Why we had nothing tucked away for a rainy day. Why we've had no help from the Friendly Society or the Buffs. Well, it's because we've been on the breadline for years. There are no savings because we needed every penny to survive. And Harry let his membership of the clubs lapse for the same reason, though I didn't know that until we needed financial help.'

'Is that the reason he got involved with Golledge and the others? Because his wages weren't enough for you to live on?

She sighed. 'That might have been the trigger, I suppose, if he really did do something awful. And I'd have liked to think he was doing it for us, so that we could have a better quality of life. But that wasn't the reason. He had expenses I knew nothing about, and he wanted to keep it that way. Didn't want me to learn the truth. I knew there had to be some reason he gave me so little to keep food on the table and clothes on the girls' backs, but I thought he was gambling, betting on the football pools or the horses.'

'And it wasn't that?' Bradley prompted her gently.

'I wouldn't be feeling this way if it were,' she said. 'I'd have been angry, of course. Betting is a mug's game. But at least I'd have understood why he wanted to keep it from me. But this . . .' Her eyes, which had been blazing, were suddenly full of tears.

'Tell me,' Bradley said.

They went into the living room, sat down on the sofa, which hadn't yet been taken away, and she told him.

Chapter Twenty-Two

Harry Harrison was a worried man. When Lorna and Bradley had left, and the girls had gone back to the parlour to continue with their card game, he sat alone in the kitchen and thought of the problems that confronted him.

Everything, it seemed, was conspiring against him. He'd never expected for a moment that Greta's sister would come looking for him and threaten to dump Frank on him if he didn't send her some money. But even that paled into insignificance beside what Lorna had told him – that bloody Bradley Robinson had somehow found out that he'd played a part in the explosion that had brought the roof down. If he could prove it, Harry and the others would go to prison for a very long time, and the thought of it made Harry's gut churn.

As if he wasn't already feeling poorly, Lorna's egg and bacon pie had brought on his indigestion again. Her pastry was usually light as a feather and crumbly, but today it had settled like a dead weight in his chest. She'd done it on purpose, he wouldn't be surprised.

He groaned and heaved himself up from the dining chair. Pouring a cup of tea from the pot that was keeping warm on the kitchen range, he added a generous tot of Bradley's whisky, then sat down again.

Ah, that was hitting the spot! By the time he'd finished it, and another tot of whisky besides, he was feeling better, and some of his natural resilience had returned. Greta's sister was all talk, always had been. And Lorna would agree to paying whatever was needed to hush it all up. She wouldn't want the boy upsetting their family life any more than he did, or all the talk it would cause.

The roof fall was a different matter, though. Harry didn't suppose Robinson had any real proof of his involvement; if he had, the police would have been knocking on the door long before now. But he couldn't take any chances. He thanked his lucky stars he'd been able to get back to Northfield Terrace to collect what he'd been forced to leave behind when Robinson had moved them out all of a rush and Lorna had stopped him from going upstairs. He'd been fretting about it ever since, that whoever was sent in to clear their things might find it first. If they'd recognised it for what it was . . . well, the consequences didn't bear thinking about. Now he permitted himself a wry smile to think he'd brought it all the way here right under Robinson's nose.

He poured himself another whisky. Good stuff, this was, and it was helping him to think straight for the first time since Lorna had dropped the bombshell that he was under suspicion. The first thing he needed to do was hide the evidence where nobody would find it. When Robinson had dropped him off, he'd managed to make it up the stairs and stash the battered old attaché case on top of the wardrobe in Lorna's bedroom. He'd thought it would be safe enough there; now he wasn't so sure. There was always the risk that Lorna might spot it and wonder what was in it. Especially if she had suspicions of her own, which it seemed she had. He'd best take the opportunity to put it somewhere safer while he was alone in the house and the pack of cards was keeping the girls entertained. Somewhere in the garden, maybe. Nobody was likely to see it there.

He reached for his crutches. Hobbled to the stairs and hauled himself up, dragging his injured leg behind him. But he'd no sooner got to the bedroom than Marjorie was calling.

'Daddy? Where are you?'

He swore through gritted teeth. 'Up here! What d'you want?'

'You're upstairs?' She sounded amazed.

'I'm doin' me exercises. Wot is it you want?'

'Nipper's on the sofa and he won't get down. Mammy says—'

'Awright. I'm comin'.' Resigned, he began to manoeuvre himself back down the stairs, clutching the banister rail tightly. Bloody dog! But he supposed he'd been a bit optimistic to think he could manhandle the case down and into the garden while the girls were in the house. He'd just have to wait until Robinson was at work and Lorna out shopping or at the cottage.

As he reached the foot of the stairs, the pain caught him again, a sharp twinge high in his gut. Trapped wind, that was what it was. Damn Lorna's heavy pastry.

He turfed Nipper off Robinson's sofa and got his crutch under the dog's backside for good measure. Then he went back to the whisky he'd poured and not finished.

Thinking of what was hidden in the attaché case had given him the germ of an idea that would solve the problem of Robinson's suspicions once and for all. He'd show the bloody man. If he thought he could pin the blame for the explosion on Harry and then get off with his wife, he was in for a shock. Harry's lips curled in a smile that was both triumphant and satisfied. He raised the whisky to his lips and drank a toast to the brainwave that would solve all his problems.

* * *

Just today, George Golledge had been deemed fit to return to his usual job underground. Like many miners who had an early start to the day, when he'd finished his evening meal he liked to sit down with the paper, read for a bit and look at the cartoon strips until his eyes drooped. He'd just dropped off when there was a knock at the front door.

Lil was in the kitchen, washing the dishes, and she called out, waking him. 'See who that is, will you, George? My hands are all wet.'

Not best pleased to be disturbed, George put his newspaper down beside his chair and did as he was told. More than likely it would be one of those women from the Temperance Society, shaking a collecting tin and lecturing him about the evils of the demon drink. If it was, he'd send them packing with a flea in their ear. Then again, it could be youngsters playing knockout ginger, though they usually targeted the back door for their pranks; it was easier to get away along the track without being seen.

When he opened the door, however, he got a nasty surprise. Standing on the doorstep was the man who had attacked him in the Miners' Arms. George tried to close the door again, but the man got his boot in the way.

'It's awright. I bain't goin' to' hit you this time,' he said. But George didn't care for his tone.

'If you don't take your foot out'a my door, I'm callin' the police!' he threatened.

'An' 'ow you gonna do that?' the man chuckled. 'I just got one question fer you, tha's all.'

'I got nothin' t' say t' you!' George blustered.

The man caught him by the neck of his shirt and jerked him forward. 'We'll see about that!'

'Wot's goin' on 'ere?' It was Lil, alerted by the commotion.

'You keep out'a this, missus,' the man warned. But he'd picked the wrong adversary in Lil, who was brandishing a carving knife, wet and gleaming with soap bubbles.

'Let go o' my hubby, or I swear . . .'

'Aw right, aw right!' He released George, holding up his hands in surrender. 'I reckon you've learned your lesson. 'Tis Harrison I want now; 'tis time 'e learned 'is. I was told 'e lived in this rank.'

'Well you've got the wrong 'ouse,' Lil snapped.

'I know that. One o' your neighbours told me they've moved out but you and 'e were friendly and you might know where 'e'd gone.'

'Well we don't, so on yer bike, mister.' Lil waved the carving knife threateningly.

'Put that knife down afore some bugger gets hurt,' George warned her, then addressed the man. 'She be right, though. We don't know where they'm gone. But I can tell you somebody who does – or says she'd know, leastways. The barmaid at the Miners' Arms. Pretty girl. Fair-headed. Mercy Comer, 'er name be.'

The man was instantly alert. 'You sure?'

'That's wot she said. Me an' me mates wanted a word wi' 'un. She wouldn't tell us, though.'

'How would she know where they've gone?' He sounded dubious.

'Mercy knows a lot o' things, far more than's good fer her. Nosy little cow, more's the pity. Now get yer foot out'a my door and let us bide.'

'Awright, I'm goin',' but if you'm telling me porkies, I'll be back. An' that's a promise.'

'Does she know?' Lil asked as they watched the man walk away down the path and disappear into the darkness.

'Search me,' George said. 'Got rid o' 'im, though, didn' it?'

'Well if she does know and she's got any sense, she'll tell 'im. He's a nasty piece o' work an' no mistake. I wouldn't want to be in Harry's shoes if 'e finds 'im.'

'True,' George agreed. 'Just as well 'e don't know 'twas 'cos o' wot you done that they bain't livin' 'ere no more. 'Twas a bloody stupid idea, Lil.'

She bristled. 'I wanted to show 'em they bain't welcome here after wot 'e put you and t' others through.'

''Twas still stupid. The whole bloody rank could've gone up.'

'Well it didn't,' Lil said.

She didn't want to talk about what she'd done. George was right, she knew. Setting the fire at the Harrisons' could very easily have turned into a disaster. She'd been mad as a hatter with Harry at the time, and with Lorna too, for starting a baking business. She'd crowed with delight to think the bake oven would be out of action. But she hadn't been thinking straight. She was lucky she wasn't up in front of the magistrates for arson, or even manslaughter. But at least she didn't have to see that prissy woman every day, swanning around as if she thought she was better than anybody else and expecting folk to feel sorry for her when it was all Harry's doing.

'Let's go in,' she said. 'I've got the washing-up to finish, and you want your snooge.'

They went in and closed the door. George made sure it was locked, checking it twice, and for once he shot the bolt for good measure. The disaster had made folk do stupid things, and he wasn't going to take any chances.

Mark Wheeler didn't go directly to the Miners' Arms. He wanted to catch the barmaid on her own, and in any case the landlord would most likely recognise him and throw him out.

Instead he walked up the hill. There was a little pub not far up; he'd wait there until closing time. Then with any luck he'd be able to find out where Harrison was hiding out, and give him some of the medicine he'd meted out to Golledge without him having three mates there to defend him.

'Oh Lorna, what can I say?' Bradley was stunned by what she had told him, his thoughts and emotions running riot.

'Well, now you know,' she said with a small, sad smile. 'I honestly don't know which I blame him for most – keeping it all a secret from me or abandoning his son like that. Because that's what he's done. I can't forgive him for that, Bradley. And I honestly don't know what to do.'

He saw that her fingers were knotted around her wedding ring, pulling it up and down towards the knuckle as if undecided whether to take it off or leave it there, the outward sign of commitment to the man who had deceived her for the whole of their married life.

'I don't want to be with him,' she said slowly. 'I haven't wanted to be with him for a very long time, if I'm honest. But I've stayed because the girls need a stable home life.'

'Do they have that with Harry?' Bradley asked gently. 'They must see the way he treats you, speaks to you. They're growing up. They'll begin to notice it more and more, if they haven't already. And to be honest, he treats them in much the same way. But they're close to you. You're a wonderful mother. Don't you think that's all they need?'

She shook her head helplessly. 'I truly don't know what's best for them. And then there's the boy – his son. I can't help worrying about him too. Poor child, none of this is his fault. But if he comes here to live with Harry, he'd be torn away from the only family he's ever known and landed on a father and grandmother who want nothing to do with him. What sort of a life would that be? It doesn't bear thinking about. If Harry and I were still together, at least I could be a mother figure to him. Stand up for him, give him the love he'll never get from Harry or his mother.'

Bradley's heart swelled with love and admiration for her, thinking of others before herself, even the boy she'd met only once, and briefly. But he was angry too that Harry should place her in this position. Heap yet more worries on her slender shoulders. He was silent for a few moments, thinking, then he made up his mind.

'Supposing I paid you enough so that you could afford to send whatever this aunt wants for his keep? That way he can stay with her.'

Tears filled her eyes. 'Oh Bradley, that is so kind! But I couldn't expect you to do that. None of this is your responsibility.'

Nor yours, he wanted to say. But he didn't.

'I'm being purely selfish, Lorna,' he said instead. 'I've seen the house come to life these last few days. I don't want to lose that. I don't want to lose you and the girls. I want you to stay with me. And if the aunt does send the boy back, I'd be prepared to take him in too, and give him a good home.' She was silent, and he added: 'You must know how I feel about you.'

Her expression was unreadable now. Had he overplayed his hand? Alarmed her?

'I don't expect you to feel the same way,' he went on quickly. 'And I don't expect anything from you beyond keeping house for me. But if giving the boy a home too is what it takes, I'd be prepared to do that.'

'But I do,' she said softly.

For a wonderful moment he could almost believe it, and then

he remembered the heartache and pain he'd suffered after he'd lost Ella.

'You don't have to pretend, Lorna,' he said lightly, as if it really didn't matter to him at all.

She was no longer twisting the wedding ring on her finger. Faint colour had risen in her cheeks.

'I'm not pretending, Bradley,' she said. 'I feel just the same way as you.'

For a long minute, in the aftermath of the enormity of what they had both confessed, neither of them spoke. Then Bradley reached for Lorna's hand, turning her to face him.

'So,' he said, 'what's it to be?'

His touch was sending shivers of warmth prickling into her veins, and her heart pounded, but she could scarcely believe this was happening. It was the dream again. At any minute she'd wake and nothing would have changed. Yet at the same time she knew that this was a pivotal moment that could change her life for ever, and from which there could be no going back. As if she was standing on the edge of a cliff, half eager, half afraid to step out into the void.

'Lorna?' His eyes met hers, questioning but filled with promise, and they gave her the courage to take that step forward.

'I'll stay with you,' she said, softly but decisively.

His eyes met hers directly. 'Are you sure? You realise it's not going to be easy for you, or the girls? There will be all sorts of repercussions.'

'I know that. But good things always come at a price, don't they? And quite honestly, I can't face living the rest of my life the way things are. I might be seen as a scarlet woman for a while, but it can't be worse than what I've put up with these last few years.'

'What will you tell Harry?' he asked.

'That I'm going to keep house for you. I might even suggest he stays too. He'll refuse, I know he will, and it will make the decision to separate his rather than mine.'

He raised an eyebrow.

'I know my husband,' she went on quickly. 'He'll choose to move into the cottage, at least until he's fit to work again and can find something closer to wherever his new job takes him.'

'And the girls?'

'I'll tell him he can see them as often as he likes.'

Bradley's mouth curved upwards, and his smile evoked a sharp reaction deep inside her, as if all her nerves were stretched tight and singing, like the strings of a violin. It was a sensation that was new to her, but the most delicious, exciting feeling she had ever experienced.

Tentatively she leaned towards him, wanting to feel his arms around her again as they had been on the day he'd first brought her to view the cottage, and her mother-in-law and the witch woman had upset her so. Bradley was clearly remembering that too. 'You're not going to cry on my shoulder again, I hope,' he said in a tone that was simultaneously teasing and tender.

Matching his mood, she smiled back. 'Not today. Though I wouldn't mind trying.'

'Come here then.' He pulled her towards him so that her head rested on his shoulder.

The touch of his lips on her forehead sent the warm tingles rushing through her veins again, and the sharp sweetness tugged deep inside her. She lifted her head and he kissed her nose, then his lips hovered over her mouth and the waiting was almost unbearable.

He kissed her gently at first, then, as she wound her arms around his neck, more deeply. The masculine smell of him heightened her awareness, the feel of his hard muscles beneath her hands made her head swim. She pressed against him, unable to think of anything but his nearness. She was lost. Drowning in desire . . .

He pulled sharply away, and she almost panicked at the feeling of desolation and disappointment that enveloped her.

'Not here, Lorna. Not now,' he said.

For a moment she was incapable of understanding. 'Bradley . . .'

'Don't you know you're driving me crazy?' His voice was ragged. 'But this isn't the time or the place.' He pushed a strand of her still wet hair away from her face. 'We really should be getting back. Harry and the girls will be wondering what's become of us.'

I don't care about Harry, she wanted to say. *I owe him nothing*. But the girls were a different matter entirely. It would soon be their bedtime, and yes, they would be wondering why she wasn't there to kiss them goodnight.

'Our time will come. Be sure of it,' Bradley said. He got up and went to the window. 'I think the rain's stopped now. Have you got your purse? Better not go back without that!'

'Better not,' she said shakily.

They put on their coats, still wet from the heavy storm, and went out. Sure enough, the rain was now nothing more than a fine drizzle. Bradley locked the door and pocketed the keys, and when they reached the lane, he took her hand.

'When are you going to tell him you're staying on as my housekeeper?'

'Not tonight. If he takes it badly – which he almost certainly will – I don't want the girls upset by hearing us rowing.'

'I agree. But I should be there when you do. If he loses his temper . . .'

'I don't think he'd hurt me. He never has yet.'

'I don't want to take any chances.'

Again Lorna felt a surge of warmth. That someone should care so much for her well-being felt indescribably good. And that that someone was Bradley . . . She glanced up, and his strong profile, though seen only dimly, made her heart sing with love and happiness.

'This son of his.' Clearly his thoughts had turned to practicalities. 'How long did the woman who's caring for him say she was prepared to wait for her money before she brings him back?'

'She didn't say. Just that she couldn't let it go on any longer.'

'And where do they live?'

'Out Charterhouse way. It seems Harry met the girl – Frank's mother – when he was working in the quarries there.'

She was suddenly aware of a change in Bradley's demeanour, and though she had no idea what the cause could be, it unsettled her.

'What is it?' she asked.

'Nothing.' But his tone was different too. It was as though he was shutting her out. 'I was just wondering what would be the best way to get the money to her.'

Though it made sense, she wasn't convinced. But she let it go. It was probably nothing, and she didn't want to spoil those special moments they had shared in the cottage. She wanted to hug them to herself, treasure them. Go to sleep remembering his arms around her, his lips on hers, and drift away to a place where they would be together for ever.

When they reached the house, she was surprised to see the front door open and Harry standing there, silhouetted against the lamplight, looking out.

'I'm sorry if you were worried,' she said. 'We had to wait for the storm to pass.'

'I weren't worried.' He was his usual contrary self. 'I'm just letting the dog out, that's all.' As if for confirmation, Nipper came bounding out of the bushes, jumping up at her legs.

'That's all right then,' she said, and went inside to find the girls.

Frowning, Harry turned to watch her go. He didn't like this. Didn't like it at all. He'd suspected for some time that Robinson was sweet on Lorna, though he hadn't imagined for a moment that she would reciprocate or allow any funny goings-on. That wouldn't be like Lorna at all, with her highfalutin principles. But now he wondered if he might have been wrong. They'd been gone a bloody long time. Sheltering from the storm, she'd said. But that sounded like a tall story to him, and it had him rattled.

He made up his mind. From now on he was going to keep a careful eye on the pair of them, and woe betide them if he caught them crossing the line.

Bradley poured himself a large whisky. The self-control he'd had to exert so as not to give in to the demands of his body and take Lorna there on the old sofa in the cottage called for it. But there was something else on his mind too. Something he should be feeling triumphant about but that was evoking mixed feelings.

Harry had once worked in the Charterhouse quarries. Perhaps he still had friends there. It was too much of a coincidence to be ignored. It seemed entirely possible that was where the explosives had come from.

He sipped the whisky, pondering for a few moments what his next move should be. But his thoughts were wandering back to all that had happened between him and Lorna and he felt a surge of happiness. His enquiries could go on the back burner for the time being. Tonight he was going to think of nothing but her and the future he hoped they would one day share.

Mercy was on her way home from the Miners' Arms, walking in the deep shadow of the path that led to her house, when the man stepped out in front of her.

'Right, missy,' he said. 'I want a word wi' you.'

She almost jumped out of her skin. 'Frighten a girl to death, why don't you?' she flared, though she was shaking inwardly. 'I told you before. I don't know where George Golledge lives. An' I'll 'ave the law on you if you don't look out.'

''Tisn't he I'm after. Matter o' fact, I've bin talkin' to 'im, an' he reckons you can tell me where I can find Harry Harrison. Be that right?'

Quick as a flash, Mercy realised what this meant. How the man had found George she didn't know. But no matter. He had. And George had repeated what she'd told the clique of miners – that she knew where the Harrisons had gone after the fire at their old house.

Instantly all her resentment of the woman she had seen with Bradley in the market rushed to the fore, along with the suspicion that Bradley was toying with her purely to get information. This man had every intention of causing trouble for the Harrisons, and if they were where she thought they were, that would mean trouble for Bradley too. Well, she owed him nothing. He'd played her for a fool, and as for *that woman*, well, Mercy hated her guts. This was her chance to get her revenge on both of them.

She wasn't going to make it easy for the man, though. He had to think he'd dragged it out of her.

'Why should I tell you where they are?' she demanded boldly.

'You will if you d'a know what's good fer you,' the man

threatened. 'It'd be a shame if that pretty face of yourn weren't so pretty any more.'

'You wouldn't dare!' She was pushing her luck, she knew, and the man's hand shot out, imprisoning her wrist.

'Wanna try me?'

Though she was trembling, Mercy tossed her head carelessly. 'I don't know for sure.'

'Never mind that.'

She drew a deep breath. 'I think they're staying with Bradley Robinson, the safety officer.'

'An' where do he live?'

'In the manager's house at Oldlands. As far as I know, anyway.'

The man released her. 'You'd better be tellin' me the truth, or I'll be comin' lookin' fer you again.'

'And much good will it do you,' Mercy said haughtily.

Her heart was thudding as she walked away up the cinder path, but she was feeling pleased with her night's work.

If Harry Harrison and his wife were roughed up, and Bradley Robinson too, it was no more than they deserved.

Chapter Twenty-Three

Bradley had been undecided whether to tell Cameron that he planned to visit the Charterhouse quarry where Harry had once been employed. On the one hand, he felt he should keep the manager informed, and it would be in his best interests to have his approval should his enquiries have any unexpected repercussions. On the other, he was reluctant to stack up further evidence against Harry until he was completely sure of the part he had played in the disaster.

In the event, the decision was made for him. Cam was not in the office when he arrived for work, but had left a note for him to the effect that he would be out all day, and Bradley could find him at Littlecote Colliery should the need arise.

Bradley checked his in-tray and scanned through a new directive for safety procedures. It was long and wordy, couched in official language, and he put it to one side. He would need to study it thoroughly later, but he couldn't see that it was urgent, and finding out what he could about where the explosives had come from and who had obtained them was a far more pressing matter.

Last night's rain had finally stopped and the sun was trying to break through, but the wind still had a bite to it. He turned up the collar of his coat as he cranked life into the Ford's engine and set out for Charterhouse, which nestled in the Mendip Hills to the south of Hillsbridge.

As he drove, he noticed signs that spring was at last on the way: catkins hung in the trees, and he spotted some lambs gambolling around their mothers on one of the grassy slopes. The sight cheered him. Though he was not a superstitious man, it felt to him like an omen, a promise of the new life he could still scarcely believe could become a reality for him and Lorna. He'd hardly slept last night for thinking about it, elated yet cautious. Things could still go badly wrong. There were many hurdles yet to be overcome. And the spectre of Ella and how she had let him down still haunted him, a dark shadow that coloured his expectations of lasting happiness.

A loud boom suddenly shattered the peace of the countryside, echoing and re-echoing until it died away in a low rumble. The quarry was blasting. It was a sound that could be heard faintly as far away as Hillsbridge; now he realised just how powerful it was close at hand and out in the open. A thunderbolt in comparison to the charges used by shot-firers in the mines. If the explosives used to bring down the pit roof had come from here, it was small wonder they'd done far more damage than the plotters had intended, especially in the light of their lack of experience. But surely if Harry had worked at the quarry he would have known that? Unless, of course, his job had been well away from the blasting zones.

A cloud of dust was rising in the sky to his left, and as he rounded a bend in the road, Bradley saw a junction up ahead with a turning that led in that direction. He slowed and pulled into a lane wide enough to accommodate the wagons that took the quarried stone away. After a couple of hundred yards, he came to a gap in a high wire fence giving access to the quarry itself.

A gaggle of buildings constructed of what he imagined was their own stone fronted the lane. He pulled up on a patch of grass to one side of them and turned off the engine, then climbed down and headed for the nearest. A painted wooden sign proclaimed: *Charterhouse Quarries*, and a plaque on the door read: *Reception*.

As he knocked and made to turn the brass doorknob, he heard a loud clacking sound from within. For a moment he was puzzled, then realised it must be one of the new writing machines that by all accounts were becoming popular with forward-looking businesses.

Sure enough, as he stepped inside, he saw it – a shiny black cumbersome-looking contraption that sat on a desk at right angles to the enquiry counter. A young woman was seated in front of it, and the clacking stopped as she realised she had a visitor to attend to.

Bradley was mightily impressed. Very few women were employed as office staff, let alone typists, but this one certainly gave every impression of efficiency in her pristine white blouse and black woollen skirt, her hair pulled away from her face into a tight bun at the nape of her neck.

'Good morning, sir. Can I help you?' Her tone was brisk, with only the slightest hint of a Somerset burr.

Bradley introduced himself. 'I was hoping I could speak to the quarry manager.'

'May I ask in what connection?'

'A rather delicate matter concerning explosives.'

'Oh, I see.' For the first time, she displayed a hint of indecision.

'I'd be grateful if he could spare me a few minutes. It's very important, and I've come quite a long way.' Though it wasn't his usual style, Bradley thought this called for a certain amount of charm, and sure enough it worked.

'I know the manager is out at the quarry face. We're blasting today and he likes to oversee operations. But Sir Henry Corsley, the owner, is on site, and I could ask if he would be willing to talk to you,' the young woman said. A delicate flush had risen in her cheeks – why he had this effect on the fair sex, Bradley had no idea, but there were occasions when it could be useful.

'That would be a great help,' he said. 'Thank you.'

'Who exactly did you say you were?' The flush was deepening.

Bradley repeated his name and job title, and she disappeared through an inner door.

As he waited, he looked around. The walls were hung with framed photographs, formal portraits of what he assumed to be the founder's family. One showed a distinguished-looking gentleman and his wife, with two small boys and a little girl, and a baby on the wife's knee. All were attired formally and were bookended by a pair of large potted palms. Another was a head-and-shoulders portrait of a handsome young man, and from the change in dress fashion and hairstyle, Bradley guessed it was of one of the small boys grown to manhood. Sir Henry in his younger days, perhaps. There was also a picture of a wedding party made up of several generations that had been taken on the steps of a grand house. It seemed there was money, and plenty of it, in the Corsley family.

It was the writing machine that fascinated him the most, however. His fingers itched to depress one of the circular metal-edged buttons and see the strut jump up to impress a letter on the sheet of paper that jutted out from the roller, half obscuring the name across the top of the contraption: *Underwood*.

'Sir Henry will see you now.' The young woman was back, holding the door to the inner sanctum open, and Bradley was glad he hadn't been caught touching the fascinating machine.

'Thank you.' He smiled at the secretary as he passed her, and saw the rosy blush stain her cheeks again.

The room he found himself in was the very model of what an office should be: a large leather-tooled desk, files neatly stacked on copious shelving, framed certificates hanging on the walls. And to Bradley's amusement, since it looked completely out of place, a paraffin stove similar to the one that heated Cam's office.

There were two men in the room, one tall, spare and courtly, who rose from a captain's chair behind the desk to greet him, and another, younger man who remained seated on a chair that was also drawn up to the desk.

'Good day, sir.' The older man's voice matched his appearance, rich and cultured. 'You wished to discuss explosives, I believe.'

'I did. Sir Henry, I presume?'

'Indeed. And this is my son, Quentin, who will inherit when I depart this mortal coil.' Sir Henry threw a disapproving glance in the direction of the younger man, who finally rose to his feet with bad grace.

Bradley nodded to him politely, but his first impression of Sir Henry's heir was far from favourable. Though of similar build to his father, there the resemblance ended. Rather than the neatly cropped hairstyle Sir Henry favoured, a cowlick flopped over one eye. His aquiline nose somehow gave the impression of haughtiness, and his mouth was fleshy yet oddly feminine. Bradley disliked him on sight.

'Do please sit down.' Sir Henry gestured towards an upright chair on the opposite side of the desk to his own. Bradley did as he was bid, and the two gentlemen also resumed their seats.

'So – explosives,' Sir Henry began. 'You are a safety officer for Montague Fairley's coal mines, Miss Sobey tells me.

I assume therefore your visit might be to further your knowledge of best practice in the use of gelignite.' He removed a pair of rimless spectacles and raised his eyebrows slightly as he regarded Bradley questioningly.

'It's a little more complicated than that, I'm afraid,' Bradley said. 'You may have heard that there was a roof fall recently at Milverton, one of the Hillsbridge mines?'

'I believe I did hear something of the kind.' Sir Henry twiddled the stem of his spectacles between finger and thumb. 'An accident with fatalities, I believe?'

'Two fatalities and some serious injuries, yes,' Bradley confirmed. 'Whether or not it was an accident is debatable.'

Sir Henry's eyebrows rose a fraction higher. 'How so?'

'It has been suggested by some of the men who were underground at the time that the roof fall was preceded by an explosion,' Bradley said carefully. 'The district inspector who investigated didn't get to hear of this, and consequently it wasn't taken into consideration in his report. I am attempting to find out the truth of the matter, and I am hoping you may be able to help in that regard.'

'In what way?' Sir Henry was clearly puzzled.

This was not going to be easy, but Bradley continued anyway.

'Unfortunately, there is a good deal of unrest amongst the Milverton miners over their pay and working conditions. I'm given to understand that a coterie of hotheads were planning to somehow draw attention to their grievances. It's my belief that they used explosive to cause the roof fall, and being inexperienced used far more than they needed, with catastrophic results. I have a pretty good idea of the identity of the culprits, but what I don't know is how or where they obtained the explosive.'

'A good question certainly,' Sir Henry said. 'But I fail to see how I can be of any assistance. Surely the answer must lie with whoever is responsible for its safe keeping at the colliery?'

'That was my first line of enquiry, of course,' Bradley assured him. 'But I've become convinced it wasn't Milverton's own stock that was used. The shot-firer is adamant that no one but him has access to his stock, and I have no reason to doubt him. He's a long-standing employee whose competence, trustworthiness and loyalty are not in doubt. And had he been involved, he has enough experience to ensure the foolish plan didn't have such devastating results. Which is why I've checked the stock at our nearby collieries and am now exploring other avenues.'

'Good God!' Sir Henry expostulated. 'Surely you are not suggesting . . . ?' He broke off, shaking his head in rebuttal and disbelief.

'Of course I don't think for one moment that you would know anything about this,' Bradley said, attempting to placate the quarry owner. 'However, I've recently learned that one of the most militant of the miners, one who was on the spot at the time the roof came down, and who was in fact badly injured himself, was employed here at Charterhouse some years ago. Which leads me to wonder—'

'This is preposterous!' It was the younger man who interrupted, his pale eyes shards of ice. 'How dare you presume that we take less care with the safe keeping of our explosives than you do? We have nothing further to say to you. This meeting is at an end. Kindly leave, sir.'

Bradley's heart sank. He'd learned nothing and had enraged the quarry owners into the bargain. But what had he expected?

'Thank you for your time, and I'm sorry if I have caused you offence. I assure you that was certainly not my intention.' He made to stand, but to his surprise, Sir Henry raised a hand.

'Stay where you are, Mr Robinson.' He turned to the younger man, clearly angry. 'I am the one who decides when this meeting is at an end, Quentin. And I'm not done yet.' He returned his attention to Bradley. 'I apologise for my son's rudeness. But you will agree that the allegations you appear to be making are serious indeed. I think I am entitled to ask who this former employee is. And how do you suppose he was able to gain access to our explosives, if that is indeed what he did?'

Before Bradley could answer, Quentin had scraped back his chair and was on his feet. High spots of colour burned in his pasty face like the painted cheeks of a cheap china doll.

'I'm sorry, Father, but I am not prepared to listen to any more of this.'

'Sit down, boy!' Sir Henry roared, but Quentin ignored him, marching across the room, opening the door and slamming it behind him as he left.

Sir Henry shook his head despairingly. 'While there is no excuse for my son's behaviour, if there is any truth in what you say, he no doubt feels responsible. One of his duties is overseeing the regular inventories of our stocks of gelatine.'

'And he might have failed to notice or report that some was missing?'

'That may well be what he is afraid of,' Sir Henry conceded. 'He knows I have had my doubts in the past as to whether he will be up to the task of running the quarry when the time comes. Now, however, he is making every effort to convince me that his days of sowing his wild oats are behind him and he will be a suitable guardian of our family interests. If he has failed in something so important, he will no doubt see it as a serious setback.' He sighed heavily. 'Children, Mr Robinson, can be a burden as well as a blessing. Are you a father?'

'No, sir.'

'Ah well.' He sighed again and placed his spectacles on the desk in front of him. 'Please continue, Mr Robinson.'

'You were asking the name of the employee,' Bradley said. 'It's Harry Harrison. I don't know if he still has friends here, but if so, I wondered if there was any possibility that he had obtained the explosives through them.'

'Mm.' Sir Henry's expression darkened. 'Highly unlikely, I'd say, if not impossible. Very few people have access to the explosives store. The security surrounding it is of the highest order.'

'Of course,' Bradley said hastily. 'I'm not for one moment suggesting . . .'

Sir Henry nodded, apparently appeased. 'Do you know the names of anyone this man Harrison might have worked with here?'

'I'm afraid not.' Might Lorna know? Bradley wondered. 'I'll do a little more digging,' he said aloud.

'I think that would be your best course of action, and if you are successful, come and see me again.' Sir Henry tapped his fingers on the desk for a moment. 'Rest assured I shall be making some enquiries of my own. As I said, it is most unlikely our security has been breached, but should that be the case, it is a most serious matter. For the moment, however, I don't think I can be of any further help to you.'

'Well, thank you for your time anyway,' Bradley said. 'I always knew it was a long shot.'

Both men rose and Sir Henry held out his hand.

'Good luck, Mr Robinson. I quite understand how anxious you are to get to the bottom of the matter. And be sure to let me know should you learn anything that might indicate we are involved in some way.'

'I will. And thank you again.'

The two men shook hands and Bradley left.

In the outer office, the young secretary was turning the pages of a ledger on a table close to the door to Sir Henry's room, and

Bradley realised he hadn't heard the clack of the typewriter keys while he had been in there. Had she stopped using it so as to listen to what was being said? Like Mercy Comer at the Miners' Arms, she was probably privy to most things that went on here, and would be a fount of information. She was too young to have been working here at the same time as Harry, but she might have heard his name mentioned by the absent manager or one of the other officials. Or perhaps she would be able to point him in the direction of someone who would remember him.

'Thank you, miss,' he said by way of attracting her attention.

She looked up from the file, the flush rising once again in her cheeks. 'I hope Sir Henry was able to help you, sir.'

'Unfortunately not.' He moved towards the outer door, and as he had hoped, she followed him.

'Allow me . . .' She reached for the knob and opened the door. Bradley stepped out, then stopped and turned.

'I don't suppose you know Harry Harrison? He was employed here about ten years ago.'

'I'm sorry, but that would be before my time,' she said regretfully.

'Pity.'

'But some of the men probably would.'

'And where might I find them?'

'At the moment, quite a few of them are in the canteen, taking their mid-morning break,' she said, looking pleased with herself. 'I saw them through the window heading that way five minutes or so ago.'

'And where is the canteen?'

'Just a little further along. If you turn left, you can't miss it.'

'You've been a great help,' Bradley said.

As the door closed after him, he hoped he hadn't given the young woman the wrong idea as he seemed to have managed to do with Mercy. But in the great scheme of things, getting to the bottom of the explosion at Milverton was really all that mattered.

The building that housed the canteen was very similar to the one Bradley had just left, except that it was a large open space filled with tables and wooden forms. A counter ran along one of the shorter walls with a tea urn and a cash register at one end, and sandwiches heaped on a platter behind a glass partition and jars of pickled onions and eggs at the other. Behind the counter a plump woman in a wraparound apron was pouring tea for an orderly queue of men in dusty working clothes. The amenities here were far superior to anything at the mines, Bradley thought, though of course these men weren't confined below ground for the whole of their working day.

He joined the end of the queue, aware of the curious glances of some of the men.

'Don't know you, do I?' the plump woman said when it was his turn.

'I had an appointment with Sir Henry. Does that entitle me to buy a cup of tea?' he returned easily.

'S'long as yer money's good.'

'A cup of tea then, please.' He fished in his pocket for some loose change and put it down on the counter. 'Take what you need.'

'Well at least this is clean,' she said, picking out a few coins and pushing the rest back in his direction. 'Some days there's more stone dust than money in my cash box.'

'Did you know Harry Harrison?' Bradley asked as she filled a cup at the urn. 'He used to work here.'

The woman sniffed. 'Oh, I knowed 'im all right. Miserable bugger. Got that flighty piece wot used to work in the Three Feathers in the family way an' 'ad to marry her.'

'That's him.' Bradley was glad he knew a little of Harry's past history. But he had no intention of discussing it now. 'I'm looking for anyone he was friendly with in those days. Would that be any of these men?' He gesticulated in the general direction of the quarry workers, who were now seated on the wooden forms in their own particular cliques.

'Don't know about friendly,' the woman scoffed. ''E worked wi' most of 'em, though. Wot d'you want wi' 'em?'

'I'm trying to catch up with him and wondered if any of them had seen him lately,' Bradley lied.

'Hmm.' The woman eyed him suspiciously. 'Try that lot over there.' She pointed to one of the tables. 'You'll 'ave to speak up, though. Most of 'em are deaf as posts from years of blastin'.'

'Thanks.' Bradley took his tea and approached the table.

'Missus over there thinks one of you might be in touch with Harry Harrison.'

The men looked at one another and then at Bradley, shaking their heads.

'A name from the past, that be,' one said.

Another spoke up. 'Ah, but funnily enough, I seen 'im a few weeks ago. Or could 'ave bin longer. I do lose track o' time. Quite a shock, it were, like seein' a ghost. An' that weren't the best of it. 'Twas who 'e was with surprised I. Told you at the time, didn't I, Jackie?'

'Ah, that's right, Bill, you did,' the man called Jackie agreed. 'We put our 'eads together, didn't us, tryin' to work out what they could 'ave to talk about.'

A tingle ran up Bradley's spine. 'Who was it?' he asked.

'Well, the last man you'd expect.' Bill seemed to be enjoying this. 'An' talk o' the devil, there he be! Comin' to tell us ter get back ter work, I shouldn't wonder.' He nodded towards the window. Bradley swung round, and could hardly believe what

303

he was seeing. Heading for the canteen door was none other than Sir Henry's unpleasant son, Quentin.

'Are you sure?' he asked, astonished beyond belief.

'Course I'm bliddy sure,' Bill retorted, indignant. 'I might be 'ard o' 'earing, but there's nothin' wrong wi' me bliddy eyesight. I'd just like t' know what Harrison wanted with his lordship.'

He fell silent as Quentin entered the canteen.

'Best drink up, lads, or he'll be dockin' our wages,' one of the others muttered, and Bill drained his cup and put it down on the table.

'Good luck to you anyways, mate,' he said to Bradley. 'An' if you do catch up with Harrison, you can ask 'im yerself what he wanted with gentry.'

A little way along the lane, Bradley pulled into a gateway that gave access to the fields beyond. His head was spinning, and quiet as these roads were, the concentration required to drive safely was beyond him for the moment.

Could it be true that Harrison had obtained the explosives from the son of the quarry owner? Surely not! Much more likely that the man named Bill had implicated him to settle an old score. Clearly there was no love lost there.

On the other hand, it did make some sort of sense. If security was as tight as Sir Henry had insisted it was, only a handful of men would have access to the explosives store, Quentin being one of them. Apparently none of the stock had been missed, which it surely would have been had one of the shot-firers taken out more gelignite than he needed, or if the store had been broken into. And who was responsible for the regular inventories? According to Sir Henry, that too was Quentin.

Even so . . . Had it been one of the quarry employees who had been seen talking to Harry, Bradley would have had no hesitation in taking his suspicions to the police. But to accuse the owner's son on no more evidence than the word of a disgruntled employee was a different kettle of fish entirely. It was highly unlikely he'd be believed, and whether or not he was, the repercussions would be serious. He needed to talk this through with Cameron. The next step could only be taken with his authority.

The note Cam had left for him had said that he would be at Littlecote Colliery all day. In a way, that was fortunate, Bradley thought. Littlecote, like Charterhouse Quarries, lay to the south of Hillsbridge. A short detour on the way home would take him there.

He made up his mind. He'd head there now, and share what he'd learned with his immediate superior. If he didn't find Cameron there, he'd go back to Milverton, get through some of his paperwork, and hope the general manager would call into the office before going home for the day.

Chapter Twenty-Four

Harry had hoped Lorna would be going out to the shops today, giving him the opportunity to move the attaché case from the top of the wardrobe in her room. He'd decided on what he thought was the perfect hiding place. The ramshackle shed in the garden was surrounded on three sides by a thick tangle of bramble and knee-high weeds. It didn't look as if it had been cut back in years, and he couldn't imagine it ever would be. Or at least certainly not until he'd long since left Bradley's house. But to his annoyance, Lorna was showing no signs of going out. When her usual daily chores were done, he'd heard the clatter of pans coming from the kitchen and found her there measuring out flour into an earthenware bowl.

'Wot you doin'?' he'd asked irritably, and she had answered him equally shortly.

'What does it look like? I'm making soda bread.'

'I thought you said you couldn't be doin' wi' this range. You'll mess it up like you'm messin' everything up. Go down the village and buy some. 'Tisn't as if his lordship is short of a penny or two.'

'I've got to get used to it sometime, and it might as well be now.' She tipped salt and baking soda into the mix.

'Wot fer? We'll be gone soon. An' wasn't that the last of the

306

bacon we 'ad fer breakfast? His lordship won't like it if there's no bacon tomorrow.'

Lorna didn't answer him, and the stiffness of her back turned towards him told its own story. Harry swore under his breath. There was no way he could move the attaché case out to the garden with her there in the kitchen.

Oh well, he told himself, there'd be other chances before they left. As long as she didn't spot the case on top of the wardrobe and wonder what it was doing there. But even if she did, and looked inside, he didn't think she'd give the game away. She had too much to lose. She might be in a strop with him now, and she would be again if she stumbled on the truth, but she'd get over it. And once his leg was better, things would go back to being the way they always had been.

Mercy's conscience was pricking her. She really shouldn't have told that man where he could find Harry Harrison. In the moment her jealousy had got the better of her, but now she'd cooled down, she was feeling dreadfully guilty and anxious. She'd seen the way he'd gone for George Golledge, and that was in a public bar, in front of witnesses. Who knew what he'd be capable of on a dark night in the middle of nowhere? He was big, strong and furious, and Harry was presumably still incapacitated. It wasn't beyond the realms of possibility that he could end up seriously hurt, or even dead. If that happened, she wouldn't be able to live with herself.

She thought of the fire at the Harrisons' home. It was still a mystery as to how it had started, though it was common talk that someone with a grudge was responsible. For all she knew, it could have been that same man. He was mad enough for any-thing. Supposing he tried the same thing again, and set fire to the safety officer's house? With Bradley and the Harrisons in it?

Mercy shivered, her stomach clenching and bile rising in her throat. She had to warn him. Risky as it was going to see him at the pit, she'd left herself no choice.

She put on her coat and headed for Hillsbridge, and as the pit yard came into sight she was enormously relieved to see Mr Robinson's little Ford parked outside the office block.

She tapped on the door and opened it without waiting. Mr Robinson was sitting behind the desk, a pile of paperwork spread out in front of him. He looked up, surprised.

'Mercy! What are you . . . ?'

'I'm sorry, but I really need to talk to you . . .'

'You're lucky to catch me. I've been out most of the morning.' He put down his pen, giving her a straight look. 'You'd better tell me what's so urgent then,' he said.

Mercy took a deep breath and told him.

To her enormous relief, Lorna's soda bread had cooked to perfection. She lifted it out of the oven and set it down beside the cooling rack. The smell that rose from it was mouth-watering, and when she tapped the crust, it sounded pleasingly hollow. She took a clean tea towel, laid it over the loaf, and was about to tip it out when a shadow fell across the kitchen window. She looked up and was surprised to see Bradley heading for the back door. It wasn't yet dinner time, and in any case she'd made him a packed lunch. Nevertheless, a warm glow of pleasure coursed through her veins. The exciting turn in their relationship was still new enough that just the sight of him could set her pulses racing and her spirits soaring.

'Bradley! I wasn't expecting you home!' she exclaimed.

'It seems I've come at just the right moment, though.' He nodded in the direction of the soda loaf, which she was holding balanced on the tea towel. 'You've been busy.' But there was an underlying seriousness in his tone that gave the lie to what might have passed for easy banter.

Lorna flipped the loaf onto the wire tray. 'I'll cut you a slice when it's cool enough.'

'Good!' But he was showing little real interest in the soda bread, instead looking around almost warily before asking in a whisper: 'Where's Harry?'

'In the sitting room. Asleep, last time I looked.' She spoke in the same low voice, but she was puzzled. Bradley didn't usually enquire after Harry's whereabouts.

'I need to talk to you,' he said. 'Let's step outside.'

'Now?'

He nodded and she followed him.

'I think I've discovered where Harry got the explosives,' Bradley said without preamble. 'When you told me he used to work at Charterhouse Quarry, I decided to pay them a visit.'

Lorna was staggered, and also annoyed with herself that the connection hadn't occurred to her. 'Oh! The quarry! I never thought . . .'

'Why would you?' Bradley said reasonably. 'You've had other things on your mind.' He hesitated. 'I don't suppose he's ever mentioned knowing Quentin Corsley, the owner's son?'

She shook her head. 'Never. I didn't even know he used to work there until that woman told me. But why? Surely it can't have been him who . . .'

'I'll explain.' Bradley launched into a brief summary of his visit to the quarry, while Lorna listened in astonishment and growing anxiety.

'What are you going to do?' she asked when he had finished.

'I don't know yet,' he admitted. 'I had hoped to catch up with Mr Cameron at Littlecote Colliery, but he was underground and not expected up for some time. I doubt he'll come back to

Milverton today, and I need to talk to him before I do anything.'

'Yes, of course. But . . . the owner's son! It's beyond belief.'

'There's something else,' Bradley went on urgently. 'I've been warned that the man who gave George Golledge a beating – the uncle of the carting boy who died – might come here looking to pick a fight with Harry. I'm told he's of average height, but well built, with hands like hams, and he's all too ready to use them. Be sure to keep the door locked until I get home, and don't open it to anyone else. No one, Lorna. Do you understand?'

She nodded, but her concern must have been clear on her face. He reached for her, pulling her into his arms and kissing her forehead, where a stray lock of hair trailed.

'Don't worry. It probably won't happen, but I don't want to take any chances. I have to go now, but I'll see you when I bring the girls home from school.'

'Of course. You go. I'll be fine.'

She didn't want him to go. She wanted to stay there in his arms for ever with the comforting touch of his hand on her cheek and the smell of him – tobacco, soap and maleness – in her nostrils.

'Take care, sweetheart.' He kissed her lightly, on the lips this time, and then he was gone. She stood for a moment, watching until he turned the corner of the house, then went back inside, locking the door after her as he'd instructed.

Something was different. She sensed it immediately, and although she couldn't put her finger on what it was, it made her uneasy. It was almost as if the very atmosphere in the kitchen had changed.

Oh, she was just being foolish, she scolded herself. Everything Bradley had told her had upset her, and no wonder. Not so much the threat of a man with hands like hams. No, it was the fact that Bradley thought he had unearthed Harry's connection to the explosion that had unsettled her the most. If it could be proved, the stigma would be devastating for the children. And what lengths might he go to in order to avoid arrest?

The feeling of unease intensified, and she tiptoed to the sitting room door and peeped inside. He was there in the easy chair he'd adopted as his own, a cushion behind his head, his eyes closed, just as he had been when she had last looked in on him. But he wasn't snoring gently as he had been then, and she wasn't entirely sure he was asleep.

Again she told herself she was being paranoid. With an effort she pulled herself together, and went back to the kitchen to finish clearing up and make a start on preparations for a light lunch.

Through half-closed eyes Harry watched her go, then sat bolt upright. His leg ached, his head ached, and that damned indigestion was back, a nagging pain in his chest, but just now he scarcely noticed. He was reeling from what he'd overheard – and seen.

He'd just woken up when he'd heard Bradley arrive, and wondered what he was doing here. At first the exchange between him and Lorna had seemed innocent enough, but when they'd begun whispering too quietly for him to hear what was being said, his suspicions had grown, and when they faded away completely, he'd got up and limped into the kitchen. They weren't there. His suspicions aroused, he headed as quietly as he could for the back door, which had been left ajar. If bloody Robinson thought he could cuckold Harry and get away with it, he was making a big mistake.

Using the door as cover, he risked a look outside, and yes, there they were, between door and kitchen window, deep in conversation. He edged closer, so as to be able to listen to what they were saying. And could hardly believe his ears.

They weren't whispering sweet nothings. That bloody bugger was telling Lorna how he had been to Charterhouse and somehow discovered that it was Harry who had acquired the gelignite that had brought the pit roof down!

For a few moments Harry was too shocked to think straight. He knew only that the balloon had gone up. He barely heard Bradley's warning of a man looking for trouble; that was the least of his worries. But when he risked another quick look outside, his blood pressure rose to fever pitch as he saw Lorna in the bloody man's arms.

He'd been right! For an instant he almost hobbled out to confront them and vent his rage, but then his instinct for self-preservation kicked in. That would have to wait. The last thing he wanted was for Robinson to know he'd overheard their conversation – and they could come back at any minute and catch him there, listening. No, he had to give himself time to think. Work out how he was going to save his skin. Stop Robinson from acting on what he'd discovered.

Now, however, having convinced Lorna he was still asleep, the enormity of it all hit him like a blow from a sledgehammer, and his heart began to pound just as it had when the roof had come down on that terrible day.

He had nightmares about it still, from which he woke in a cold sweat. The ear-splitting explosion. The chunk of stone striking his head, dazing him. The hailstorm of rock, clinker and dust knocking him off his feet. Clogging his mouth and nostrils, weighing down on his chest so that for what seemed like an eternity he couldn't draw breath. Struggling in pitch darkness to dislodge some of the debris, somehow managing to create a cavity around his head. Hawking sludge from his throat and mouth, gasping in air. Huffing out dust from his nose.

Desperately trying to move the lower part of his body. And drifting in and out of consciousness as shock set in and the effort became too much for him.

He relived it now as if it was happening again. Trapped. Helpless. And all because he'd been daft enough to want to play the big man in front of his pals, who were plotting a way to make that bugger Sir Montague sit up and take notice. And especially to get one over on George Golledge, who was the hero of the hour for having come up with the idea of a roof fall.

The conspirators had discussed it over a pint or two in the Miners' Arms, enthusiastic, excited. Only Moses Whittock had voiced his doubts, but George had brushed them aside.

''Tis perfect. 'Twould show his lordship just wot we'm faced with every bliddy day.'

'Just s'long as we'm all well out o' the way,' Moses had muttered, realising he would be outvoted when it came to a decision. 'But where be you gonna get the explosives to do the job? Not from Dick Penny, that's fer sure. He d'a guard his stock like the crown jewels.'

'That's true enough,' Ticker Greedy said. 'An' there's no way we'd get 'im onside. If 'e found out wot we'm up to, he'd be straight to management afore you could say Jack Robinson.'

It was Shorty Dallimore who reckoned he had the answer.

'Didn't you used t' work at Charterhouse, Harry? The quarries?'

'That's right, 'e did! There's yer answer!' George turned to Harry. ''Ow about it, my son? You must 'ave mates wot'd filch a bit fer you.'

Harry shook his head dismissively. 'I 'aven't seen any o' them in years. Besides, there's even tighter controls there than we got. 'Tis pretty strong stuff, an' it's only the shot-firers that gets to 'andle it, same as 'ere.'

'You must know somebody,' George exclaimed, frustrated, and with the circle of eager faces waiting on his reply, Harry had an idea.

Quentin Corsley, the quarry owner's son. Harry was pretty sure that checking the stock of explosive was one of his duties. And Harry knew something about Quentin that he was sure as heck Quentin wouldn't want to come out, even after all this time. Something he'd found out when he'd married Greta. A shotgun wedding if ever there was one.

'You'll 'ave to wed 'er,' Greta's father had told him decisively when it had come out that she was in the family way. 'There'll be no bastards in this family.'

And her mother had added: 'The shame of it! I thought we'd 'ad our fair share of trouble – all that business with our Wally. At least 'e 'ad the decency to get away afore anybody found out. But I'm not goin' t' lose me daughter as well as me son through letting theirselves down.'

Harry had never so much as heard Wally's name mentioned before, or even known Greta had a brother, and his curiosity was piqued. At the time, no more was said about it, but later, when he and Greta were alone, he'd questioned her.

'Wot was all that about your brother?'

To his surprise, her face had flamed. She wasn't a coy girl, but he could see this had thrown her.

'Nothing,' she said shortly.

'Come on,' he'd urged her. 'Tip the skeletons out o' the cupboard, do.'

'I can't. Just leave it.'

Harry had no intention of doing any such thing. 'If we'm goin' t' get married, we shouldn't 'ave secrets. I might change me mind if you won't tell me.'

'I can't, Harry, honest. 'Tis shameful.'

'Wot? Did 'e murder somebody?'

'No. Worse.'

What the devil was worse than murder? Harry wondered. And then it occurred to him. Something not only illegal, but to many folk as much a cause for shame and disgrace as an unmarried girl having a baby.

'He bain't a nancy boy, be he?'

The horrified look on Greta's flushed face was enough to give him his answer.

'Oh my Lord!' It was all he could do not to laugh out loud.

''Twasn't 'is fault!' Greta burst out. 'He was forced.'

This time Harry couldn't help grinning. 'That's wot they all say.'

'No. Really.'

'Why didn't 'e go to the bobby, then?'

'Nobody would've believed 'im. No more'n you do.'

'I'll believe it if you say so.'

'They wouldn't, I tell you. If you knew who it was . . .'

'Go on then.'

Greta was biting her lip, deliberating. Eventually she said: 'Promise me you'll never tell a soul.'

'Promise.'

Another long pause, then: ''Twas Pa's boss's son.'

Harry's scepticism melted away like snow when the sun came out. The quarry owner's son. Quentin Corsley. That wet streak of lardy bacon. He could see why Greta's brother had had to keep quiet about it. His father's livelihood depended on it.

'That's why our Wally 'ad to go away,' Greta said bitterly. 'He was a lovely boy. Looked like an angel, 'e did, with his ruff and surplice an' all when 'e was younger an' singin' in the church choir. Quentin Corsley took a fancy to 'im when 'e went to work at the quarry. Tricked 'im into stayin' late one night.

315

An' . . .' She broke off, tears filling her eyes. 'Well, you can guess wot 'appened. An' it wouldn't 'ave stopped with the once, an' folk would've got suspicious. 'Twould 'ave ruined our Wally's life if it 'ad got out. Quentin bloody Corsley would've got off scot free. He'd 'ave said our Wally tempted 'im, led 'im on, an' Wally would 'ave ended up in court. For buggery! That's why you mustn't say anythin'. Ever. Promise me.'

Harry had promised, and he'd kept his word. Over the years he'd more or less forgotten about it. Sitting with his mates in the Miners' Arms, though, it had all come back to him.

God alone knew where Greta's brother was now. But Quentin was still here, lording it over the quarry, and he'd do anything, Harry reckoned, to make sure it stayed that way. Including raiding the quarry explosives store.

This was Harry's chance to make himself a hero in the eyes of his friends and put George Golledge well and truly in the shade.

'Well, I can try,' he'd said. Though already he had been pretty confident of his chances of success.

Now, sitting in Bradley's front room, his gammy leg stretched out in front of him, Harry swore to himself as he remembered just how much he had enjoyed the power his knowledge had given him over Quentin Corsley. How easy it had been to get what he wanted – the fellow had been putty in his hands, terrified by the threat of exposure. And how he had revelled in the admiration of his pals, and George's surprise at his success. It hadn't occurred to him that things could go so horribly wrong.

That fateful morning, he'd taken some of the sticks of gelignite to work with him and given them to George, feeling smug that he had still more stashed away in his old attaché case. He hadn't realised just how powerful the stuff was, though he supposed he should have done, nor that George would make such a hash of setting it off. It was only as he lay badly injured and trapped that he'd realised his own stupidity, and God only knew he'd had plenty of time for regret ever since.

But he'd still been confident that he would never face any sort of punishment for what he'd done. The Inspector of Mines had ruled the disaster an accident. None of his mates would rat on him, and Quentin Corsley would be too afraid for his own skin to admit his part in what had happened. Certainly no one would ever think for a minute that Harry might have blackmailed the son of the quarry owner.

Only now once again it seemed the roof of the world was falling in.

Somehow Harry marshalled his churning thoughts, rerunning the conversation he'd overheard in his mind and latching onto the one thing that offered him any hope.

So far the only ones who knew what he'd done were Lorna and Robinson, and it had sounded as if Robinson wouldn't have the chance to speak to Cameron until tomorrow about how they should proceed. That meant that he had just a few hours to save his bacon. And with a flash of inspiration, he knew exactly how he was going to do it.

For the first time, he was glad that Lorna hadn't gone shopping this morning and he hadn't had the opportunity to smuggle the gelignite out of the house and hide it behind the garden shed. It was still here, and he would use it. He'd blow up the house and the two people who could expose him with it. The same two people who were carrying on right under his nose and making a fool of him. Fury boiled in his veins as he thought of them together, and he tried to control it so as to be able to think straight. It was imperative he work out exactly how he was going to do it yet escape himself and make sure the children weren't harmed.

His heart was thudding again, but he scarcely noticed. All he could think of was getting rid of the two people who could incriminate him. And the satisfaction he'd feel when it was done.

Chapter Twenty-Five

'I'm going to take the children down to see their granny and grandad,' Harry said.

Bradley had brought the girls home as usual, but he'd simply dropped them off and returned to work, and Lorna had had no chance to talk to him. Now she looked up from the vegetables she was preparing for the evening meal, surprised by Harry's suggestion.

'Are you sure you can walk all that way and back again?' she asked dubiously.

'Gotta do it sometime. Might as well be now.'

'Well, if you're sure.' She was concerned he might not be able to manage it. Dr Mackay had said he should take exercise, but he'd never yet gone as far as Littleton Lane. And in light of what Bradley had said about the man who might come looking for Harry, she was worried about the children leaving the house. Supposing they were to meet the man on the lane? If he was seeking revenge, heaven only knew what he might do.

'I don't think it's safe,' she said. 'When Bradley came home this morning, it was to tell me that there's a man after you – the same one who gave George a beating – and it seems he's found out where we are.'

'So?' Harry's lip curled. 'I can look after meself. I could brain

319

a man with me crutches soon as look at 'un.'

Lorna shook her head, exasperated. 'But what about the girls? He's dangerous, Harry. For all we know, he's the one who started the fire at Northfield Terrace. We can't take any chances.'

'All the more reason to get 'em down to Ma and Pa's. They can stop with them.'

Lorna was horrified. With this hanging over them, she didn't want her daughters out of her sight.

'Your mother won't have that,' she said. 'She's made it plain.'

A little voice piped up behind them; Vera had crept up unnoticed. 'Why are we going to Granny's?'

'You're not,' Lorna said.

'Oh yes you be.' Harry was at his most belligerent.

'Why?'

'Never mind why. Get yer night clothes an' put yer coat on. And tell Marjie to do the same.'

Vera pouted. 'I don't want to go to Granny's. Mr Robinson is going to play snap with us this evening.'

'You'll do as ye're told.' There was no arguing with him in this mood.

'Just for tonight,' Lorna said, doing her best to pacify Vera, who looked to be on the verge of tears. 'And I'll come with you as far as the end of the lane. Nipper could do with a walk.'

At least she could make sure they got that far safely, she thought.

But as she stood at the top of the rise and watched them disappear along the track that led to the cottages, she had the most awful feeling that she might never see them again.

The sinking feeling was still there in the pit of her stomach as she unlocked Bradley's back door and locked it again after her.

Without the children, the house felt horribly empty, and tears pricked her eyes. Stupid really, she thought. During the week they were always at school, but at least she knew they'd be back at going-home time. The thought of not being able to give them their tea and tuck them into bed tonight outweighed everything else. Never mind that Harry was going to be charged with manslaughter at best, and perhaps even murder. Never mind that there could be a dangerous man trying to break down the door at any moment. Nothing was more important than her children.

Still, she consoled herself, they'd be safe with Harry's mother and father. They might not want to be there, but at least they wouldn't witness violence that might traumatise them. At least they wouldn't be burned in their beds if this man had been the one to start the fire at their old house and attempted to do the same here. And whatever was to come in the next weeks and months, she had a future to look forward to. A future with Bradley.

How she wished he was here now! But it would be hours before he came home.

So lost in thought was she that before she knew it, she'd peeled enough potatoes for the five of them. Shaking her head as the awful feeling of emptiness overcame her again, she put some in a small saucepan and covered them with water. Hopefully they'd keep for tomorrow. And hopefully by then the children would be back.

Harry didn't stay long with his parents. Though his father had been understanding about the children's need for safety, and had spoken to his mother more forcefully than he usually did, she was in a miserable grump about having them foisted on her.

Besides, he had things to do. He wanted everything set up

and ready so that when his chance came he would be able to take it, and he still had to figure out the final details of how he would make his plan work.

At least the girls were out of the way now, but he was still pondering how he could incapacitate Robinson. He needed to die in the explosion while Harry himself escaped. Though he'd come off best in more than one brawl, he knew he wouldn't be able to overpower the man given the state he'd been reduced to – his comment about using his crutches to brain a man had been nothing more than bravado. As he saw it, his only chance would be to creep up behind Robinson when he was sitting down and crack him over the head with something good and heavy, hard enough to knock him out. The flat iron, perhaps. It lived on a shelf in the kitchen. He'd seen Lorna take it down and set it on the range when she had some ironing to do.

And there were sharp knives in a wooden block on the worktop if he needed one. Or – even better – his cut-throat razor, which hung on a nail beside the sink.

His plan was coming together. With renewed confidence, he walked the rest of the way back to the house.

Bradley was finding it impossible to concentrate on the paperwork that was piling up on his desk. He could think of nothing but what he'd learned this morning, still scarcely able to believe it. But the pieces fitted. Either Harry and Quentin had been friends, which seemed highly unlikely, or Harry had known something he'd been able to blackmail the quarry owner's son with. That he had been secretly selling explosives, perhaps?

If he was right, Bradley knew all hell was going to break loose, and it was imperative he talk to Cameron so that they could decide on a course of action. Anxious though he was to get home and make sure Lorna and the children were safe, he decided he would stay on a while in the hope that Cam might return here before going home himself. Sharing what he had discovered with his superior was best done as soon as possible.

The sun that had broken through the cloud that morning with the promise of brighter days to come had gone into hiding again, and as Lorna made the final preparations for the evening meal, the light in the kitchen was beginning to dim. She wondered whether to light the oil lamp, but decided against it. The wick needed trimming, and she didn't want to take her eye off the vegetables that were simmering on the range. Bradley should be home before it got too dark; he'd do it. Pointless to ask Harry.

He'd been in a very strange mood since he'd got back from taking the children to Littleton Lane. Surly as ever – snapping 'Of course they'm all right' when she'd asked how the children had been when he'd left them – but at the same time radiating a sort of nervous energy. Fussing and moving things. Pacing, moving them again, and generally getting under her feet.

Eventually she hadn't been able to stand it any longer.

'For goodness' sake go and sit down, Harry,' she'd said. 'I'd have thought you'd have tired yourself out walking down to your mother's and back.'

'P'raps I will 'ave a snooge,' he'd said, surprising her. Usually any suggestion she made was met with derision and rejection.

She looked out now at the gathering dusk, thinking that Bradley should have been home by now and hoping he'd be here soon. Something must have held him up, she decided, and wondered if it might be connected to what he'd learned this morning.

She checked the vegetables – almost done. She took them off the heat and drained them. They'd finish cooking in the steam but still be warm when Bradley got home. Perhaps she would see to the lamp after all.

She looked around for it, but it wasn't in its usual place. Harry must have moved it when he was so restless earlier. Taken it with him into the front room, perhaps. She went through, expecting to find him asleep in the chair he seemed to have made his own, but he wasn't there, and she heard a floorboard creak above her. Had he gone upstairs, elated, perhaps, at having walked all the way to Littleton Cottages and back and thinking he'd try another challenge? Maybe hoping that if he could make it, he'd be able to sleep in a bed instead of on the sofa? *Her* bed? Oh please no! The thought of him beside her turned her stomach.

But she didn't want him falling down the stairs as he had once before and ending up in a heap at the bottom. She hurried through the living room and saw his crutches propped up against the newel post at the foot of the stairs. Dismayed, she hurried up, her stockinged feet making no sound. Her bedroom door was open, and through it she could see Harry apparently lifting something from the top of the wardrobe.

'What are you doing?' she demanded.

At the sound of her voice, he started and almost dropped whatever it was he was balancing with both hands, but managed to steady it. To her surprise, she saw it was his old attaché case.

'Mind yer business, woman,' he growled.

'What's your case doing there?' she asked, puzzled. 'Have you been up here before?'

'Wot if I 'ave? It's a free country, in't it? Are you spyin' on me, or wot?'

'I was going to help you down the stairs, but I'll leave you to it if that's what you want,' Lorna said crossly. 'Just don't blame me if you fall.' She swung round and marched back across the landing.

'You can take this for me.' Harry was following her, still clutching the case. Lorna didn't reply. She had no intention of helping him now. If he wanted the case downstairs, he could do it himself.

As she started down the stairs, she could hear him coming down behind her, one tentative step at a time, the case bumping on each stair as he went. Let him struggle! she thought crossly.

Exactly what happened next was something of a blur to her. Harry must have stumbled – she heard him swear – and lost his grip on the attaché case. She was aware of a *thud, thud, thud*, and something struck the back of her legs, taking them from under her. Her head banged back on the stair above, and then she was tumbling in an awkward tangle of arms and legs, the attaché case bumping down in front of her.

For a long moment she lay against the bottom stair, stunned. Harry scrambled past her, intent on reaching the case, which lay on the floor to her left. She turned her head, trying to see what he was doing, and a dart of pain shot up her neck, making her gasp. The bottom of her spine was hurting too where she had landed on it, and her head was spinning, but she could see that the case had burst open, spilling its contents onto the floor. Harry was trying to push them back inside. A bundle of reddish-brown and orange sticks that might almost have been candles with cords attached . . .

'Harry,' she murmured groggily. He ignored her.

She attempted to get up, but everything was unfocused, unreal, fading. Darkness was closing in and she sank into it.

In a blind panic, Harry picked up the attaché case, not waiting to click the fastenings closed, and, leaving Lorna lying at the foot of the stairs, hurried to the kitchen as fast as his gammy leg would allow. Nipper was out of his basket, woken no doubt by the commotion, and Harry pushed him into the front room and shut the door. The bloody dog under his feet was the last thing he needed.

Why the devil had Lorna come upstairs at just that moment? he wondered bad-temperedly. He'd thought she was busy in the kitchen and he would have plenty of time to unload what he needed and get it downstairs and out of sight. But no, she'd had to upset everything. Served her right if she'd hurt herself badly. She'd tumbled down the stairs from at least halfway up and she'd certainly looked out of it when he'd left her. Fainted, perhaps, or passed out from hitting her head on the stair. He remembered how he himself had drifted in and out of consciousness when the rock had hit his head. He was pretty sure she'd come round again soon, and that would spell disaster. She'd seen what was in the case. He doubted she'd know what it was, but if she told Robinson, he certainly would. And Robinson could be home at any time now. Somehow Harry had to take care of this, and fast.

His head felt as if it was about to explode, and his heart was pumping furiously, but he knew that somehow he had to rescue his plan. He tried to marshal his racing thoughts, and as he did so, he felt his spirits rising. In some ways Lorna's fall could make things easier. If she was still at the foot of the stairs when Robinson came home, he would almost certainly go to her aid, and hitting him over the head with the flat iron would be child's play. Much easier than having to wait for his chance. But he must make darned sure she was still there.

There was a length of thick twine in the case; he'd used it once to hold the thing together when he'd stuffed it too full for it to stay closed on its little catches. He got it out and put it in his pocket, then found a book of matches, the flat iron and his cut-throat razor, and took them into the living room together with his attaché case.

Lorna was still slumped at the foot of the stairs. She'd come around now, but she still looked dazed. 'Harry, help me! I can't get up,' she said weakly.

He retrieved the twine from his pocket and bent down, grasping her by the shoulders and yanking her upright so roughly that she gasped. He ignored her reaction, twisting first one arm then the other behind her back and holding her wrists together with one hand while he wound the twine around them as tightly as he could and knotted it. Her eyes were wide now, her face a mask of bewilderment, pain and horror.

'Stay there,' he growled between gritted teeth, though he knew there was no danger of her going anywhere. If she couldn't get up with her hands free to use as a lever, there was no chance she could do it with them tied behind her back.

He put the case out of sight behind an easy chair that stood to the right of the door. The cut-throat razor he hid beneath a cushion on the chair, while he pocketed the book of matches and debated where would be the best place to conceal the flat iron. But did that really matter? Robinson was going to be too concerned with Lorna to notice it even if it was in plain sight. He put it on one of the dining chairs and pushed it far enough under the table so as not to be immediately obvious, but within easy reach for him to pick up the minute Robinson approached her.

One last thing. If Robinson was only stunned, he would have to be restrained, and for that Harry needed some more twine or rope. He thought he'd seen some coiled on a shelf in the garden shed when he'd been in there poking about. He'd have to be quick, but he'd feel much safer if he knew he could tie the man up if necessary. He hurried out, leaving the kitchen door open to save time, and hobbled across the uneven ground, all the while listening out for the sound of Robinson's motor in the lane.

It was almost dark in the shed. It had only one small window, which was dirty and draped with cobwebs, but by the flickering light of one of the matches he spotted the rope on a shelf just as he'd remembered. He grabbed it and hurried back to the house. He was breathless from the exertion and his heart was pounding erratically, but he didn't dare to slow down.

He found Lorna struggling to free herself – useless, of course. But he gave her a shove anyway so that she fell back against the stair. Then he dropped the rope onto the easy chair and covered it with the antimacassar.

'Why are you doing this, Harry? Let me go, please!' she begged, desperate, pleading.

'I can't do that, Lorna,' he said.

'But why?'

'You'll find out soon enough.'

He fetched the oil lamp and lit it. By its light he could see that Lorna was chalky white, and he felt a glow of satisfaction. There was nothing left to do now but wait for Robinson to get home. And then it would be showtime.

Chapter Twenty-Six

Lorna wriggled helplessly as she tried to free her hands, but every movement sent fresh waves of pain through her spine and her poor stretched shoulders, and the knots held firm.

What in the world was Harry thinking, tying her up like this? He must have taken leave of his senses. Did it have anything to do with the blow to his head he'd suffered when the pit roof had come down? She'd thought his constant bad temper was due to the pain of his injuries, but certainly he'd seemed to be getting progressively worse. Could it be a bleed on the brain? She'd heard that could happen. Whatever, he was behaving now like a dangerous madman.

And where was Bradley? He wasn't usually this late. Why tonight of all nights? Thank goodness at least the children weren't here. It would have been even more terrible if they'd had to witness this.

A sudden thought struck her. Had he deliberately got them out of the way? If so, he'd planned this. But why? She couldn't hazard a guess, unless . . .

A sudden thought struck her. She'd thought he was asleep when she and Bradley had been talking outside. But what if he had been pretending? What if he'd heard Bradley say that he knew where Harry had got the explosives?

Jennie Felton

The explosives! Lorna's blood turned to ice. Was that what she'd seen when the attaché case burst open? She had no idea what gelignite looked like, but might it have been that? Oh surely – surely – Harry couldn't be meaning to end it all . . .

He was pacing, wired up with the same sort of nervous energy as when he'd returned from taking the girls to his parents' house.

'Harry,' she said, her voice trembling like the rest of her, though she tried to control it, 'has this got anything to do with the roof fall at the pit?'

He laughed harshly, accusingly. 'You'd know all about that, I s'pose.'

'You got the explosives that brought the roof down from the quarry, didn't you?' she said. 'How could you have been so stupid?'

'Stupid, eh? To try and get more money to put food on the table and keep a roof over yer 'eads?'

She was annoying him, she knew, but she was praying she would be able to talk some sense into him.

'Much good it did us,' she said. 'Is this going to work any better? Think of the children, if not me. You love them. You must do or you wouldn't have taken them to safety. What's going to happen to them? For heaven's sake, Harry, stop this now before someone gets hurt, or worse.'

'The children'll be fine. A damn sight better than if their father's in jail.'

That puzzled her a bit, but she persisted. 'You did wrong, Harry, but this is going to make things worse. If you just face it like a man—'

His face darkened with fury. 'Be you sayin' I'm not a man? I'll show you . . .'

He was across the room in two short strides, striking her full

330

in the face so forcefully he almost lost his balance. Lorna's head jerked back, and with a muffled cry of shock and pain she fell against the stairs, stars exploding before her eyes. And at that very moment, through the ringing in her ears, she heard Bradley's voice.

'Hello? Where is everybody?'

'Quick! Here!' Harry called. Lorna watched aghast as he picked up the flat iron from a chair and held it out of sight behind his back. 'Lorna's fell down the stairs, an' she's delirious!'

'Oh my God!' Bradley appeared in her line of sight.

'Brad!' she gasped but her jaw, stiff from Harry's blow, wouldn't work properly, and it came out as 'Rad'.

'Lorna!' He dropped to his knees beside her, and Harry moved behind him, the flat iron raised above his head.

'No!' At the same time as she managed to scream the warning, she kicked out hard. Her foot connected with Bradley's gut, knocking him off balance, and he fell to one side just as Harry swung the flat iron down, so that instead of connecting with its intended target, it caught Bradley on the shoulder. With a grunt of surprise and pain, he rolled over, clutching his arm, and made to rise. But before he could do so Harry had grabbed his cut-throat razor from the easy chair. With his free hand he yanked Lorna upright, lifted her chin to expose her throat and pressed the razor against it.

'One wrong move and she gets it,' he snarled.

'What the hell are you doing?' Bradley demanded, levering himself up on his uninjured arm.

The muscles in Harry's arm bunched as he pressed the razor against Lorna's throat so that it cut the skin and a trickle of blood ran down.

'Stay where you are, Robinson! I'm warning you . . .'

Bradley froze, not daring to risk another move with the razor so perilously close to Lorna's jugular vein. He was in no doubt that Harrison would do as he threatened. The man had gone completely mad.

By the light of the lamp he could see an ugly weal already darkening to a livid bruise across her cheek and jawline, and her eyes, huge and urgent, seemed to be trying to tell him something. From the taut stretch of her shoulders he guessed that her hands were tied behind her back. This was a trap, set for him, presumably because he had been investigating the explosion at the pit, and for the moment Harrison held the trump card. With the razor at Lorna's throat, there was nothing Bradley could do but try to reason with him.

'Why are you doing this, Harrison?' he asked levelly.

'Why the devil d'you think? To stay out'a stir, o' course. I heard you this morning. Wot you said. You've been pokin' around. Askin' too many questions. An' you think you've got me. But I'm telling you straight. It ain't goin' t' 'appen. You won't be tellin' any other bugger wot you think you know.'

So he'd been right, Bradley thought. Harry had been behind the explosion at the pit. And he was holding Lorna hostage in the mistaken belief that he could escape the consequences. But it was how he planned to stop Bradley from taking action on what he'd found out that was both puzzling and worrying. And the man really didn't look well. It wasn't easy to tell by the light of the oil lamp, but his colour was somehow unnatural, waxy almost.

'All right, Harrison,' he said. 'It's me you want, and that's fair enough. But for God's sake, let Lorna go. She's your wife. The mother of your children. Let her go, and then we can talk about this.'

Harry laughed, the crazed laugh of a madman. 'Talk? 'Tis

too late fer talk. 'Tis time fer action. An' you'm goin' t' see plenty o' that.'

Another veiled threat. Bradley grew ever more desperately worried for Lorna's safety. 'Just let her go, and I'll do whatever you want,' he said.

'You expect me to believe that?' Harry asked scornfully.

'I give you my word.'

Harry was silent for a moment, as if considering the offer. Bradley wanted nothing more than to lunge at him, but he dared not.

'Well?' he prompted. 'What do you say? Do we have a deal?'

'You'll do anything?' There was a crafty look now in Harry's eyes and he was smirking unpleasantly.

'Anything.'

'Awright.' He seemed to have made up his mind. 'There's a little case behind that chair.' He jerked his head to indicate where he meant. 'Push it over t' me with yer foot. But I'm warning you, try anything stupid an' I'll finish 'er off.' To emphasise the point, he drew the blade across Lorna's throat, lightly, but enough to graze the taut skin, and Lorna gasped.

'Don't worry, sweetheart. It's going to be all right,' Bradley said, attempting to reassure her, and immediately realised his mistake.

'Sweetheart, eh?' Harry snarled. 'I bloody knew it.'

'I care for her, yes, which is more than you do,' Bradley said. 'I'll do as you say, but I won't come any closer. I swear.'

'You'd better bloody not.'

Bradley inched his way to the back of the chair and nudged the case towards Harry with his toe.

'You want'a see wot's inside?' Harry taunted him. ''Tisn't locked. Go on, open it an' 'ave a look. But no sudden moves, mind, or she gets it.'

Bradley leaned over, careful not to do anything to alarm Harry, and slid his fingers beneath the worn leather lid. As the contents were revealed, a shock wave flashed through him like a bolt of lightning.

Gelignite. Not just one or two sticks, but a whole bundle, with detonators and fuse cable attached. Harry's intention was to set off an explosion that would destroy the house and anyone in it.

Seeing the horrified realisation on Bradley's face, Harry smirked. 'Satisfied?'

'Harrison . . .'

'*Mister* Harrison to you.' He jerked his head in the direction of the dining table. 'If you want me to let 'er go, fetch a chair, bring it back 'ere and sit down.'

Bradley had no choice but to do as he was told. As he placed the chair where Harry indicated, facing the stairs, Lorna's eyes, dark with terror, met his. But he knew that to communicate with her in any way would only inflame the dangerous situation.

Harry tossed him a length of rope. 'Tie yer feet to the chair legs. Go on, do as I say an' I'll let 'er go.'

So he'd been right. Lorna was the bait. Though he knew he was facing certain death, Bradley felt nothing but enormous relief. At least she would be spared.

He bent double, winding the rope between his ankles and the legs of the chair, wondering if he could somehow fudge the knots without Harry noticing. But mad though he plainly was, Harry was not stupid. He reached for his crutch with his free hand and used it to test the knots. Finally, satisfied, he removed the razor from Lorna's throat, throwing it onto the easy chair, and Bradley breathed a sigh of relief.

But it was short-lived. Leaning heavily on the crutch, Harry retrieved the gelignite and set it down on the floor before laying

334

the length of fuse across the room so that it reached almost to the kitchen door. His plan was clear to Bradley now. He'd made sure the fuse was long enough to allow him to escape before the flame reached the detonator. He stood for a moment regarding it with satisfaction, and rubbing his arm as if he'd suddenly developed an itch. He really didn't look well, Bradley thought. But it was a fleeting thought only as Harry cackled, 'This is cheerio, then.' He took a book of matches from his pocket and lit one, grinning inanely.

A fresh wave of alarm flooded through Bradley.

'Let Lorna go!' he said urgently. 'You've got me. For God's sake, let her go!'

Harry laughed again, that crazed cackle. 'More fool you to think I'd ever do that. D'you think she'd keep quiet? Course she wouldn't. She'd be straight to the rozzers.'

'Then take her with you. You can make sure she doesn't talk,' Bradley begged desperately.

'An' 'ow am I goin' to do that, eh? She d'a know where I got this stuff too, don't she? I heard you this morning, tellin' 'er.' His mouth twisted into a snarl. 'An' I saw you all over 'er. Oh no, mister, you and she want'a be together. Well I'm goin t' see you bloody well are. For all eternity.'

The match had burned out. Harry lit another and held it up, mocking them. 'Be this the one t' do the job? Or shall we bide a bit longer?'

He was clearly enjoying this. The threat. The power. Bradley was no longer in any doubt that he meant to kill both of them. And there was nothing he could do to stop him.

Ignoring Harry completely, he looked directly at Lorna so that their eyes met. 'I love you, Lorna.'

Her lips moved, and at last she managed to whisper, 'And I love you, Bradley.'

Fury twisted Harry's features. 'Right. That's it.' He dropped the spent match, lit another and set it to the fuse. It flared briefly, then went out, and Bradley dared to hope that it had got damp somehow. But on Harrison's next attempt it caught, and the flame began to inch slowly along its length, towards the bundle of gelignite.

Harry grinned at them, triumphant. 'I be off then.' He turned for the door and went out, leaving Bradley and Lorna to their fate.

He'd done it! As he emerged into the darkness that had fallen, Harry was exultant. He didn't feel at all well, but what did that matter? He'd done it! Now all he had to do was get as far away from the house as he could before the place went up. If he could make it to the end of the garden, he might be able to scramble over the low wall and into the field. That should give him some cover. Trouble was, he'd left his crutch behind and the damned contraption on his leg wasn't helping. Somehow he waddled on, staggering now, until he reached the wall, and there he stopped to get his breath before trying to hoist himself up.

No good. He couldn't do it no matter how he tried. And the effort was making him feel very ill now. His heart was thundering, too fast for comfort, and the pain that he'd thought was trapped wind was worse than ever, tightening his lungs and spreading down his arm.

What the hell was the matter with him? He'd just have to rest and hope that when the house went up he was far away enough not to be hit by flying debris. Oh well, that had happened before, and he was still here to tell the tale . . .

He leaned against the wall. His head was swimming now and the pain was becoming unbearable. He gasped. Slid down the wall. Experienced a moment's blind panic. But he'd done it! He'd done for them both! It was his last lucid thought.

'Right. I'm off to deal with Harrison.' Mark Wheeler tied a muffler round his neck and headed for the door.

'Don't, Mark, please! I'm begging you! We don't want any more trouble.' Edie Maggs caught at her brother's sleeve, but he shook himself free.

'I'm gonna make sure 'e gets rough justice, 'cos that's the only sort 'e will get,' he snarled. 'Thinks 'e's gettin' away wi' it? I'll show 'im 'e's not.' He strode out, banging the door behind him.

He faced a long walk to the other side of Hillsbridge, but if he cut through to the trammy that took tubs of coal down to the railway sidings and scrambled up the other side, it would be a much shorter route. Just as long as there wasn't a herd of cows and a bull in the field leading up to Oldlands. But it was still early in the year for them to be out of the farmyard. He'd just have to take a chance on it.

He started down the steep incline, almost missing his footing a couple of times. But he carried on regardless, fired up with anticipation of the punishment he was going to mete out to that bugger Harrison.

Bradley wasn't ready to give up yet. He could see the cut-throat razor lying in the chair where Harry had thrown it; if he could reach it, he should be able to cut himself free. He began rocking the chair he was tied to, trying to walk it across the floor, but his progress was minimal. He'd never reach the razor in time to saw through the rope and get himself and Lorna out of the house before it went up. But he had no intention of simply sitting here watching the little flame creep relentlessly towards the gelignite.

He managed to wrestle his arms out of his coat, then bunched it up and tossed it over the fuse, which was now dangerously short. His aim was true; the little flame disappeared under the bulk of heavy wool. But was it extinguished? Or was it going to flare up again? He didn't know. With a superhuman effort, he managed to rock the chair sideways until it toppled and he landed heavily on top of his coat, pressing it down onto the fuse with his body weight.

So engrossed was he in what he was attempting to do that he didn't hear the knock at the door. But Lorna did, and despite the injuries to her face, she managed to call out: 'Bradley! There's someone there!'

Bradley raised himself with an effort on his uninjured arm and shouted with all the strength he could muster. He heard the creak of the handle being turned, shouted again. He only hoped it wasn't the man Mercy had warned him about. But even he might be their salvation. Then the door burst open, someone rushed in, and in the shadowy light thrown by the oil lamp, he recognised Cam's solid figure.

'Get Lorna! She's hurt!' he yelled. 'Get her out of here and take cover, both of you. There's explosives . . .'

'What? Where?' Cam sounded totally bewildered.

He blundered forward, and swore as he almost tripped over Bradley's prone figure. 'Bradley?'

'Never mind me! Just get Lorna out! She's on the stairs!'

To his enormous relief, Cam sprang into action, heading past him to where Lorna lay.

'It's all right, lassie. I've got you.'

Bradley heard her gasp of pain as Cam picked her up.

'Go!' he yelled, and only breathed again when a blast of cold air hit him as Cam threw the back door wide. They'd made it out. Thank God!

* * *

Cam still didn't know what the hell was going on. When at last he'd finished at Littlecote – a job that had taken him all day – he'd driven to his office to deal with the paperwork it had engendered whilst it was fresh in his mind, and found a note from Bradley propped up on his desk. Bradley had stayed late, it seemed, as he had something he wanted to talk to Cam about, but had eventually given up and gone home. From the tone of the note Cam had gathered it was important, and he had decided to drive out to Littleton and visit Bradley this evening rather than waiting until next day.

He had, of course, been totally shocked by the scene that had greeted him, but with Bradley's desperation to get Lorna out of the house, and the mention of explosives, he hadn't stopped to ask questions, or even to free her hands, which he could see were tied behind her back. He simply hoisted her up into his arms and raced out.

His motor was parked on the road; he hurried to it and lifted her in as gently as he could. But he knew that if there were explosives primed to go off in the house, as Bradley had seemed to think, this wouldn't be far enough away to be out of danger. He hurried to the front of the motor and cranked the engine to life, then, as he clambered into the driving seat, he realised Lorna was trying to say something.

'Go back for Bradley, please!' He was just able to make out her words over the roar of the engine.

'When I've got you to safety,' he shouted over his shoulder, then let out the clutch, drove for dear life along the lane and pulled into the colliery yard. This was far enough to be out of range of any flying debris if the house went up, he thought.

'You'll be safe here,' he said, turning off the engine.

'But Bradley . . .'

'I'll go back now.'

He took a few moments to untie the rope around her wrists, take off his coat and cover her with it. Then, puffing from the exertion, he ran back along the road to the house.

For a few moments Bradley had lain still, unsure whether he'd managed to stifle the flame or whether it would reignite and begin inching once more towards the bundle of gelignite. But when he managed to swivel around enough to see the snaking fuse, he could see no sign that it was still alight. Cautiously he moved his coat to one side. He could smell scorched wool – he'd ruined it, no doubt, but it had done the job. What did a coat matter when his whole house could have gone up, and him with it?

He could move, he realised, by using his arms to worm his way across the floor, dragging the chair behind him, and he made for the chair where Harry had left the razor. When he reached it, he tested it with his finger; it was sharp enough to draw blood. Harry could so easily have cut Lorna's throat with it! Bradley's gut clenched. Damned man! Where was he now? Anticipating the big bang? In hiding somewhere waiting for it? He was going to be disappointed, Bradley thought grimly. But disappointment was going to be the least of his worries when they caught up with him.

He put the razor to the rope around his legs. A few strokes and he'd cut through the loops and was free. He scrambled to his feet, made for the door. All he wanted now was to get to Lorna, hold her and comfort her, and if she was as badly hurt as he thought she was, get her to medical attention.

As he passed the door to the front room, he heard a whimper and realised that Harry must have shut Nipper in there. He opened the door, but instead of bounding out, Nipper crept forward, ears flat to his head, tail between his legs.

'It's all right, boy,' Bradley said, but Nipper looked up at him with huge soulful eyes. A look of shame that he hadn't been able to protect them, Bradley thought.

He found Nipper's lead, clipped it on and took him outside. The last thing he wanted right now was for the little dog to run off. Lorna would never forgive him. Ridiculous to think such a thing in the light of the disaster they'd faced, but there it was.

'Robinson!' Cam came panting round the side of the house. 'Lorna's in my motor up in the colliery yard . . .' He broke off. 'You were tied to a chair the last time I saw you. How did you . . . ?'

'Long story. Let's go to Lorna.'

'You mentioned explosives. What about . . .'

'I've made them safe.' Bradley slammed the door behind him.

'Shouldn't you lock it? ' Cam cautioned him.

'I very much doubt there'll be anybody out here except perhaps a few poachers,' Bradley said, but he locked the door anyway.

They started up the lane, Nipper dragging a bit on his lead, apparently still feeling ashamed.

'I take it this is all Harrison's doing?' Cam ventured.

'It certainly is,' Bradley said grimly.

'So where is he now?'

'He ran off after he lit the fuse. I don't know where he is, and I don't much care.'

'Mightn't he go back and have another go?'

'The door's locked now, remember. And anyway the remaining fuse is too short to be safe. He'd blow himself up.'

'But your house . . .'

'The least of my worries.'

All that mattered to Bradley right now was getting to Lorna.

From the moment Cam had carried Lorna out to the car, everything had been jumbled together in a hazy blur of shock, pain and overwhelming fear. The jolting of the motor as it raced over humps and ruts in the lane, each one eliciting a silent scream of agony. The nightmarish aura that enveloped her. And the sickening knowledge that Bradley was still inside the house, which could be blown sky high at any moment, bringing with it unbearable loss.

She was dimly aware of Cam freeing her arms and tucking something heavy but soft around her, and of moonlight falling on her face as it emerged from behind fitful cloud. And an image of her mother, crystal clear against the darkness amid the trees where the moon could not reach. In the midst of all the confusion and terror, Lorna experienced a moment of joy. Mam was here. She would make everything better. But her mother was shaking her head, and Lorna seemed to hear her voice from somewhere inside herself. *No, my love. It's not time . . .*

And then a moment she would remember for ever.

'Bradley!' she murmured.

He was beside her, gently smoothing her tumbled hair away from her face, kissing her cheek. Was he real? Or, like her mother, a dear lost soul? But she could hear his breathing, feel it close to her ear, and smell the familiar well-loved scent of him, tobacco, soap and maleness.

She closed her eyes and drifted, away from the fear and pain and mayhem, to a place where nothing mattered but that he was with her, whole and alive.

Chapter Twenty-Seven

As soon as they had taken Lorna to the cottage hospital and been assured she was in good hands, Bradley and Cameron had dropped Nipper off at the house, having made sure there was now no danger of the explosives reigniting, and driven to Bath. This was too serious a matter for Sergeant Love to handle, and the two men were in agreement that it would be best if they went directly to the divisional police headquarters.

In the event, things hadn't worked out quite as they had envisaged. There were several people ahead of them in the queue waiting to speak to the desk sergeant, and when at last it was their turn, the sergeant was reluctant to allow them access to a detective. Eventually, however, he had shown them through to the office of the duty inspector.

Bradley wasn't overly impressed by the man behind the well-worn desk, who indicated that they should sit on the two hard upright chairs facing him. Detective Inspector Bowen was a portly man attired in a waistcoat and tartan trousers, and he exuded an air of pomposity.

'Correct me if I am mistaken, but I was given to understand that the roof fall at the colliery was ruled by the Inspector of Mines to have been an accident, and the coroner at the subsequent inquest into the death of a man and a boy reached the same conclusion.' He regarded them smugly. 'Unless you have new evidence, you are wasting your time and mine.'

'We have new evidence all right,' Cam said shortly. 'And you'd do well to send a man to Oldlands House without delay so that he can recover it.'

The DI assumed a smile that did not reach his eyes. 'Perhaps you'd care to explain, Mr . . . ?' He raised a quizzical eyebrow.

'Cameron,' Cam said. 'I'm general manager of Sir Montague Fairley's mines. And this is Mr Robinson, the safety officer, who pursued an investigation of his own since he was dissatisfied with the inspector's findings, and as a result came close to being blown up by one of the perpetrators this evening.'

Some of the wind appeared to have been taken out of the DI's sails. He was more used to bullying anyone unfortunate enough to cross his path than coming face to face with a man who was his equal and not averse to using intimidation himself when the situation warranted it.

'What exactly are you alleging, Mr Cameron?' he enquired, fixing Cam with a cold stare.

'A man by the name of Harrison obtained gelignite illegally and used it to cause the roof fall that killed a man and a carting boy,' Cam stated. 'For the moment, the details of that are irrelevant. The more pressing matter is that tonight he attempted to use more of the gelignite to murder Mr Robinson when he discovered he'd been found out. Fortunately he failed, but he is now on the run. The gelignite is still in Mr Robinson's house, with the fuse attached though now inactive, since Mr Robinson managed to extinguish the flame before it reached the detonator. I suggest you send an officer to the scene immediately.'

'And where is this house?' the DI asked in a supercilious tone.

'On Oldlands Lane, just a few hundred yards from the colliery of the same name. Our local police station is in Hillsbridge.'

'So why did you not report this to the sergeant there?'

Cam had had enough. 'We supposed we would save valuable time by coming direct to you,' he said sharply. 'Clearly we were mistaken. You seem incapable of recognising the urgency of the situation. And I warn you, your chief constable will hear of this if you continue to delay taking action.'

'Very well. I will contact the Hillsbridge sergeant.' High colour had risen in Bowen's paunchy face, and he made a great show of checking his timepiece, which hung on a chain straining across his ample gut. 'There should be at least one constable still on duty who can be deployed. If not, Sergeant Love will have to deal with the matter himself. We shall need full statements from both of you, of course, and none of my detectives are available at the present time. But I must insist that you leave the police work to us from now on.'

'We'll see about that.' Cam got to his feet. 'I'm only surprised you don't consider this serious enough to warrant coming out to Hillsbridge yourself. It doesn't inspire much confidence in you, that I can tell you.'

Without another word he strode out of the office and the police station, Bradley on his heels.

'We'd best get back. I don't trust that man any further than I could throw him,' Cam growled as they reached the street.

'I think your threat of the chief constable worked,' Bradley said. 'The rest was just bluster to save face.'

Cam snorted. 'I damn well hope you're right. We hand him evidence on a plate, and he throws it back in our faces. Get the motor going for me, laddie. You're younger than me.'

In spite of himself, Bradley smiled. Cam was one of a

kind, and Sir Montague was lucky to have him as his general manager.

Mark Wheeler was creeping around the side of the house when he heard voices. Not from inside, though he could hear a dog barking there, but coming from the direction of the road. He flattened himself against the wall, then inched along and peeked around the corner. To his utter shock, he saw the lights of two bicycles being wheeled up the path, and what looked like the silhouettes of two policemen's helmets.

Dear Lord, he'd almost been caught red-handed! Thanking his lucky stars for the deep shadow at the side of the house, he made a run for it towards the garden. Too late.

'Hoi! You!'

'Stop, thief!'

Mark ran as fast as his legs would carry him. He could see the outline of a garden shed against the skyline. He made a dash for it across a patch of rough ground, and slid out of sight in the narrow space between the shed and a wall.

The voices were coming closer, and he saw the beam of a powerful torch slicing through the darkness. He inched a little further behind the shed and his foot brushed against something lying on the ground. A sack of rubbish maybe? He didn't know, but he didn't dare risk trying to step over it for fear of stumbling and alerting the policemen to his whereabouts. He stood stock still, holding his breath. The policemen passed right by the shed, shining their torches into the darkness beyond, and he heard one of them say: 'We've lost 'im.'

'Yeah, he's legged it all right.'

As the voices grew fainter, Mark heaved a sigh of relief. But his heart was pounding so hard in his chest he was surprised the policemen hadn't heard it.

He turned to face the wall. Beyond it, a field stretched away. He grabbed the top and was hauling himself up when one of his boots loosened a stone, which came away in a shower of old cement. Unbalanced, Mark lost his footing and fell back with it, landing heavily against the shed and sliding down to hit the ground with a bump.

He swore, and remained where he was for a minute or so, afraid he might have given himself away. But the policemen didn't come running back. Mark reached out a hand to lever himself up and encountered something soft – the sack of rubbish, he supposed. Except that it didn't feel like a sack of rubbish. It felt like . . .

A body!

The moon emerged from behind a cloud and he saw it, spread-eagled there, unmoving but not yet completely cold. He jerked his hand away as if he had touched a hot coal. His stomach was turning over, filling his mouth with bile. In utter panic, he scrambled to his feet and stumbled to the wall, where he grasped the top once again and this time managed to hoist himself up and over. When he landed on the other side, he didn't even stop to brush the dirt from his hands. He ran, stumbling, across the uneven tussocks as if the devil himself was after him, and didn't stop until he had no breath left and his legs would no longer carry him.

He sank to the ground, his mind racing. He had no idea who the body belonged to, and he had no intention of going back to find out. His determination to teach Harrison a lesson had dissipated as if it had never been.

All Mark Wheeler wanted was to get away from this accursed place, reach the safety of his sister's house and pour himself a stiff drink.

* * *

Jennie Felton

Contrary to their expectations, as they drew up outside Oldlands House, the lights of the motor showed two bicycles propped up against the hedge, and a torch beam was cutting a swathe through the darkness beside the front door.

'Ye gods and little fishes!' Cam exclaimed. 'You were right, laddie.'

He turned off the engine, and he and Bradley headed up the path to find the Hillsbridge sergeant and a constable waiting.

'I didn't expect to find you here,' Cam greeted them.

'Orders from on high. And his lordship's on his way from Bath,' Sergeant Love replied glumly. Since receiving the call from the detective inspector, he had seen his chances of an early night receding fast. 'What's bin going on, then?'

Bradley fished in his pocket for his keys. 'You'd better come in. But tread carefully. There's live explosive, and I don't know how stable it is.'

'Explosive?' The sergeant was startled – and alarmed. 'Bowen didn't say anything about that.'

'Well, I'm sorry, but there it is. It's all down to Harry Harrison.'

'Him that was hurt when the roof came down at Milverton?'

Bradley nodded grimly. 'Yes, him. And tonight he tried to blow me up, and his own wife too, to stop me from reporting that it was him that caused the roof fall.'

'Where is he now?' Sergeant Love asked.

'I don't know. He ran off after he set light to the fuse. He could be anywhere by now. But come in and I'll explain.'

Everything in the living room was exactly as they had left it, and the two policemen eyed the bundle of gelignite sticks warily.

'A drink would oil the wheels,' Cam said. 'Where do you keep your whisky, Robinson?'

348

'In the chiffonier.' Bradley glanced at Sergeant Love.

'Not for us. We're on duty,' Love said, but Cam was having none of it.

'Rubbish. A wee dram won't do you any harm.' He fetched glasses and the bottle of whisky and poured generous measures. 'Robinson and I need it, and you will too before the night's out, if I'm not much mistaken.'

Sergeant Love sipped judiciously, but the constable, whose name Bradley did not know, was less cautious. He took a healthy drink of the golden liquid.

Bradley could hear Nipper scratching at the front room door and whining.

'I need to let the dog out,' he said to Cam, who was prowling the room, glass in hand, inspecting the gelignite at a safe distance. 'Can you begin explaining while I do?'

'I will,' Cam agreed.

Bradley took Nipper out into the front garden, and was waiting for him to finish his business, which seemed to be taking longer than usual, when he heard the sound of an engine and saw lights coming up the track. He whistled to the dog and took him back inside.

'I think Bowen's here,' he said, and went out again to meet the detective inspector, leaving the two local policemen scurrying to get rid of the whisky glasses before they were caught red-handed drinking on duty by a senior officer.

While Bradley and Cam talked to the DI and a young detective constable took copious notes, a uniformed officer Bowen had brought with him, and who he said was an expert in such matters, made the explosives safe, packed them in a box and took them out to the motor.

'So where is this Harrison likely to have gone?' Bowen asked when they had finished. 'He's a dangerous man, and it's imperative we find him without delay.'

Bradley hesitated. It was a question he had been dreading, but Cam spoke out.

'His mother and father live in Littleton Lane.'

Bradley's heart sank. The last thing he wanted was a couple of burly policemen banging on the senior Harrisons' door and frightening Marjorie and Vera half to death. This was going to be bad enough for them without the trauma of being woken and seeing their father taken away in handcuffs.

'He wouldn't go there,' he said quickly. 'They don't get on. But he'll have a key to the cottage he and his wife were going to move into, next door but one. If you want to try there, I'll show you where it is, and I'll check on his parents while you search the empty cottage.'

The DI nodded. 'Right. We'll do that. My DC can carry out a search with one of the local officers. If that is unsuccessful, I think we need to pull this Golledge in without delay. If Harrison is able to warn him, we may have two dangerous men on the run. Perhaps you would be good enough to drive me to the police station, Mr Cameron, and we can talk further about any other men you believe were involved in the explosion at the pit. I'd like this all wrapped up tonight if possible. Do I make myself clear?'

Though still pompous, Bowen's attitude had changed completely now that he saw the chance to shine as the hero of the hour. It wouldn't do his chances of promotion any harm at all, Bradley thought.

His wrenched shoulder was hurting badly and his old leg injury was aching, but he wanted to be sure they did not blunder into the wrong house. And if they did find Harrison, he was determined to be there to see the evil man taken into custody.

* * *

George and Lil Golledge were fast asleep in bed when they were woken abruptly by a loud hammering on their door.

'Wot the devil?' George muttered, pushing aside the blanket and wincing as he reached for his dressing gown. As he made his way down the stairs, with Lil, also in her dressing gown, following, the insistent knocking came again.

'Awright, awright, I'm comin'!'

Opening the door, he was startled to find Sergeant Love and Patrick Foster, the young detective constable, standing there.

'You'd better get some clothes on, Golledge,' the sergeant said shortly.

'Wot fer? Why?'

'You're coming with me. You've got some questions to answer.'

'I'm goin' nowhere!' George protested belligerently.

'In that case, I shall have to arrest you. Is that what you want?'

''E ain't done nothing wrong!' Lil butted in forcefully. ''Twas all 'Arry 'Arrison's doing!'

'And he'll be questioned too – when we find him.' Sergeant Love was becoming impatient. 'Now, are you coming quietly, Golledge, or not?'

''Twas 'Arrison, I tell you!' Lil repeated. 'He's the one wot got hold of the explosives!'

George rounded on her furiously. 'Shut up, you stupid woman!'

'Right, that's it.' Sergeant Love had had enough. 'Hold out your hands, Golledge. I'm arresting you on suspicion of murder.'

At the far end of the rank, Dolly Parsons had been woken by her baby kicking out strongly – Flossie had been right; she was much

351

further on in her pregnancy than she was prepared to admit. She was in her kitchen, making a hot drink that she hoped would help her to sleep, when she saw lights and heard voices.

Going to the window and looking out, she was startled to see George Golledge, her next-door-but-one neighbour, being led away in handcuffs by two uniformed policemen. She knew there was talk that George had been involved in causing the roof fall at the pit, and guessed right away this must have something to do with that.

She'd never get back to sleep now, she thought, hot drink or not. She was thrumming with excitement and couldn't wait to share what she had seen with her neighbours.

When they reached Littleton Cottages, Bradley made straight for Number 3. The house was all in darkness, and when the door was opened by Harry's father in nightgown and slippers Bradley was fairly certain nothing was amiss here. 'Sorry to disturb you,' he said apologetically, 'but I'm looking for Harry, and I wondered if I might find him here.' It wasn't an outright lie, but it wasn't the whole truth either. If he told the Harrisons what had happened, the girls would be sure to find out, and he didn't want them upset.

Harrison senior wiped a dribble of spittle from his chin and shook his head. 'No. He left the kiddies here this afternoon, and he hasn't been back since. Why? Wot d'you want 'im for?'

'Nothing that won't wait until the morning. I shouldn't have woken you up. I'm sorry.'

He turned away quickly to avoid further awkward questions and hurried back along the track, leaving a sleepy – and puzzled – Harrison senior to close the door and go back to bed.

The search of No 1 had proved equally fruitless, he discovered, and he decided he would drive directly to the cottage hospital rather than the police station. He'd have to make a full written statement sooner or later, he knew, but for now Cam could tell the DI anything he wanted to know. Bradley's over-riding concern was to get news of Lorna. He wasn't sure whether he'd be able to see her; if she was on a ward, he guessed the patients would have been settled for the night. But at least he could speak to someone who would hopefully be able to set his mind at rest.

As he had expected, the cottage hospital was in darkness, with the exception of the reception area and the nurses' station, where gas lights cast a warm golden glow. He rang the bell on the desk and a pert little nurse came bustling out.

'Can I help you?'

'I'm here to enquire after Mrs Harrison,' he said, trepidation bubbling in his gut. 'I brought her in earlier, semi-conscious and suffering from a number of injuries.'

'Are you a relative?' she asked.

Bradley was uncertain as to how to reply. 'She lives with me,' he said, hoping the rules weren't such that information could only be given to family members.

The little nurse chewed her lip, looking worried.

'Please,' he said. 'She doesn't have any family nearby and I have to know how she is.'

As always, the effect he seemed to have on women worked its magic, and the nurse relented.

'She's comfortable,' she said. 'Doctor has given her a sedative, and she's sleeping. All being well she should be discharged tomorrow.'

Bradley heaved a silent sigh of relief. 'I don't suppose I could see her, just for a minute?' he said, knowing full well he was pushing his luck.

'As I said, she's sleeping.' Another pause, then: 'She's at this end of the ward and the curtains are drawn around her bed. But it is just for a minute, and you mustn't make a sound. The other patients mustn't be disturbed.'

'I won't,' Bradley promised.

Using a small flashlight, she led him through a pair of double doors and into the ward beyond, where she opened the floral curtains that were drawn around the nearest bed.

Bradley's heart contracted as he saw Lorna lying there, her hair spread out across the pillow, a dark bruise blooming on her cheek. Her hand was lying on top of the covers and he stroked it gently.

'I'll leave you alone for a minute or two,' the nurse whispered. She handed him the flashlight and tiptoed out.

'Oh Lorna, I'm so sorry to have brought you to this,' he said softly. 'I don't suppose you can hear me, but I'm here. I'll always be here for you.'

She didn't stir, but it seemed to him her features softened into the semblance of a smile.

'I'll be back tomorrow when you're awake.'

He bent and kissed her on the hand that he had been holding. Then he turned away, slipping quietly between the curtains and pulling them closed again behind him.

Back home once more, Bradley took Nipper out into the garden, then locked and bolted the door and checked that all the windows were securely fastened. With Harry still on the loose, he didn't want to leave anything to chance. Who knew what the man might do next? He gave Nipper a biscuit and sent him to his basket, then went to bed himself.

He'd thought sleep would be difficult to come by, but he'd been wrong. Exhausted by the events of the day, he was asleep almost as soon as his head touched the pillow.

Next morning, however, he was awake early, his mind racing. He made himself a pot of tea and a pan of porridge, already missing Lorna and the bacon and eggs she had been cooking for him.

When it was time, he drove down to Littleton Lane to collect the two girls from Harry's parents. As he reversed along the track he glanced at the cottage that Harry and Lorna were to have moved into, but saw no sign of life. Not that Harry would be likely to make his presence obvious, but he certainly hadn't been there last night, and Bradley still thought it unlikely he would have stayed in Hillsbridge.

Not wanting to be questioned by Mrs Harrison as to why he'd called on them last night, and fervently hoping that neither she nor her husband had talked about it in front of Marjorie and Vera, Brad knocked on the door and then returned to his motor to wait for the girls. As they came running out and climbed up into the motor, their grandmother appeared in the doorway. Brad raised a hand to her, then pulled smartly away. He didn't feel in the least guilty for virtually ignoring her. A woman who could treat Lorna the way she had didn't deserve his respect. In any case, they'd find out soon enough; if Harry was still missing the police would no doubt soon be paying them a visit. It was up to them to tell the Harrisons what had happened and maybe interview them if Harry was still missing.

'So how was your stay with your granny and grandad?' he asked when they got into the motor, holding his breath as to what their answer might be.

To his relief they seemed totally unaware of the late-night disturbance. 'It was fine,' Marjorie said, though she was less than convincing.

Vera piped up. 'No it wasn't. It was horrible. Granny wouldn't let us have a hot water bottle, or have sugar in our tea.

And she always sounds so cross! A bit like Daddy, really.'

'Vera!' Marjorie reprimanded her, an echo of Lorna. 'You shouldn't say things like that.'

'But it's true! You know it is!'

At any other time this would have amused Bradley, but not now. He had too much on his mind. He hoped he would be able to bring Lorna home today as the little nurse had suggested he might, but he was wondering if he should prepare the girls for the possibility that she might not be well enough.

Better not, he decided. They would only worry all day, and if Lorna was there when they came out of school, it would all have been unnecessary.

The girls chattered between themselves for the duration of the journey. He dropped them off at the school gates, wishing he could go directly to the hospital, but he knew it was far too early. He supposed he should go to the police station and get his statement over and done with, but first he wanted to call on Flossie Price. As a close friend of Lorna's, she should hear the news from him rather than anyone else. Then he'd go home and get things straight. He didn't want Lorna to come face to face with anything that would remind her of her ordeal.

Although he'd only met Flossie the once, and briefly, when she saw him on her doorstep she recognised him straight away. Her motherly face was a picture of concern and her first words were: 'Is it Lorna? Is she all right?'

'She is,' he assured her. 'But she's in hospital, and I thought you'd want to know. Can I come in?'

'Yes – yes, of course!' She led the way into her kitchen. 'What is it? What's happened? It's Harry, isn't it? What's he done to 'er?'

'If I tell you, I'd ask you not to repeat it to anyone, for the moment at least. It's a police matter.'

'Oh, you can trust me,' Flossie said with fervour.

'Very well.' Keeping the explanation as short as possible and trying to downplay the more grisly details, he related the events of the previous evening while Flossie listened in horror.

'I knew it!' she said when he'd finished. 'The times I've tried to warn her about that man. But would she listen? And I'm guessing George Golledge is mixed up in this too. Taken away in handcuffs last night, by all accounts.'

'You know about that?' Bradley asked, surprised.

'Dolly Parsons, wot lives next door but one to the Golledges, was awake and saw it all. So as you can guess, 'twas all along the rank by breakfast time.' The mention of breakfast brought her up short. 'Oh – where be me manners? Can I get you a cup of tea?'

'Thank you, but no. I'm pressed for time. But I did want to ask you a favour.'

'If it's fer Lorna – anything.'

'I was hoping you'd say that. Even if Lorna's out of hospital I don't think she will be up to looking after the children, and I don't want to take them back to their grandparents Do you think I could bring them to you when they finish school this afternoon?'

'Well of course you can! Those poor little mites . . . They can stay with me overnight, and for as long as they need to. Don't you worry about that,' Flossie said emphatically.

Bradley thanked her and left, acutely aware of neighbours peeking from behind their curtains as he walked back to his motor. There was bound to be speculation and gossip, and he suspected there weren't many who couldn't hazard a guess as to why George had been driven away in a police car. Most of them would already know a great deal more than they had been prepared to say.

Back at his house and keeping an eye on the time, he tidied up the kitchen and living room. The gelignite and half-burned fuse had been taken away by the police, of course, but he was surprised to find that the rope he'd been bound with and the cut-throat razor were still there. He put them in a cardboard box and placed it on the kitchen table, thinking he could take it to the police station when he went there to make his statement. If Harry was caught and it came to trial, the items would almost certainly be required as evidence.

If Harry was caught. He was beginning to think that was unlikely.

He debated whether he should take Nipper for a walk, and decided a good run in the back garden would have to suffice. He could always find a stick to throw for him; the winter winds had brought down quite a few branches from the trees that stood sentinel around the perimeter.

The weather had turned milder and the smell of spring was in the air. He really must do something with this wilderness of a garden, he thought. And the prospect of Lorna and the children moving in with him was just the incentive he needed. He'd get a lawn laid where they could play, and put up a swing for them in the beech tree. There would still be plenty of room for growing vegetables and herbs. Lorna would like being able to step outside the back door to pick sage and parsley, peas and beans, perhaps soft fruit too. He remembered the loganberries that had twined up a wooden fence in his parents' garden, could almost taste their sharp sweetness and see his hands stained purple from their juice. As for the old shed, that would be just the place to store potatoes and apples.

Clearing it all would be a mammoth task, though, and Bradley wasn't sure he'd have the time to do it himself. Perhaps Amos would be prepared to work on it at weekends if he paid him well enough; failing that, he'd hire a gardener.

As he stood on the path looking around and planning a layout, he briefly forgot the terrible events of last evening that had been playing and replaying in his head ever since, and instead looked to the future. A future he would share with Lorna and the children. A future he had never expected when he'd come to Somerset. A love that had taken him unawares but that felt so right, as if it had always been meant to be.

Suddenly the urge to see her was overwhelming. The doctor might have completed his rounds by now and Lorna could be ready to be discharged. He looked around for Nipper, but the dog was nowhere to be seen. He whistled and called his name, and after a moment Nipper emerged from behind the ramshackle shed, looking at Bradley but making no move to go to him before turning and disappearing once more. Bradley whistled again, but to no avail. Nipper must have found something of interest in the tangle of weeds that surrounded the shed, he thought, and hoped it wasn't a dead bird or badger. If he'd been rolling in it, he'd have to be washed before he could be allowed into the house, and that would delay him further.

None too pleased, Bradley picked his way across the moss-choked grass and rounded the corner of the shed. He could see Nipper's frondy tail and hindquarters at the far end as the dog sniffed at something.

'Here, Nipper!' he called sharply.

The dog backed up a little and looked round, then once again returned to whatever it was he'd found. There was nothing for it, it seemed. Bradley would have to go and fetch him himself. But no way was he going to fight through the tangle of weeds and bramble. He retraced his steps and went to the other end of the shed. Then stopped, shocked.

It wasn't a bird or a badger that was claiming Nipper's

attention. It was the body of a man, slumped against the wall.

Harry Harrison. And from the look of him, he would never be threatening anyone again.

Chapter Twenty-Eight

Inspector Bowen had arrived at Hillsbridge police station soon
after eight o'clock to be greeted by a bleary-eyed Sergeant Love.
He'd had little sleep himself, but he was fired up with determination to solve the case that he believed would hasten his rise
through the ranks. He'd got little out of George Golledge the
previous night beyond his insistence that it was Harry Harrison
who had obtained the gelignite and set off the explosive that had
brought down the roof of the mine, but he was hoping the man
might be more forthcoming after spending a night in the cells.
According to the safety officer, there had been others involved
in the plot, and he needed names. And unless Harrison had been
found, or had turned himself in, both of which he thought
unlikely, Golledge was the man who could give him the
information.

Fortified with a cup of tea, he settled himself in the poky
office, behind the desk that Love had cleared for him last night,
and told the sergeant to bring the prisoner in.

As he had anticipated, Golledge was a good deal more
subdued, though still truculent.

'I hope you're going to be more cooperative now that you've
had time to think things over,' Bowen said by way of opening
the interview.

'I told you. I ain't done nothing wrong. You didn't 'ave no right to keep me in that cell all night. 'Twas freezin' cold, and the 'ard bed played me up summat terrible. I could 'ave you fer wrongful arrest.'

'That's where you'll be staying, Golledge, unless your story is corroborated.'

'Corrora . . . what?'

'Backed up by others. So, are you going to give me names? And tell me where I can find them?'

'Well, they'll be underground b' now.'

'Where? Milverton?' George nodded. 'So who are they?'

George rasped his hand over the stubble on his chin but remained silent.

Bowen fixed him with a steady stare. 'Come on, man.'

George huffed breath over his top lip. He couldn't meet the inspector's eye. 'Shorty Dallimore . . .'

'Shorty? What sort of a name is that?'

''Tis wot we d'a call 'im. Just like we do Ticker Greedy. An' Moses Whittock.' He raised his eyes briefly, defiantly. 'He were christened Moses, if you do want'a know.'

'And we'll find them at Milverton Colliery?'

'You should do. If not, the boss can tell you where they do live. Now can I go 'ome?'

Bowen was silent for a moment. He'd already decided that he would release George on bail when he had the information he needed. There was simply not enough room to interview more than one suspect at a time, and the station had only two cells. His detective constable should be arriving very soon and that would make the place even more congested. But at the same time he couldn't risk losing Golledge as well as Harrison, or have him warning his mates before he'd had the chance to speak to them.

Through the window he saw a uniformed constable approaching the station. Just beginning his shift, he imagined. He might provide a possible solution, escorting Golledge home and remaining to ensure he didn't leave the house. But the search for Harrison would require all the manpower they could muster, and the Hillsbridge police, with their local knowledge, would be the most useful.

'Not until I've spoken to the men you've named and satisfied myself that you've been telling me the whole truth,' he said bluntly. He got up, went to the door and opened it.

'Love!' he barked. 'Return this man to the cells. And then I'll speak to you regarding the next steps that need to be taken to clear this business up once and for all. I need one of your officers to go to Milverton Colliery and bring three men in for questioning.'

Alice Love was not best pleased. Her home was as crowded as the market hall on a Saturday, and she didn't like it one bit. She was used to folk knocking on the door at all hours, and she didn't mind that. In fact she quite liked it, since it meant she was one of the first to hear about the goings-on in the town. But this was something else. She'd had every officer who could be brought on duty tramping through her kitchen and expecting mugs of tea to fortify them before going out to search for Harry Harrison. Worse, there was a young constable she presumed must be a detective, since he wasn't wearing a uniform, in her front room. If it had just been him, it wouldn't have been so bad, but Moses Whittock was there too, sitting in one of her chintzy armchairs, and he was black with coal dust. How she'd ever get it clean again she didn't know.

Ticker Greedy was in the office with that overbearing inspector from Bath, and Shorty Dallimore was occupying one cell while George Golledge was in the other, where he'd spent the night. She'd had to make breakfast for him, and the man had had the bare-faced cheek to complain that the bacon was too fatty and the egg overcooked. And now, to cap it all, the inspector had sent out for tea for himself and Ticker Greedy.

She was at the sink, swilling out a couple of mugs – she hadn't got around to washing up the ones the search party had used, and she didn't have any more spares – when she heard a knock at the front door. She groaned. Not somebody else! But nevertheless she went to the doorway leading to the little lobby so she could hear who it was and what they wanted.

Her husband was already opening the door. Alice craned forward, listening. She didn't recognise the caller's voice, but she heard what he said all right. And it was dramatic enough to make her mouth drop open.

Harry Harrison had been found. In the caller's garden. And he was dead. Probably had been for hours.

As she heard her husband say, 'You'd better come in, Mr Robinson,' she scuttled back to the sink and hastily dunked a couple more mugs into the washing-up bowl. They'd probably be needed. And she didn't want to be caught eavesdropping either.

But oh my goodness! Now she really had something to think about!

Lorna felt as though she was emerging slowly, like a butterfly from a chrysalis, through a mist that was not stifling but welcoming her back.

'Where am I?' she asked. As she spoke, her jaw felt stiff and sore.

'You're in the hospital, my love.'

Flossie's voice. What was Flossie doing here? For a moment Lorna thought she must be dreaming again, but as her eyes focused, she saw that it was indeed her friend sitting beside her, holding her hand. Fragments of a remembered horror pierced the fog, but she couldn't make sense of any of it.

'Where's Bradley?' she asked.

'Taking care of things.'

'What things . . . ?' Lorna suddenly realised it was full daylight. 'What time is it?'

'Just gone half past eleven.'

'But . . . the sun's shining.'

Flossie chuckled. 'Half past eleven in the morning. You've had a good long rest, Lorna. They gave you something to make you sleep.'

Lorna's eyes widened. 'Oh – but the children! They should be in school . . .'

Flossie patted her hand. 'Stop worrying. They are in school. After they're coming to mine. So are you, when you're fit enough.'

Lorna scarcely heard the last bit. Her fuzzy mind was still on her girls.

'They'll like that. But what about their father . . .'

Flossie was not at all sure how much Lorna remembered of what had happened, or of why she was here. But for the moment she didn't want to get into that. 'Don't you worry your head about any of that,' she said. 'All you've got to do is concentrate on getting better.'

'I suppose . . .'

She was feeling tired again. Her eyes so heavy she could barely keep them open. She gave up the struggle and drifted off again into a deep and dreamless sleep.

* * *

The shocking news Bradley had delivered had galvanised Inspector Bowen into action, relieved, no doubt, that the search for a dangerous man could now be called off. He instructed Sergeant Love to send the three miners who had been brought in for questioning to be sent back to the pit after warning them that they would be required for questioning again later, but for the time being George Golledge was to remain in his cell. The police surgeon was sent for, and then Bowen, his detective constable, and a Hillsbridge officer, who could confirm that the body was that of Harry Harrison, set out for Littleton, Bradley following. Although it seemed certain that Harrison had died from natural causes, a thorough search was made for any evidence – not an easy task given the overgrown state of the garden – while they waited for the police surgeon and the mortuary wagon.

First to arrive was the police surgeon – a Dr Goodenough. He was a stout man who spoke little but bristled with importance as he made a cursory inspection of the body.

'Well?' Bowen said impatiently. 'We can discount foul play, can we not?'

'Until I conduct a full post-mortem, I couldn't possibly say,' Goodenough replied shortly, without troubling to look at the inspector.

The mortuary wagon was next to arrive, and as he watched Harry being loaded into it, Bradley was surprised to feel not loathing for the man who had terrorised Lorna and intended to kill them both, but pity. He hadn't been evil, just terribly disturbed. Driven by who knew what to save his own skin when he'd been found out. Perhaps weakness had led him to turn his back on his son, lie to Lorna, and resort to joining the militant men when he could no longer afford to keep up the payments he was making to his sister-in-law. From there, things had snowballed out of his control and eventually driven him mad, helped along, no doubt, by the injuries he'd suffered and the blow to his head. Insanity was the only possible explanation – apart from anything else, how had he thought he could get away with what he'd planned for them? As for how he had died, Bradley could only suppose the exertion, excitement and stress had proved too much for him and his heart had given out. In the last resort he was not so much a monster as rather a tragic figure.

When the mortuary wagon had pulled away, with Goodenough following in his motor, Bradley was anxious to leave too. He was already much later than he'd planned in getting to see Lorna, and he thought he should call in to Milverton and update Cam on the latest developments on his way.

Fortunately Bowen raised no objections – there wasn't much more they could do here until he got the results of the post-mortem, and he wanted to call the three miners back for interview without further delay.

As he drove, Bradley's concern for Lorna was compounded by worry about the best way to tell her that Harry was dead. Whatever her feelings towards him now, it was going to come as a shock, and he didn't want to do anything that might set back her recovery. If it was decided she should remain in hospital for another day or two, he'd say nothing, he decided. If she was being discharged, though, she would have to be told.

The red-brick hospital building loomed up at the side of the road as he breasted the hill, and he was surprised to see Flossie standing in the porch outside the main door. After he'd told her Lorna was in hospital, she must have walked all the way from Hillsbridge to see her. What a good friend she was!

He pulled into the open space beyond the building, turned off his engine and walked back.

'Mrs Price—' he began, but before he had the chance to say more, Flossie spoke.

'Oh, Mr Robinson, I'm so glad you're here!'

Bradley's heart lurched. 'Is Lorna . . . ?'

'The doctor's bin to see 'er not ten minutes ago and says she's fit to go 'ome if there's somebody that can fetch 'er. The nurse is gettin' 'er dressed now – that's why I'm out 'ere – but you were the only one I could think of and I didn't know 'ow to get 'old of you.'

'Well, I'm here now.' Bradley was enormously relieved.

'An' thank the Lord you are. They'll come and tell us when she's ready.'

Almost immediately, the door opened and a nurse popped her head out. 'You can come in. She's decent.' She glanced uncertainly at Bradley. 'Are you . . . ?'

'I'm here to take her home,' he said.

The nurse's face cleared. 'Ah, right. She's in the day room. We just have to wait for her medication to be put up and then she can go. But she's to take things easy for a few days, the doctor said. And be sure to call him if there's any problem.' She opened the door wide and stepped back to allow them in. 'It's just down there on the right.'

'I know where 'tis,' Flossie said. With her large family, she was no stranger to the hospital, and she strode out confidently, Bradley following.

The day room was small but welcoming, with comfortable chairs and a couple of occasional tables, and bright yellow curtains hanging at a window that overlooked open country-side. Lorna was seated in one of the chairs, her hands clasped in her lap. She looked small and vulnerable, the multicoloured bruise covering her chin and one cheek, and the dark circles beneath her eyes accentuating her pallor. But her face lit up when she saw that Flossie was not alone.

'Oh Bradley!' She winced, as if it was still painful to speak.

'How do you feel?' he asked. Stupid question, but at that moment it was all he could think of to say.

'I'm all right,' she said gamely. 'They wouldn't be letting me go if I wasn't.'

'And she's comin' home with me so I can take good care of 'er,' Flossie said. 'I've told 'er you're bringing the children to mine after school, and we can make the space for one more.'

'You're so kind, Flossie, but it would be an awful squash,' Lorna said. 'We can all go to Bradley's.'

Bradley felt a rush of joy. All he wanted was to have her back under his roof, where he could take care of her, help her to recover and give her all the love and respect she had lacked for so long. But Flossie spoke out with fierce determination.

'After what 'appened? I don't think that's wise, my girl. How d'you know Harry won't try again?'

Lorna's expression turned to one of uncertainty. She had fully regained her memory now, and Flossie's words sent a shiver down her spine. 'He wouldn't, would he, Bradley?'

''E's still out there, Lorna,' Flossie insisted before Bradley could say anything. ''Tisn't safe. 'E's capable of anything, he's proved that much.'

Bradley made up his mind. This was the moment to break the news.

'Harry isn't a danger any more,' he said evenly.

Two pairs of eyes fastened on him, puzzled, disbelieving.

'Wot d'you mean?' Flossie challenged him.

'Harry's dead,' Bradley said quietly.

There was a moment's silence, then Flossie demanded, 'How d'you know that?'

'I found him in the garden when I went home after coming to

see you, Mrs Price. I think he must have suffered a heart attack or a stroke.'

'Oh my Lord!' Flossie exclaimed, and Lorna uttered a small gasp. Her already pale face had turned chalky white and her hand flew to cover her mouth.

'It's all right, Lorna. I'm sorry it's come as a shock, but it's as well you know before I take you home. And you can rest assured that you and the children will be perfectly safe now.' He reached for her free hand, but she jerked it away.

'No!'

'Lorna, sweetheart, it's what we planned . . .'

'But don't you see? Everything's different now.'

'Yes, Harry can't hurt you any more. That's what I'm trying to tell you.' He could see she was getting more and more upset. 'Let's go home,' he said gently. 'It'll be just the two of us. The children can stay with you, can't they, Flossie, until Lorna's feeling stronger.'

'I can't come with you, Bradley.' Lorna stood up. Her hands were balled to fists in the folds of her skirt. 'It wouldn't be right. It would be disrespectful. He was my husband! Marjie and Vera's father!'

Bradley was staggered that after all that had happened, she could still remain loyal to him. Defend him.

'Lorna, my love, you're not thinking straight.' He moved towards her, but she shrank back.

'Go away, Bradley! I can't take any more. Leave me alone, can't you?' She was shaking now, swaying slightly. 'Just go away and leave me alone!'

Bradley hesitated, stunned, hurt, puzzled.

'Lorna!' Flossie said sharply. Too late. Lorna was crumpling like a rag doll.

In the nick of time, Bradley reached for her, caught her in

his arms as her legs gave way beneath her.

'Nurse!' Flossie dashed for the door and shouted into the corridor. 'We need some help here!'

It could only have been moments before a nurse appeared, older than the one who had shown them in and wearing the uniform of a sister, but Bradley had already sat Lorna in a chair and was pushing her head down between her knees.

'She fainted,' he said.

'We don't know that.' The sister quickly took charge. 'She suffered a blow to the head, didn't she? Dr Mackay is still on the ward. Fetch him!'

Flossie hurried out while Bradley stood, anguished and helpless, unable to tear his eyes from Lorna's chalk-white face and limp body.

Dr Mackay arrived, Flossie on his heels.

'She's collapsed,' the sister told him.

'So I see.' He turned to Bradley and Flossie. 'Could you both wait outside?' His voice was calm, but there was no mistaking the tone of authority, and they did as he said without question.

'This is my fault. I upset her. I shouldn't have pressed her . . .' Bradley was pacing the reception area, while Flossie had sat down on one of the upright chairs against the wall.

'She was takin' it all wrong,' she said. 'She ain't right yet. They shouldn't 'ave been sendin' 'er home.'

'I thought she'd just fainted, but they seem to think it's more than that,' Bradley said worriedly.

'Let's not put the cart before the 'orse. We'll know more when they've 'ad a proper look at 'er. She's goin' t' be right as rain, you'll see.'

Bradley raised his eyes heavenward as if in silent prayer, and Flossie went on: 'I reckon 'twould be best though if you keep away fer a bit. Once we've 'ad a word with the doctor, why don't you go 'ome? They won't be lettin' 'er out now this 'as 'appened, an' I can stay with 'er as long as you can 'ave the girls when they come out of school.'

Sad though it made him, Bradley knew she was right.

They waited in silence, each lost in their own thoughts, for what seemed like a lifetime, though in reality it could not have been more than ten minutes or so.

It was Dr Mackay himself who came to speak to them, and the news he gave them was optimistic.

'Mrs Harrison is conscious now, though clearly she suffered a relapse of some kind,' he said. 'Perhaps the whole business of getting dressed and the excitement of going home proved too much for her. But I've no reason to suppose she has suffered any permanent damage. We'll need to keep her under observation for a little longer, of course, and I'm sorry about that, but it would be irresponsible to discharge her until we're sure there won't be any further incident such as this one.'

'Thank God!' Flossie crossed herself. 'How long do you think that'll be?'

'It's hard to say. A day or two, maybe. But if you'd like to reassure yourselves, you are welcome to go back in and see her for a little while.'

Flossie threw Bradley a warning glance.

'I'll come in, certainly, but Mr Robinson has to get back to work, don't you, Mr Robinson?'

'Yes. I'm sure Mrs Price will let me know how she finds Mrs Harrison.'

It broke his heart to say it, but what choice did he have?

Word was spreading through Hillsbridge like wildfire. It had started with Dolly Parsons telling all and sundry about George

Golledge's arrest, news that had been repeated over and over again, enthusiastically by some and received with dismay by others. The miners who had known about and supported the militant action had even more cause for concern when they learned that Moses, Ticker and Shorty had been taken in for questioning. Though they hadn't played any active role, the very fact that they had known what was going to happen could implicate them, and they feared for their jobs, if not much worse.

There was much wild speculation after the three men were sent home. Someone had been found dead, though no one was quite sure who, and the story changed like Chinese whispers as it spread. Some folk had seen the mortuary wagon passing through the town and turning, so they said, onto the road to Frome. But it was Mercy Comer who came closer to the truth than anyone.

Though they had been told to go home and stay there, Moses, Ticker and Shorty had never been ones to respect the law. They needed to talk, anyway, and so they disobeyed the instruction and met up in the Miners' Arms.

'Why aren't you lot at work?' Walt Bray asked them when they came in and ordered their pints of beer.

'We've got other fish to fry,' Moses said non-committally. But they all looked worried.

Mercy soon realised they were being less careful than usual about keeping their voices down when she was within earshot. She moved closer, wiping down the table nearest to them even though it was already spotless.

'I reckon 'Arry must've blown 'imself up some'ow,' she heard Ticker say. 'I don't reckon 'e gave all the stuff 'e got to George.'

Shorty's reply was just as audible. 'At least if 'e 'as, it'll put George in the clear. For the best all round, if you d'a ask I. We can say 'twas Harry set off the explosion an' there's nobody can say different.'

Mercy was shocked. She couldn't believe Harry had blown himself up; if he had, she was sure it would have been common talk by now. That wasn't the sort of thing you could keep quiet. But it certainly sounded as if he was dead, and the surviving conspirators were going to lay all the blame on him. Which just wasn't right. She hadn't liked Harry, but then truth to tell she didn't like any of them very much, and she liked them even less for lying about a man who could no longer defend himself.

When her shift was over, she'd go and see Bradley, she decided. And she no longer cared if she was seen. This lot wouldn't be around for much longer if she knew anything about it. They'd be in prison, where they belonged.

Chapter Twenty-Nine

Bradley called in at the police station and gave a statement to Sergeant Love, then drove home. He made himself some bread and cheese, which he had no appetite for, let Nipper out to do his business, and went back to Milverton.

Cam was in the office, sitting at his desk smoking his pipe and staring into space.

'Have you brought Lorna home?' he asked.

'No, she has to stay in for a couple more days. What's been happening here?' Bradley didn't feel like talking about it, and Cam didn't press him. The dispirited slump of his shoulders had told him all he needed to know.

'They're doing the post-mortem as a matter of urgency,' he said instead. 'Inspector Bowen and the constable are observing. Can't say I envy them. I've had to watch a few in my time, and I couldn't get the stink out of my nose for days'.

'Smelling salts,' Bradley said. 'A good pinch of them should do the trick.'

'Aye. I dare say. Anyway, once they have the result, they'll be pulling the three wise monkeys back in to get to the bottom of the whole grisly business as soon as possible. There's no doubt that it was Harrison who was responsible, but they'll want to know how he got hold of that gelignite.'

'I already told them that,' Bradley objected.

'They'll be wanting corroboration before they go arresting landed gentry, mark my words.' Cam puffed on his pipe.

Good luck with that! Bradley thought. He couldn't see the quarry owner's son being brought before a court. Money would talk, just as it always did. There would be friends in high places who would bring their influence to bear. But at least Quentin wouldn't get off scot free. From what he'd seen of it, Sir Henry already had a poor opinion of his son and he would be justifiably furious with him. There would be consequences, he had no doubt of that. And in the last resort, perhaps Quentin was a victim too. Weak, but not evil. An easy target for Harrison's blackmail, if that was indeed what had happened.

'You'll be wanting to get back to the hospital, I expect, so if you wish, I can pick up the bairns from their school and take them to the neighbour who's going to be looking after them,' Cam said, and Bradley realised he could avoid the subject no longer.

'Actually, I'd be grateful if it could be the other way round. For some reason Lorna seems to have taken against me. Mrs Price is with her now, but she'll need to get home. If you would be so good as to fetch her, I'll collect the children, take them to her house and wait for her there.'

Cam raised an eyebrow. 'Is it the injury talking?'

'I don't know,' Bradley admitted. 'She's not recovered, that much is obvious, but it was learning that Harry is dead that set her off. As you know, she was going to move in to Oldlands House as my housekeeper . . .'

'Housekeeper!' Cam interjected with a wry smile.

'. . . but she's saying now that it would be disrespectful to Harry's memory,' Bradley went on, ignoring the knowing comment.

'Aye, well, I can see she has a point. But I'd have thought that now she's free, she would be only too pleased to have work, and a roof over her head for herself and her children.'

'I'd have thought so too, but it seems not. In fact, she doesn't even want to see me. But I can't have Mrs Price walking all the way back to Hillsbridge. So if you could fetch her, I'd be most grateful.'

'Of course I will. And don't you be fretting. Things will improve as she recovers her strength, I'm sure of it.'

'I hope you're right,' Bradley said. But he was still smarting from the way Lorna had turned on him. He could hear her now, telling him to leave her alone. It had sounded to him as if she despised him. Perhaps it was just because she was still suffering from the injuries Harry had inflicted on her. But if so, did it mean she was brain-damaged in some way? He couldn't forget how the roof fall had affected Harry's already volatile temperament. If something similar had happened to Lorna, it might well be that he had lost her for ever.

Cam had not long left for the hospital when there was a knock at the office door. Before Bradley could call 'Come in!' it opened and Mercy Comer appeared, checking over her shoulder to make sure she had not been seen, then quickly entering and shutting it behind her.

'Mercy!' Bradley didn't feel in the least like coping with the barmaid just now.

'I had to see you.' There was nothing flirtatious about Mercy's manner today. She looked, and sounded, panicked.

'You'd better sit down then and tell me what it's about,' Bradley said.

Mercy sat in the chair opposite him. 'The men are goin' to pin it all on Harry Harrison,' she blurted.

'What?'

'He's dead, in't he? And they'm goin' to say 'twas him as did it. The roof fall.'

'He *was* responsible for it, Mercy,' Bradley said patiently. 'We know beyond a shadow of doubt that he obtained the gelignite.'

'But 'twasn't him that set it off,' Mercy persisted. 'I heard the men talking. 'Twas George Golledge.'

Bradley was developing a headache. He could feel it tightening around the base of his skull and spreading into his temples.

'You'd better explain,' he said wearily, and sat back, massaging the nape of his neck.

Mercy told him.

'You'll have to go to the police with this,' he said when she'd finished. 'They're in charge of the investigation now.'

'Oh! I don't know about that. Can't you do it?' Mercy sounded alarmed.

'No, Mercy, I can't. That would be hearsay. They'll want to take a full statement from you. I've had to give one myself.'

The girl was silent, chewing her lip, and Bradley wondered why she was so reluctant. Had she, or one of her family, had dealings with the police before? Whatever, she was going to have to speak to them herself. He checked his watch. Almost going-home time for the children. But he would be passing right by the police station on his way to the school.

'Look, I'll drive you there and explain that you have important information for them. But I can't stay. I'm sure they'll want to speak to you alone. Come on.'

Without giving her time to object, he got up, reached for his coat and made for the door. Mercy followed reluctantly.

Sergeant Love was in his office with the young detective constable when they arrived.

'Mercy has something important to tell you,' Bradley said without preamble. 'I'll leave her with you.' He urged the nervous girl forward, giving her arm a reassuring squeeze, then turned and left.

Soon after Bradley arrived at Northfield Terrace with the children, he heard the sound of a motor engine. Arthur, who had been raiding the biscuit tin, must have heard it too, for he was at the window in a flash, his interest in the shortbread forgotten. Motors fascinated him, and when Bradley had picked him up along with Marjorie and Vera, he'd asked hopefully if they could go for a ride before returning home.

'Not today, Arthur. Your mam will be back soon,' Bradley had said. 'I promise we'll have a trip out before long, though.'

In contrast to Arthur's unbridled enthusiasm, the girls had been subdued and anxious. Bradley had gently explained that Lorna wasn't here because she'd had a bit of an accident and had had to go to hospital.

'She is all right, though, isn't she?' Marjorie had asked, looking very worried indeed. It wasn't so long ago that the mother of one of her classmates had died very suddenly, collapsing on her way home from taking her daughter to school, and the sad news had made a very real impression on Marjorie.

'Of course she is,' Bradley had assured her, wondering just when would be the right time to tell the girls that their father was dead. He thought Flossie might be the best person to do that. 'She just needs to rest for a little while.'

'Is it our fault?' Vera had asked, her lip trembling.

'Not at all. But you must be really quiet and let her take things easy when she comes home.'

'We will,' they chorused.

As he saw his mother emerge from Cam's motor, Arthur

dashed back to the biscuit tin, anxious to return it to the shelf before he was caught red-handed. Too late.

'Are you at those biscuits again, Arthur?' Flossie demanded as she came into the kitchen, but she didn't tell him to put back the ones he'd taken. Instead she suggested he should take the tin and share some with Marjorie and Vera in the front room. 'And play a game with them,' she added, and Bradley realised that she wanted the children out of the way so that she could talk to him in private.

'Well? How is she?' he asked as soon as they were alone.

'Not too bad. She started to calm down soon after you left. I think Dr Mackay gave her somethin', because after a while she got sleepy. But I 'ad time to talk to 'er, an' she seemed to be takin' on board wot I said.'

'What did you say?' Bradley asked.

'Well, I told 'er 'ow silly she was being. That you'd bin good to 'er, an' 'twas a shame she'd spoken like that to you. An' I told 'er nobody would blame her fer movin' in as your 'ousekeeper when she's got nowhere else to go. Specially when they find out what 'Arry did to 'er. But I didn't think 'twas a good idea to say anythin' about 'ow much she means to you, or you to 'er.' She's very fragile, poor lamb, and who knows wot might set her off again.'

'So it's best if I stay away from her?' Bradley said.

'Fer the time bein', yes. She'll come round, she just needs a bit o' time. Never mind wot she said; anybody can see the way she feels about you, an' that's wot's botherin' 'er if you ask me. She feels guilty, an' she took it out on you.'

'I hope you're right,' Bradley said. 'It is all right to leave the children with you tonight, is it? I don't think I should take them home with me. There were police everywhere earlier on, and they might be back, for all I know.'

'I already said so, didn't I?' Flossie said. 'It's a pleasure 'avin' them around. But wot are we goin' to tell them about their dad?'

Though he had considered asking Flossie to break the news to them, he had since had second thoughts. 'I think we should leave it until Lorna can be there. If we do it while she's in hospital, they'll be afraid they're going to lose her too.'

Flossie nodded her agreement. 'I'll go over to the hospital tomorrow morning – I thought about twelve. The doctors should 'ave finished their rounds by then, and we'll know more about when she can come home.'

'How are you going to get there?' Bradley asked.

'Well, by Shanks's pony, o' course! The walk will do me good.'

'You've proved yourself a true friend, and I am so grateful,' he said. 'But you shouldn't have to walk. Either Cam or I will take you.'

Flossie shrugged. 'I don't want to put you to any trouble. I'm just doin' wot anybody would do in my place.'

It was far more than that, Bradley thought as he insisted he'd make sure Flossie had a ride to the hospital, then said goodbye to the two girls and left. She was one in a million. What a difference between her and Harry's mother!

That thought led to another. It was unlikely that the senior Harrisons knew yet that their son was dead. It wouldn't be long before it was all over Hillsbridge, but the jungle drums wouldn't have reached Littleton Lane so soon. Though closer to the scene, they were far more isolated there, and the news would only reach them when a tradesman or someone who had been into town went into the little village store on the crossroads and spoke of it. As for the police, although they would no doubt get around to notifying the family in due course, at present they had their hands full and might not have found the time.

He'd go and see them, Bradley decided. It was only right. And he could do it on his way home.

Much to her surprise, Mercy was actually enjoying herself. Well, who wouldn't when the detective who had questioned her and was now taking her statement was as young, good-looking and sympathetic as this one. DC Foster, his name was, and he was nothing like the bullying detective sergeant who had interviewed her once when Walt Bray had discovered money missing from the till. She'd tried to be helpful then, though she'd known nothing, but he had seemed set on pinning the blame on her. As if she'd ever do such a thing! In the end he had reduced her to tears, and that had only made things worse, convinced him that the reason she was crying was because she was guilty. It was only when Walt had intervened and vouched for her that the horrible man had backed off. A couple of weeks later, Walt had caught one of the lads who acted as sticker-up in the skittle alley with his hand in the till and she'd been completely exonerated, but the experience had left her with a fear and hatred for plain-clothes policemen.

But this one was a different kettle of fish altogether. Mercy thought she was in love. Never mind Bradley Robinson. DC Foster was much closer to her in age, he didn't have a ring on his finger, he knew her address and where she worked, and she was confident her charms were working.

Having information of interest in the inquiry had turned out to be lucky for her after all. She'd be seeing more of DC Foster if she wasn't much mistaken.

As Bradley turned into Littleton Lane, he saw two women at the end of the track engaged in what appeared to be a heated argument. The older one he recognised as Harry's mother; the other seemed vaguely familiar, though for the moment he couldn't think where he'd seen her before.

'Go on! Go!' he heard Mrs Harrison shout as he turned off his engine. 'An' don't you dare come back!' She was gesticulating wildly, and sounded almost hysterical.

'Oh, I'll be back!' the other woman shouted. 'An' next time I'll 'ave Frank with me. He's your grandson, an' he's your responsibility, not mine!'

As she strode furiously away, Bradley realised who she was. Harry's sister-in-law. The woman who was taking care of his son. He and Lorna had passed her and the boy walking up the lane. He'd only seen her from behind; it was her coat and hat he recognised. Lorna had told him she was threatening to return the boy to Harry if he didn't resume regular payments for his keep. But why was she here today of all days?

'An' you! I want to talk to you!' Harry's mother was approaching the motor now. 'Get out 'ere an' act like a man. How *could* you? That I should 'ave to find out like that! From *'er* of all people.'

Close to, Bradley could see that Mrs Harrison was not only angry, but dreadfully upset, and before she could say another word, he understood. This was the reason Harry's sister-in-law had come to see her. She lived in Charterhouse. No doubt the police had been to the quarry, and word that Harry was dead had got out. If she'd heard of it, she would have known she'd get no more money from him, and she'd set out again on the long walk to sort things out with his mother.

'Mrs Harrison, I am so sorry,' Bradley said, getting down from the motor. 'It's the reason I'm here – to break the news to you.'

''Tis true then, is it?' Rose Harrison's chin wobbled and her eyes bored into his as if willing him to tell her this was all a mistake.

'I'm afraid it is,' he said.

Her neck drooped so that her chin rested on her floral pinafore, and she pressed her clasped hands against her mouth. But when she lifted her head again, the cold anger was back, her way of expressing her grief perhaps.

'So why didn't you come an' let us know before? Why did I 'ave to 'ear it from that woman? You were 'ere pickin' up the girls this mornin', an' you didn't say a word about it!'

'His body hadn't been discovered then, Mrs Harrison. And things have been rather hectic ever since.'

'Well where was 'e? What were the matter with 'im?'

'He was in my garden. As to what he died of, I'm afraid I couldn't say. We'll know more when the post-mortem's been carried out.'

'Post-mortem! Oh no!' Mrs Harrison wailed. 'They'm not goin' to cut up my boy! I won't let 'em.'

'I'm afraid there's nothing you can do about that, Mrs Harrison,' Bradley said, thinking it ironic that in death he was 'my boy' when she'd seemed to care so little for his welfare when he was alive.

'Whatever's goin' on?' It was the neighbour Lorna called an old witch. She'd been hovering unnoticed but was now determined to butt in, and Bradley took his chance to escape.

'Mrs Harrison has had a bad shock,' he said. 'Perhaps you'd take her in and give her a cup of tea. Strong and sweet.' He turned back to Harry's mother. 'Once again, I can only apologise and leave you in good hands.'

As he reversed into the lane, he looked back and saw the witch woman leading Mrs Harrison into the house, her arm round her back. She'd be all right. She was as hard as nails, and if she wept, it would be crocodile tears. But Harry's son and the woman who was caring for him were another matter.

He made up his mind. She couldn't have got far. Certainly not all the way back to Charterhouse. He'd catch up with her, give her a ride home, and tell her that he would send her enough money each month to pay for the boy's keep and extra besides. The thought of the poor child being dumped on that dreadful woman's doorstep was more than he could bear. He'd offer him a home himself if it came to that, just as he'd promised Lorna. But it wasn't really the best solution. Living with his aunt might not be ideal, but it was the only home he knew. He'd have friends there as well as family.

He opened the throttle and set off in pursuit of the woman.

Chapter Thirty

Bradley had no need to take the girls to school next day, as they were back within easy walking distance, and Arthur would accompany them. But he felt a huge responsibility for them, and besides, he wanted to update Flossie on his encounter with Harry's mother.

Needless to say, Arthur was delighted to see him when he knocked at the door ten minutes before they were due to leave, excited by the prospect of another ride in the motor. But both Marjorie and Vera were still looking anxious.

'How is Mummy?' Marjorie asked. 'Have you seen her?'

'Not yet,' Bradley hedged. 'But I'm hoping she'll be able to come home today.'

While they were getting their coats on and collecting their bags, he told Flossie what had happened since he had last seen her.

'How much should I tell Lorna?' she asked when he had finished.

'Just that I've arranged to send Frank's aunt the money she needs for his keep,' he said. 'There's no need to worry her with anything else. And be sure you wait for either me or Cam to take you to the hospital.'

'We'll see.' Flossie cherished her independence.

The children were now ready and waiting and he left with them, promising that they could all take their turn at sitting in the front, and that perhaps this afternoon he would take them for that drive. With all they were going through, the girls certainly deserved a treat, he thought. And he had the perfect one for them in mind if things worked out as he hoped.

Sir Montague Fairley's butler tapped respectfully on his library door.

'Mr Cameron is here to see you, sir. Do you feel well enough to see him?'

Sir Montague grunted. 'I suppose I shall have to.' Phlegm rattled in his throat as he spoke. He had been suffering from a severe bout of influenza for more than a fortnight, and although the worst of it was over, he had been left with a chesty cough that nothing, not even his best whisky, could help. He tired easily, too, and had taken to retiring early and rising much later than he was accustomed to, and frustration at his continuing weakness was making him even crustier than usual.

Neither had his mood been improved by the recent disturbing developments in his coalfield. Fred Gardiner, his agent, had spoken to the detective inspector when he had called, explaining that Sir Montague was 'gravely ill' and not to be disturbed, but had kept him briefed as to what had transpired, unable to hide a certain sly relish at the demise of Harry Harrison and the downfall of George Golledge. But that was Gardiner all over, and it was one of the things that made him a good agent in Sir Montague's eyes. He was never squeamish about carrying out his employer's orders regarding the profitability of his mines and estates, however much hardship that might bestow on individuals.

Cameron, on the other hand, was a different kettle of fish. He

Jennie Felton

empathised with the men a little too much for Sir Montague's liking, though he could be firm when necessary and his good standing amongst the workforce was often useful in defusing situations.

Not this time, however, Sir Montague thought, gearing himself up for a confrontation that would probably do nothing for his blood pressure.

'Come!' he barked as another knock came at the door, much harder and more decisive than the butler's tentative tap.

There was a purposeful set to Cameron's craggy features as he strode into the library, but that was not going to deter his lordship.

'Sit down, Cameron,' he said, indicating a chair facing his own. 'You are here, no doubt, to explain how you came to be unaware of the disaster that was brewing right under your nose.'

'Not at all, sir,' Cam said firmly. 'I warned you there was considerable unrest among the men and trouble was brewing, though I confess it never occurred to me that any one of them would be so stupid as to do what they did. If anyone failed in their duty it was the Inspector of Mines, who was clearly too lazy to look into the affair as he should have done and should be reported to his superiors. No, I am here to set the record straight. You were all too ready to accept his verdict that the roof fall was caused by a fault in the seam, and to blame Mr Robinson and the deputy for oversight in spotting it. In fact Mr Robinson has gone far beyond what is expected of him, and very nearly lost his own life as a result, as I'm sure you will know by now. If he had not suspected the cause was something entirely different and pursued an investigation of his own, none of this would have come to light. I believe he is owed an apology at the very least, and some recognition of his efforts.'

Sir Montague, quite unused to being spoken to in such a fashion, had retreated further into his wing chair. Now he sat forward again.

'Have you quite finished, Cameron?'

A wry smile twisted the manager's lips. 'I've said what I came to say, aye. Robinson has been unfairly blamed, and as you know, unfairness is one thing I cannot abide.'

Sir Montague was feeling weary again, too weary to argue or prolong this interview, and in any case Cameron was making to rise and leave.

'Very well. I'll give it due consideration,' he said testily. As Cameron reached the door, however, a thought struck him. What impact was this going to have on the smooth running of the colliery? 'Just a moment, Cameron. With charges against the men highly likely, how many of my workforce am I going to lose as a result of this debacle?'

'At a guess, sir, I'd say just Harrison – who is dead – and possibly Golledge, the other ringleader. But I'm doubtful he will ever be charged. The men are sticking together, saying nothing and protecting their own. Unless someone breaks the wall of silence, there may never be sufficient evidence for a court case.'

'Hmm. Well, get rid of him anyway. I don't want a man like that in my employ.'

Cameron nodded. 'For once, Sir Montague, I am in agreement with you.'

Determined as she had been to make her own way to the hospital, by mid morning Flossie was looking ruefully at her swollen ankles, which were rolling over the top of her black button shoes, and decided it would be wise to accept Bradley's offer.

He was at the door by a quarter to twelve and dropped

her outside just after midday, promising to be back to pick her up at one.

Flossie, who had been a little apprehensive as to what she would find, was heartened to discover that Lorna was dressed and in the day room. She was being kept in for a further twenty-four hours, just to be safe, but she hadn't had any more funny turns, the nurse told Flossie, who didn't even stop to think it was an unusual way for a medical professional to describe yesterday's episode. 'Just make sure you don't do anything to upset her,' she added.

'I won't,' Flossie promised, wondering whether it would be best not to mention Bradley at all, never mind his promise to pay for Frank's upkeep.

In the event, after asking after the children, it was Lorna who instigated the conversation.

'I've been thinking about what you said. I shouldn't have spoken to Bradley like that. I just snapped, I think. Suddenly it was all too much and I couldn't take any more.'

'I know,' Flossie said. 'With wot you've bin through, 'twas only natural.'

'D'you think he'll be able to forgive me?'

''E already 'as,' Flossie said bluntly. ''E understands, course 'e does.'

Lorna looked relieved. 'And what you said about it being all right for me to move in as his housekeeper . . . D'you really think it's not too soon? If he still wants me, that is.'

'Course 'e wants you. An' you've got nowhere else to go, 'ave you? Oh, p'raps there'll be a bit of talk. Some folk can't 'elp themselves. But it'll be a nine-days wonder and then they'll forget all about it.'

'But the children . . .'

'They think the world of 'im, and 'e thinks the world of them.

He'll take care of all of you an' make you 'appy. Goodness knows, it's what you deserve. It'd be a mean tyke who'd deny you that.'

'But supposing they get bullied at school?'

'That's not goin' t' 'appen,' Flossie said firmly. 'They'm well liked, your two girls.'

'I suppose.'

Whatever she said, Flossie knew it wouldn't be as simple as that. But if the girls were bullied, it would only be because of what Harry had done. Bradley was highly respected, and he would do everything in his power to protect them, she knew.

'Do you think he'd come to visit me this evening?' Lorna asked. 'I need to tell him how sorry I am for the things I said. And I really do want to see him.'

'Oh, 'e'll be 'ere, no doubt of it.' Flossie patted her hand. 'Now, there was something 'e wanted me to tell you. But I've half a mind to let 'im do it 'imself.'

'Oh Flossie! You can't just leave it at that.'

'Awright. As long as you don't mind me mentioning Harry's son.' She saw Lorna's face change and hurried on. ''E's goin' to make sure the boy is provided for. Send money regular like, an' if I know anything about it, the lad won't want for a thing. 'E spoke to the aunt yesterday. Made arrangements.'

'He is such a good man.' Tears shone in Lorna's eyes. 'Oh Flossie, I am so, so lucky.'

Flossie nodded. 'Yes, I think you are. And not before time! So I'll tell him to come for evening visiting, then?'

'Please,' Lorna said with feeling.

When Flossie left, Brad was already waiting for her outside.

'How is she?' he asked as he helped her up into the motor.

'Much better. They're keepin' her in for one more night just to be on the safe side, but they reckon when the doctor's seen 'er in the morning she'll be able to go home.'

'Thank goodness for that!'

'And there's something else,' Flossie went on, unable to keep the good news to herself for a moment longer. 'She wants you to go and see her this evening at visiting time. You will go, won't you?'

'Just try and stop me,' Brad said with a delighted smile, then added: 'You're a wonderful friend to her, Flossie.'

'Oh get away with you.'

They drove in silence for a few minutes, then Flossie said: 'You can drop me in town today. There's some'ut I want to do before I go home. Somebody I want t' see before it's too late.' Brad threw her a questioning look, and she laughed. 'Awright, I might as well tell you. I'm goin' to see the man wot manages the market. I'm gonna take that stall if it's still goin' vacant. I don't want t' tread on Lorna's toes, but I don't s'pose she'll be wantin' it now.'

'I think you can safely say you won't be doing that,' he said, smiling. 'But rest assured we shall be among your first customers.'

'That's awright then.' Flossie smiled broadly. 'I reckon things are turning out just fine, don't you?'

Brad nodded. 'I certainly hope so!' he said.

'I'm very sorry, sir.' A shamefaced and quaking Quentin faced his father across the big leather-tooled desk in Sir Henry Corsley's office at Charterhouse Quarries.

'Sorry? I am afraid that barely scratches the surface this time, let alone cuts the mustard.'

Given the circumstances, the quarry owner's tone was remarkably restrained, but there was no mistaking his anger –

and deep disappointment. 'Do you not realise the seriousness of what you did?'

As Quentin lowered his head, unable to meet his father's eyes, the cowlick of hair fell over his forehead, exacerbating Sir Henry's despair with the son he had hoped would one day take over the running of his empire.

'A man and a boy were killed, Quentin. Because of you.'

'He threatened me, sir,' Quentin mumbled. 'He said—'

'I know what he said. You've already told me.' Sir Henry sighed. 'Have you any idea of the lies I have had to tell in order to protect you? I was forced to assure the police that no explosives were missing from our store. Rubbish the reputation of the man who told the safety officer he had seen Harrison talking to you. I have put my own honour at risk to save this family's good name and that of the business I have spent my life building up. It is just fortunate in the extreme that all the evidence is either hearsay or circumstantial. Harrison is dead and his cronies are uncooperative. That, it would seem, will mean the investigation will be wound up. But as far as you are concerned, Quentin, you are no longer my son and heir.'

'What? Where will I . . . ?'

'I haven't yet reached a decision as to your future. And I want you out of my sight until I have. But rest assured, you will not be running Charterhouse Quarries. Now go!'

With one last pleading look at his father, Quentin rose and headed for the door.

'And get that damned hair cut!' Sir Henry shouted after him.

The Miners' Arms had been far from busy, and Mercy was watching the hands of the clock above the bar move all too slowly towards two, time to close for the afternoon. She hated it when there was not enough to do and no one she could eavesdrop on or share a joke with. She was rubbing polish into the stains left by beer glasses on the dark old wood, without much effect, when the door swung open. Well, if someone thought they were going to get a pint now, they'd be lucky.

'We're closin',' she called. Then, as a young man stepped inside, she wished she could bite off her tongue.

It was Patrick Foster, the young detective constable who had taken her statement.

'Oh!' she said, momentarily lost for words.

'Sorry,' he said apologetically. 'I just popped in on the off-chance I might catch you.'

Mercy gave a little laugh. 'Well, it looks as if you have,' she said, recovering herself somewhat. 'You want to ask me some more questions, is that it?'

'Just one,' he said. 'We're wrapping up here for the time being and going back to Bath. And . . .'

'Yes?' Mercy prompted him, though she already had a good idea what was coming.

'Just wanted to ask if I could see you again,' he said nonchalantly.

All her confidence returned with a rush. 'Well, you know where to find me,' she said pertly. 'I'm here most evenings. And lunchtimes too.'

'Don't you get any time off?'

'Sometimes.'

'I was thinking maybe . . .'

'Yes, why not,' she said, putting him out of his misery.

'Foster!' a voice from outside shouted. 'Come on, or we're going without you!'

'I'll see you then,' the young DC said, and made a hasty exit.

Mercy smiled delightedly as she retrieved her duster and polish. She was very glad Walt hadn't decided to lock the door early for lack of customers. Sometimes things were meant to be. And she was very much looking forward to seeing DC Foster again.

It was mid afternoon. At Cam's insistence, Bradley had taken the rest of the day off, and the general manager was alone in the office when, through the window, he caught sight of George Golledge crossing the yard. Cocky as ever, from the look of him. Cam strode to the door.

'Golledge! Come here!'

Smirking, George sauntered across the yard, and Cam indicated with a jerk of his thumb that the man should go inside.

'What are you doing here?' he asked when the door was closed behind them.

'Come to see me mates. Tell 'em I'm in the clear. The police've 'ad to let me go, 'aven't they? Didn't 'ave nothin' on me.'

'I presume what you mean is you've been released on bail,' Cam said.

George shrugged. 'All the same, i'nt it? So I can come back to work, can't I?'

'No, Golledge, you can't,' Cam said shortly. 'The police may not have enough evidence to charge you – yet – but you and I both know you were the instigator of what happened, and very probably the one who set off the explosive. Sir Montague is adamant. He won't have you working in any of his pits again. And you'll have to vacate your house.'

George's expression changed to one of shock.

'Wot? Wot we gonna do, me and the missus?'

'I really don't know, Golledge, and I care even less. You will have to take it up with Sir Montague's agent when he visits you to give you notice.'

'But where be we gonna go?'

'That isn't my problem. Now, will you kindly take yourself off these premises before I have you arrested again – for trespassing.'

He stood at the window and watched George go. The man might be escaping a long prison sentence, but he certainly wasn't getting off scot free, and Cam thought it was as satisfying a conclusion as they were likely to get.

The evening visiting hour had begun, and Lorna waited in nervous anticipation as the first trickle of visitors passed the day room on their way to the wards. Despite Flossie's assurances, she was not at all sure Bradley would come. She didn't know what had come over her yesterday that she could have behaved so to the man she loved with all her heart.

They were soulmates, she thought. From the moment they had met, there had been something between them, something inexplicable but compelling. Through everything that had happened he'd been there for her, and from him she'd somehow found the strength to go on. And more than simply the chemistry between them, their relationship had the feeling of rightness. As if it had always been meant to be.

The problem was that she'd been torn between the loyalty she felt she owed her husband and the powerful feeling that was drawing her to Bradley. She squirmed inwardly now, remembering the way she had spoken to him. He had been ready to die for her, for goodness' sake, but yesterday she'd sent him away with cruel words she could scarcely believe she'd uttered, and if she'd lost him, she simply couldn't bear it. She closed her eyes, pressing her hands to her mouth and praying that he would be able to forgive her. That he would come to see her tonight . . .

'Lorna?'

She opened her eyes, and as if by some miracle, he was there in the doorway.

'Oh Bradley, you came!'

'Did you think I wouldn't?' he asked ruefully.

'I didn't know. Oh Bradley, I am so, so sorry!'

'Shh!' He was across the room in two strides, taking her hands, bending his head close to hers. 'You were still in shock, and no wonder. I'm the one who should be apologising. If I'd gone straight to the police when I learned it was Harry who'd got hold of the gelignite, none of this would have happened. But no, I had to have proof. And it almost cost you your life.'

'And yours . . .'

'I had no idea he had heard us talking. But I shouldn't have taken that chance. The truth is, I was more worried about what the carting boy's uncle might do, and I missed the threat that was under my nose. Dear God, if Harry wasn't dead, I'd kill him with my bare hands.'

He leaned closer. 'I love you, Lorna.' His breath was warm in her ear. 'I've loved you from the first moment I laid eyes on you.' He raised his head, looking directly into her eyes, and a small smile played around his mouth. 'And right now I have a surprise for you. One I think will please you.'

'What is it?'

'Ah, if I told you, it wouldn't be a surprise, would it? Patience, Lorna.'

He smiled at her again teasingly, then got up and left the day room. Puzzled, Lorna wondered what it could be. Flowers? The first daffodils, perhaps . . .

A few minutes later he was back. And . . .

'Mammy! Mammy!'

Marjorie and Vera came rushing into the room, their faces alight with excitement. Running to her, throwing their arms

397

around her, one on each side, nestling into her.

'Oh!' Overcome with emotion, Lorna could barely speak. She hugged them to her. 'Girls! Oh my loves!'

Marjorie inched slightly away, looking at her. 'Are you all right, Mammy? Bradley said you'd hurt yourself. We were so worried.'

'Did you fall over?' Vera asked.

'No. Nothing like that. I just . . .' She hesitated. She certainly wasn't going to tell them what had really happened. Perhaps she never would. She didn't want them to think badly of their father. 'I just slipped on the stairs and banged my head.'

'So you won't have a thing on your leg like Daddy?' That was Vera, sounding perhaps just a little disappointed by the lack of drama now that she was satisfied Lorna was still the same mammy she always had been.

'No.' Lorna glanced at Bradley, silently asking the question. Did they know Harry was dead? He shook his head – no – and she wondered if this was the moment to tell them. Or should she wait until she was at home with them?

'Will Daddy be there when we get back from Mrs Price's house?'

The irrepressible Vera had given her the perfect opening, but she decided against taking it. She didn't want to spoil these precious moments. Giving them the news could wait.

'He won't be, no,' she said. 'We're going to stay with Bradley, and Daddy didn't want to.'

'Where is he going to live then?' Vera asked.

'With Granny Harrison, I expect,' Marjorie said.

Vera wrinkled her nose. 'Just as long as we don't have to live with her too!'

'We won't,' Marjorie said patiently. 'We're staying with Mr Robinson. Mammy just told us that.'

'Oh yes!' Vera turned to look at him. 'I'm really glad! Will you take us to see the cows every day? And take Nipper for walks?'

Bradley laughed. 'Maybe not *every* day. But often.'

'And the market on Saturdays?'

'Yes.'

'We'll like that, won't we, Marjie?'

Marjorie nodded. 'I'm glad we're staying with you, Mr Robinson. It'll be like we're a family.'

Lorna met Brad's eyes and they exchanged a smile. Then Brad knelt down, pulling the three of them into a close embrace.

A family. A *happy* family. Warmth spread through Lorna's veins and her heart sang. Yes, her bruises were still painful. Yes, her back and her face were stiff and sore. Yes, it would be a long time, if ever, before she was able to forget the awful events of that evening. But what did she care? All she had gone through was worth it for what she had gained. True happiness at last, with the ones she loved most in all the world. And tomorrow she would be going home with them.

She was, she thought, truly blessed.

Author Note

I was born and brought up in Radstock, a small town which was the hub of the Somerset coal-mining industry. It sits in a valley surrounded by steep hills, some eight miles south of Bath. Once the whole surrounding area was dotted with pits, as far afield as Bristol and the Mendip Hills, but by the time I worked for the NCB (the National Coal Board) in the early sixties, just six remained. Even Ludlows, the closest to my home, had closed, though I have clear memories of the team of ponies pulling a string of coal carts across the main road – I believe they mostly contained spoil that was headed for the 'batch' at nearby Writhlington – and miners, still black with coal dust, squatting against the wall opposite the pit yard.

In days gone by, spoil had also been deposited along the route of the main railway line to Bath, and though the embankment was now covered with scrubby brush, it was often set alight in hot summer weather by sparks from passing steam engines. Watching the fire brigade deal with it was great entertainment for us children. If left unchecked, the fire would have spread beneath the surface for days, if not weeks. (Incidentally I was obsessed with the fire engine and always rushed to look for it when the hooter – the 'all-clear' siren during the war –

sounded. The brigade captain suggested putting me on the front of the engine as a mascot!)

Perhaps, by now, you have recognised Radstock as the Hillsbridge of my Somerset mining sagas. My father had been a carting boy in one of the pits, and when the stories he told me about the old Radstock inspired me to write my first novel, *The Black Mountains*, Radstock became Hillsbridge. I dedicated that book, the first of many under my real married name, Janet Tanner, to him. Sadly, he did not live to see it published, but he carried my draft in his wallet, so he knew of my intention.

When, in 2013, I began my Jennie Felton mining sagas with *All The Dark Secrets*, Hillsbridge was reincarnated. Nowadays, only one 'batch' as the slagheaps were known, is recognisable, towering above Old Mills in Radstock's twin town, Midsomer Norton. The rest are wooded over.

But in the centre of town, the pit wheel from the last Radstock pit to close, in 1973, stands proudly in the centre of town, beside what used to be the market hall, but which is now an amazing mining museum. Within its walls are countless exhibits, as well as a mock-up of a coal seam which you can walk through; a Victorian schoolroom where a volunteer sometimes takes classes; and a Co-operative grocery store complete with the aerial cash railway system – I was always fascinated by the wooden cups zinging across the wires to the central cash desk – and a full-size delivery cart and horse drawn up outside. From time to time, they also host exhibitions and illustrated talks. I promise you, it is well worth a visit, and I'd be honoured to think my books had inspired you to experience first-hand the setting, and the history, of the place I am proud to call my home.

Jennie Felton grew up in Somerset, and now lives in Bristol. She has written numerous short stories for magazines as well as a number of novels under a pseudonym. As well as the standalones *A Mother's Heartbreak*, *The Stolen Child*, and *The Smuggler's Girl*, she is also the author of the Families of Fairley Terrace Sagas series, about the lives and loves of the residents of a Somerset village in the late nineteenth century, which started with *All The Dark Secrets*.

Stay in touch with Jennie!

Visit her on Facebook at
www.facebook.com/JennieFeltonAuthor
for her latest news.

Or follow her on Twitter **@Jennie_Felton**

If you loved *The Coal Miner's Wife*,
don't miss Jennie Felton's gripping

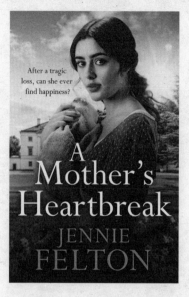

When her father dies, Abigail Newman is forced to leave her mother
and the vicarage she was raised in and take up the position of
governess to the son of Sir Hugh Hastings. Arriving at the grand
estate of Bramley Court, Abi, who is concealing a heart-breaking
secret, finds a family haunted by a tragic loss.

But Bramley Court is also filled with secrets. Why is Sir Hugh's
wife, Lady Imogen, so sure she can still hear the cries of the little
boy she lost eighteen months ago? And what is the history between
the mysterious, glamorous visitor, Constance Bingham, and
complex, charismatic Sir Hugh?

As Abi weaves herself into the fabric of the house and family, she
longs to help the people she's come to care for so deeply. Will they
find peace and Abi heal her own broken heart?

HEADLINE

And discover another sweeping saga from Jennie Felton . . .

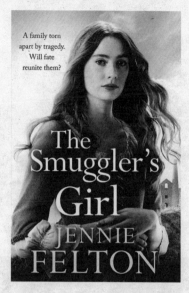

A family torn apart by tragedy. Will fate reunite them?

The Smuggler's Girl

JENNIE FELTON

Cecile has been raised to a life of privilege at Polruan House, by her widowed father and aunt. Now she's of age, they are determined that she make a proper match, but Cecile's heart belongs to their coachman, Sam – most definitely *not* suitable marriage material.

When Sam turns to his friend, smuggler Zach Carver, for help eloping with Cecile, Zach tells of a recent encounter with Lise, a beautiful but poor girl in St Ives, who is the mirror image of Cecile.

And so a daring plan is born to briefly swap the girls. But bringing Cecile and Lise together will uncover an astonishing family secret of a bold escape from a loveless marriage, a treacherous shipwreck and a sister thought lost to the sea long ago . . .

HEADLINE

Have you met the Families of Fairley Terrace?

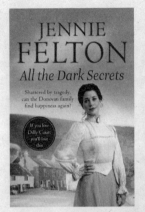

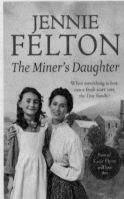

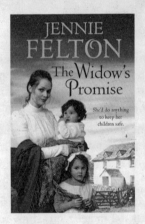

Jennie's compelling saga series
is available now from